Simon Wi_____

# Oblivion's Forge

BOOK ONE OF THE AONA SERIES

*Oblivion's Forge* by Simon Williams
Book I in the Aona Series
© Simon Williams 2011

First published 2011
Second Edition 2012

*For Jayne.*

# APHENHAST

THE PINNACLES

UI-CHORAN

CHOR VALLEY

MORTHANIEN'S CASTLE

RUAN-TOR

THE OLD ROAD

THE PLAINS

THE OLD ROAD

RAND CASTLE

ETHANALIN TUR-MORN

THE CRESCENTS

ALHAR

RIVER'S EDGE

CULVANNEM

FISTELKARN'S TOWER

ROCKMIRE

ALINNARA'S HAVEN

FIRSTWOOD

RIVER ALTAMEUR

NISSTAR

KVARLSWOOD

MIDFORD

CAI

THE MIRK

MIRKWALL

EMBERTON

ALHAR

DARKENHELM

THE SOUTH OCEAN

4

# I - A Single Word

As the blackness closed before him, and the fury of the void flung him half-broken to the rocky ground, he thought for a certainty that this would be his last moment.

A dull red sun hung in the distant west, on the point of dissolving into the dusty horizon. Behind him, a scream that seemed to come from the earth itself was cut short savagely, and the black portal that had spat its fury at the unwilling watcher vanished from the world forever.

Vornen opened his eyes hours later with the sun a faint memory in the west and a biting cold wind tugging at his ragged clothing. Already the first hint of frost settled upon the ground.

He could not move without searing agony crippling him, as if razorwire cut through every muscle in his body, nor could he raise his voice to a whisper, let alone shout for help. He wondered how soon the warm sleep of exposure would claim him. In all likelihood he was stranded leagues away from any settlement. Even more likely were the chances of internal wounds killing him before the frost had a chance.

He tried to sit up, collapsed to the swiftly freezing ground and waited half-aware as the world around him grew dim. Familiar constellations emerged to dot the chilly sky. Neither moon had risen yet. *It must be a fourth-night,* Vornen thought as the icy breeze numbed his face and brought tears to his eyes. *Why couldn't I remember that before? A fourth-night in the month of Neardark, early winter.*

The last scraps of light disappeared in the west. Vornen felt blood flow into his mouth; when he spat it out, a sudden agonising convulsion in his stomach gripped him, and for a moment even the sky faded as pain consumed what remained of his world. *Gods, let this end soon*, he thought weakly.

But with the onset of full darkness came steady footfall accompanied by a faint jangling, and then a *chulan* woman- all harshness and sinew, perhaps chief among the huntspeople of her village judging by the amulets she wore. Gazing without expression upon his sorry form, she stood above him for a moment as he stared wordlessly up at her. Pain stabbed through him in a dozen places as she gathered him up. Unable to scream his agony, he could utter only a faint gasp before passing out.

She bore him back to her cart and then along a stony track to her settlement. Later, in a moment of lucidity, Vornen heard low murmurs of excitement, vaguely remembered lamp light and sometime afterwards the smell of meat as it cooked over an open fire. Voices were raised at one point. The argument took place between two people- one male, one female- both of whom appeared as nothing more than shadows across the canopy of the tent in which he lay. In time the sky grew lighter, and he slept again. Voices came and went, murmurs that drifted through the periphery of his dreams.

Nightfall approached, and with it came silence so deep that for a while he wondered if he had been abandoned. Sometime after that- he fancied it might be growing light again, but couldn't be sure- he heard the laughter of children as they ran past outside. A wind gathered strength around the place where he rested, until it sounded like a continuous howl of grief.

All these things became memories, or perhaps dreams. He slept deeply, perhaps for days. From time to time he was brought out of his slumber by a *chulan* healer, to take sips of water that felt like silk inside his throat. Perhaps it contained something to aid his recovery. His voice

6

having fled, he could not ask for more, so he gestured weakly instead, which did no good. The healers gave him only as much as they thought he needed.

Then one morning, suddenly he woke of his own accord, with sunlight upon his bed and a sharp ache throughout his body, as if all his muscles had been beaten to a pulp. As he lay in the unexpected warmth, a healer's assistant came to feed him hot, thick broth laced with spices and the first bread of the morning. The food was offered a little at a time, the timid girl squatting patiently by his bedside. She fed him as one might feed a helpless child, in considerate silence, the ritual perhaps familiar to her and repeated endlessly without thought.

A while later, agonising pain ripped through his stomach. He had just enough strength to cry out before his breakfast passed out of him in a haze of heat and pain. In silence his rescuers cleaned and bathed him, and then made him drink water laced with sour-root, mint and fennel and another, bittersweet herb that he failed to recognise. He rested afterwards and even managed the weakest of smiles as he observed the pan that had been placed in a helpful position by the side of his bed.

Another day passed, and he recovered sufficiently to walk. The healers occasionally came to watch him take tentative steps, or to help him if he felt unable to. Most of them could not speak Hastian or any language but their own, yet their words of encouragement could not be clearer.

Finally, when his recovery was judged to be sufficient, he was taken by a green-clad healer's assistant to a hut where the woman who had found him waited. Vornen had already guessed that questions would be asked. The *chulan* lived closely attuned to the earth and its shapings and had a certain sensitivity to murmurings and movements that changed the Existence. Perhaps that was why he had been found as quickly as he had. He wondered if this woman had also been drawn to the opening, that savage moment when the Gate suddenly appeared.

Vornen was admitted into the sparse darkness of the woman's dwelling where she sat cross-legged upon the ground. Despite the chill air, she wore only a thin cotton shift and skirt. Several necklaces glittered faintly in the gloom. Her grey hair hung unkempt and lank to her shoulders. The remains of a fire gleamed sullenly in the hearth, faintly illuminating her on one side. The other lay in thick shadow.

"I am Ona," she said simply. The *chulan* people rarely bothered with titles of any sort, viewing them as pointless. It was a custom that Vornen admired.

He bowed slightly and winced as a sudden savage pain flared in his neck. It would be many days before he moved without some physical reminder of what he had witnessed, even though his actual memories had already lost some of their edge. "I am Vornen." After a moment's hesitation, he felt as if he should explain himself further, given her stony, expectant silence. "I am... well, a traveller in a sense..."

"I know what you are," she intervened. "I know how you came to be here. Tell me what you have seen."

Vornen smiled warily. "What I've seen?"

She leaned forward. The hearth-light moved slowly across her face and illuminated her harsh countenance. "You *will* tell me, Vornen, or you will not leave Ui-choran alive. How did you come to be there, at that exact moment? I will have answers."

Vornen felt the smile drain from his face. "As you wish. The truth is, I am drawn to them. I have always been drawn to them. I can help that fact no more than you can help breathing."

She reached out and touched one of his new scars, a curiously curved gouge that he had first seen for himself when one of the healers had given him the use of a looking-glass. A sudden hungry look entered her eyes. "You are a *witness*," she accused him. "You were there as it happened. You were there at the opening and the closing." She licked her lips and nodded in agreement with herself. "I have never witnessed that exact moment. I feel them from afar sometimes, but they are gone before I arrive. Long gone. All that is ever left for me is the odd... *emptiness* in the air."

"I would have perished were it not for you," Vornen said, hoping they might talk of her people's good deed rather than the Gate. "I thank you for saving for me, and your people for nursing me back to some sort of health." He winced as another spasm in his back reminded him that his recovery would not be complete for a while yet.

"Never mind that," Ona said dismissively. "Had I found you anywhere else, I would have left you to stiffen in the frost." She sat back, now almost entirely cast in shadow. "I must know what you *saw* between the opening and the closing. If you won't..." She shrugged. "I can have our healers undo their work. I am sure with some effort we can create again the state you were in when I picked you from the hillside."

Neither of them spoke for a long while. "I saw the darkness of the void," Vornen said eventually. His voice had changed, although he did not notice. As he spoke, it seemed that even in the gloom of Ona's hut, something blacker and deeper opened before them. "I saw stars. *Other* stars, not those we see above us. I heard things... noises. Numbers. *Directions.*"

Ona said nothing, but she leaned forward intently. Perhaps without knowing, she touched each of her necklaces in turn, as if to evoke the protection of whatever Gods the *chulan* worshipped these days. Suddenly Vornen recalled something else, a terrible truth he had sensed whilst staring into the abyss of space. "Gods, I remember," he whispered. "I *remember* now."

9

"What?" The fear in his heart glittered in her eyes. *"What?"*

"The voices..." Vornen shivered. He could not even describe those voices to her. They did not belong to any creature, any *life* that he could understand. They were disembodied fragments from some distant corner of the Existence. They were the harsh noises of *something* that had spent an eternity looking for a world, the most important of *all* worlds...

"They are coming." He blinked and looked at her. "They have found Aona."

"Make sense. *Who?*"

Vornen shook his head. "I don't know any name for them. I don't know what they are." Suddenly he began to shiver, and the shivering became uncontrollable. As he collapsed on his side, his sight becoming a hot feverish blur, Ona cursed and barked out something in the *chulan* language. Someone rushed in through the doorway. Vornen lost consciousness as he was taken back to his bedchamber.

He woke sometime later. It was dark outside and Ildar had just risen in the east. Vornen lay on his mattress and contemplated an altogether different sky. *I will not see that one again,* he thought. *It's never the same one. How many stars are there across the Existence, hanging in the void? Some uncountable number?*

Then a name came to him, and he knew it was the name to which the voices belonged.

*Marandaal.*

He whispered the word over and over, not knowing what it meant, but fearing the strange resonance that it had.

*They are coming.*

The unspeakable fear that clawed its way through his mind was impossible to bear. He opened his mouth and screamed. He continued screaming until three of the *chulan* folk held him down and sedated him.

10

Ona came to see him hours later. Weak and disoriented from the sedative herbs he had been given, he could not speak coherently, but she had no questions for him in any case. The *chulan* woman stood and regarded him in silence for a long while, and it seemed to Vornen that she was torn between the need to ask him more questions and fear of what he had already told her.

A week later, recovered fully, he left the *chulan* village. His saviours supplied him with gifts of winter food for whatever journey lay ahead. He thanked them, humbled by the generosity of people who had little enough to feed themselves, and then he left, heading south-east.

A deep, nagging unease tore at him as he walked the narrow trail through the vastness of the Chor Valley whose southern end opened out into the Plains. It was a far worse sensation than the physical wounds that still caused him pain, and it would not fade. It nestled in his stomach, an invisible invader.

*The name,* he thought, although he dared not speak it or even think of the sound it made. *I always thought that names were immaterial, nothing more than signatures that had filtered down through the Ages, possibly a different one for every race in Aphenhast or even the whole of Aona. But* this *name is different.*

*Has this happened before? Has anyone ever withstood them?* he pondered on the third day after his departure from village, as he rested on the threshold of the great Plains, eating.

There was no answer, of course. A nagging sensation troubled him, told him that perhaps they had reached this world before. But surely these were ancient events, unwritten anywhere here. No parallel existed that he had heard of. The script was itself unwritten. This was a world that had long since moved on and forgotten about the myths of past Ages.

*What can I do, except spread rumours and fears?* he thought as he stared morosely across the moorland. *The* chulan *woman knew I spoke the truth. She felt it as much as heard it. But that means nothing.*

*Forget about it,* his sly and lazy part told him. *Soon you'll be drawn elsewhere, you'll find other truths. You can do nothing, so do nothing.*

The wind rustled his shoulder-length brown hair. His wary, greyish eyes took in the distant scenery for a long while, until it seemed he had lost himself. This haggard, scarred man who looked washed free of life's colours, would have seemed utterly transfixed to anyone passing by. But here, no one passed by. This had always been a barren part of the land- *a vastness in which to lose myself,* he thought.

A grey mass of cloud gathered to the east and north, stretching across the vast heights of the Pinnacles. In all likelihood it bore the first severe snowfall of the coming winter. It would arrive sometime tomorrow, and had probably already blanketed the *chulan* village.

He ate what little he needed to satisfy his scant appetite, and at length he lay down to sleep. But as he stared up at the canopy of stars, ill thoughts raced through his mind. A measure of the rapture he had felt fleetingly as a child, face upturned to the heavens, returned- a quiet excitement and wonder. But now it was tinged with real, tangible fear.

Vornen could not sleep, and dawn found him on the move again. He strode over the frosted ground and silently wished the burden that was his could be erased.

II

Three days passed. Weariness had seeped into him long before the late sun slanted across the light covering of snow that had fallen on that third afternoon. But it was only as sunset approached that Vornen finally stopped, by a

12

windswept tree whose roots had nearly been ripped from the ground. His left foot had begun to bleed; carefully he removed his boot, and wrapped what remained of the spare bandages provided by the *chulan* around the area where the skin had come away. He had no healing ointment left. A hurried inspection of his backpack revealed that nothing remained of the food the *chulan* had provided.

Vornen sat and leaned against his backpack with a sigh and considered each direction in turn. To the south lay the empty plains, with the nearest village many days' walk away, and wandering gangs of thieves and cut-throats posed a constant threat. He did not have days to spare even if he accepted that risk. To the west, equally empty lands lay for as far as the eye could see, until at some point they became the Huurin swamplands of distant Harn, two hundred leagues away. Vornen laughed, looked north to the vastness of the Pinnacles, utterly inhospitable regardless of the season, and then last of all, east, along the edge of the mountain range.

He knew, deep within himself, that he had looked eastwards last because this would be the direction he had to take. He could not see it yet, but Morthanien's remote fortress lay in those foothills, almost directly east from here. He remembered its location perfectly.

*But then I would,* he thought with a faint smile. *I always know my exact directions. Exact east, west, north and south, like lines that no one else sees. Other people point vaguely in directions when asked; to me they're bright, straight paths, each of which might as well go on forever.*

*Unless I choose to freeze,* Vornen thought bitterly, *I will have no choice but to plead with Morthanien. Damn him! Did he know I would end up there, one way or another?*

Peering up into the empty sky as if for an answer, he wondered if the aged warlock would even listen to what he had to tell him, much less believe it, before exacting whatever punishment he deemed necessary. Vornen had

13

neatly escaped the punishment that had been due him for the theft of two books from Morthanien's library during his only previous visit, something that possibly he alone in the world had the recklessness to attempt. Of course, the knowledge they had supposedly contained had gone forever now, reduced to nothing but motes of ash in the air after the books mysteriously caught fire one night and almost burned him in his sleep.

He smiled thinly. *To this day, I can't remember why I stole them. But then there are many things I can't remember.*

Vornen regretted that rash theft, but it was by no means his heaviest regret. A part of him wanted to be caught and imprisoned because the only alternative would be simply to continue from place to place- and occasionally from Gate to Gate as and when forces compelled him. *The natural forces own me,* he thought, *and every time they stir, they pull at me and take another little part of my life. Perhaps incarceration in a warlock's prison would be preferable, if it doesn't send me mad of course.*

But no, Morthanien had not known of the books' disappearance, or perhaps he had not been sufficiently moved to hunt Vornen down and visit justice upon him. Maybe he had correctly seen the theft for what it was- an act of madness and nothing more- and left Vornen to run headlong into the rest of his miserable life. It was the kind of callous harshness for which Morthanien was well known.

Swiftly Vornen considered the possibilities that lay before him. He was cold, wounded, he had little food left, and dozens of leagues separated him from the nearest settlement. In these conditions and with the promise of more snow to come, it would take him weeks to reach safety, and he could not even afford days.

In his darker moments over the last few years, he had often drifted to sleep fervently wishing he would never see the dawn, but now he suddenly found himself almost passionate about his survival and angry at the odds ranged against him. It was an unusual feeling.

Morthanien's castle stood a morning's walk away- perhaps a day's struggle if the blizzards came again tomorrow and his foot grew worse. It would be warm, or at least it would be warmer than remaining outside in winter's embrace. It would also be safe- except from the warlock himself, of course, on whose uncertain mercies he would have to throw himself.

*The first time,* Vornen recalled, *he didn't know me. I was just another wanderer without purpose. I said enough about myself over time to see displeasure in his eyes, but I think this time I'll see much more than simple displeasure.*

Vornen sighed, and gathered twigs for a fire. Later, as the flames flickered in the darkness, his thoughts wandered, and he found himself wishing, for the first time in months, for a pinch or two of *kyush* to smoke, just to gently set him on his way to blissful dreams. Dreams were so much better after the haze of *kyush*, or so he had always told himself.

But he had no *kyush*. And he did not dare sleep.

### III

The gate of grim iron, framed in thick grey stone the colour of the sky, and the empty courtyard that lay beyond were as he remembered them. Nothing ever seemed to change here, and in all probability nothing of any note *had* changed for many more than his thirty-eight years.

Vornen slipped through the gate and limped across the courtyard, shivering as he glanced up at each of the myriad arched windows that glared down from the towers. The fortress almost gaped indignantly at him as if astonished at his daring to return.

15

Wearily he struck the vast iron knocker on the double door in the wall of the fortress and listened to the echo as it reverberated down the hallway beyond.

Morthanien, if he was in the fortress, either did not hear or chose not to pay heed. Vornen waited for as long as he could bear standing there, then with an effort pulled open the door a little way. He was not at all surprised to find it unlocked; Morthanien had better and more macabre means of defence at his disposal than mere locks. If he was curious enough about a visitor to his remote homestead, then he would allow them entrance and decide what to do with them later. As he contemplated that, Vornen almost turned and fled.

Gloom and dust greeted him, the deep and melancholic atmosphere of a hallway unused to the tread of visitors. The place smelled of the many old libraries it contained, a combination of grim silence and vast, all-pervading knowledge. Vornen closed the door with an effort to shut out the icy breeze and then stood, listened, and imagined that the fortress listened back at him. *What next?* he fancied it might be whispering. *Now that you dare to come back, which of my libraries will you choose to pilfer from?*

Taking a deep breath, he set off towards an archway on the far side of the entrance hall. His footsteps echoed harshly in this empty, high-ceilinged place. His heart hammered. He wished Morthanien would appear and be done with it, but of course the old warlock would know well enough that that was what he wanted. And so Morthanien would wait awhile, lurking in some upper chamber, listening with enjoyment as he wandered haplessly, dreaming up some suitable fate for the trespasser.

Vornen swallowed with an effort- days had passed since he had last spoken and his mouth felt full of dust- and tried to call out, but the shout he attempted was nothing but a faint croak.

He had almost reached the archway when his sight began to fade, colours and shades shimmering and bursting in his vision. When he fell to the floor, his legs giving way underneath him, he was already unconscious.

"Did you enjoy reading my books, Vornen?"

He slowly opened his eyes, barely able to take in his new surroundings- a low-ceilinged bedchamber stripped bare of all but the most minimal furnishings- before Morthanien's grim visage- grey beard, grey eyes like storms, a face of old age and yet without age of any sort- loomed above him, a dreadful expression of amusement and fury on his face. Together they looked like madness.

Vornen tried to concentrate on the stone ceiling. Grey afternoon light came in through a small window in one wall. On the other side of the room an oil-lamp burned low.

"Did you find what you were seeking? Did the knowledge serve you well?" He heard a mocking edge to the warlock's voice. "Or did you fail to understand, in your blindness and your greed, and sell it to some interested stranger?"

Vornen knew that there was no point whatsoever in lying to him. Morthanien had at least picked him up from the cold stone and given him shelter rather than throw him out into winter's embrace, but he might well change his mind if Vornen gave anything but a truthful account of what had happened. Morthanien had given his hospitality, and truth would be the least he expected in return.

"The books burned." Vornen cleared his throat and continued in a cracked whisper, "I tried to read them, but I couldn't, so I put them to one side. And then they caught fire as I slept. I gained nothing from my misdeed."

Morthanien nodded, seeming pleased with the answer- if he could ever be said to look pleased without some other, more savage expression lurking beneath- and held

Vornen's head up whilst placing a cup of water to his lips. Vornen drank thirstily until the cup was withdrawn.

"Just think." Morthanien's voice was calm, but menace laced his words. "If you had managed to read them, or worse still, *understood* what the words truly meant, you might have caught fire yourself. One might say you have had a lucky escape."

Vornen nodded. He was about to thank Morthanien for sparing his life rather than leaving him in nature's less than tender care, but then he considered darkly that his life might not be spared. Morthanien might change his mind. *My life has been a series of lucky escapes, if I think the glass half full,* he considered, *but all things must eventually end.*

"There is more water for you," Morthanien said abruptly, placing the cup on the floor next to the bed. "After you've rested, I daresay you will need something to eat." He stared briefly around the room, as if he had seen something that Vornen could not- and then he left abruptly. Vornen listened to the warlock's footfall echo down the passageway outside the room, and drifted off to sleep without a further thought.

When he woke, day still held- or perhaps this was a different day- and the snowstorm had truly arrived. The blizzard howled at the window, swirling in a chaotic dance as Vornen slowly moved from the bed and walked over to gaze into the white world outside. The fearsomely bright scene had a stark beauty to it.

*I should tell Morthanien about everything I saw and heard when the Gate opened,* he thought suddenly to himself.

The idea became persuasive as it lingered. The knowledge would then be Morthanien's problem, to do with as he wished. He would have the power and influence to do something about it. Even the Council of Priests that held sway in the southern cities had heard of Morthanien.

Vornen resolved to tell the warlock what he knew. Perhaps when the storm eased, he would be free to go, and put this in the past.

*I could go back to Ruan-Tor,* he mused. *My two years of exile will have passed. Then I might travel down to Darkenhelm again, or perhaps even the South Ocean Islands if I can find enough work and save some money. That would be good. Gods know the weather will be an improvement down there. Perhaps I'll sail to that island- damned if I can remember the name of it now- where those wonderful red and yellow fruit grow on the trees, where those fine black women wander shirtless in the streets, where they play the finest music...what was the name of that inn at the port...*

The door opened suddenly and Morthanien stepped in. Vornen jumped; he had not even heard the warlock approach.

"I see you are feeling better," Morthanien remarked. "Would you care for something to eat?"

Vornen nodded gratefully, relieved and surprised.

They sat together in one of the smaller chambers upstairs. Vornen took a sip of sour yellowgrass liqueur and grimaced. Some concoctions improved as time went on. Yellowgrass, however, remained as potent and as abrasive as ever. Still, the fire in his belly was welcome. He sat back in the armchair and watched Morthanien, who glared into the flames of the hearth as if divining something from them. Shadows cast by the fire danced around the walls, upon the many books and ornaments that occupied the room. Something small and dark with many legs scurried across the top shelf of the bookcase, where fewer books allowed greater freedom to move. Vornen averted his gaze in a hurry.

"You have something to tell me, Vornen," the warlock said eventually, although his gaze remained fixed upon the fire. "I can see it in your eyes."

19

Vornen felt a surge of fear followed by a feeling of relief, a kind of release. "Yes," he said tiredly. "I'm a poor liar even before I open my mouth." He took a gulp of yellowgrass and swallowed it before continuing, "But I'm not sure how to say it."

"I am sure you will find a way."

Vornen sat back. "When I was here before, did I tell you about my... *compulsion*? About the Gates?"

Morthanien's cold eyes looked him up and down. "You did," he admitted, "although I have to say, I couldn't decide whether to believe you or not. Such people have long been known to exist, attuned more than others to the web of forces that hold the world together, but..." He shrugged. "You struck me as a storyteller, a man who had perhaps met such a person and liked the idea of their existence in some way- and so adopted it as his own."

"I was in the *chulan* lands to the west," Vornen told him, "perhaps a ten-night ago, or more." He frowned, trying to remember. "It was a fourth-night, close to dusk. Neither Ildar nor Archaon had risen, at first. A Gate opened up before me on the hillside, for just a moment. And I..." He shrugged helplessly. "I remember only a little, and less each day. But I do recall a word. A name. *Marandaal.*"

Morthanien gazed sharply at him, suddenly intent. "How can you know that name?"

"I don't know it through choice, I assure you."

Morthanien's chair creaked unpleasantly as he leaned closer. "Very few people alive today know that word, Vornen. Even fewer know what it means."

Vornen tried to recall the other details- the voices from the void, the particular shapes made by the strange constellations he had seen. But even at the *chulan* settlement, as he rested, he could feel some of that detail grow dull at the edges. *A few more weeks and it might disappear entirely*, he thought. *But perhaps something will*

20

*remain, some little dark knot, even if it's just the fear without the memory.*

"They are coming here," he whispered. "They want this world for their own."

"Tell me, storyteller." Morthanien's voice had a dangerous edge to it. "How can you know that?"

Vornen shrugged helplessly. "I simply know something that I can't prove."

Morthanien sat back in his chair and regarded his visitor in stony silence. "So," he said eventually, "the last man I expect to beg for shelter comes bearing the last tale I expected to hear. I certainly did not expect to hear of *them* again. But then, I never expected to see you again, Vornen Starbrook. I had thought you dead, or mad." A faint smile twitched at the corners of his lips. "Or at the very least, badly burned."

Vornen grimaced as he finished off the yellowgrass. "The fever hasn't enslaved me yet, although I am sure it will in time. You may linger on for another hundred years, Morthanien, but I've probably already lived longer than I should, given my affliction." As Morthanien raised an eyebrow in vague curiosity, Vornen nodded. "Yes. I call it an affliction. Who would willingly choose to be bound so, by forces that no one can control? I feel the threads of the world itself, pulling me in directions on a whim. Why should I want to live?"

"I have no sympathy to give you, Vornen, and your self-pity fills me with disgust."

He could not help but laugh at that, and watched as Morthanien refilled his glass. "By my reckoning, your exile will be over now," the warlock commented, as Vornen took another sip of the fiery drink. "Will you head back to Ruan-Tor?"

"Perhaps." Vornen stared guardedly at him. "When the weather permits, I will be away from here- if you allow me to remain that long, of course."

21

"There's enough room," Morthanien replied, which did not entirely answer the question.

"You comment on my exile," Vornen said, "but should we not speak of these... *marandaal?*"

"There is nothing to be said on that matter." Morthanien stared coldly at him. "You may as well have told me a star was about to fall to earth and send us all tumbling into darkness."

Vornen nodded. A strangely familiar emptiness stirred within him. "I understand. I wouldn't believe me, either." He gave a tight little smile. "Perhaps some madness has taken me after all, Morthanien, and I simply haven't realised it. Why else would I dare to show my face here?"

The warlock stared contemptuously at him. "Maddened or not, I care nothing for you. You may stay until the storm passes, then you will leave. I will provide you with food and water, enough for the journey to Ruan-Tor, as long as you are sparing with it. I don't wish for you to remain here longer than necessary. As for our discussion- well, it is touching to find that you care so much about the world, Vornen."

The warlock's expression darkened as he leaned forward. "Would you care to know what I really think? I think you *are* mad. Mad from being half-torn time and again by these... *events*, perhaps, if you are truly what you claim to be. Mad from *kyush* and drink. Mad because, as you say, your mind and body are slaves of the natural forces. Well, to one extent or another we all are. *You* are nothing, Vornen, less than nothing, a small stain upon the world. If *marandaal* were truly about to return, *I* would know about it."

Vornen shrank back, dumbfounded. He opened his mouth, though in truth he had no idea what he would have said given the courage- but the warlock fixed him with a stare that made him want to crawl away to the furthest recesses of the castle, like an unwanted insect to be crushed if he dared to utter another sound.

Morthanien said nothing more and strode contemptuously from the room. Vornen remained in his chair, not daring to move, and he stayed there for hours, even the sour temptation of the yellowgrass forgotten as he stared into the hearth and the flames, colder inside than he had ever felt in his life.

IV

The storm passed during the night and Morthanien sent Vornen on his way the following morning with enough food for five or six days.

Two days later, as the sun still hovered in the distant west- though it may as well have been hidden for all the warmth it gave- Vornen chanced upon a campfire in a shallow valley bordered by the wind-blasted remains of withered trees. The flames burned brightly even in the sunlight, and the best efforts of the stiff breeze that slanted across the valley had failed to snuff them out. After a moment's hesitation, Vornen walked on towards the lone figure sitting a few paces from the fire.

As he drew nearer, hands raised to show he meant no harm, the man by the campfire- a thin, gangly youth with lank black hair and a week's worth of untidy beard- sprang to his feet and grabbed at something by his side. Vornen had his sword in hand before the young man had even got to his feet, and was about to shout at him to stop- *I'm in neither the mood nor the condition for a fight,* he thought desperately- but then he relaxed, firstly amused and perplexed by what he saw, and then saddened.

The youth held a small, banded-together wooden sword- the sort that children might use for mock fights- in both hands, and brandished it fiercely. "I will slice the flesh from your bones!" he shouted.

23

Vornen stopped immediately and wondered what to do. *I've turned away from such as him before,* he recalled. *I've never known what to say or how to behave around those who have lost their minds- have they not already lost everything they can lose?*

"Please, put the... put the sword away," he said finally. "I mean you no harm. I was simply passing by. You see so few folk around here, so I just thought I'd wish you good day. And the path does lead past your fire." He shrugged. "My apologies, friend. May I pass?"

But the long, uncomfortable moment persisted. The young man stood, swaying slightly, eyes wide and fixed intently on Vornen, who frowned as he saw perspiration trickle down his forehead. Gods, the man was sweating in *this* weather? What could be wrong with him, aside from the obvious?

*If he has some fever or illness then I'd best steer clear of him,* Vornen reminded himself. He began to fervently wish he had given the campfire and its unfortunate owner a wide berth, despite the sympathy he began to feel for him. But this path was the quickest way to Ruan-Tor.

Eventually the young man placed the wooden sword on the ground, though he remained crouched protectively nearby, ready to snatch it up again in an instant. Vornen took a few relaxed steps closer and glanced quickly around the little encampment. The youth had no real weapons that he could see, and to Vornen's bemusement, neither did he appear to have any belongings except for the clothes he wore and his wooden sword. How had he survived the savagely cold nights? Vornen noticed a thin, torn robe which had been tossed carelessly aside. *Too hot for him?* he wondered worriedly.

"My name is Vornen," he finally ventured. What else was there to say? He extended a hand in greeting, still not sure if he ought to. "And yours is?"

"Larien," the youth said flatly. His stare remained fixed on Vornen like that of a feral animal even as he took a step back.

"And where are you headed?"

Larien grinned suddenly. The expression was one of pure savagery. "I follow the clouds."

"And on a day like this, when there are no clouds? Where do you head then?"

"They come eventually."

Vornen took a deep breath. *This could have been my fate,* he found himself thinking. *And it might yet be, in time. How often have I felt myself drift, my own grip on the world slipping away almost without my knowledge?*

*I can't walk away from him. He's lost in every possible way.*

Vornen looked into the boy's wide, frantic eyes, and said softly, "Larien, I'm headed for the town of Ruan-Tor. I suggest you come with me, regardless of where you think you're going. Look at you! You've no shelter, no food, and the snowstorms are coming early this season. You'll die here unless you come with me."

"Ruan-Tor," Larien mused. He stared into the distance for a long while- so long in fact that Vornen began to suspect he had fallen into a trance.

Finally, Larien stirred. Blinking, he glanced at Vornen once again. "Ruan-Tor," he said, more clearly. His voice held a slight tremble. "Is it a good place? Will I find a welcome there?"

*A better one than me,* Vornen thought, but he forced a smile. "It is, and I'm sure you will. You may well find yourself some sort of employment, which will be good for you. Provided you're not too fussy about the jobs you're given. Work and you'll be fed and given somewhere to sleep with a roof over it- and that's a start at least. So, will you come with me? I know the way and I have enough food to last the journey, if we're sensible with it."

Larien returned a tight little smile, probably the sanest expression he had shown throughout this odd exchange. He said nothing, but it became slowly obvious to Vornen that his words had had the desired effect. Larien carefully placed the wooden sword through his belt, as if it were a delicate splinter. Then he picked up his robe and walked at Vornen's side as they made their way through the valley, the icy breeze sighing through the bare trees like a lost spirit.

His new companion made no conversation for the rest of the day, and Vornen lapsed into a long period of reflection, brought on mostly by the thought of Ruan-Tor itself.

Four years had passed by since he had last set foot in that town, but Morthanien's derisory words had brought his time there painfully back into focus. It was odd how news of such an almost political nature- the demise of a bodyguard to the overseer of Ruan-Tor, Lord Vothangrane- had been picked up by a famously solitary warlock, but there it was- Morthanien knew many things, and many of the things he chose to know were surprising.

Vornen wondered bitterly if Morthanien had learned the more minute and painful details of his ignominious exit from the town of his birth and upbringing- his humiliating march through the streets to the western gates, to be banned from the town for exactly four years. It was a strange sentence, but then it had come about from compromise. The local militia- headed by the coldly religious Rocan Cartwright, had bayed for his blood and demanded a hanging. Lord Vothangrane had denied them that enjoyment at least, but such was Vornen's unpopularity that an example had to be made. "I'm grateful that I'll not see you hang," Vothangrane had said to him, as Rocan's men prepared to march him through the streets like an exhibit of justice, "but you cannot remain here. The people need time, as do you."

26

"Exile, then," Vornen had said dully, and he wondered what he might do with those four years. Even in that moment his head had been spinning from *kyush* smoke and liquor. He had not been able to look Lord Vothangrane in the eyes, so had stared at the ground. "Exile, *your Lordship*," one of Rocan's nearby curs had hissed, and bloodied his lip with a casual swipe.

At sunset, as Vornen had stumbled down cobbled Gate Street, the father of the man he had almost killed kicked and spat at him, urged on by the cheers of those who had gathered, many of whom had had good reasons to celebrate his forthcoming exile. A grim-looking Rocan waited at the western gate, coldly austere and resplendent in black chain armour. *Only the churchday best for Rocan on a day such as this,* Vornen remembered thinking, that being one of the few cohesive thoughts to remain in his addled mind.

"Four years," Rocan had said to him as the outer perimeter gates were pulled open and the sentinels stood aside to allow him through onto the Old Road. He looked in that moment like a great stone silhouetted in the dying light, remorseless, immovable. "Is that enough for you, I wonder?"

"There's nothing here for me," Vornen had retorted.

"There is nothing for you anywhere," Rocan had said as he was shoved out onto the road, and the gates creaked shut behind him.

Much as he hated to admit it, Vornen had come to realise the truth in what Rocan had said that day. The emptiness within him- which he had sought to fill with drink, with violence, even with the vile *kyush* weed that had almost brought him to his knees all by itself- was not something that left. Perhaps it simply could not leave. *I can't cut away a part of myself any more than cut my own head off and walk away,* he had considered many times. *So why can I not live with myself?*

Then an answering thought would come to him, each time: *You're a slave and always will be- and what hope is there in such a life? Eventually one of those rips in the air, those moments when the forces binding everything together fall apart, will destroy you, and that will be the end of it all.*

Days of silence had followed his exile, for he was in no mood to speak with anyone and avoided all the settlements in the plains. The days became tennights without him having noticed. They stretched through the silence of his solitary existence- long periods of travel, reflection, rest and thought.

After a month or two, he would occasionally find a settlement in which to sate what lingering need remained for *kyush* or drink, but as time passed and he became leaner, even more withdrawn and detached from all that had gone before, shedding substance and somehow gaining emptiness along the way, he found that those needs faded, just as memories dulled. He cared less; he avoided the towns and villages once again, and for part of this time he almost entirely forgot how to talk to people.

And meanwhile the Gates called to him more strongly than ever before, as if leaping to fill the void. Four times he was drawn to them, but he remembered little before or after except for the final journey that had ended in the Chor Valley and almost in his own slow and painful death.

Of the other journeys, he remembered nothing but the beginning and the end, and these only vaguely. He recalled babbling incoherently under the stars, about the light being the end of all things and the darkness the beginning, before starting his fractured monologue again, only this time the light was the beginning and everything ended in complete darkness and cold, where nothing remained to be seen and nothing moved.

The experience terrified him, because throughout it all he could still hear a small voice, some grim knot of remaining sanity that cried out as if in torment. *I lost a little more of myself,* he would think when eventually he regained his wits, shivering and wretched. *I'm thrashing against an ocean, and I lose something of myself each time.*

Sometimes Vornen imagined that he had travelled, only to wake and find that the whole episode, which he supposed had taken weeks or months, had been a dream during a single night. He would weep, fearful that he could no longer tell dreams from reality. Then, he would feel even colder, even more detached from everything that had once been so meaningful in his life. It was better that way, he decided, but there were some days and nights when he needed to spend time convincing himself of that.

The winter was particularly full of such days and nights, when he would dwell on the whereabouts of Suli Garranson, his former love. Even these thoughts of lost passion now took the form of tired distraction.

*I thought I'd always feel the same after she left,* he would often remark, *but now each time I think about it all, it feels further away, smaller, less important. Why must everything mean less over time?*

It saddened him that the past had become the distant past, but he had found that whilst many things saddened him, none of them did so as much as they once had.

Vornen roused himself from his melancholia and glanced across at his silent companion. "How long have you been travelling, Larien?"

The youth turned his oddly vacant stare at him and shrugged.

*Perhaps he's lost track of the days,* Vornen considered. *Easy enough when little of importance separates them. He might mark the shapes of the clouds, but he probably fails to count the cycles of the moons.* "Where are you from?"

"Ethanalin Tur-morn," Larien said quietly.

29

Vornen merely nodded but was surprised to hear that name. Few people born in that place admitted to the fact. It was well-known as the blight of the entire north with good reason. For a number of years, it had been caught in a spiral of neglect; once a prosperous centre for the silver trade- the hills to the south-east of the town were riddled with long-deserted silver mines- these days its identity and wealth had been largely lost, the little that remained hoarded by the church or local militiamen. The town was mired in lawlessness and savagery. Vornen had even heard that a different militia ran the place from one tennight to the next.

"I think you did well to leave," Vornen commented, this being the greatest encouragement he could come up with. Larien gave him a flat stare that could have meant anything.

By the end of the day, they had reached the end of the valley and found a path that Vornen knew led to the Old Road, which would take them to Ruan-Tor. The Old Road was seldom used these days, mainly for superstitious reasons, but the standing stones that marked its route every dozen yards or so still stood as usefully as they ever had. Vornen knew a road for a road, and nothing more or less than that.

For perhaps the hundredth time that day he tried to work out why he had decided to return to Ruan-Tor, and still he could not. Was it idle curiosity? Or to see what reaction he might receive from the townsfolk? Or did part of him hope to make amends in some way? That could prove difficult and painful, and he suspected that he was still very much the same man he had always been- a Powers-maddened slave, an outcast by definition and behaviour.

*Oh, I'm treading water well enough,* he thought, *but it would be so easy to stop, to sink back down. That's simply the way it is. And the town is no doubt riddled with drink and* kyush *as much now as before.*

30

He pointed to a small copse of withered trees just off the path. "We'll rest here. The trees will make a windbreak. We've made good progress today."

Larien said nothing as they put together sticks for a fire, and a while had passed as they sat eating Vornen's preserved rations of cured meat and cheese, before he spoke up. "How long until we are there? How many days?"

"Three, perhaps four. If the snows come again then our journey will be far more difficult. But"- he glanced towards the north and the west and saw no clouds- "perhaps we'll be lucky."

Larien smiled into the flames, an expression that Vornen found oddly unsettling.

Knowing that his companion was unarmed- not that his wooden sword could not administer some painful blows- Vornen allowed himself to doze off into the lightest of slumbers after they had eaten, with one hand on his sword-pommel. But that lightest of slumbers became something more and he woke suddenly, roused by the sound of distant laughter.

The fire burned low. His pack remained untouched, or at least it lay exactly where he had deposited it. Larien, meanwhile, had wandered off somewhere. Vornen sighed and rose to his feet, grabbed his pack and slung it over his shoulder, then followed the man's footprints through the snow.

The path taken by his companion looked erratic, as if he had wandered one way and suddenly chosen another, over and again. But Larien had walked without any problem throughout the day. Had he been hiding a bad wound which had since opened up? If so, he was unlikely to make it as far as Ruan-Tor. Or had he simply intended to wander off into the snow in any direction? Could this be what "following the clouds" meant? Randomly staggering through the darkness, on a night when no clouds could be seen?

31

Vornen could now see him up ahead. Ildar's light was bright enough for him to see that Larien had stripped off his shirt with savage urgency, ripping part of the fabric. He knelt on the hard snow and leaned forward slightly, the bones of his spine jutting out in painful detail. Welts of fresh blood that looked like the result of some manic knife or whip frenzy adorned his back and his arms. *How is that possible?* Vornen thought in bemusement. *How could he have done that?*

Then he realised that Larien was simply *shuddering* in some bizarre way, almost as if in latent reaction to those wounds. Vornen could not tell whether he was crying or laughing, nor could he be sure any longer if it was laughter that had awakened him.

Swiftly he glanced around in all directions. For one moment he felt certain that some other presence watched from nearby, but there was no one else here. The only sounds were the gentle sigh of the breeze and Larien's muffled groans as he shivered half-naked on the ground.

*I can smell his blood,* Vornen thought suddenly as he turned his attention back to the suffering before him. *Even from here I can smell it.* And he saw that the wounds upon the man's back had indeed opened up again. Were there more of them now? Vornen thought so.

Larien's wooden sword had somehow been driven halfway into the hard ground, and stood before the kneeling man like one of the carved crosses that marked some of the older graves in the South. Larien continued to shudder, and blood dripped from his back and arms onto the snow, dark streams that gleamed in the harsh moonlight. A moment later, he raised his head to look at the wooden sword and began to speak to himself- a strange, repetitive mantra in a language Vornen had never heard before. It continued over and over and rose slowly in pitch and urgency before it lulled again, until Vornen could bear the sound and the incomprehensible sight no longer and crept back to the fire.

32

He stood for a moment ensnared by indecision. *I should help him,* Vornen thought, but he didn't know how that might be possible.

*Or I should put him out of his misery.*

But his instinct screamed at him to flee, and that was all Vornen needed. He strode away from the fire and headed south-east towards the Old Road, whose standing stones would show him the way in the worst of blizzards. After a while, he broke into a run, and for the first time in many years, he raised his head and gave fervent thanks to Gods he had never worshipped, when snow began to swirl down to cover his footprints.

## V

Three days later, numb with the cold and with two toes already frostbitten, Vornen reached Ruan-Tor's tall wooden perimeter fence. Forty hands high, the sharp-tipped fence posts, standing and bound close together, made a formidable barrier. Vornen uttered a weak laugh of relief as he leaned against it for a moment. He dared not lean and rest for too long, knowing that he could so easily sink down here and fall asleep.

*And many would find that a delicious story to tell amongst themselves,* he told himself, wiping freshly-fallen snow from his hair. *Vornen came crawling back in the middle of winter of all times, only to fall and give up just outside the town.*

So he forced himself to continue along the fence, leaning against it when he had to, until eventually he reached the west-facing entrance gates. Just beyond the snow-topped iron bars a square tower loomed, and Vornen looked up to see the pale face of a single guardsman staring out from a small window high up. Summoning the last reserves of his energy, he shook and pounded at the bars, and called up to the lone sentinel, until at last the man

33

turned his attention to the gaunt stranger at the gates. The questioning face disappeared from the window after a moment, and Vornen closed his eyes and waited, forehead pressed against the iron bars.

The guardsman's words startled him out of near-slumber. Perhaps this was a moment or two later, but it could easily have been an hour. Vornen found that one of his hands would not come free from the gate bar he was clutching.

"Where are you from?" The guardsman edged closer, sword carried loosely at his side.

"Please," he whispered, but what little sound he produced was carried away by the breeze. "Let... me..."

*"Where are you from?"*

Vornen could have wept, had he the strength. He could no longer even think of the words to speak. He watched as the young sentry stared nervously at him, and then, without another word, he turned and walked, not back into his watchtower but down the snowbound, walled track that led into the town proper.

Vornen watched until the departing guardsman was no more than a faint dark mark against the haze of white, and then his legs gave way. He fell to the ground and the welcome cold press of snow.

Rocan Cartwright watched impatiently as the physician bound the man's feet. "Will he live?"

The physician seemed to find that amusing. "Do you want him to? Starbrook himself would no doubt find that interesting, should he wake."

"I *am* interested in knowing what he's done with himself for the last four years years," Rocan confessed, "although once my curiosity is satisfied you can cut off as many parts of him as you like."

The physician smiled uncertainly- never in his life had he considered cutting off body parts for sheer

34

amusement- and left the dormitory, hurrying along to his next patient.

Rocan walked over to the mattress where the sleeping man lay. His head had been propped up with three straw-stuffed pillows. Rocan's gaze took in the gaunt, almost shadowy visage, the scars from various wounds, and finally the bandaged feet, two toes of which had been amputated.

"Who would have thought," he said to the otherwise empty room, "that you of all people could become even less of a man, Vornen?"

Rocan was of Vornen's age, an Ildarian month older. They had been schooled in the town Guild together and even as far back as that they had clashed on numerous occasions, whether it be over who made the better swordsman, who was the stronger arm-wrestler, who could run the faster, and...

"Suli," Rocan whispered hatefully, as the memories loomed in his mind.

That Suli had chosen Vornen over him was a fact Rocan had never and could never understand, nor forgive. *I should never have pleaded with her,* he thought, *but what else was I to do, when I saw Vornen for what he was- a violent madman even at the age of fourteen summers, a lunatic and a wastrel who was thrown out of the Guild?*

*Ah, but she became the same sort of creature,* he sharply reminded himself. *Somehow she fell under his spell, or under the same spell that Vornen had already succumbed to, and after that their fate was more or less the same. The sudden violence, the visions and madness... possession, I would have called it then, but these days I would be far less certain. The times when they would suddenly leave on some journey or other, only to return days or even tennights later as if they had never been anywhere...*

*They were far worse together than apart.*

He recalled the day when Suli had suddenly left Ruan-Tor, eight years or so later. She had left a message for no one except, strangely, the innkeeper of the Last Stone

35

Standing, whom she had barely known. Suli had been an orphan, cared for in her younger years by the one and only orphanage in Ruan-Tor, so she had no family to bid farewell to. Rocan had heard a rumour that she had been left here as an infant by passing travellers, but the orphanage would not divulge anything that related to her family, if indeed they knew anything.

The message had been addressed to no one in particular, and perhaps to everyone in general: *I have left Ruan-Tor. I will not return.*

Whilst the populace of Ruan-Tor gave a quiet sigh of relief, glad that one troublemaker in their midst had departed, Vornen and Rocan both raged- Rocan inwardly, or outwardly in private. Vornen lashed out at anything and everything he could. He drank, he fought, he was arrested for the attempted murder of a man he barely knew, he desecrated the church, and then, perhaps a month later, he too vanished from Ruan-Tor, and was not seen for many months.

*And so it continued, long past his youth and long past his prime,* Rocan thought, *if it could ever be considered thus. I became knight-commander, and he became simply a bigger and uglier copy of what he already was. And this wretched excuse for a man stole from me the only love I ever had.*

So suddenly consumed by hatred did he become, that he considered smothering Vornen with one of the pillows. Would that not be justice? Had Vornen not always been on the cusp of self-murder, yet never quite possessed the vile courage to remove himself from the world? And, Rocan tried to convince himself, would it not be a kindness to Vornen himself?

He was standing over his foe's sleeping form, still undecided, when Vornen opened his eyes.

Rocan's heart skipped a beat, but still he gazed resolutely and met the man's pale grey-blue eyes. Vornen said nothing; for a moment he thought he was still dreaming.

Eventually he spoke, although his voice was still barely capable of a low murmur. "Rocan. A pleasure to see your face again."

"You may remain here for now," the knight-commander said quietly, "but set so much as one foot wrong, Vornen, and I will see you banished forever from Ruan-Tor. Or hanged. I think hanged might be best."

"That hardly sounds like a welcome to me, Rocan," Vornen said.

"You're *not* welcome, in truth. But Lord Vothangrane was told of your arrival before I was." Rocan's lip curled in distaste. "Perhaps your luck has turned."

"My luck doesn't turn. It knows only one direction." Vornen swallowed and then grimaced. "Would you fetch me some water?" As the knight-commander stared at him, Vornen added wearily, "Is that too much to ask? *Water?*"

Rocan looked at him as if he had asked for blood. Finally he departed and came back a while later with a large canteen of water, but by then Vornen had fallen asleep again.

Rocan left the water by the mattress, then turned and left. He could no longer bear the sight of his lifelong foe, returned from the wilderness like an unwanted gift.

## VI

Ruan-Tor remained much the same as Vornen remembered, all grey and black stone and hardwood with little ornamentation, but then he had not really expected the town to change in two years. The grim, black-stoned church on the hill, the walls of granite and gates of thick iron, all stood darkly resplendent against the snow. The people, *his* people, though it was hard to think of them in such a way, were as hard-faced and resolute as the place in which they lived. The town had a harsh beauty that stood out in almost painful relief against the snow.

In the four days he had been up and about, Vornen had encountered all manner of reactions- all, that was, except broad honest welcome. He had been spat at, had a dagger waved in his face along with a promise to decapitate him or at least cut his balls off should be put so much as a foot wrong, and he had been asked half a dozen times why he had bothered to come back at all. A few people had at least muttered a good-day or good-morning, although he noted with some sadness the wariness in their eyes.

*Even the ale is the same,* he thought with a faint smile as he supped the dregs from his tankard and set it aside. Rocan leaned slowly forward from across the table, a measured but quietly threatening gesture. Most of Rocan's movements felt like threats. *I'll need to keep my wits about me,* Vornen silently noted. *But then, I've always had to where Rocan's concerned.*

Rocan's cold blue eyes surveyed him as if he were vermin. "I will watch you and wait," he said. "I don't believe for a moment that you have been cured of your madness, nor your capacity to bring ruin. In the meantime, Lord Vothangrane wishes to see you at the earliest possible opportunity."

Vornen frowned, taken aback. "Lord Vothangrane wishes to see *me*? After everything that's happened?"

Rocan gave him a contemptuous look. "You think I have any idea why? He has been... ill for some time. He's hardly been in the land of the living for the past year and a half. Now he's stirred at last, but..." Rocan looked decidedly uncomfortable, an expression that Vornen had seldom seen on that face before. "You will have to see for yourself, Vornen. You have been summoned, and you will go to him. Then you can ask your questions and hope for answers. Tomorrow morning, at daybreak."

With that, the knight-commander rose from his chair and strode out of the tavern without looking back, eager to be out of the smoke-filled hovel. It seemed that those few

38

who were present breathed a heartfelt sigh of relief as the door creaked shut behind him. Vornen smiled wanly as a thought occurred to him: *I doubt if Rocan is that much more popular than I am.* Then he caught sight of hard, searching looks cast his way, and the smile faded.

*Gods, I would rather not do this,* he thought. The idea of meeting Lord Vothangrane again filled him with a sense of dread, not to mention shame. One of the many things that Vornen regretted from his previous life in Ruan-Tor was that he had brought such humiliation and embarrassment to the man who had taken him into his household at an early age and ensured that he was looked after, schooled and trained, after his expulsion from the Guild.

The drink and debauchery, the hazy sessions of *kyush* with the town's most infamous whores, the fighting and the troublemaking- somehow his return had brought the memory of these events clearly back into focus, as if they had happened only a few months ago rather than years. Out in the wilderness it had been easy to push those events to the back of his mind, but that was impossible in the place where they had occurred. Some of those very events had taken place here in this tavern.

*Vothangrane almost understood,* Vornen mused. *Certainly he understood that I needed to bury the pain so often, even if he had no idea what caused it. Well, for much of that time I had no idea either. I became nothing more than a symptom of myself.*

He remained in the tavern for the rest of the day, winning enough money in a game of fourdice to pay for five more tankards of ale. He allowed himself no more than that, knowing he could not afford to let his guard down.

Vornen wondered briefly if Suli had come back to the town, but knew that to be an idle, wistful thought born more from recollection than hope. What reason could she possibly have to return? She had left of her own accord; no one had

39

forced her out. The thought had first occurred to him as he caught sight of Ruan-Tor from a distance, but he had dismissed the idea as fanciful long before he reached the town gates.

Suli Garannson had been an enigma to all, darkly beautiful- so much so that Vornen had lusted after her in vain long before he had fallen in love with her- but reclusive and possessed of a terrifying temper. She had sought neither friends nor lovers but had succumbed to Vornen's attentions at a time when they both struggled to come to terms with the nameless curse they shared, the pull of Gates. Vornen could not remember which of them had revealed it first, but he could recall in perfect detail the tearful aftermath, the overwhelming relief they had both felt at the discovery that they were not entirely alone. Of course, the following morning they realised that in the cold light of day the fact changed nothing.

A few people- Vornen did not know exactly how few- were simply attuned to Gates, to the forces that fashioned them, and there was nothing that could be done about it. No cure existed. No choice could be made. One could only try and live with it. If that meant a forced journey, being drawn towards a Gate or the imminence of a Gate, then so be it; no alternative ever existed.

Vornen recalled that he had once tried to explain it to someone. It was also a little like being able to see places and the way they were joined or linked, in a way unrelated to the works of cartographers, although it was said that his kind shared a part of this talent with the witches and warlocks who sought and identified the lines of natural force that traversed the land and the oceans. Suli's version had been better- "The world is like a jewel at the centre of many spider webs," she had said.

To be born with this *Gatesight* as some old books called it, effectively meant a death sentence for most people. The visions, the dreams of places beyond Gates, of lines of

40

power, plagued almost all who bore this "gift" and worse, drew them towards the Gates themselves, vast portals that linked places throughout the Existence.

Vornen likened it to being a human lodestone, helplessly drawn from time to time to these portals as they formed, as the lines of power and attraction fluctuated. No one knew why they fluctuated, and no one knew how or why the Gates even existed. Most people were unaffected by them, could not even see or detect them. Gatesight effectively imprisoned those afflicted by it in a separate world to other people.

Vornen's family had never comprehended this curse, but he felt no animosity towards them for that. The condition was impossible to understand.

Vornen still marvelled at the fact that most folk in Ruan-Tor considered themselves Gods-worshippers, and yet he had never heard of more than a handful who so much as believed in Gates.

Suli and Vornen had shared as much as two people could possibly share in the eight years they had spent together, until after Suli's departure, when Vornen's insistence on cloaking his muddled visions and nightmares with alcohol and *kyush* brought about his ruination and eventually- long years after Suli's sudden departure- his exile.

Vornen had caught sight of Ilhar, the orphanage's warden shortly after Suli's disappearance, coming out of church. The man had apparently thought of her almost as a daughter, although Suli had either not known or chosen not to care. Vornen saw a man weighed down by her departure, but still a man less weighed down than he had been. Not that Ilhar was glad that the girl he had cared for over the years had fled to some distant place to shriek out her madness in the company of strangers or the wilderness, but Vornen had nevertheless seen a small measure of relief in the man's eyes. He could not begrudge him that.

41

As he observed the patrons of this dank place, it occurred to him that they all looked the same; middle-aged men who resembled even older men in their appearance and manner. They were faded, wrinkled and yellow like ruined books. Their trembling hands, covered in veins that bulged with knotty complexity, held pints of cheap ale and paper tubes of smoking-herbs. A faint whiff of *kyush* hung in the air. They spoke of things they had never done, and things they could do nothing about. Their thin but unhealthy frames heaved as they occasionally coughed or even retched.

Vornen shuddered, sipped his ale, and tried not to see the furtive glances that still were occasionally cast his way.

## VII

The following morning, he stood in the study-chamber of Ruan-Tor's overseer, in front of the desk. That Lord Vothangrane was up and about so swiftly after having been "hardly in the land of the living for the last year and a half" was remarkable, but closer inspection revealed him to be a man who had no business being up and about. He had lost a great deal of weight and had aged perhaps twenty years or more in the space of four. Gone was the belligerent, generous and easy-going man, latest in the long Vothangrane line, leaders of Ruan-Tor for a century or more. The man Vornen had known had been replaced by a grey and worried creature.

Vornen felt a weight of guilt descend upon him as he beheld his former master. Perhaps if he had been able to hold his own life together at that time, and remained in Ruan-Tor, this might not have happened. Perhaps whatever strange malaise had gripped Lord Vothangrane was in part a product of his, Vornen's, ignominious exit from the town.

Lord Vothangrane whispered something to himself, as if answering a thought of his own. More wraith than man

42

to look upon, he sat back into the vast ornate chair that he had once occupied much more of. A shaking hand briefly touched his cheek, then fell limply by his side as if the life had suddenly fled from it.

Vornen shifted uncomfortably. He needed to speak. "My Lord, I must beg your forgiveness for everything I did. I became lost in myself. It was entirely my own fault that I was exiled. Everything that led up to that time was my fault. If only I'd..."

"What did you do, Vornen?" Lord Vothangrane stared wearily at him, vast shadows under his milky eyes.

"What did I do?" Vornen was completely taken aback. Had the overseer lost his wits entirely? "My lord, where to begin... I..."

"No, no. What did you do when they shut you out of Ruan-Tor? Did you wander the empty land?"

"Mostly. I travelled, and I thought a great deal. I had too little direction and too much time. But at least I lost my appetite for the *kyush*."

"And your appetite for trouble?"

"I sincerely hope so, my lord."

Lord Vothangrane smiled at that. "Some good came of it, then. Now, I need to tell you what I can about these last few years, Vornen. Not that I have much to tell, as there is so little I remember... but I need to speak of it to someone, and it might as well be you, now you've returned. You were always a good listener. You knew when to speak and when not to."

Lord Vothangrane moved with painful care towards the ornate window that looked out over the town. Vornen moved to help him but was waved away. "I'm not bedridden," he was told, "and I intend to make the most of that fact."

Together they surveyed the snowbound town. Winter had paused for breath once again, and Ruan-Tor lay still and silent. Here and there a few townsfolk wandered along the roads which had been partly cleared of snow.

43

"The ruling council have managed affairs much by themselves over the last few years, and done well by all accounts," Lord Vothangrane said. "The morale of our people is in good shape, considering. Rocan has also been of great help. He is a good man, Vornen, and a fair one, though you might be reluctant to agree."

Vornen shrugged. "He is a pious man, certainly."

"He takes himself seriously. Perhaps too seriously. Whereas in many ways you do not take yourself seriously enough. You do not look after yourself as you should. You allow yourself to be shackled to the past. At least, that's how I remember you, and I still see a desperate unhappiness in your eyes. An inability to forgive yourself. *I* readily forgive your transgressions, Vornen, but my forgiveness is not the issue here."

"I..." Vornen struggled momentarily for the right words, in the wake of that insight. "I need to make amends for the past, my Lord, then perhaps I can think of what to do in the days to come- however many there are. I'm not sure how I can do that, but I'll find employment of some sort, any sort..."

Lord Vothangrane raised a weary hand. "If you wish to make amends, which I am sure you do, then you will have ample opportunity in the months ahead. There are reports of events out in the open land that no one has been able to understand. People in some villages are being seized by a madness of some kind. Other settlements have been destroyed, without obvious reason, and the perpetrators remain unknown. In some places, there have been sacrifices..."

"*Sacrifices?*" Vornen blinked. "Even in the outlying villages, there have been no sacrifices for hundreds of years." He shook his head. "Have some new Gods been imagined into being?"

"No one knows who or what drives it." Lord Vothangrane's fingernails tapped a sharp and restless rhythm on the windowsill. "But nothing happens without reason."

Vornen suddenly half-remembered something, perhaps from a dream or from his most recent Gate-journey; a vision of light, a myriad of doorways, stars that changed position, an important word... *I must remember!* he thought frantically. *I need to remember, but I've forgotten whatever it was! Did I tell Morthanien? I am sure I must have. But he didn't believe me. I remember that much, but...*

"Vornen?"

The world came sharply back into focus. Vornen placed a hand upon the cool plaster of the wall to steady himself.

"We seem to be headed towards chaos, in the outlying territories," Lord Vothangrane said bleakly, "and we have no idea why."

"I remember some years ago a group of religious madmen tried to start a war between the plainspeople's clans," Vornen said. At the same time, what remained of the sudden memory slipped further from his mind.

"This is something else, something far greater. There are fears that Ruan-Tor itself will come under attack sooner or later. If you seek employment, then you should look no further than here. You were a good guardsman on your sober days, and I need good guardsmen. I need *sober* guardsmen, so if you can promise me a clear head on duty then I'll see a position for you is found."

"I never finished my training, as I recall," Vornen observed dryly.

"No, well that can be remedied. You should return to the household. Where are you staying at the moment? Some low tavern?"

"One of the lowest. I thank you for your offer, my Lord. And certainly I will help you, and help Ruan-Tor, in any way I can."

"Good." Lord Vothangrane managed a wan smile. "I am glad you've returned, Vornen. Are you?"

Vornen nodded. "If I can be of service to you, my Lord, then yes- at least, I *will* be glad. To be returned into the household is more than I could have expected. More than I deserve, certainly."

"As you know, I made a promise to your parents before they left," Lord Vothangrane said mildly, "but we'll not talk of that." He sighed. "I had hoped to describe to you what happened to me after you left, but it seems that the more I try to recall the early days of my illness, the more that recollection shrinks back and fades. It becomes confused when I try to study it. One thing I do remember, however, is a dream. A dream that I had over and again, and every time the same."

He paused to stare vacantly through, or possibly at the window, and his lips moved soundlessly. To Vornen he appeared to be counting motes of dust in the air. When the old man failed to continue, Vornen quietly prompted him: "This dream, my Lord. What did it concern?"

"I walked through a forest. The trees were dense, close about me. The air felt like ice." His voice had become dreamy, almost distant. Vornen felt oddly disturbed by its tone. "I walked deeper into the forest, and all the daylight became shut away from me. Yet a different light shone, from the trees themselves, from out of the earth itself. A thudding sound came, and I could not tell if it came from the ground or within me, or both. A heartbeat, but not the beat of any heart I could know. Some inner voice assured me that one day all this would pass."

Again he lapsed into silence. Vornen felt his skin crawl. Something about Lord Vothangrane's words deeply worried him, though he could not say why. "What happened after that?" he asked.

"I started to hear things. Strange cries came from above. I could not tell what made them, as the sky was far

46

above and could not be seen through the pressing darkness of the trees. The ground grew soft, but not because of water. Something had transformed the place where I stood. All living creatures had fled, except me. I headed into the heart... the dark heart of something, at the centre of the forest. I had become lost, with no hope of ever finding my way out. But Vornen..." Lord Vothangrane's eyes widened as if he had suddenly remembered another detail. "One time, I caught a glimpse of something... shadows that danced at the edges of my vision as they pulled... other shadows out of the earth."

Vornen said nothing, but the vague memory of his last encounter with a Gate returned for a moment, fainter than ever, a fluttering at the periphery of his mind. Then it was gone.

Lord Vothangrane was not done with his recollection yet. "I remember something else. Words repeated themselves over and over in my mind, as if the darkness at the heart of this place spoke to me. *This is not your world,* it said."

He nodded and glanced at Vornen. "Those exact words. What can they mean?"

"I couldn't say, my Lord. I'm not sure a dream always means anything at all." Worriedly, Vornen recalled Lord Vothangrane's words concerning events out in the plains. *People in some villages are being seized by a madness of some kind.* Lord Vothangrane did not seem mad precisely, but he did seem... *disturbed,* Vornen decided. Preoccupied by a dream, or by some perceived portent within it.

*I need to remember my own dream, or vision,* he thought again, but the words themselves felt empty, pointless.

They both jumped, startled, as the chamber door burst open and one of the guardsmen appeared, dressed in the grey and brown livery of Lord Vothangrane's inner court. Vornen saw the man's glassy-eyed panic and knew something terrible had happened even before he spoke. "My

47

Lord, fighting has broken out in the market place! A slaughter, I'm told..."

Lord Vothangrane raised a tremulous hand to his forehead. "Gods, as if we have not had enough hardship..." Lost for further words, he moved to a chair near to the fireside and sank into it.

Vornen turned and strode out of the room, past the guardsman who stood to one side to allow him passage.

*With any luck, it will be over by the time I get there,* he thought to himself, trying to ignore the panicked thumping of his heart. Fights and even killings were not uncommon in Ruan-Tor, especially when times were harsh. *I expect Rocan will already have meted out his particular brand of justice,* he added as an afterthought, realising how much his hatred of the knight-commander had been rekindled since his return.

Vornen had reached the outer gates of the fortress and was being admitted out onto the broad street when the first faint sounds of the disturbance came to him. As he stopped and listened, he realised with a sudden cold feeling that these sounds, carried by the icy breeze, were not those of a drink-fuelled quarrel or even a swordsman's duel. They were- as the guardsman had said- the sounds of slaughter. Faint screams rose into the air, sounds of panic and horror. Vornen took a deep breath and turned to the gate sentinel. "Do you know if Rocan's knights are on their way?"

The sentinel frowned worriedly. "I don't know. I've not seen them pass by."

Vornen made his way cautiously down the cobbled hill towards the marketplace area. The few people he saw along the way hurried in the opposite direction, eager to be as far as possible from the chaos. Soon enough he reached a point in the road from which he could see a little of what had happened, for the road continued down and widened out into the market place a little over a hundred paces away. Normally crammed and bustling, now overturned stalls and debris lay scattered everywhere, winter vegetables and other foodstuffs spilled and trodden on.

He noticed the bodies- perhaps twenty or more men, women and children, scattered amongst their produce. Then he beheld the cause of this carnage, and a sensation of horror and bewilderment overcame him.

Larien, surrounded by six or seven men, presumably the only ones who had not already fled, wielded a sword the like of which Vornen had never seen before- plain-hilted but with a blade that looked utterly black. Vornen watched in shock as Larien used it to cut straight through one of the men, who fell to the ground. Blood sprayed through the chill morning air. A moment later, the sword slashed out again, like a sliver of darkness cutting through the morning sunlight, and another man fell.

Then, as the others shrank back, their resolve broken, Larien calmly strode on through the abandoned marketplace, reached the other side, and walked on through the archway, swallowed up by the shadows and soon out of sight.

Vornen leaned against the wall of a nearby house and tried to collect his thoughts. *This is impossible,* he thought frantically, though the scene before him screamed otherwise. His mind kept flitting from one scenario to another as if desperate to gather scraps of sense. Somehow the events of the last few days- his meeting up with Larien, the man's strange behaviour, the ritual- all *meant* something, but Vornen had no idea what. A crazed man with a wooden sword had become a crazed murderer with a sword that looked like a black rip in the day itself. How had he even survived the journey here, given his condition when Vornen had last seen him? Who had let him in? What story had he concocted in order to gain entrance?

And above all else, why this senseless slaughter? Could it simply be a random act of madness?

When eventually Vornen forced himself to go and witness the results of that massacre to see if anyone had survived, he found it far worse than it had looked from a distance. Many of the bodies had been disembowelled. Blood and gore lay strewn in the snow. Vornen counted twenty-eight dead bodies in all and no one left alive, before he gave up.

His desperate thoughts wandered again and drowned out all reason.

*I could have stopped him. Whatever sorcery he was calling upon when he knelt on the ground, I could have slain him then. I could have cut him in half and stopped this evil. But I ran. Why did I run? Why do I always run?*

Yet he had no strength for running or even walking now. Vornen sank to the ground, the sounds of Larien's rampage echoing in his mind, and he remained there on the cold flagstones even as the sounds of Rocan's approaching horsemen echoed around the blood-spattered marketplace.

# II - The Compass of Pain

## I

Two days had passed since her arrival at the castle, and Amethyst remained far from impressed with the hospitality provided.

An austere, unfussy place of grey, imposing columns and walls, the Rand Fortress lacked beauty and imagination, but more importantly, it lacked warmth. Amethyst felt as if she should have liked the straightforward design of the castle- it was markedly different to many of the garish and often pointlessly ornate castles of southern Aphenhast, whose architects were artisans above all else, and even celebrated as such on certain days of the year. But with the coming of the winter blizzards, the unforgiving and plain interior made her feel all the colder. More than anything, it made her long desperately for the comforts of home.

*This is a place without nooks and crannies,* she had observed, knowing that that was not quite true. *Everything is in plain sight. Everything is large and grey and joyless. It matches the snowbound plains to perfection.*

Amethyst had found most of the people here cold, grim and unfriendly. Her tanned, olive skin and her accent betrayed her as a woman far from home, which did not help matters. Indeed, she was probably further from home than any of the merchants and travelling folk who were staying at the castle. Most of them were in the process of finishing off their trade until the spring, and would soon be hurrying south to warmer climes before the snow made the trade routes in the valleys of the Crescent Mountains impassable for months. Some merchants had already departed, forsaking even profit in their hurry with one eye on winter's approach.

It had not escaped Amethyst's notice that if she remained in this grim part of the land for much longer, then she too would be trapped until the spring came.

*But I can't go back,* she reminded herself. *And I may never be able to.*

Not for the first time today, her thoughts wandered back to the event that had led her here. In time it would lead her elsewhere, dragging her on an invisible leash.

"Damn it," she muttered, scowling out of her bedchamber window. Her forgotten meal cooled on the mantelpiece and thin tendrils of steam rose into the chill air. "Why *me* of all people?"

*The old woman in Alinnora's Haven had been delirious, gravely weak and on the verge of slipping away, yet she had grasped Amethyst's hand with a sudden, final ferocity. Her veins loomed like roots out of her withered hand as she shook with desperate effort.*

*And then the woman with the iron-grey hair, who had brought her to that dank bedchamber in the house at the edge of the village soothed her patient as the rain hammered down outside, hissing on the dirt-streaked road. Amethyst had wanted nothing more than to be away from that place, as the old woman's milky eyes opened briefly, opaque and unseeing in the gloom.*

*A clear picture had blossomed in her mind at that exact moment- an image of a young girl who stood directly in front of her, in a large house somewhere in a town she had never been to. Somehow, she knew that the girl was staring into a mirror from the way she peered.*

*I am the mirror,* Amethyst remembered thinking in her shock.

*The moment passed, but the vision had imprinted itself on her mind. Afterglow shimmered behind her eyes as*

*she shook her head in bewilderment. "What did you... how..."*
*Instinct took over and she reached for the knives in her belt,*
*but for the first time in her life she was thwarted, her hand*
*melded to her trouser pocket as surely as if the two had been*
*sown together.*

*"That would not be wise." The healer- not healer, but*
witch, *Amethyst thought fearfully- stared levelly at her.*
*Amethyst felt a sudden pressure grow over her fingers as she*
*tried to move her hand again. A little more and it would*
*crush her bones. And then she would never use her knives*
*again, or anything else with that hand. She nodded*
*reluctantly.*

*"What you saw was Imiera's last vision," the woman*
*said softly, stepping in and out of shadow as she paced*
*around the bedside. "As you see, she is dying." There was*
*neither sadness nor regret in her voice. Somehow Amethyst*
*doubted that the woman indulged herself with such*
*sentiments.*

*"Why did you bring me here?" she demanded.*

*"Because Imiera's quest has passed to you. I have*
*made it so. The memory of what you saw will not fade. It*
*belongs to you now. And to me, of course, through you." She*
*smiled faintly.*

*Imiera shuddered. Her head moved suddenly,*
*violently to one side and it seemed that she whispered*
*something into the gloom. The witch moved to touch her neck,*
*then her forehead as the old woman became still. "She has*
*passed back into the world."*

*Amethyst found herself out in the rain a moment*
*later, as if the intervening moment had been cut from her life.*
*Perhaps it had. She shivered and drew her cloak about her,*
*then turned and headed back down the road towards the inn*
*where she had been staying.*

*A while later, with the witch's words tumbling in her*
*head, she stared out at the downpour and tried to remember*
*the detail of what had happened. But with each passing*

53

moment it faded a little more- except for the vision, which remained bright and vivid.

She could recall arriving at the village. She could even remember talking briefly with the witch-woman, but she could not remember going with her to the ramshackle house at the end of the road.

With her mind brimful of unasked questions, Amethyst remained in the corner by the hearth in the otherwise deserted tap-room, her drink forgotten, her appetite for lunch diminished. Why me? she asked herself, but the answer was obvious. She had simply been in the wrong place at the wrong time, an unfortunate traveller passing through. When the woman had approached her, full of despair over the illness of her mother, Amethyst had protested that she knew nothing about healing, and had been about to pass on her way. But the woman had touched her hand, just briefly, and then...

Then I was in her cottage, Amethyst thought numbly, as if she stole time from me.

A short while later, she could remember almost nothing but the vision itself, and the painfully detailed image of the girl, still so bright in her mind, staring into the mirror in quiet desperation as if she wished for the power to step through the glass and into some other existence.

Amethyst shuddered. She could not warm herself up. She felt as if a taint lingered within her, invisible, intangible. A parasite, but not one that could be excised.

Before this event, which would change her life more than she could have ever foreseen, Amethyst had languished in a strange torpor, a product of homesickness and lack of purpose. She had left Darkenhelm full of hope and excitement, burning with the desire to see the world, or at least the rest of Aphenhast.

But she had become tired, disillusioned, jaded by people who were either suspicious, devious or simply

54

*unpleasant. Over time the flames of her youthful excitement burned lower and lower. They had gone out entirely by the time she had reached the village of Alinnora's Haven, where her life would change forever.*

*Although a city girl by birth, she knew some of the "odd ways of the middle lands" as her father had once sardonically described them.* They believe in the strangest things, *he had warned her more than once, after meeting her for luncheon outside the Guild she was studying at in Darkenhelm.* They hold to those beliefs as strongly as you or I might hold to logic and reason.

*He had warned her of misguided, superstitious folk, but he had not warned her of witch-women who had the power to steal her freedom with a simple touch.*

*Amethyst had slept poorly the night after her encounter, but nothing could have prepared her for what happened the following morning as she left Alinnora's Haven and headed along the south road towards Rockmire. A nagging headache became a full-blown hammering inside her skull, accompanied by flashes of vivid colours and shapes that became so bad she could barely see where she was going. A four-horse carriage almost ran her down as she meandered into the middle of the road. With the curses of the coachman a faint whisper amidst the noise in her head, she staggered to the side of the road and collapsed in the mud. The agony receded a little as she lay there, sobbing; enough for her to get shakily to her feet and continue tentatively on.*

*But then the pain slammed into her again, this time a dozen times worse. Crying out, she collapsed at the side of the road again. Colour and light stabbed through her head as if slicing her brain apart.*

*When the agony dissipated sufficiently, Amethyst dared to sit up, and rummaged in her pack for some of the herbs she had bought the other week for headaches. She found none. Cursing in frustration, she staggered to her feet and started to walk back towards Alinnora's Haven. She would be able to buy a good stock of medicines there. She recalled seeing a herbalist's shop on the main road that opened every day except Alea's Day.*

*Amethyst stopped suddenly. "That's impossible," she whispered.*

*Every ounce of pain had been lifted from her. Her vision was clear. She felt almost as good as she had ever felt.*

*Slowly, a dread realisation crept up on her. She turned and abruptly walked several steps due west, as far as the stone wall bordering the road on that side. Immediately the pain loomed again- not as severe but still debilitating. The same happened when she turned and headed east. Amethyst did not dare turn south again, knowing in her heart what would happen if she did. She headed north, with a clear head and troubled heart. After only a short while, the magnitude of what had happened struck her, and she wept as she stumbled along.*

Gods, I'm being pulled in one direction, *she thought miserably,* and all others are denied me, if I wish to retain my sanity...

In the castle chamber, Amethyst pulled herself out of her thoughts with an effort. *What's done is done,* she tried to tell herself. But if only it could be undone.

If only, if only. How often in her life had she said that, even when she only half-meant it? Few things had a more bitter taste than hindsight.

She had been intent on travelling to the lands north of the Crescents in any case- a journey no one else in her family had even considered. Another of her idiot schemes, her mother had scoffed, although in truth that was partly out of worry that she had made up her mind to wander so far from home. Amethyst had left Darkenhelm with the fading of summer, just after her twenty-fifth birthday, and her family had fretted about her travelling lands such as these with autumn rushing into winter's embrace. But even they-

and her father a weather-seer in his spare time- could hardly have foreseen a snowstorm such as the one that howled outside and lashed against the windowpane, so early in the season. Even as far north as this, such heavy snowfall was apparently uncommon at this time. And she was only a dozen leagues or so from the northern edge of the Crescents here. Had it not been for the blizzard, and of course if she had been given a chamber on the other side of the castle, she could have enjoyed a view of those mountains, rising like a vast row of gleaming teeth that stretched east to west as far as the eye could see.

Amethyst turned away from the window, sat on the edge of the bed and tentatively tried some of the stew that the servant-girl had brought her. Despite the off-putting oily swirl on top, perhaps some mysterious local touch, it tasted good- far better than she had expected. Within a short while she had finished it off and mopped up the last of the stew with the final piece of freshly-baked bread.

Her surroundings were basic, and the reception as frosty as the weather. But Amethyst, now with a pleasant warmth in her belly, decided that the food almost made up for it. Almost.

She smiled for a moment as she recalled how the clerk in the guest-hall had not known how to spell Darkenhelm, having asked for the place of her birth. Perhaps he had never heard of Aphenhast's largest city. It seemed likely, especially given the curious look he had given her when he thought she was too busy signing her name to notice. *It's hundreds of leagues to the south and means nothing here,* Amethyst admitted to herself, *but how could he have never even heard the name? I may as well be in a different land altogether here.*

Nevertheless, her mood had improved somewhat. She moved to sit cross-legged on the bed and began to sharpen her array of belt-knives. They numbered eight, and each one was subtly different in weight, balance and blade length. The sharpening was an unnecessary task, as the weapons were already frighteningly sharp, but the activity often helped her to think things over.

On occasions during the last few weeks Amethyst had felt an indescribable hatred stir within herself, a deep fury at the situation in which she had become trapped. Inevitably that rage had found a focus, and sharpened itself around the girl whose image remained perfectly clear within her mind. There had been moments when she had wanted to kill the girl when she found her. *Because I will find her,* Amethyst reminded herself. *It may take a long time, but I'm being pulled towards wherever she is. The witch made it so. I can remember that much even now. And when I do find her...*

Amethyst smiled bitterly as she briefly caught sight of her reflection in one of her blades. She was a free woman in name, yet all she yearned for was freedom.

Since the age of fifteen, Amethyst had taken on various roles- bodyguard, spy, acrobat and scribe's apprentice amongst others. Oddly, the apprenticeship had been the most fulfilling, although it had largely involved copying and looking after old texts that the world had forgotten. The past, her old master Scribe Harran had said to her, was the most important thing of all. "But you can't change the past," she had argued early on in her training, to which he only smiled and remarked, "Nor can you learn from the future."

Harran had displayed an annoying habit of pointing out facts of life, the Existence and everything, which were obvious enough once she considered them but which somehow had still needed to be pointed out to her. Amethyst remembered they had debated whether societies of each Race ever learned from the past. Often those debates had persisted long into the evening.

Reason and common sense, she supposed, were not amongst her greatest assets. She smiled sardonically, tracing a finger carefully along the back of one of her blades. *These* were, perhaps. She could juggle six of them at a time without impaling herself. She could fling each one and strike a target no larger than a sling stone at more than fifty paces. Oh yes, she had poise, balance and no small amount of fighting ability, yet she could not even work out what she wanted to do with her life- once or *if* she was free again- beyond endless exploration.

But had she not already grown weary of adventure even before the course of her life had been changed? And what lay beyond that final disappointment?

*Maybe I should have been a dancer all along, just as Mother wanted,* she thought bitterly. *I would never have found contentment, but neither would I have found myself in* this *situation.*

Amethyst sprang from the bed and strolled over to the window once again, hands in the pockets of her breeches. She wondered whether to take a tour of the castle and see which areas were permitted to her and which were out of bounds, especially to a strange southern woman who had yet to declare her business beyond "travelling through." If nothing else, it would keep those humourless guards busy.

Something was happening out in the main courtyard. Although the storm remained as fierce as ever, a contingent of the castle's soldiers had ventured out on patrol- one of several that had taken place in the last few days. This time they had brought other people back with them. That these people were not castle folk was obvious even to Amethyst; they wore ornate, decorative robes, and one of them, a grim-looking old man who refused to be helped even as he slowly negotiated the slippery slabs of the courtyard, wore a vast array of amulets, necklaces and charms around his neck and wrists.

*Plainsfolk,* Amethyst supposed, *and he is their elder, or shaman, or whatever they call spiritual leaders around here.*

Some of them, she noted, had been wounded, and two could not walk at all. Looking at the bloody, ruined knee of one man, untended and open to the air, she doubted that he would ever walk unaided again. She wondered what had happened and why they were being brought here. For their own protection, she reckoned, but from what? Perhaps some of the plainsfolk were invited to shelter within the castle each winter, but large as this place was, it did not have room for an extra two hundred, let alone thousands.

The last to be brought into the courtyard was a small child who the soldiers almost dragged down from the pony he had clutched desperately onto. The boy staggered to the ground when helped down from the saddle, and the soldiers picked him up with swift impatience, their hurry to be inside obvious. As they bore him through the inner gates and into the castle, out of the gathering snowstorm, the child's feet barely touched the ground.

*Whatever their story, they were lucky to have been rescued in this weather,* Amethyst mused, flipping a knife in the air and catching it blade-down between her fingers without even looking- a trick that had long been second-nature to her but which elicited alarm and admiration in equal measure wherever she displayed it.

Shrugging, she returned briefly to her thoughts, but finding them uncomfortable and restless, she soon left her chamber for the raucous distraction of the main downstairs hall, where at least a little drink and conversation- or what passed for conversation in these lands- might pass the time until the storm dissipated.

She drank, and she talked- even amongst these haughty people there were a few who found her interesting enough to converse with- and later, as a blizzard howled around the castle and an alcoholic warmth afforded her temporary contentment, Amethyst made her way back to her room.

60

But during the night, she discovered that the witch's curse held a malevolence even greater than she had feared; it could no longer abide her remaining here, not yet striding on her way.

## II

Amethyst rolled off the bed and collapsed to the floor. She doubled over and coughed blood onto the carpet. Her body shook with pain. Silently she raged against the invisible prison in which she had been placed, but her fury did as much good as ever. Curling herself up tightly, she closed her eyes and prepared herself- as best she could- for the torment.

The crippling agony came and went in waves, like fingernails that scraped through her head. This time it seemed vengeful, like a live creature that screamed its hatred through her mind. It grew steadily worse, a cacophony that threatened to send her tumbling into madness, until she screamed for mercy over and over. Only then came a lessening of the terrible sound to a dull roar, as if a beast from her nightmares paced restlessly outside, snarling threats.

She fell into a kind of slumber. When she woke in the morning, her head felt like mud. Only when she turned to face east could she manage to think at all. *East,* she thought numbly. *I am far enough north, and now it turns me to the east.*

Sometime later, a sob escaped her lips. The realisation came to her that the time had come for her to leave. A faint but urgent pounding sounded in her head. If she did not head east this morning, the curse would crush her brain.

*Oh, I will do as bidden,* she swore as she staggered to her feet. *I will find your precious witchling. I will rid myself of this evil. Then I will come for you.*

61

But she did not, could not, do any such thing. As she made her way downstairs a short while later, Amethyst fancied that she could feel the torment return, ready to pull her mind apart. In her panic, she missed her footing, and tumbled a dozen yards down the stairs. Her head struck one of the stone steps and the world faded from her eyes.

Amethyst woke suddenly. *It's a different room,* she noted almost immediately. *And something has changed...*

*It's still there,* she realised after a while. *The witch's eye inside my head. But it's...* less, *somehow. How can that be?*

The pain in her head had subsided almost completely, replaced by a kind of dullness as if her senses had been smoothed over. *Something has happened to me,* Amethyst thought. She remembered falling down the staircase and hitting her head. *It must have been the impact. It did something.*

She sat up and wondered fearfully if the agony would suddenly return. It did not. She felt simply tired and a little disoriented.

The room was a small, sparse bedchamber with a low, slanting ceiling and great dark beams of wood stretching from wall to wall. Sunlight shone in through a plain, small window set in the most distant wall. A faint aroma of something like perfume or flowers hung in the air. Amethyst wondered whereabouts in the castle she had been taken. Some place where casualties were treated perhaps? *At least they have looked after me,* she considered. *The way I've seen some people looking at me, I should be grateful that they didn't leave me where I was or throw me out into the courtyard.*

The door in the side wall opened, and a man of perhaps forty years walked in. He had to stoop through the doorway because of his height. Iron-grey hair hung lank to his neckline and touched the faded leather jerkin he wore.

He smiled as he observed her sitting up, and remarked, "How does your head feel?"

Amethyst frowned. *How can he know?* she thought, but even as he added, "You struck your head as you tumbled down the stairs," she realised what he meant. *Of course he can't know,* she told herself. *No one does, and no one will. I need to work out by myself why it's faded. Was it something to do with my head striking the stone stair?*

"I remember," she said, then awkwardly added, "Thank you."

"Oh, I didn't pick you up and bring you here. But I am able to help you."

As he stood and regarded her without expression, Amethyst suddenly tried to figure out what he might mean. "Help me?" she repeated.

"You regained your wits briefly as you were being brought here," he said. "Ah- I see you don't remember. No matter. The servants who brought you here told how you shouted and ranted, but that's to be expected. It happens. You spoke of the lights and colours, and the dreams. Only a little, but enough."

Amethyst averted her eyes, her heart sinking as she contemplated his words. *Gods, first I fall downstairs and then I shout to all and sundry about everything,* she thought miserably. *How much longer until I lose control forever?*

"You are not alone," he told her as he walked a little nearer. Now in the way of the bright afternoon sun, he appeared almost a silhouette.

"My head hurts less now," she said. "Have I been... given anything for it?"

"A little medicine for the accident, and something else for the dreams," he said, "to help you deal with them." He walked over and sat on the edge of the bed. "My name is Fenmor. I command the army that protects the Rand castle and estate, but I also have a certain talent as a herbalist.

63

Something to pass the time on those rare occasions when I have time to pass. And your name is?"

"Amethyst."

"A pretty name. Where are you from, Amethyst? The far south I'd guess- Darkenhelm perhaps?"

She nodded. "I don't mean to be disrespectful, but I long to be back there."

"One day, perhaps you will be." Fenmor watched her in silence for a while before he added quietly, "You're not alone anymore, Amethyst. It can be frightening when the visions start, when the lights and the colours and the dreams whirl around in your mind... but it simply means that you have been chosen. The pain is the worst thing of all, but it passes." He smiled and patted her hand. "Soon enough you will feel at peace."

Amethyst stared at him, not sure what to say. *How can he know that much about it?* she wondered. *Has he been cursed in the same way?* Aloud she asked him, "Have *you* had them?"

"Oh yes." His voice had developed a wistful, almost dreamlike quality. "Had, and continue to have. They tell of a new Age, of new Gods. That is why we have these visions, Amethyst. That is why so many of us have had the same dreams of the Great Light. The world is about to be made anew, in the image of new Gods, of light and revelation."

He squeezed her hand, his smile broadening all the while. "The pains ebb and flow, but after several days they usually disappear. Sometimes they linger on awhile, but I have developed a brew that keeps them at bay for the most part. It does leave you feeling a little light-headed, but there are no other ill effects, and the dreams still come, without the pain. You are blessed. Truly blessed!"

Amethyst lay back in the bed, concentrating on the ceiling, looking everywhere but into Fenmor's eyes, afraid of what she would see there. *This man has lost his sanity,* she realised, *but worse than that, he thinks that I somehow share*

64

*his madness! Do the powers that be in this place realise that their soldiers are commanded by a religious lunatic?*

"I will let you rest and recover your strength," Fenmor said, much to her relief, but that relief was short-lived. Rather than depart, he wandered over to the window and stared out. He nodded to himself a few times, turned and smiled at her, and after a while came and sat on the bed again. "This is no season to be travelling on your own," he observed.

"No," Amethyst agreed carefully. "I think I will remain here in the castle awhile, if I'm allowed to, if you can help with the pain. I can work to pay for my lodging and food..."

"Oh, there's still travelling to be done." His expression darkened so suddenly that Amethyst felt a chill within her stomach as she watched him. "Evil grows in strength, out in the plains."

"What sort of evil?" Amethyst asked despite herself.

Fenmor took a long while to reply. "An ancient darkness, thought gone forever," he said finally. He looked uncomfortable even speaking of it, as if by discussion it might be somehow invoked. "This is a remote part of the world, Amethyst, and settlements are far apart from each other. The old and barbaric ways are still remembered amongst some of the tribes. Ways that we- by which I mean the castle folk- left behind centuries ago. Many places have been attacked by..." He shook his head. "We don't need to speak of it now. Perhaps when you're on your feet again, we can talk of such things. You are here now, so when you are well enough, you should know what we are fighting against."

He smiled, and then left her alone, closing the door softly behind him.

*An ancient darkness, and new Gods of light and revelation,* Amethyst thought weakly. *How much of what he said is grounded in truth and how much is some fanciful notion from his own mind?*

65

Suddenly she recalled the plainsfolk she had seen being ushered through the courtyards, brought into the unfamiliar surroundings of the Rand castle. *For their protection,* she thought. *Or might there be some other reason?*

*There is still travelling to be done,* Fenmor had said. But why? If the wild parts of the land were under attack, surely this was the worst time to travel- not even considering the season. *Does he mean me?* she wondered. *Does he mean the entire castle? Or should I read nothing into what he said?*

Amethyst dozed off, and hours passed before she woke. Sitting up again, she saw that all the daylight had disappeared; a few stars and a white glow from Ildar's face lit the portion of sky she could see through the window. Amethyst swallowed, suddenly thirsty, and noticed a jug of water and glass on her bedside table. She frowned, certain that they had not been there earlier. A servant must have come in and placed them there, going about her task quietly so as not to disturb her.

She sat up a little more, poured herself some water and drank. It was cool but not too cold. She finished the glass off and lay down again.

Sleep had almost returned when she felt the pull, the pain, of the witch's curse again. *The tide was going out, but now it's coming back in,* she thought in a panic, and sat up, then threw back the bedclothes and sat on the edge of the bed, horror rising within her as she realised that this time it was going to be worse than ever. She had sudden visions of her body being found slumped on the bed, eyes burst out of their sockets, skull split apart, heat and froth spilling from the cracked shell that housed her burnt mind.

"*No!*" she screamed and ran for the door.

It was bolted on the other side. Amethyst shrieked and pounded as loudly as she could on the door, over and over, until finally someone on the other side threw back the bolt and the door opened.

Amethyst almost collapsed into the arms of the girl in the doorway, who was stoutly built and held her up easily. "M'lord Fenmor is on his way," she murmured. "You'll be at peace again soon."

"It will kill me!" Amethyst shouted, but the servant, if that was who she was, shook her head and motioned for her to be quiet, holding her arms forcefully. A moment later, Amethyst heard someone approach in the corridor beyond, and then Fenmor appeared. "Thank you," he said to the servant girl, who gave a quick bow and hurried away.

Fenmor calmly bore Amethyst to the bed and gently placed her back into the dishevelled bedclothes. Even in her panic, Amethyst marvelled at his strength. She was slightly built, but the act apparently required no effort whatsoever.

He poured some fine brown powder into her drinking glass and added water from the jug, whereupon the powder dissolved and left the water as clear as before. He was about to hand her the glass, but Amethyst had began to shake violently, the agonies too much for her. Her view of the room disappeared in a red haze, came sharply back into focus, disappeared again. She could taste blood in her throat.

Dimly she felt Fenmor pinch her nostrils together, open her mouth and pour the water. Some of it she choked on and it came back up. But she swallowed enough of it.

Amethyst imagined herself sinking into soft sand. Before her, the tide receded, an evil foam that raged endlessly yet had no choice but to retreat.

She lay back, dimly aware of Fenmor lighting a lantern. He placed it on her bedside table. The pain receded further, nothing but a distant line now. "Better?" he inquired as she blinked and the room swam back into view.

Amethyst nodded weakly, and watched as he placed a small cloth bag on the table. "This is *cahreu* root, dried and powdered," he said. "For those whose visions are more powerful- worse, you might say- than others, it keeps the worst of the pain at bay. Sprinkle a little into water- or wine or ale or the juice of fruits- and it will help."

Amethyst no longer cared if the commander-at-arms of the Rand Fortress was a religious lunatic. He could babble his nonsense about new Gods and Great Lights as much as he wished. Relief and gratitude almost overwhelmed her.

"Thank you," she managed to whisper.

Fenmor smiled and said nothing. After a moment he left, and Amethyst slept peacefully without stirring even once for the remainder of the night.

III

She woke with barely a murmur of the curse lurking in her head, and almost wept as she sat up.

Amethyst felt well enough to rise and dress. Afterwards she wandered over to look out of the window, greeted by the brightness of mid-morning. Barely a cloud could be seen in the sky. Beyond the castle grounds, the plains stretched into the distance, covered in pristine snow.

As if he had sensed her stirring, Fenmor walked in a short while later. "Ah," he said, looking her up and down as he stood by the doorway. "I see the *cahreu* root and some good sleep have helped you. Are you well enough to travel?"

"I... I hope so." *That might depend on the direction in which you take me,* Amethyst thought darkly. She knew that the witch's eye still lurked inside her head, however subdued and faint its reach might be. "Are we headed east?" she asked. *Please, let it be so!*

Fenmor nodded and sat on the edge of the bed, pondering something. Finally he said, "I promised you an explanation, and I think now would be a good time." He paused, perhaps working out how to word that explanation. "Well, the truth is, Amethyst, we are living at the end of an Age. What else could it be? A hundred or more people within this castle alone have dreamed the same dream, of the great

68

light that comes out of the east. And it will come to others, as it did to you. The eyes of many thousands shall be opened." He smiled. "There you have the fact of the matter. It sounds incredible- but I can assure you, it *is* true."

"The east." Amethyst could barely hide her relief. It seemed that the witch's hold abated a little further at her utterance of that direction. *East,* she thought, and almost smiled. "I will come with you," she said.

"Yes," he agreed. "You will. You *must,* because you have been chosen. But we digress. I told you of a darkness spreading. Already it has tainted many of the plainsfolk, killing some and corrupting others. Quarrels between villages have become bloodbaths. There are stories of sacrifice and ritual burnings." Fenmor shook his head grimly. "These are all signs of a return to darker times, the peeling back of long centuries- but we cannot allow that step back to be taken."

"Why is it happening?" Amethyst asked.

"Because of the promised salvation, because of the light of our dreams." He smiled at her as if the answer was obvious. "It is the response of a great evil, one that once ruled over all the Races, in an Age now all but forgotten." He nodded, his smile growing sad at Amethyst's blank expression. "You've never heard of any of this," he remarked. "Well, such truths were forgotten first in the South, but they're forgotten everywhere now. Or were, until the dreams came. I knew only a little before the dreams, and had dismissed it as myth, or at least a history so distant as to be of no consequence."

"What will happen," Amethyst asked, "when the great light comes out of the east?"

"The Old Dark will be burned away forever," Fenmor said, "and the Gods will walk throughout Aona." He smiled, and then gave her a considering look. "Tell me about how they were for *you,* Amethyst- the dreams. I know you don't

69

wish to recall the pain, but the light, the endless light- that must echo still through your waking thoughts."

Amethyst swallowed, trying to force down her sudden panic. "It does," she stammered. "The... the light... so beautiful despite the pain..."

"Yes. *So beautiful despite the pain.*" He strolled casually over to where she stood, though it seemed he took only an instant to reach her. She found herself looking down at the floor, but he tilted her chin upwards. "Look at me," he said softly, and Amethyst forced herself.

"Now," Fenmor said, his voice softer than ever, "tell me again what it was like. Tell me what you saw."

His eyes were like hard grey stones, the colour of boneyard slabs. She could not look away from them. *What can I tell him?* she thought frantically. *How am I to know what answer he requires?*

"I saw light," she whispered eventually. "Light that went on forever. Light from the east."

"Anything else?" His voice was barely audible.

Amethyst imagined a silver crown tumbling through the air, each side in turn catching the light as the opposite face was cast in shadow. *I must choose,* she thought in desperation. *I must choose, and boldly.*

"No," she told him. "There was nothing else."

The blow that struck the side of her head sent her flying halfway across the room. As she reeled on the floor, Fenmor hauled her up and struck her across the jaw, not powerfully enough to break it but enough for the sour taste of blood to flow into her mouth as two of her teeth came loose. "You lie," he said to her, sounding almost hurt. "Why would you lie?"

He dragged her over to the bed and loomed over her. Amethyst coughed, flecks of blood staining the pillow.

"Why would you *lie?*" he repeated.

70

Amethyst struggled to speak at first. Fenmor waited impassively. "Because I don't know your *dream*," she said finally. "I want nothing to do with this madness..."

"Then your visions..." Fenmor nodded suddenly. "Ah. I understand now. Yes. Something else afflicts you. What is it, I wonder? Sorcery of some sort. I don't understand sorcery." He shook his head and looked down at her, as if considering something. "Yet the *cahreu* gives you peace, for a while."

She nodded weakly.

"I have more of it," he said. "I have as much as you need. Tomorrow, the amount I have already given you will have been exhausted, as you piss it out. You will need more, or else whatever is *wrong* with you will return. You will be as you were last night before I soothed you, Amethyst. Ranting and screaming, but *unchosen*."

She stared up at him, full of hate. "Will you let me have some, when I need it?" she asked finally.

Fenmor's lips moved to form a predatory smile. "You're no use to me with your mind lost, woman. I want you to be *aware*, you faithless whore. I want you to be aware each night as we head east, and I take my fill of you."

Amethyst said nothing, but closed her eyes, willing herself to remain calm. Fenmor laughed, drew a fingernail down her cheek as if pretending to cut her with a knife. *He's going to rape me,* was Amethyst's only, panic-stricken thought.

But he did not. He kissed her upon her lips, mockingly, and then he left.

Only then did Amethyst open her eyes, and allow her emotions free rein.

# III - Dreamers

Early morning sunlight cut savagely into Amethyst's eyes as she struggled awake. The tent opening flapped in the chill breeze. Perhaps the sudden influx of cold air had woken her. She saw Fenmor walk away towards a few of his men who had gathered together. From what she could tell, an argument had flared up over some points on a map.

*I hope they're all lost,* she thought dully. *Because I already am.*

Last night, the black tide of pain had drawn back in, and with it had come an involuntary panic, despite her attempt to remain calm and emotionless in front of Fenmor. He had observed her as one might observe an animal struggle in a trap. The small pouch of *cahreu* root dangled from his fingers and he frowned thoughtfully as if he couldn't decide whether to eventually give some to her or throw the entire pouch onto the communal fire out in the encampment. Finally he had let her have a little- enough to keep the agony at bay- and then...

Amethyst suddenly leaned to one side and retched. The effort left her weak and shaking, but she felt a little better for it. She wiped her mouth and sat up, then watched Fenmor and the other two men as they continued to point and argue.

*I'll kill him somehow,* she swore, but that was an empty promise and she knew it. She had no plan, and she could not even steal any of the *cahreu* from him. He might be a lunatic but he was far from stupid. He kept the ground herb with him always, tightly wrapped up, although she suspected he had a supply of it elsewhere in the camp.

*But I must find a way to get it myself,* she thought. *And I need to find a way to kill him.*

She wished she could not remember how many times he had raped her since their departure from the castle. "Four," she said absently to herself.

Amethyst continued to watch as Fenmor grew more and more irate with his minions. She hoped fervently that one of them would take a knife to his belly. But that too was wishful thinking. No one would dare.

*And what about* my *belly?* she wondered fearfully. *If some seed of his grows within me I'll tear it out with my bare hands!*

Their progress had slowed over the last few days, not because of the weather, which had held fair with clear skies, but because of Fenmor's insistence that they visit each settlement they passed near to. They rested in every such place, but that was not the main reason that they stopped and camped there.

Fenmor issued a warning to everyone who lived in these villages that great evil roamed the plains, but he tempered that grim warning with a promise that the hour of salvation was close at hand. As she watched from a distance the suspicious expressions of those who gathered to listen, Amethyst could be sure only that they were frightened of something. *Yet they mistrust Fenmor and the castle folk,* she had realised. *Something else is amiss. Fenmor spoke the truth when he talked of events here in the plains- amidst the madness of his ramblings.*

The commander-at-arms turned abruptly from his argument and raised a hand as he walked away as if to show he was no longer interested, or that his will would hold sway regardless of opposing ideas. Amethyst immediately looked away from the tent opening, and she stared at the floor, face to one side, as Fenmor stormed in.

"They presume to know better than me," he fumed, and glared at her as if she also presumed to know better than him. Amethyst wisely said nothing, but he was not done with her. Was he ever?

73

Fenmor turned her head so that she faced him. With an effort, Amethyst kept her expression as neutral as possible. *If I went for him suddenly,* she thought, *I might be able to bite his nose or his cheek, or stab a finger through his eye, at least disfigure him in some awful way. Would that be worth it? Maybe he would beat me to death, and that would be the end of it. No longer trapped by this creature, or by the curse.*

She pictured Fenmor standing over her, his boots and his fists stained with her blood, as the haze of fury slowly drifted out of him. She imagined the witch-woman's distant scream of frustration as the link, the black tide as Amethyst likened it to, fragmented and fell apart.

*Free,* she thought. *I could be free.* Her gaze fixed upon his nose, his cheek. Finally, she concentrated on his neck. *That would be best of all,* she reckoned. *If I somehow bit through his windpipe, he might not even live for long. Maybe I would live long enough to know of his demise.*

"I don't like the way you look at me sometimes," Fenmor told her. His grip upon her jaw tightened; the now-familiar predatory gleam entered his eyes. "How many lessons must I teach you?"

"May I have something to eat?" she asked, hoping to deflect the accusation.

"In a while." He pushed her back to the ground and smiled suddenly. "You will thank me when all this is done."

Amethyst felt a hysterical laugh force its way through her. She looked away and swallowed it down. But Fenmor was already too caught up in another of his monologues to notice.

"Many of the plainsfolk are forsaken already. Yes, I see it in their eyes whenever we stop at one of the settlements. They are blind to the dreams, or have no wish to see the truth for themselves, or worse than that, the Old Dark has them bound, and they can serve only their old masters who have stirred once again. They were always the

74

closest to those ways. Every time we ride away from one of their villages, I wonder to myself how many of their own kind they have sacrificed..."

Amethyst turned her head, interested despite herself. "How are your people not the same as them?"

"I would say the folk of the Rand castle and lands are quite different." Fenmor sounded almost reasonable, and Amethyst dared to sit up. "Once, perhaps we were the same as the plainsfolk. But over time some people change and others stay as they are. Some built great castles and cities, and others remained out in the cold. This is the way of people across the known lands." He gave her a measured look. "You think I'm a madman, leading a hundred people across the plains in the middle of winter to behold the end of an Age. I see the looks you give me from time to time. But every one of these people- *my* people- have shared a dream, and it's the *same* dream. How do you explain that?"

*A madness that spreads like a plague,* Amethyst thought, but she said only "I can't explain it," which was the nearest thing she could think of to a safe answer.

"You cannot explain, and you cannot judge, because *you* have not had this dream." Fenmor tapped her on the side of the head. "No, something entirely different afflicts you, woman. *We* have all had visions of a new age of enlightenment, but *you*..." He drew back, giving Amethyst a hard, contemptuous look. "You have a darkness in your head, which only the *cahreu* subdues. But it can't cure you."

"Perhaps when I see the light that you all dreamed of, that may cure me," Amethyst said. *And if I see this mythical radiance, maybe I'll believe in it myself,* she silently echoed.

He smiled thinly at that. "Pray that it will." He looked her up and down, a hard, distant expression in his eyes.

*What will he do now?* Amethyst wondered, but sudden intervention came, for just at that moment someone

75

out in the encampment shouted, "M'lord Fenmor! There are..." The voice cut off suddenly; Amethyst heard a faint thud, and then other sounds rose from out in the cold. They were sounds of panic and confusion, and even as she listened to them the cacophony grew louder. There came a drumming of many hooves, and the clash of blades.

Fenmor cursed and strode outside. It was the last time Amethyst ever saw him.

## II

An eternity passed, punctuated by the sounds of fighting and dying. All the while the icy wind sighed around the tent where Amethyst sat still. She clutched at her blanket, stared at the tent flap and wondered who or what might come through.

*Plainsfolk,* she thought dully. *Who else would it be? Fenmor said that a great darkness had infected them.*

Amethyst pictured in her mind something monstrous that would tear through and reach for her, but with an effort she remained calm. The sounds outside were horrific, but they were the sounds of men and women butchering one another. *There are no monsters here,* she told herself, over and over. *Or, there are only human monsters.*

Suddenly, just when she wondered if escape might be possible amidst the confusion, the tent flap opened and a hard-looking plainsman loomed before her, shutting out most of the light. His leather armour was torn in several places, and Amethyst noticed drying blood on his forehead and on both of his fists. He stared at her for a moment, then he turned and called out to another of his people, "Craddan! Here!"

Presently another, older man appeared at the opening. Amethyst suspected that he had not been involved in the battle, judging by the lack of even the merest cut or splash of blood upon him. He scratched at one weather-beaten cheek, perhaps contemplating what to do with her.

"She looks different to the others," the younger man noted. "Look at her light brown skin. Pretty, isn't she?"

Craddan frowned. "I have my own eyes, man. Suspect she's a far-southerner. Where are you from, woman?"

"Darkenhelm," Amethyst managed to say. A sudden idea occurred to her, and it involved no deceit whatsoever. "They kept me prisoner." Warming to her relation of events, she continued, "They beat me and raped me. They said they were going into the distant east. They were all mad! The commander-at-arms talked endlessly of dreams and a great light..."

Craddan held up a hand and frowned. His blue eyes held a sudden sharpness. "We know about their dreams and their gods of light."

"Fenmor, the commander-at-arms, said that they had all had the same dream." Amethyst sat up, suddenly fearing what she might have started. "But how might that be possible? Perhaps he was lying, or mad." *Mad, certainly,* she echoed silently.

Craddan's expression grew solemn. He exchanged a look with the other man, but neither of them said a word. "Will you let me go?" Amethyst asked eventually. *Gods, let them say yes,* she thought desperately.

Craddan shook his head. "First, you will be taken to Edlun."

"Who is he?"

"He is our priest." Both men stood up and the younger one left. Craddan glanced back at Amethyst before leaving. "He will determine whether you are also one of the afflicted. If you dream of the star-demons, Edlun will know, and you too will die."

*Gods, they're as mad as Fenmor's people,* Amethyst thought as her heart sank. "And if not?" she asked him.

77

Craddan shrugged. "That is up to him."

*Well, I certainly haven't had such dreams,* Amethyst consoled herself as Craddan left. *So, if I'm lucky perhaps they will see I'm no enemy of theirs, and let me go.*

As she listened to the wind howl around the encampment, Amethyst then wondered if that was such a clever idea. Would they perhaps allow her to stay with them, at least until they reached a sizeable settlement where she could stay awhile? And equally to the point, would she want to?

Amethyst got up and unsteadily made her way outside. The scene of carnage that greeted her almost made her faint, for it was far worse than she had imagined.

Bodies lay impaled on spears, some of them with their innards strewn over the snow, bright red and pink harsh against the otherwise pristine surface. Eyes gazed sightlessly up into the blue sky. A few of the castle folk had been beheaded. Others lived, barely. They shuddered and moaned as they played out the final ignominious moments of their lives. Some distance away, carrion crows hopped about impatiently. One or two dared to go amongst the plainsfolk to claim their prize.

Amethyst tried to tear her eyes away from the scene, but it was impossible, for the dead lay everywhere. Craddan stood a few dozen yards away and watched with grim satisfaction, arms folded as six of the plainsfolk piled bodies onto a great pyre ready for burning. As Amethyst made her way over to ask him more about the priest, she noted that many plainsfolk were also amongst the dead. These, however, were being carried to a separate location where their surviving comrades made valiant attempts to dig graves in the snow.

"I was only their captive," she said, and glanced around in every direction. *Could I escape?* she wondered for one unreasoning moment. *If I ran... would they bother to come after me? Would they perceive my flight as guilt? Would they chase after me and butcher me in the snow as well?*

Craddan gave her a considering look. "The world is changing, Amethyst. We too must change. The Ages are like the coming and going of the tide." He smiled as he saw her bewilderment. "Yes- I have seen the ocean, stood at its feet," he said, misinterpreting her expression. "I've travelled, and learned from each journey."

Amethyst smiled uncertainly. *Tides,* she thought, and it seemed that something shifted in her head, a sullen, malevolent movement. For just a moment, pain flared up, but then it dwindled away to nothing. "Do you have any *cahreu* root?" she asked, hoping that she looked much calmer than she felt.

Craddan shook his head, not seeming at all bewildered by her question nor even interested. "No. Perhaps Edlun does. Come- I'll take you to him now. The sooner he sees you, the sooner we will all learn your fate."

They walked a short distance across the bloody remains of the encampment towards the eastern side, where a cloaked man stood and surveyed the scene, flanked by two tough-looking plainsmen in leather armour. Amethyst noted that neither of them looked as if they had been involved in the fighting. *Like Craddan,* she thought, and could not help but wince and look away as the plainsman kicked aside the body of a young castle woman as if it were a dog carcass.

"Some of these people are still alive," she pointed out. "Could you not at least give them all a quick death?"

Craddan turned to her, a hard look on his face. "You think they deserve it?"

"Surely even your enemies deserve some sort of mercy in death?"

He stopped suddenly, and with a sudden movement seized her forearm. Amethyst grimaced, for his grip was as strong as iron. "Listen, woman. You know nothing of this part of the world, so I'll forgive your insolence. These lightdreamers have murdered hundreds of our people. Some have even been taken into their stronghold on the false promise of safety. And the castlemen have no idea of events in our lands. They speak of disappearances, sacrifices, of some hidden evil that spirits people away... hah!"

"Is any of it true?" Amethyst asked as she pulled her arm free.

Craddan said nothing for a long while. He stared southwards, and the breeze blew his hair across his face. One hand scratched idly at his three days' growth of beard, the other tapped restlessly on the pommel of his longknife. "You have to understand the old ways," he said finally. "If you know nothing of them, then..." He shrugged. "You're a woman of Darkenhelm. You people have only one God: commerce."

"And what Gods do you worship?" Amethyst asked, fearing the answer even as she spoke.

Craddan turned to her with a smile that was almost friendly. "Why, the Earth Lords. Who else? Who else but our masters have protected our entire world, since the very dawn of time?" He regarded her awhile longer, and his smile grew sad. "Your world has grown far apart from ours, Amethyst. So far that they mean nothing to you- but they will, in times to come. Tell me, when he was neither raping nor beating you, did the glorious commander of the castlemen speak of an end to the Age?"

Amethyst nodded.

"Well, he was right about that. And he was right about the eastern light."

Amethyst stared at him. She thought her legs might give way under her. "You mean... you... your people have also had those same dreams? Then why..."

"No." Craddan shook his head. "But on occasion the Earth Lords reach out and guide us, sometimes through dreams or portents. So we know about the destroying light."

80

"And I suppose they told you to murder all these people?"

Craddan had not listened. Once again he watched the building of the grisly pyre. Amethyst took the opportunity to look around as thoughts of escape loomed large in her mind once again. *But even if I could, what then?* she reminded herself. *I have no food, no clothing except what I'm wearing, and I wouldn't last more than a day in this weather.*

They trudged onwards. Amethyst flinched as a dying man reached out a hand towards her. *Craddan is as mad as Fenmor,* she thought. *Earth Lords and dreams and light... why has everyone here lost their grip on sanity?*

As they neared Edlun and his guardsmen, the pyre was lit. Flames began to swiftly engulf the wood and the bodies and a great cheer went up, followed by a peculiar chant. Amethyst looked away, and instead found herself drawn in some awful way to Edlun, to his yellow-brown eyes that drank in the sight of the burning, to the thin crack of a smile upon his lips and the dirty, sallow complexion of a man old beyond his years, a visage like filthy parchment.

"You spared one of them," Edlun complained as he turned to look at her and Craddan. "Ah- but she's a southerner. A pretty southerner. Had you presumed to have her for yourself, Craddan? Do you like such folk?"

"I brought her so that you might see if she bears the taint," Craddan said warily. *Is he afraid of Edlun?* Amethyst wondered. "If she does, then of course she must die. But if not, I say we set her free. She is not part of the struggle against the starspawn."

"Is she not?" Edlun's grin revealed a rotting graveyard of misshapen teeth. "Everyone is a part of the struggle, Craddan. Everyone must take a side, sooner or later."

"Even so, if she is no lightdreamer then she deserves her freedom. Are we agreed?"

81

Edlun looked Amethyst up and down. "Agreed," he said, and then, "Come here, woman. Kneel before me."

"Do as he says," Craddan said harshly, as Amethyst hesitated. She took a deep breath and walked to Edlun, then knelt down in the snow and tried to ignore the stench of the man. *I'm no lightdreamer,* she thought desperately. *If he can see that, I am free. Free!*

She almost panicked when Edlun's hands embraced her head; the touch was warm and damp. *They're not hands at all,* she thought briefly, and told herself to be rational.

The grip tightened a little, and then, inexplicably, Edlun suddenly removed his hands as if her head had become a mass of writhing snakes, and screamed.

Amethyst stared at him and scrambled to her feet, then backed away. The plainsmen around them each drew their longknives; one of them pressed his blade against the flesh of her neck.

Abruptly Edlun ceased his noise and sagged to the ground. He looked up at her, and Amethyst was shocked to see a thin trickle of blood run from his eyes. *Oh Gods,* she thought numbly. *He's going to say I'm a lightdreamer.* She looked down at the snow and pictured her body lying there in a splash of gore, kicked around by Craddan and the other plainsmen. *This is it,* she thought, and a sudden calm came over her, even as tears leapt unbidden to her eyes. *This is finally it. The whole journey was a disaster. I should have stayed at home. I suppose no one will know what became of me.*

"Is she?" Craddan quietly asked the priest.

Edlun did not take his eyes from her. His tongue reached out and licked at a thin rivulet of blood that had reached his lips. "No," he said. "She is not."

Craddan blinked, taken aback. Then he glanced at Amethyst. "You are free to go," he said.

Edlun stood up. His hot, lupine stare remained fixed on Amethyst. "No. She is *not* free to go."

82

"We agreed..." Craddan began, but Edlun raised a hand to silence him. Amethyst noticed a deep, roughly circular gouge in his palm and wondered what could have caused it. "She is not poisoned by the light. She does not dream of it. But there's something else."

"What is it?" Craddan demanded.

Edlun smiled knowingly. "Two women stare out through her eyes."

He glanced at one of the men next to Amethyst and nodded. *Make it quick,* she thought and closed her eyes.

But the expected cut never came. Instead, a blow struck her on the side of the head and she fell, senseless before she reached the ground.

## III

Amethyst woke to the sight of a dark wooden ceiling, and a pounding in her head. Slowly she moved her head to one side and tried to comprehend her new surroundings, but the pain rose to a crescendo and she cried out.

She became dimly aware of daylight on her other side, pouring in through a window. *Some kind of hut,* she thought, *or someone's dwelling.* Suddenly the memory of Edlun came back to her, and despite the agony she almost managed to sit up. Panic flared as brightly as the pain. *Is this place his?* she asked herself as she looked around. She lay on a stuffed mattress which had been placed on a wooden pallet. The hut was otherwise unfurnished, except for a cold hearth built into the wall on the other side. With a sigh she lay down again. She lacked the energy to sit up for long.

Hours passed, and the day grew dim. Finally with the dusk came the sound of boots crunching over the snow outside. The door opened and Edlun walked in. His body obscured what remained of the daylight as he stood and regarded her in silence. He carried firewood, a large can of water- or perhaps some other liquid- and dried provisions.

Putting them down, he busied himself rebuilding the stick-fire in the hearth, although he also glanced occasionally around at Amethyst as if he expected her to have changed into someone or something else.

"We are alone now, or as alone as we can be," he said suddenly, as new flames began to lick around the fresh wood. The priest crept nearer, his eyes fixed on hers. His matted beard stank. Some indeterminate dark substance lay clotted behind his thick yellow fingernails. Amethyst thought at first that it might be soil, but it smelled oddly like putrefied flesh.

"We are?" she said faintly.

The priest nodded with strange eagerness. "Yes, *yes*. I told them to leave, and so they went. And we have travelled far. Yes." He grinned suddenly, and Amethyst recoiled at the sight. "Drink!" He lifted Amethyst's head, and pressed the flagon of water to her lips. She resisted, and he said, "It's snow-melt, nothing more. What, you think I wish to poison you? How would that benefit me?"

Amethyst drank thirstily and pushed the flagon away when she had had her fill. The coldness of the water made her teeth hurt, but it was nothing compared to the pain in her head.

"What will you do with me?" Amethyst asked as she stared up into the gloom of the ramshackle roof.

"I only do as my masters command." He took some saltmeat from one of the provision packs, tore it in two and placed one half in his mouth. "Only as they command," he repeated once he was done chewing. "This is a good place. They are strong here. My masters will want to know of this..." He jabbed a finger towards her forehead. "This powerful *compelling* that you have been placed under."

Despite the fear and revulsion she felt, a seed of hope began to grow in Amethyst's heart. "You can see it? You can see what happened to me?"

"Oh yes." He flashed a boneyard smile at her, proud of his perceived insight. "I see the compelling, and I even see the creature that made it. A woman, a meddler, a hedgewitch who dabbles in matters she knows littleabout."

"Can you do anything about it? Can you free me?" She barely dared to hope.

"Through you, the Earth Lords may reach *her*," Edlun whispered, wide-eyed as if in wonderment at the power of his Gods. He looked to each wall in turn, then to the fire, and finally he spoke again. "She will die."

"And what about me?"

Edlun knelt by the fire and placed his hands so near to the flames that Amethyst was certain they would start to blister and burn. Unbelievably, they did not. "It's not for me to say," he said finally, then added, "It's safer here, now that those poisoned with the light-dreams have made their... *pilgrimage*. Those who avoided Craddan's men, at least." He laughed out loud, a sharp, uncontrolled sound almost like the bark of a maddened dog.

"Why didn't you go with them? Why bring me here?"

"The Earth Lords speak to me. They tell me to keep you here, until they come to see the compelling for themselves. *Yes.* She borrowed it from them, you know, as do all the hedgefolk who scratch the surface."

His frantic smile became a grimace, almost inadvertently, as if some unseen force reshaped his expression. One side of his face glowed faintly with the light from the flames. The other, cast deep in shadow, looked slack and inanimate as stone.

Amethyst took a deep breath and struggled to sit up. She tried not to show an inkling of the pain in her head. But her body would let her move no further.

Edlun loomed over her suddenly. "You cannot walk yet. You must rest."

Amethyst stared up at him through a haze of pain. For a moment she fancied that Edlun's eyes were darker than before, with a tinge of green around the edges that made them look like distant and abandoned wells. She shrank back as the madman's hand patted her own, hot and dry like the roar of the hearth.

"The *marandaal* thirst for the death of all things," came a whisper in her ear, carried on foul earthy breath. "But this place is safe from the dreams of light..."

Amethyst turned away, unable to look into the eyes of her captor any longer. Blood pulsed madly through her head, and as if to mirror that frantic course, flames- the only light left in the world- rose higher and brighter. Now it seemed that she lay surrounded by light without shadow, except for the creature of cold madness and dark earth that loomed at her side.

## IV

Amethyst woke suddenly from a nightmare in which flames had engulfed her from the inside out.

Deathly cold air surrounded her. In the hearth, nothing but black and grey ash remained, apart from where the charred remnants of sticks had been placed to lean against each other.

*How many days have passed?*

Amethyst saw a slight movement in the shadows across from her. Edlun appeared almost to detach himself from the wall as he emerged and crept nearer. "I have watched you for three days," he whispered.

Amethyst had no idea what to say to that. She glanced again at the madman, and a sudden cold feeling washed over her. Had his eyes changed colour again? And was his jaw somehow less pronounced, as if the bone had started to sink backwards into the rest of his skull? The man's chin looked dead and grey under the tangled beard. Before he could avert his eyes, Edlun caught her glance and smiling, pulled away a small piece of skin and put it in his mouth. Chewing slowly, he retreated to the hearth where he sifted through the ash and placed the charred sticks together on the ground. Carefully he examined each in turn, as if he searched for a sign.

*Three days without water,* Amethyst thought to herself. *How can I still be alive? Or does he lie?*

"My masters value those such as you." Edlun's voice had a gleeful edge to it, as if he might be rewarded imminently for all his efforts.

"The Earth Lords? Do they have names other than that?" Amethyst was surprised that she could speak properly. *If only the rest of me worked,* she thought grimly.

Edlun turned, slack mouth open as if in astonishment. "Do you expect me to name them? I would burn, or drown, or sink into the earth if I did that. The only other word we may use for them is *choragh.* But your questions don't matter. You only need to remain here, and soon they will come. A message was sent in the flames." He pointed eagerly to the hearth as if he expected Amethyst to plainly see that message for herself.

*Will they?* she wondered. All she had seen in her travels was madness heaped upon madness, men and women bent on destroying one another- and for what? Having the wrong dreams?

She lay back and thought quickly. Somehow she had to escape from this place, but she would have to kill Edlun first. Did he have any weapons? Amethyst suspected that there might be all sorts of dreadful sorcery he could evoke if he needed to, and besides she was in no condition to fight anyone or anything.

Edlun chuckled, as if he knew her thoughts, or more likely interpreted the movements of her eyes. "The call through the flames brings close the attention of my lords."

"What do they want with me?"

"No more questions. I'm your keeper, nothing more." Edlun looked at her for a long while. He seemed about to say something when suddenly he turned- or at least, his head turned with a sickening scraping sound, and he gazed at the doorway of the hut. Then, muttering to himself, he scampered back, all the while keeping his eyes on the doorway. To Amethyst it seemed that the light had grown stronger. A strange humming sound started up; judging by his reaction, Edlun could hear it also, and could not bear it. Putting head in hands, he commenced a terrible screeching, but Amethyst could barely hear his agonised screams. The hum grew louder and all-pervasive.

A figure appeared at the doorway. She could not tell who or what it was. White light suffused everything now, except for the babbling, shrieking bundle of darkness that was Edlun, a miserable creature that pulled itself apart as it shuddered in a corner of the chamber, face turned from the light. Nails dug deep into its head and its spinal bones jutted out of its back.

*Is this it?* Amethyst thought faintly. *Is this the promised light in the east, which Fenmor spoke about and his people dreamed of? Can it be real?*

The light that had turned Edlun inside-out ceased so abruptly that Amethyst had no time for shock or struggle as, in the utter blackness that followed, she was gathered up and carried away.

V

She woke under a deep blue, sunlit sky. Immediately she closed her eyes against the brilliance of the sun that sparkled on the snow, and cried out at the sudden pain. When finally she dared open her eyes again, she saw that someone had wrapped her in a thick robe, and a fire burned nearby. A pot of something bubbled over it.

"You're a long way from home," said a voice near her right side. Amethyst jumped almost out of her skin, and turned quickly to face the man who sat a few yards away.

The breeze rustled his silver hair as he regarded her calmly. He was middle-aged, she reckoned, but he had a lithe, intent look to him that made him appear many years younger. His skin was very pale, almost like that of a *luyan*. He put the book he was holding into his pack and turned to look at her. "A long way from home and in the heart of winter, north of the Crescents."

*A long way from home.* Amethyst shuddered, and suddenly a thought occurred to her as the events of the last few weeks rushed back into her thoughts. "Which do you worship?" she asked him without thought to the consequences. "What mad faith do *you* follow?"

"Ah. The stirring of the old ways. Yes, I've witnessed it too, though I've kept as far out of harm's way as I can." He took the pot from the fire using a stick, and placed it on the ground where it made the snow hiss and melt. "Would you like some soup?"

"Soup." Amethyst blinked, and was about to ask the same question again, then suddenly realised how hungry she was. When had she last eaten properly?

"There's nothing better in the winter," he remarked. "Even those mild and wet winters that you're probably used to. My name is Elluron." He extended a hand in greeting, and after a moment's hesitation Amethyst shook hands with him. "I'm Amethyst. Did you come to the hut?" she asked on an impulse. "Did you take me away from there? All I remember was a light... I thought it was..." She stopped suddenly and gave him a wary look. "I need to know. Are you one of these dreamers? Do you follow the light, or the Earth Lords, or..."

A hard look crossed Elluron's face. "Now they call themselves the earth-lords." He shook his head. "I'm no dreamer." He wrapped cloth around his gauntleted hand and poured soup into one of two battered mugs placed nearby. "Did you want any?"

89

Amethyst nodded and watched as he poured out a generous helping of the thick, aromatic vegetable broth and passed her the mug. She wrapped her hands around it and savoured the heat and aroma, then tried a little once it had cooled in the chill air. It was delicious.

"Thank you," she said, remembering her manners a little late. He nodded, poured himself some and sat in contemplation for a while. He gazed south-east towards distant hills. Somewhere over the rolling plains, carrion birds circled and cawed. Amethyst wondered if they hovered above the scene of another massacre.

She returned her attention to Elluron, and watched him for a while, before finally she spoke again as the memory of Edlun's hut loomed large in her mind. "Thank you for saving my life."

When Elluron turned slightly to look at her, his expression was strangely sad. "Will you say that a year from now, I wonder?"

She finished off her soup and set the mug down. "Why do you say that? What will happen before then?"

"You've seen for yourself how easily the puppet strings of humankind are pulled one way or the other," he said. "How well do you know your history?"

"Well enough, I suppose. I studied it for a year at my local Guild in Darkenhelm."

"That means nothing to me, Amethyst. As the names of the Old Dark and the starspawn mean nothing to you."

She stared warily at him. "I've heard those words before, but only in the last few days."

"Their old names are *choragh* and *marandaal*." He almost spat the words. "Some day soon, I think those words will be remembered again. Their true names are, I'm sure, much older than that, from an even more distant Age." He slowly began to pack up, as if making ready to leave. "Where are you headed, Amethyst?"

"Before I was captured, I was headed east."

90

Elluron shook his head and washed out his pot with half-melted snow. "I wouldn't do that, were I you."

"I have no choice," Amethyst told him. Even as she spoke, she could feel the faint shifting in her head as if in response, not pain but certainly the threat of pain. *Will I ever be rid of you?* she thought miserably.

He stared at her, and she noticed for the first time an odd colour to his eyes, not blue but a strange opaque violet with flecks of gold. *Why did I not notice that before?* she wondered, and then: *Where is he from, I wonder? Is he entirely human?*

"I understand," he said finally. For the briefest moment a look of sympathy crossed his face. "Do what you must."

Elluron took from his pack a small bottle that contained a colourless liquid and passed it to her. "This will keep you warm enough, along with the cloak," he said. "No more than a sip each day, mind. Ethanalin Tur-morn is five leagues from here due east. There should be enough to get you that far, at least. Once you're there..." He shrugged. "As you say, you have no choice. But beware of everyone and everything you see, if you need such a reminder."

"You give me this, *and* this cloak?" Amethyst was baffled. "But what about you?"

"I have a spare," he said. "I'll be warm enough." He smiled at her continued bewilderment. "I have spoken with so few people since I came here. It's odd to converse again after such a long time. But it was good to talk with you, Amethyst."

"Where are you from?" she asked. The light caught his eyes strangely again, and for a moment they had an intense gold sheen to them. *I've never seen eyes anything like them,* she thought, as she tried to observe without being obvious.

91

"Ah. Now there's something I certainly could not tell you," he remarked, "even if I was permitted to. A long way from here, shall we say."

He completed his packing. Amethyst watched him, caught up in a sudden panic. There were so many more questions he might be able to answer- and yet he was about to leave, and she suspected he would not permit her to travel with him. *He warned me against going east,* she recalled, *yet I know I will have to.*

"Can you at least tell me what's happening?" she pleaded. "Why do the castle folk and the plainspeople wage this war against each other? What are all these dreams, about Earth Lords and starspawn? Are they real? Or is everyone here under some vast spell? How can that be?"

Elluron stood up, brushing snow from his clothes, and slung his pack over his shoulder. "Oh, they are real enough," he said softly, "but until now their reach had diminished, the *choragh* shrivelled into the furthest corners of Aona, and the *marandaal*- well..." He shrugged. "Some say that when they were first cast out of this world, they were unable to find their way back."

"Is *this* their world?"

"Oh no. Their world..." Elluron smiled and shook his head. "That was longer ago than you or even I could possibly imagine, Amethyst." He raised a hand in farewell. "Be careful in the east town."

Then he turned and walked away across the snow.

# IV - Doorways

Night after night Jaana would hide her face away in the pillows as Danyl slept- hide it until she *knew* he was truly asleep. Only then would she turn to view the ceiling, to stare up at the cracks and the cobwebs and the dirt until she too drifted into a slumber.

She no longer wept, because it was a waste of time and energy. No one except Danyl could hear her, and she neither wanted nor needed his concern. He was a good man- as far as she could tell- but she had no time for men good or bad. She would move on soon, out of this village and away. In fact, she ought never to have stopped here. She ought never to have ceased her journey. The curse of settling down had begun to set in like rot. And with recent events in the village, the need to leave- for she felt utterly helpless here, a healer who could not heal- had grown ever stronger.

Danyl did nothing of any substance, as far as she could tell. A tall and languid youth, he spent his days on the veranda, under a parasol if the weather suited, and his evenings either reading or making love with her- at least, he assumed it was love he was making- or entertaining himself and others of his kind at the tavern. Stone had only one inn, a low-ceilinged den of blue smoky air and tables in which generations had etched names and partnerships. It was a place of old ritual and determined inwardness.

The rain came down again briefly as she sat on the veranda. Rivulets poured from the roof. Jaana wondered absently if the thatching was good for the whole season. Well, if not, it would give Danyl something to do. He was sinking ale at the *Traveller's Rest* and would wax lyrical later on, considering himself a bard or a poet, especially if the promised thunder arrived. The elements moved and excited him. She would open her legs for him and watch his face frozen by flashes of lightning.

Jaana watched the downpour, as inside her the feeling of restless unease grew and grew, like a cold hunger without end.

She jumped, startled by the knock upon the door of the cottage. Taking a deep breath, she went to answer the call, although she suspected with a heavy heart that she might know the reason for this visit even before she opened the door.

The sight of the old man on the doorstep, soggy cap in hand as if to apologise for daring to call, or in case he might have to beg, served only to confirm her weary expectation. The rain had nearly halted, and the mist clung in droplets to his thin, lank grey hair and beard, like dew on spider webs. A picture of abject misery stood before her, a creature washed free of colour and life.

Jaana suppressed a sigh. Even here, a considerable distance from the place where she had originally practised her healing, word had spread that she could help with all manner of ailments and illnesses. In fact, she simply used what had once been common knowledge in the middle lands, the lore that her mother had passed down to her. She did not say as much, worried by what the response would be wherever she went, but went quietly about her business and helped and advised where she could.

In Stone, however, amidst the ramshackle huts and ancient redstone houses, she had found a sickness that had perplexed her, to the point where she craved the anonymity to hide away and take no part in anything to which duty bound her. Never before had she felt as helpless as this, and her mother's old saying- *You can do only what you can, and you can never fix everything-* provided scant comfort.

The old man looked apologetically at her, and opened his mouth to explain, but Jaana only needed to look into his haunted eyes. She managed to force a smile born of long practice. "I'll come with you," she said, all the while thinking, *Show me another patient who cannot be cured, to remind me of my own inadequacy.*

They hurried through the narrow street, the mist close about them. Jaana's companion limped along and yet still managed to cover the ground swiftly. It would be dark soon, Jaana noted. Already the few traders who were open for business today had shut their shops and stalls, weary of waiting for custom that seldom showed its face. Stone had no standing lanterns in its streets; after dark, the only light generally came from the *Traveller's Rest* or from the hand-lamps of folk on their way back home from it.

Jaana shuddered as she considered just how fragile this community was. If that tavern should ever burn to the ground one night, what would they have? These people were superstitious rather than religious- Jaana had never decided which of the two was worse, but that was by the by- and unlike the folk of Nisstar and other Mid-Hastian cities and towns, they had no church or temple to retreat to for solace, nor did they have a spiritual leader of any sort. The Warden of the town was a man of figures and details, dry sense and firm logic, and the only leader here.

The small stone house to which her companion led her was set off from the main street, barely more than a two-roomed hut, with a small, dank-smelling loft. A persistent dripping came from up in the hay.

Her companion fumbled around and eventually managed to light a lantern which he placed on a hook that reached down from one of the beams. Moving through to the back room, he lit another, and by its light Jaana saw a young woman no older than herself lying on a bed. Perhaps she was the man's daughter or grand-daughter. Then again she might be his wife for all Jaana knew. She decided not to ask.

95

"I performed the warding ritual," he said suddenly as he turned to face her. Tiny lantern reflections danced in his eyes. "Perhaps it was not the right one. Sometimes I forget them..."

Jaana had no idea what warding ritual he referred to, and did not especially want to know. In her experience, the act of mumbling strings of words in the hope of some supernatural intervention was simply a prayer by another name, and she had as much time for superstition as she did faith.

The girl's eyes were closed, and her face looked so pale in the dim lantern light of the bedchamber that it appeared almost translucent. Around the bed the old man had placed various trinkets and supposedly magical ornaments, perhaps obtained from the merchants who visited villages such as this simply to peddle such useless goods. Jaana knew they meant nothing and could never work, but there was little sense in telling him that. Instead, she nodded gravely and knelt by the girl, then reached out to gently touch her cheek. Her skin was hot despite her pale appearance, her breathing irregular and her heartbeat slow. Too slow. That weary, ponderous thud belonged to someone three times her age.

All these symptoms together made no sense, and yet they were the same as she had seen five times already in this little town alone. *This is an unwinnable battle,* a weary voice whispered in her mind. *Walk away.*

"How long has she been like this?" she asked.

"Two days now. She will not be roused. I gave her the restorative water..."

"Restorative water?"

"From the well. It has special properties on account of the depth from which it's drawn. I could make her swallow the water, but she wouldn't wake. I had no wish to trouble you, but I..." His voice trailed away and he shrugged miserably. "What else could I do? She has no one else. I must do what I can. No one else will look after her."

"You mustn't worry about that," Jaana said gently. "What's her name?"

"Ilun. My grand-daughter."

"Ilun." Jaana gently clasped the girl's hand as she spoke the name. Ilun's eyes flicked open instantly.

Jaana knew it was only her imagination, but she felt almost certain that the temperature in the sparse little bedchamber dropped suddenly. A groan came from the hayloft, as if the boards were about to give way. Somehow the dripping of water through the roof sounded a little louder, more insistent. Jaana wondered if the leak had become worse. She even imagined that something might be forcing the water through, as if the rain was eager to break through the roof and drown the three of them. Was it raining harder outside once again?

*Hail. It's just hail*

Jaana heard, and saw from the corner of her eye, Ilun's grandfather step back, whispering a warding passage to himself.

She let go of the girl's hot, limp hand, suddenly uneasy. "Can you hear me?" she whispered.

Only Jaana's reflexes saved her from a mauling. Ilun's long-nailed hands sprang at her, grasping, reaching to rip the flesh from her face and stab into her eyes. Jaana stumbled back and knocked over some of the false healing charms. She stared in horror as the girl sat bolt upright in bed, eyes blazing with fever. Her arms still reached out and clawed at the too-cold air. Jaana's hand stole to her left cheek where she had been scratched. *It could have been much worse,* she thought. Slowly she got to her feet and kept her eyes on Ilun, trying to calm herself. *She could have torn the flesh from my bones.*

As she gazed back into that desperate, empty stare, Jaana felt defeated. This was like the other cases she had

97

seen in the town- worse than most perhaps, but the symptoms were much the same. She had been unable to heal any of the others. Two had since died, the other three remained alive but only barely, and they slipped towards oblivion. *Damn it all,* she thought despairingly. *It's the same, every time I see it.*

"The stars are changing," Ilun said tonelessly to the air in front of her.

Jaana stared at the girl as an unpleasant, crawling sensation swept over her. She had never heard anyone with this illness say anything before. The others had all screamed and sobbed, or ranted wordlessly for hours before the madness exhausted or extinguished them, but none had uttered anything coherent.

"What do you mean, Ilun?" she asked quietly. The girl stared back at her, eyes dark in that drained face- but she said nothing. Eventually she sank back onto the bed, eyes closed once again. Her hands clenched and unclenched. They shook violently and Ilun's nails drew blood from her palms. Finally she became still.

"Has she said anything else since she fell ill?" Jaana asked, and turned around when no reply came. Ilun's grandfather had fled the house.

Jaana spent a while longer gazing at the girl, at the pointless ornaments arranged around her, and then back at the open front door, through which her grandfather had gone, lacking the sense or resolve to see the girl for what she was.

*Every illness has a cause and a cure,* Jaana reasoned, *only sometimes we have yet to discover them. But I can't even begin to work out a cause, and without that...*

Jaana felt a heavy cloud of defeat loom over her, worse than ever before. This was an illness with a difference; one whose symptoms made no sense and could not be eased by any medicine she knew of. The victims were of different ages, by all accounts healthy before they had fallen ill. None had consumed anything they shouldn't have. Nothing suggested a cause, nor did anything link the victims other than that they all lived in this town. That might have been a clue, Jaana mused, but she had seen similar cases in other towns, some distance away.

*The stars are changing.*

She shuddered, and turned to leave. Almost immediately she felt certain that Ilun had sat upright again and was staring directly at her. Jaana turned swiftly, only to see the girl's sleeping form. She had even started to snore gently.

When she emerged from the house, the rain had indeed returned and came down harder than ever. Jaana ran back to Danyl's house with the hood of her cape covering her as best it could. Perhaps she could prepare some mixtures that might ease the girl's suffering, lessen the fever if nothing else, but they were not a cure. In the end, her condition would fail to improve

*It will do nothing except sow seeds of false hope,* Jaana reasoned as she shut the door behind her and stood shivering in the hallway. *What good would I do, if I were to return with an array of powders and liquids that had no effect on the other victims, and would doubtless be just as unhelpful to this one?*

So Jaana did not go back. She collected water from a few of the big iron pots out in the back yard, and heated it awhile over the fire for a bath. Sometime later, bathed and feeling a little better, she sat out on the veranda once again, watching a distant thunderstorm in the far south- the rain and mist having moved slowly north away from the town- and thinking over and over about Ilun and the other victims. Briefly she wondered if Ilun's grandfather would dare make his way back to his house, or perhaps even come back here, more apologetic than ever. He did not, and Jaana was glad to see that no one else passed by either.

It would be easy to dismiss the whole matter and simply label the girl as insane, incurable. That said, all the others had, according to everyone she had spoken to, been perfectly rational and reasonable people before being struck down in this way. Digging as deeply as she dared into the ways of such close-knit folk, Jaana had discovered little in their lives to indicate that they might slip into madness- not that such a thing could be easily foretold.

She had been here for three months, and all the cases had happened during that time, as far as she could tell. Given the superstitious nature of these rural midland folk, she ought to consider herself lucky that *she* had not been blamed for any of this. Or might that be their next leap of judgement, borne out of frustration that she could not heal their sick? Would they turn on her?

*That would be just what some folk back in Firstwood would want to see,* Jaana thought bitterly. *The same fate for me as for Mother. She tried only to fulfil her calling in life, and yet she was accused of every piece of bad luck that happened in that place. Oh, they were happy enough to come to her when times were good, but then the bad harvest and the stillbirths put a stop to all that, didn't they? Did they choose to blame the poisoned water that happened at the same time as the flooding? No! Suddenly they decided that a witch practised in their midst, throttling babes inside their mother's wombs, turning the wheat black and shrivelled...*

Perhaps Ellen would be able to help.

Jaana shivered. If she went to Ellen, it would also mean having to leave Stone without any explanation, never to return. This was one little superstition that Jaana had allowed herself- never revisiting a place of pain and misery, including the place of her birth and childhood. Besides, if the people of Stone somehow found out to whom she had gone, return would be impossible. Ellen, her teacher and mentor, was feared and loathed across large parts of the middle lands, another victim of an unsought reputation based on folklore.

Thinking her a victim of her mother's witchery, people in these midland villages had for the most part taken kindly to Jaana after her efforts to practise far and wide as a healer. Some saw her efforts as a path to redemption. But that would count for nothing if they discovered her association with Ellen, one that had started twelve years ago when Jaana had been taken as a frightened ten-year-old into Knarlswood to meet with Ellen, in order for her potential to be surmised. Not that Jaana cared about any such discovery at this point, despite having gone to great pains in the past to cover her tracks. Although she felt sorry for the plight of the people here, she found herself exhausted by their ways as much as her own inadequacy. More than ever she longed to be distant from them.

*I would sooner turn my back on healing than be a failed healer,* she swore.

The thought of going back to Ellen's domain deep within the vast forest of Knarlswood filled Jaana with fear and relief in equal measure. She felt troubled and lost, full of questions to which she could find no answers. Ellen would help her find a way to deal with those questions, even if she did not have all the answers, but she also had a habit of making Jaana face uncomfortable, even painful truths.

It did not take her long to gather her possessions. Aside from a few token keepsakes from her childhood, she had only those that Danyl had gifted her with, and Jaana was not the sort of woman to take such mementos when leaving, especially if she intended never to return. She therefore left them upstairs in their bedchamber, and delioberately averted her eyes as she closed the door behind her.

*Steel yourself against sentiment, woman,* she harshly reminded herself as she made her way downstairs, *and you will save yourself untold grief.*

101

She took enough food for the journey, but no more- it would take three days, or perhaps four, depending on how the weather turned- a map, though she rarely needed one, and spare clothing.

These things she bundled into her backpack, working hastily as she contemplated the possibility of Danyl coming back early. He would complicate matters through his questions, and his inevitable pleas for her to stay. With that minor task done, she left him a brief note using parchment and stain taken from his writing desk. It said simply *I have left. I will not be back. I am sorry.*

Then, as promised in that hasty scribble, she left.

## II

Jaana found that her weariness sowed despair. Several times over the days that followed, as she headed north towards Knarlswood and shivered in the chill breeze, she cried softly, hating herself for being weak, for still worrying or even *thinking* about the people of Stone, who perhaps even now might wonder where she had gone. Danyl, meanwhile, might be viewed in time as nothing more than a witchkeeper- hence his good health and comfortable home, they would say in conclusion. He could write, and play the pluckboard- how many others could do that? And had he fallen ill? No, he had not. Perhaps he would be cast out, or worse. Ill times would foster ill thoughts.

But after some time Jaana could no longer bring herself to care. Her worries for the welfare of those folk became confused with frustration and even hatred of their ignorance and superstition. Worse, black memories came sharply back to her thoughts- of the people of Firstwood, where she had grown up. *They are all the same,* she ranted silently, knowing they were not, but unable to quell that raging, barely coherent idea.

She shunned the villages that she passed near to, keeping instead to seldom-trodden tracks, the sort that human folk avoided if they could. These were paths used by *ko xhoth* and *luyan* travellers, but Jaana had no quarrel with those beings and held no fear of them.

When she had to walk along a track that her kind might use, wide and fashioned at least partly from stone blocks, she even hid behind walls or hedgerows if she saw or heard riders or carts approaching, though this happened only a few times. The act shamed her- *a failed healer on the run from everyone and everything,* she taunted herself as she crept close to the ground with her heart thumping- but she could not bear even the slightest possibility of being recognised, nor could she bear questioning voices, nor suspicious eyes.

One time, she huddled down on one side of the stone wall, whilst on the other, a cart had stopped, one of its wheels broken by a rut in the track. Those travelling on the vehicle were soldiers of some sort, she guessed, judging by their talk, not to mention the amount of swearing, spitting, and worst of all, pissing against the other side of the wall that she hid behind. Jaana waited despondently, the rain pouring down and forcing its way through her layers of clothing, until eventually they fixed or replaced the wheel and the cart continued its painfully slow progress along the rapidly flooding track.

No, Jaana decided vehemently, she craved no human company at all, except perhaps that of her mentor. Yet in a strange sort of way, she had never thought of Ellen as human. One of the reasons that Jaana almost feared the old woman was that she always seemed more like *something* in human form than anything else, although on the one occasion when she had dared mention that- for Ellen encouraged her to be forthcoming and speak her mind- the old woman had laughed uproariously. *You imagine too much!*

103

Yet she had lived in the depths of Knarlswood, the brunt of misguided fairy tales and fearful superstition, for as long as anyone could remember, and when Jaana had first been taken to her- with her mother a silent but comforting presence at her side in the twin moonlight- her first impression had been that this was a woman who had become so much a part of her environment that she really *was* a part of it.

Jaana had realised quickly in the months that followed that the same could happen to anyone anywhere, and that it was not necessarily a good thing to allow. Perhaps that was one of the reasons she had fled Stone. *Keep moving or lose yourself* she had thought, so many times.

Jaana ran out of her food supplies before Knarlswood was even visible in the distance, perhaps eating for comfort without realising it, so she collected what late autumn berries she could find, most of them on the turn or oversweet, and every night laid a few traps in the hope of finding a rabbit or two ensnared come the dawn. None ventured her way, however, and as a hastening breeze blew from the east she wearily continued into the forest.

To say Knarlswood was ancient would have been an understatement; the forest had stood here possibly for many thousands of years even before the First Age, and few enough people could comprehend how long ago even *that* had been. Vast knotted oaks grew tall and strong, with mossy branches spread wide. Here and there, yew trees spread their mad arms across as far as upwards. Shards of late afternoon sunlight fell to earth amidst the lush greenery, as the clouds parted briefly in the west.

Sheltered from the breeze and having finally found some pears and red sourplums to eat, Jaana found her mood somewhat improved, her panic about being recognised or *found* diminishing with every step she took away from the haunts of humankind. She would make her way to Ellen's hut- an easy enough task for her- and rest there awhile. *And*

104

*then what?* she asked herself, although she had no ready answer. Ellen might welcome her- might or might not, in truth- but she would not put up with her for longer than she thought Jaana *needed* to stay with her. Then, with whatever wisdom she thought appropriate imparted, she would send her on her way.

All Jaana knew was that one part of her life- that of a drifting healer, whose abilities had now seemingly found their limit- had ended with her abrupt departure from Stone. It was time to be elsewhere, to channel what energies she had left into something else if she could.

*And I must tell Ellen of what I've seen,* she reminded herself. *I might be unable to do anything about it, but surely Ellen can. I should really have gone to her before, rather than try to help.*

Jaana shivered violently and pulled her cloak tightly about herself. The biting wind might not reach far into the forest, but the air was still fearsomely cold.

Dusk had fallen by the time she reached the broad grassy path that would lead her to Ellen, but she decided to plod onwards in any case. She could reach the arbour walls tonight at a good pace, and as she looked up Jaana saw the clouds begin to clear away. Ildar would rise soon, and by her bright light she could safely make her way.

Whilst on this path, Jaana saw the campfire of the *luyan* woman.

The *luyan* herself sat cross-legged by the edge of the flames, seemingly oblivious to the heat, whittling away at a stick to make either a makeshift spear or arrow- Jaana could not be sure as the stick seemed too short for one and too long for the other. She was of average height and girth, not unlike Jaana herself in build, but in keeping with the ways of her people, her attire was quite different. She wore only a skirt-like affair about her waist, fashioned from river-reeds and grasses knotted thickly together, and a ragged cloth that covered her breasts. A thick cape of fur had been folded neatly by her side. Her long hair was both yellowish and translucent. The light from the flames danced across it and made it appear like fine strands of glass.

Jaana also noted, as she stopped and warily looked her over, that the *luyan*'s grass skirt was belted, and the belt held several knives and darts, of varying length.

She took a deep breath and thought quickly. She had properly met only two other *luyan* people in her life. One, a man whose body had started the rapid ageing, as happened to these people past a certain age, and who had gone mad at the same time. The other, a woman perhaps a little older than the girl who sat just fifty yards away, had helped her find her way back home when she had become lost in a small forest near Firstwood many years ago. She had been eight years old and more than a little scared by the experience, but the *luyan* had led her to a road she recognised, and quite possibly even saved her life. Jaana recalled clearly the moment when she had looked up at her rescuer, begging her to come back with her to her mother's house so she could thank her properly. She had felt excited at the prospect, as if this beautiful creature was somehow *her* discovery.

But the *luyan* woman had refused, a sad look in her eyes. "My mother will welcome you!" Jaana had insisted, desperate that the two of them could meet. "She's not like other humans."

What had the woman's last words been? Jaana couldn't recall, but she remembered that a moment later her rescuer melted back into the gathering dusk, gone forever.

It had been the same time of year as now, she recalled, and with the same amount of light left in the sky. The only difference had been the warmth in the air- summer had lingered long into autumn that year.

Jaana strode on along the path; she had to pass by after all, and there was no sense in assuming the worst.

"Good eve to you," the *luyan* woman murmured as she walked by. Jaana turned to look at her, smiled and nodded, trying not to stare at the pale visage and brilliantly clear green eyes. *She is so beautiful,* she thought, embarrassed. *I musn't gawp at her.*

The *luyan* gazed at her without expression. Finally she said, "You can help me. You are a witch. I have wounds that need healing."

Jaana took a false step and stumbled to a halt, her heart hammering. All around, the trees sighed in the evening breeze as if in admonishment. "You mistake me for someone else," she heard herself mumble. "I'm no witch." The words tumbled easily from her mouth, but the *luyan* girl merely raised an eyebrow and briefly turned her attention to the sharpened stick in her hand, whittling a few more splinters from it before she again glanced at Jaana. "Why do you say that? You're not in your spirits-fearing village now."

"I... I need to..." Jaana tried to continue, but she completely forgot her words, and instead- much to her horror and despair- she began to cry. She sank to her knees and wept like the lost girl she had once been, in a vast woodland with the trees sighing all around and the night closing in, and the company of this stranger.

She did not even notice the *luyan* walk over and squat down beside her, and flinched when the woman's hand touched hers. "I don't mean to make you afraid. I shouldn't have been so forward, perhaps. Sit with me."

Jaana wiped at her eyes, struggled to her feet and did as bidden. "It's now too dark to travel," the *luyan* continued, then said abruptly, "My name is Lyya Mo'iynen."

Jaana was about to give her name but Lyya raised a hand quickly- slender and six-fingered as *luyan* hands often were- and flashed a smile at her. "I know your name already. I've seen you before. Sometimes you come to see the woman we know as El'maran – the keeper of the seasons. I have seen her teach you. I cannot pretend to understand such things, but they're of interest to me."

Jaana stared at her. "How could you find your way in without her knowing?"

"The walls that surround her domain, you mean? Oh, they're easy to climb..."

"I don't mean that," Jaana frowned. "Ellen has placed a ward of some kind. She has never told me how it works, but she knows if anyone trespasses..."

"Trespasses? Knarlswood is ours as much as hers, and she knows it," Lyya said dismissively. "We may come and go, if we respect the areas in which she chooses to live- and she is likewise allowed to come and go through our territories. We live and let live, Jaana. I believe that's also a saying amongst your people, much as they find ways to forget such wisdom."

"It is- and they do," Jaana commented ruefully.

"That said, some of my own people are less forgiving of those humans who wander blindly through Knarlswood, without thought to the consequences." Lyya's peculiarly intense eyes gazed directly at her, and Jaana blushed and looked away, feeling stupid and awkward. "It's just that... Ellen never told me about any arrangements that she had with your people."

"Ah well," Lyya said with a shrug, the matter no longer of interest. "Are you hungry?"

Jaana nodded, grateful for the change in conversation, and smiled as Lyya brought forth a freshly-caught rabbit from a cloth sack behind her. "Thank you, Lyya. But I deserve no such kindness."

"It's too much for me, and it will hardly keep," Lyya pointed out. "Better to pick the bones clean than throw good meat to the carrion."

Jaana could not disagree with that. Murmuring her thanks, she spread her cloak on the ground and sat down nearby. Her stomach began to rumble as Lyya skinned and cut the rabbit with expert hands, and then cooked it over the fire, occasionally turning it on the sharp wooden stick that she now realized was being earlier fashioned as a spit. *That must be a harshwood stick,* she noted, observing how the flames failed to eat away at it. Harshwood was notoriously difficult to burn, and remained cool even over flames.

How long had it been since she had had a good meal? Of course- the evening of the last day before she had left, when Danyl had cooked for her. He had had a peculiar talent with food. It was perhaps the one area where he had successfully focussed effort and talent.

Jaana frowned and pushed thoughts of him to one side, as Lyya glanced quizzically at her. "Why are you upset? It cannot be just weariness," she commented.

Jaana shrugged tiredly. "I found... things I was unable to help with," she said at last. "As I said to you, Lyya, I'm no great healer or witch, whatever you may think you know about me. I try to learn from one, but there are many things that she cannot teach me. That was one of the first things Ellen made clear. You cannot teach someone how to *feel* something."

"So you ask El'maran to help you now." Lyya nodded to herself. "Of course. She is very wise."

"And I have much to discover. Much to learn." Jaana stifled a yawn. "I hope she can help. People are falling ill in some of the villages, Lyya, with a kind of delirium, a madness, and it seems that nothing I do can help them. Nothing that *anyone* does seems to help, from what I've heard. So I must ask Ellen."

"Falling ill?" Lyya frowned. "I heard a story about an illness, perhaps a tennight or more ago. A sleep of some kind, and a fever. Perhaps it's the same one."

They sat and watched the flames as the meat slowly cooked. A while later they ate, picking the bones almost clean, and after washing her meal down with some water, Jaana lay back and almost immediately fell into a deep slumber, unable to help herself.

She woke into the morning light. The wind had died down and far above, patches of the sky could be seen, cloudless as far as she could tell. It was warmer than it had been yesterday, and the forest looked beautiful in the still morning air. Jaana sat upright and smiled as Lyya, who looked deep in contemplation. "You slept for a long time," Lyya commented as she glanced round. "Even for a human. You must have been very tired."

"I feel better now." Jaana sighed. "I must go to Ellen this morning." Suddenly she remembered something that Lyya had said last night. "Lyya, you told me that you had wounds that needed healing. What wounds?"

"Oh." Lyya glanced apologetically at her. "I recognised you, and didn't want you to pass by. I was curious to talk to you, and needed an excuse. So I uttered the first thing that came into my head." She paused, then added, "But there is something I want to ask you. I would like to come with you, if I may."

"Come with me? To Ellen? Why?"

"To learn- why else? She taught you, and perhaps she can teach me." Lyya looked thoughtful. "Perhaps she won't be dismissive of me, if I'm with you."

"I doubt she would be willing to teach another, Lyya. In all honesty I think she found teaching me to be trying enough."

"At least let me ask her," Lyya said. A defiant look had entered her eyes, and Jaana realised there and then that the *luyan* woman was not going to back down. If she refused to let Lyya accompany her, then no doubt she would simply follow regardless, and possibly even interrupt Ellen at some inappropriate moment. Lyya was willful and headstrong; that much was obvious. Better that she simply agree, and put up with whatever tongue-lashing Ellen chose to dish out for bringing someone to her uninvited. And she did owe this woman *something* after all, for her kindness and food.

110

"As you wish. But be prepared for disappointment. And don't expect a greeting of any warmth," Jaana warned, but judging by Lyya's grin of delight, that caution had fallen on deaf ears.

They scattered the cold ash from the fire in a circular pattern- one of many odd *luyan* rituals. Then they set off along the broad path, a way that would lead them into the heart of Knarlswood.

Leaf-filtered sunlight lay sprinkled over the forest floor as Jaana and Lyya reached the wall that marked the boundary of Ellen's domain. The ancient stones had been carved by *crommari* craftsmen in the First Age, for a purpose long since forgotten, and over time they had become smothered in layers of soft green moss and patches of green, grey and brown lichen.

Jaana breathed in the cool air, listened to the silence and felt a deep sense of relief and contentment as they drew close to the damp calm of the wall. She felt much the same whenever she came back, and as she touched the wall she wondered, not for the first time, why she had ever wanted to leave. Some vague desire to be out in the world and amongst people, perhaps, although Jaana knew it was more complex than that. The truth was, she did not get on particularly well with people, and the world mostly felt overwhelming, confusing, a place with which she often struggled to cope. Healing had brought a certain amount of satisfaction, and the gratitude of those she healed had given her perhaps a little contentment, along with the inevitable embarrassment of attention.

But now, either her gifts had begun to fail her, or she had reached her natural limit, in finding an affliction that lay beyond her skills and her understanding.

*Yet it must happen for a reason,* she reminded herself, *and therefore a cure must exist. It will be for a better, wiser healer than me to discover it.*

111

The two women walked alongside the wall and presently they arrived at a gate of worked stone and iron. It was closed, but had not been locked. There was little point-the wall might be twelve feet high, but it was scalable from nearby trees. Ellen had merely set her boundaries, using for the most part these ancient *crommar* walls, and in any case she had methods of defence she could call upon that rendered mere locks useless in comparison. Jaana shuddered as she recalled being shown examples of such methods.

"I've not seen this gate before," Lyya confessed, reaching out an inquisitive hand and then drawing it back, thinking better of the act. "Then again I've never looked for it. Whenever I've been curious, I've found my way over the wall."

"We are going to be asking Ellen for advice and help-or at least, I am. So it makes sense to enter through a gateway as she prefers." Jaana was unable to keep the sharpness from her voice. Lyya shrugged, oblivious to her reasoning. "I also have questions to ask her."

"Ellen has a habit of not answering questions," Jaana warned, "or otherwise she chooses to respond with a question herself. Remember that and you may not be too disappointed."

Jaana opened the gate. They passed through and into the forest beyond. The only paths beyond Ellen's wall were those here-there-everywhere tracks made by woodland animals, but Jaana had been this way many times before, and held no fear of becoming lost now that she had come this far.

Jaana set off along one of the less overgrown routes, and her *luyan* companion followed silently behind. The sun had already started to descend in the west when they reached Ellen's old wooden hut, set in the shadow of two oaks, and entwined with ivy and other creepers.

Ellen had emerged from the darkness of her dwelling before Jaana and Lyya were even within proper sight of it.

She stood, arms crossed, and watched in expressionless silence, as they walked up to her. Ellen made a forbidding sight- lean, muscular for a woman, wearing shirt and trousers the same colours as the surrounding woodland. Her white hair was as long and untidy as Jaana remembered it being last time she had seen her. As ever, she offered no welcome or greeting, simply stating bluntly, "I trust you have a good reason for bringing someone with you, Jaana."

"I..." Jaana swallowed, struggling for the right words, or indeed for any. Her relationship with her mentor had always been something of an uneasy one, and merely being in the presence of this fierce, seemingly cold woman was a humbling, sometimes fearful experience. "There are many things I need to tell you about, Ellen."

Perhaps it was the tiredness and tremor in her voice, but Ellen's severe expression suddenly softened a little. "Well, it has been a while," she admitted, "so of course I will hear whatever stories you bring. I expect you're hungry." As Lyya hung back, Ellen turned and looked her up and down, hands on her hips. "You too, *luyan,* unless you prefer to hunt your own meals."

Lyya nodded, and left her bow, arrows and knives by the doorway, albeit with a certain reluctance, as Ellen ushered them both inside. Jaana was relieved that Lyya knew that important custom and had adhered to it. "So, before we speak of anything else," Ellen continued as they sat on the wooden floor- she had never thought chairs to be a worthwhile addition to her home- and turned to Lyya. "How did you convince Jaana to let you come with her? What is it that you want so badly, that only I can give?"

"I want to learn," Lyya said earnestly. "Everything that you teach Jaana. The ways of healing, of the elements, the understanding, the earth..."

Ellen looked scornfully at her. "Don't tell me there are none amongst your own people who can teach you. A

113

good lie might impress me; a poor one and you'll be on your way with your belly still empty."

"They don't believe I have the potential." Lyya sounded angry for a moment. "But I *have*. So I come to you."

"And power?" Ellen responded dryly. "Is that not also something that you wish for? I have never known anyone desperate to know the ways you speak of, who doesn't also nurse a certain lust for power."

Lyya frowned, dumbfounded. Jaana smiled to herself, for she knew this conversation well. It was almost a kind of ritual, a dance that had been played out before, seven years ago when Ellen had asked her the same searching questions. Jaana, then a fifteen-year old girl with a wish to continue the healing ways of her family but also to avenge her mother- the desire for vengeance had burned especially brightly then- had not thought before answering those questions, and had panicked when those answers had appeared to be wrong. She had tried to backtrack and reach for other answers, certain that Ellen would cast her out for such stupidity.

But Ellen had merely sat and listened, allowing her to give as many answers as she chose, until finally, when Jaana had become lost for further words, she prompted her to think and give one honest, considered response.

*The hard answer,* Jaana recalled. *The one that few will admit to.*

Lyya, however, was taking considerably more care, which Jaana had certainly not expected. Her green eyes looked thoughtfully down at the ground, before she finally said, "I suppose I must."

"Why do you say that?" Ellen demanded.

"Because, without the desire to wield it, how can it come to me? How can I achieve any of these things? I must desire it, and if it then comes to me, I must learn to use it as it should be used."

114

*Better words than my own,* Jaana thought ruefully, and not without a little admiration for Lyya.

But whether or not Ellen was satisfied with the answer, she couldn't tell. "So *luyan,* imagine that you have such power, such abilities, after years of hard work and learning. What then? What do you do with them? Hide away from the world as I do?"

Lyya frowned at that. Jaana also thought it a little odd that Ellen would say such a thing, especially with such bitterness. Had she not chosen the life she led?

"I would like to do some of the things that Jaana does," Lyya finally ventured.

"Jaana must have impressed you quickly if- as I suspect- you met only very recently."

"I..." Lyya blushed. "I had heard of her before, and seen her once or twice from a distance. She is known amongst some of my people, or at least her name is."

A sudden thought occurred to Jaana. "Lyya, did you know I would be passing that way, last night?" Even as she asked the question, Jaana knew that was exactly what had happened. She would never have seen a *luyan* who did not want to be seen. They could even change their own colour slightly to better merge with their surroundings- and she would never have heard them either. They could move almost soundlessly if they wanted to.

Lyya's blush deepened. "Yes," she said eventually. "I knew that you must be on your way to see El'maran... Ellen. You only ever come to Knarlswood for that reason. I knew which route you would take as light was failing. I could think of no other way to meet you, and so to meet Ellen."

Jaana shook her head in bewilderment. The *luyan* people certainly had odd ways of going about matters. Ellen, meanwhile, barked out a derisory laugh and spat into the fire.

"But I had no idea you would be so upset," Lyya quietly pointed out, and it was Jaana's turn to blush as Ellen stared at her. "Upset? Why?"

"That's what I came here to tell you about."

"Well, you had better do that whilst I cook supper for us," her mentor said briskly.

Jaana began her story on the cold, rainy day of her arrival in Stone. She deliberately said nothing of Danyl and the time she had spent with him; it was irrelevant, and the fewer reminders of that fleeting liaison the better. That Danyl had treated her with a measure of kindness and respect, albeit in his oddly distracted fashion, only made her more determined than ever to put further distance between them. A violent or otherwise abusive relationship would at least have become a reminder not to let such obstacles to her work get in the way again. Jaana knew that that was a particularly twisted point of view- it was certainly not the one her mother would have taken, despite all the times she had suffered at the hands of others- but it had served her well.

Ellen listened and occasionally asked brief questions for clarification, as she busied herself cooking saltmeat with some root vegetables dug from her small garden. Jaana sensed that her mentor's mood grew increasingly sombre as she continued her relation of events right up to the point where she had left the village.

Later, as they ate their meal in reflective silence, Jaana glanced at Ellen several times. Rarely had she seen her so thoughtful.

Afterwards, with the crockery set aside, Ellen said abruptly, "There's a tale to be told tonight. You may not have heard it before- it is a myth, and not well-known south of the Crescents. Once, it was passed down from generation to generation; however, the original story changed over time. When the meaning of a story grounded in fact becomes lost, then the story itself is useless and dead. What I tell you now

116

is that story. It may not be entirely true, but certainly there's more truth than falsehood to it."

"Is it to do with the illness amongst the humans?" Lyya asked.

"Be quiet, *luyan,* and listen. Then you can make what you will of my words."

The flames formed the only light left anywhere except for a few stars visible through the window. Ellen stared into the depths of the fire as if for inspiration, and then she began to speak.

"The First Age is almost entirely forgotten now, thought of only as an indeterminate past when there were no human cities or towns to speak of, when forests covered the land, when many hundreds of lakes and rivers ran the length and breadth of Aphenhast, and for that matter the lands east and west. But during that time, thousands of years ago, something happened that might have destroyed the land and its entire people. There would have been nothing after that. Not for such as us, anyway, except perhaps something akin to the hells and nightmare worlds threatened by those southern Churches even to this day.

"Across the land, portents were heard of something to come, some mysterious arrival. The religious declared that their God was about to walk the earth with his people. Thousands suffered dreams of a vivid and frightening nature. Others lapsed into states of fever and madness, and screamed of death, of life itself becoming unravelled, of an end to all Ages. Life and time itself, unmade, cast into the dark. Of course, this was in a time when the younger Races such as ours were not free. But that slavery, which persisted for so many millennia, is also forgotten now, the beings that held us in chains themselves nothing more than vague legends.

"And then came other signs. Vast stones, monoliths, blacker than the night. They were Gates, points of immense power that link places together across unimaginably great

117

distances. But these were Gates that had been fashioned with a particular purpose."

"Fashioned for what?" Jaana could feel her skin crawl even as she asked the question.

"For the coming of the *marandaal.*"

Ellen said nothing more, but gazed out through the window at the stars. Jaana and Lyya glanced sombrely at each other, and eventually Jaana said to Ellen, "I have never heard of that word."

"In the old tongue, the name means "the light stepping out of darkness." As to where they came from, how they even came to be in the first place..." Ellen shrugged. "There is myth, and then there is the yawning gulf of time before myth. Ages come and go. But one thing is for certain; they have existed for a *very* long time- far longer than you or I can comprehend.

"They came through the Gates. They destroyed what they could destroy, and twisted and mutilated everything that could not be destroyed. War came to these lands and it lasted perhaps two, three hundred years. There are few records anywhere to show this struggle was even fought, so who knows how long this destruction, this bloodshed, went on for. Eventually they were defeated, as the Gates themselves were destroyed, but at immense cost. And the ancient masters of the younger Races, the *choragh-* well, they destroyed them, though with help from the slave armies they drove across the battlefields. Few survived. It was perhaps a thousand years or more before the land and its people recovered. And there is no word of *how* the *choragh* and the younger Races together managed to defeat such beings. There it is, you see. A faint echo of a story."

The three women fell silent. Ellen stared fixedly out into the dusk, but Jaana found that her gaze wandered to the warmth of the hearth, and her thoughts darkened as she recalled the feverstruck girl in the cottage in Stone.

*The stars are changing.*

118

*What does that mean?* she wondered. *The stars never change, even though the constellations move around. The patterns are eternal.*

She shuddered, and wondered if this might indeed be a prelude to some kind of *arrival.* Or was it just a disease, pure and simple, albeit one she had fathomed nothing about? After all, people maddened by fever and disease often shouted nonsense. She had to be calm and consider everything.

"Is it happening again?" Jaana asked eventually.

Ellen shrugged. "How can I say? I have not examined these people. I have not seen them. Even if I had, I'm no seer. It could be anything. You simply reminded me of an old fable." But there was an edge, almost a tremble, to her voice.

*If it was simply an old fable and nothing else,* Jaana thought, *why speak of it now? What is it that you're not telling me?* But she said nothing.

After a while, Ellen spoke up again. "You must both be tired. We can talk tomorrow and see what might be done. Perhaps we can see one of these people for ourselves, if we're allowed." Then, inexplicably, she brushed Jaana's cheek with her hand, an expression as bewildering as it was oddly affectionate. "You will have to be strong," she said. "It's always in times of weakness that the dark finds a way in."

"Strong?" Jaana blinked and tried to ask her why, but the old woman waved the question away with her customary impatience.

Jaana and Lyya lay down on the spare hay pallet at the back of the hut, and sleep came quickly to them both. Jaana sank swiftly into a deep slumber, and later dreamt that a thousand or more maddened people flocked to her, their pale and grasping hands outstretched and imploring as their voices cried out in unison. Chains and spikes had been worked into their arms and legs, cruel and rusted. Behind them, something less than a figure but more than a shadow waited, never staying in one place for more than a moment,

119

so she could not see it properly. In the sky above, angry black clouds rolled, borne by icy winds. Underfoot, the ground grew uncertain and jagged holes appeared.

She woke suddenly. The early morning sun slanted in through the doorway and lit motes of dust in the still, cool air. Lyya stirred drowsily beside her, muttered something to herself and turned over on her side.

Jaana rose and stretched, feeling a little more refreshed, and hungry despite the generous size of last night's supper. She glanced across at the other hay pallet, where Ellen was sleeping, then wandered over to the doorway where she stood for a while and gazed around the surrounding forest. *Sometimes I wish I could live as the* luyan *do,* she thought wistfully, *the woodland my home, and then I could forget the rest of the world and its pain and fear.*

The memory of Ellen's words last night stirred unease in her stomach. She sighed and walked back into the hut, then wandered over to her sleeping mentor. She tried to figure out why Ellen had said what she had, before ushering herself and Lyya to bed. *You will have to be strong. It's always in times of weakness that the dark finds a way in.* Well, she had always needed to be strong- her life had been a stark choice between being strong and drowning in despair.

As she looked down at Ellen, unease of a quite different kind stirred. Something was wrong.

Then the realisation hit her.

Jaana could do nothing but stare in open-mouthed horror, and then reach out a hand to check the old woman's heart, her pulse, her skin temperature.

Ellen no longer breathed. Her heart was still. Her body was stone cold. She had been dead for perhaps half the night.

As she bent down near to her face, Jaana caught an acrid odour- the smell of redweed, a potent and painless poison. Then she noticed that a small grinding of it had been left in a mortar at the side of the bed.

"Oh, no," she whispered. "Why? *Why?*"

Later she would remember having repeated that word again and again like a useless mantra, tearfully demanding to know the reason why Ellen had chosen to take her own life. *Why, why, why.* She would remember Lyya rising and moving to her side as her whispers became sobs, which in turn became screams of utter despair that threatened to overwhelm her.

Not knowing what Ellen would have wanted done with her body now her spirit had fled, Jaana did nothing. Numb with grief, she only barely listened as Lyya suggested quietly that she make her way to the *luyan* settlement with her.

She walked with her companion through the sunlit woodland, her entire world and all that she valued torn to pieces and wrapped in darkness.


III


For a day and a night, Jaana and Lyya made their way through the depths of Knarlswood, heading along a path that Lyya said led to Ai-Loun, her home. The thought of being invited to a *luyan* settlement would normally have filled Jaana with foreboding and excitement in equal measure, but since their departure from Ellen's hut she had felt nothing except a dull pain and a heaviness that had settled inside her like a stone.

Lyya would occasionally glance back to make sure she was still there. The *luyan* woman said nothing, perhaps knowing there was nothing she could utter that would be useful. When they rested, they did so in silence, and although Jaana saw Lyya glance furtively at her from time to time, she did not look back. She wanted to close her eyes, curl up and sleep forever, or until she and the world moved on and her pain with it.

The path gradually widened into a grassy track that took a mostly straight route through the forest and headed north of north-east. Every now and then they walked across ancient *crommar*-built stone bridges, great arches encrusted with lichen and rounded with age, or some newer wooden ones fashioned by *luyan* pathmakers, to cross streams and small rivers.

Lyya refilled her canteen with water and drank a little more straight from the river. Jaana did the same, and winced as the sharp chill hurt her teeth. "You should eat," Lyya ventured, and offered her some of the salted rabbit meat she had prepared, but Jaana shook her head. The very thought of eating made her feel faint.

The bridge they had now reached was at the end of a clearing in the forest, and longer than the others they had crossed. It spanned a larger, faster-flowing river, a tributary of the great Althameer waterway that cut through the Hastian landscape roughly from north-east to south-west, until finally it reached the sea on the south coast near a city called Darkenhelm, some eight hundred leagues or more away. Jaana had never been anywhere near that place, but suddenly the idea of letting the river carry her down to the sea, past that multitude of unknown lives, to cast her into that expanse felt almost appealing.

*I would be bashed to pieces long before I reached any city,* she thought. *But to be carried away, and no longer have to care about anything...*

Lyya cursed quietly, and Jaana tore herself away from the sight and sound of the river below, which had almost lulled her to sleep. "What...?" she began, and then she saw what Lyya was already staring at.

Jaana watched as the newcomers emerged into the sunlit clearing from one side. One was a human man, tall and well-built, with dark brown hair. The colour of that hair was perhaps the only feature he had in common with his companion, a slim, almost boyish *du-luyan* woman, whose

122

features somehow had both a sharpness and fragility about them. Her thin lips narrowed further in suspicion as she stared at them both, her yellow eyes betraying a cautious and wary nature. They man appeared to say something to his companion, and then they both walked cautiously towards Jaana and Lyya.

"I am Fauli. My friend is Tyrameer." The *du-luyan* woman seemed a little uncomfortable, reluctant even, and glanced at her companion before she continued, "He... *we* thought we may travel together, if you are headed the same way as us for a while. It's no longer as safe as it was, outside the main settlements."

Tyrameer nodded. "Even in Knarlswood. Brigands, followers of some new faith..." He shrugged. "What they are is not so important. As Fauli said, the forest is not as safe as it was."

"Odd that such people wander through Knarlswood these days." Fauli grimaced in distaste. "It was not so long ago when they would have to be dragged screaming into these woods. Perhaps their religion has overpowered such superstitions."

Jaana had heard of no new faith, not that she paid a great deal of attention to such matters. She saw that Lyya looked at Fauli as if uncomfortable with something. She recalled that the *luyan* and *du-luyan* did not get on with each other as a rule, though she had no idea why. She knew it had nothing to do with their respective light and dark skins. It was far more complex. She decided to ask Lyya about it later if the opportunity presented itself.

"We were headed to Ai-Loun," Lyya ventured at last.

"Ai-Loun? A fair way from here," Fauli commented.

Lyya scowled. "I know how far it is and I know the way."

Fauli looked her up and down as if doubting that Lyya could make the journey. "If you can bear to travel with

123

us, *luyan,* we can walk most of the way there with you. It's on our way and we can head north along the main track."

Lyya opened her mouth to say something, then paused and reconsidered. Finally she shrugged. "As you wish."

Fauli nodded. "Good. Let's not waste any more time here then."

As dusk fell, they made camp for the night in a gorge through which another, smaller tributary of the Althameer river ran. The night would be well-lit- already the bright face of Ildar had risen and stars dotted the sky. Jaana wrapped a blanket about herself to keep warm, though in truth, with only a light breeze, it was not as cold as she had feared it would be. Fauli and Tyrameer moved to sit some distance away from the fire at one point, to discuss something with each other.

"Are you going to eat something tomorrow, Jaana?" her companion asked, absently poking at the fire with an errant twig.

"If I have the stomach for it," Jaana said quietly, then recalled what she had meant to ask Lyya when she had the opportunity. "Lyya, why do the *luyan* and *du-luyan* hate each other so much?"

Lyya glanced at her in surprise. "Hate is not the word I would use for it. I suppose we simply find it difficult to like or accept one another. It's complicated by a number of things. The *du-luyan* live longer than we do, and have conquered the rage and dementia that can come upon our kind as we age more and more rapidly. Some say they've used earth magic- the Old Powers- to defeat it." Lyya shrugged, glancing quickly across at Fauli. "If that's so, then I've never heard any of them admit to it."

Jaana nodded. She had heard much about the Wasting as the *luyan* referred to it, and a little about how the *du-luyan* people did not suffer such an end to their lives.

"But no one can defeat death in the end," she pointed out. That was an obvious statement, but one that had been drilled into her time and again by Ellen.

Thinking of her dead mentor made her heart sink again. What was she to do? A picture came to her mind, of Ellen slowly rotting away in her home, turning to dust - eventually to be forgotten along with whatever secret wisdom she had carried with her and chosen never to reveal. A grim, pointless end.

"I am truly sorry about El'maran." Lyya shook her head, although Jaana could not tell whether it was in bewilderment or disgust. "I cannot understand what she did. To take her own life!"

"Humans sometimes do, Lyya." Jaana felt suddenly as if she might start weeping any moment. "I know that the *luyan* simply don't have it within them to carry out self-murder, even towards the end of their lives when the Wasting torments them. But we humans are such miserable creatures. We think ourselves the masters of the land, the masters even of nature, and yet we hide away to protect ourselves, we squabble and we make war, we fight, and we sow nothing but hatred!"

Bitterness had made Jaana raise her voice without realising, and Fauli and Tyrameer briefly looked in their direction, curiosity plain on their faces. Jaana bit her lip and looked away.

"That's what happened in the city of Nisstar," Lyya said softly. "They killed many of my people, or enslaved them, and drove the others away. That place is forbidden to all *luyan* now, except those who remain there as slaves, forced into servitude or the arenas where they're made to fight each other to death in the dust. But war will come of that, I am sure. The Rising have promised as much." A venomous look passed across her face. "Your people have much to answer for, Jaana." Then her expression softened. "I expect you don't think of them as your people."

Jaana shrugged. "I had heard some stories from Nisstar, but I've never had cause to go anywhere near there. I've never been to *any* large city. But I had no idea that *that* had happened. It seems I know even less than I thought of the world."

Lyya nodded soberly and resumed her poking at the fire. Eventually Jaana asked her in agitation, "What am I to do, Lyya? I have nowhere to go. I wanted to find out about the illness and what might be done- but I can do nothing about it now. The only person who could have helped me is gone."

"There are others who may be able to help," Lyya said. "That was why I suggested you return with me to Ai-Loun. I am sure El'maran was very wise. I *know* she was very wise. But you will be able to find the answer you seek elsewhere. She was not the only one with wisdom of such things."

"The wise don't kill themselves," Jaana told her forcefully, and perhaps Lyya knew better than to argue further.

She slipped into despondency. Lyya was trying to help, she knew that, but that very fact somehow made it worse. Yet again she tried to figure out a possible reason for Ellen's suicide. Had her mentor been driven to it somehow? Might it have been something to do with Jaana's telling of the mysterious disease she had encountered so many times? Jaana could make even less sense of that. Surely Ellen would have wanted to at least give her guidance. But if her mentor had harboured any answers, she had taken them with her.

*Why?* Jaana raged inwardly. *Why did you selfishly take your own life, and leave me with nothing? Without any help? You knew I would not have come begging for your aid unless it was truly needed!*

126

She sighed, realising her hands were trembling. Lyya reached out and put her hand in her own. "It is hard to understand."

"No." Jaana shook her head wearily. "It's impossible to understand."

Jaana clasped her friend's hand and squeezed it tight. They said nothing for a long while, and looked out over the river as moonlight moved restlessly upon its surface.

"We are going to see a friend of ours- Fistelkarn, a scholar of the arcane arts," Fauli said the following morning.

Jaana recalled that the two of them had spent a while perusing their maps last night. "I've heard the name," Lyya commented as she looked up from her ash-scattering ritual.

"It has been a long time since we last met. But there is more than that." Fauli motioned to Tyrameer, who continued hesitantly, "We heard you talking of an illness, last night. There is an illness- a madness, some say- amongst people hereabouts. It might be the same thing."

Jaana nodded cautiously. "It might."

"My father, mother and sister all fell ill in this way," Tyrameer said. "The priest in Lower Oakby, the village where we lived, did everything he could, and healers looked after them and eased their suffering as far as possible, but in truth there was nothing they were able to do."

*A priest could have done nothing regardless,* Jaana thought, but said nothing.

Tyrameer continued sombrely, "My father and mother died, and my sister... well, she was alive when I left Lower Oakby, but... well, she was not as she once was. She no longer recognised me, and when I looked into her eyes I saw nothing left of her."

Lyya gave Jaana a sidelong glance and then spoke up: "My people know of this Fistelkarn only as a collector of lore, a kind of sorcerer or trickster. He's not a healer. How might he help you?"

"I doubt that he can, himself," Tyrameer admitted, "but he knows many people, including one or two healers who might. We could have gone south to Nisstar, perhaps, but..."

He glanced at Fauli, realised what he had said, and looked uncomfortably down at the ground. Fauli smiled and clapped him on the shoulder, having to reach up to do so. "I know, Tyrameer. I know. As if I'd want to follow you into Nisstar anyway."

Jaana got the impression that Fauli probably would have done if she'd had to, and if she could have smuggled herself in. The two of them were certainly close, and entirely comfortable in each other's company. She wondered how they had met and become friends.

Jaana decided there and then to tell them of her own discoveries- or *lack* of discoveries, she reminded herself. Her existence as a healer felt over now; she could feel no urge to aid those who had fallen unwell, just a sorrow that she could do nothing about the feverish madness that had claimed so many people, including Tyrameer's family. Jaana felt ashamed but tried not to think about it. It had been her gift, her *calling* some had called it, including her own mother and later, Ellen.

*If it was a calling,* she reflected, *who or what was it that called to me? Some misguided conscience? Whatever it might have been, it calls no longer.*

"I was a healer, although I was never able to understand this affliction," she admitted. "Sometimes I could ease the suffering of those who fell victim to it, but I could never cure them." She saw hope flare up and then die in Tyrameer's eyes. "I'm sorry, Tyrameer. But I was never an especially gifted healer. I'm sure Fistelkarn will know others who can help you."

"Perhaps." Tyrameer no longer seemed as certain.

128

"We're doing no good standing here," Fauli said abruptly as she picked up her backpack. "We have a long way to walk today."

"I would like to come with you to see Fistelkarn," Jaana said suddenly. She had not even thought before speaking, but now that she did pause to consider, she realised that it was at least a way of helping, if only in a small way. "If we do meet with any healers, my experiences might help them find a cure." She shrugged. "Perhaps not. But I can try. I can at least tell them about what I've seen."

"Then I will come too," Lyya said. Jaana looked at her in surprise. "I thought you were going back to Ai-Loun."

"I can go there whenever I want." Lyya's tone was dismissive. "I would like to..." She shrugged. "Accompany you, if you don't mind. For a while at least."

"Of course I don't mind." Jaana smiled, and then realised it was the first time she had done so for many days.

They headed north, towards the edge of Knarlswood where the trees met the foothills of the Crescents. In the grey sky above, the first snow of the coming winter drifted down.

## IV

The days that followed, as they pressed on into the lowland Crescents, felt as grey to Jaana as the snow clouds that scudded overhead. She ate little, said even less, and at times shw wanted to just lie down and curl up, drift off to sleep and never wake up. Every step took an abundance of effort and seemed pointlessly leaden.

Lyya tried to lighten her mood, but even the *luyan* woman's tales of her family and her life in Ai-Loun, interesting and occasionally amusing as they were, failed to rouse her from this quiet despair. Dawn broke slowly and unwillingly each morning, the dark sky lightening only to a murky grey. Clouds rolled past, carried by the breeze and

129

threatening more snow the whole while, although barely an inch had fallen in the last few days.

"Much more will come soon enough," Fauli warned. "I don't remember winter being this cold this early ever before."

Occasionally they passed close to remote farmsteads, served only by tracks that wound through the wilderness. Most of these buildings looked in desperate need of repair work unlikely to ever be received, and some had even been abandoned.

During the afternoon of the third day, the light snow that had drifted on and off since mid-morning lessened but became unpleasant and sleety, and the four of them trudged onwards along tracks and paths that quickly became muddy underfoot. Eventually a thin mist descended, and darkness arrived early and swiftly. Soon enough the way ahead could barely be seen, and Fauli suggested that they rest for the evening in an abandoned barn a short distance away from the track. Disused and left to the mercy of the elements, the roof of this place had long since fallen in, and the stone walls were encrusted with soft moss.

The evening drifted to a starless, moonless and utterly silent night, bitterly, painfully cold, rampant with the kind of damp chill that felt as if it could seep into bones.

Jaana watched despondently as Fauli sprinkled some firepowder over the wood they had gathered to help make a fire. There were few twigs here, and those they had found were damp, yet the fire sprang up quickly, the firepowder causing it to flare briefly with greenish-blue flames and sparks and push back the darkness a little more.

Inevitably Jaana found that her thoughts returned to the evening of her arrival at Ellen's dwelling. She wondered if Ellen might have carried some terrible secret, perhaps something to do with what she and Lyya had said that same evening. But knowledge so terrible that, rather than tell her acolyte, she instead resolved to kill herself and take it with

130

her? What kind of insight could be enough to make her flee this world as a self-murderer?

"Do you fear for her soul?" Lyya asked gently.

Jaana jumped at that. She had begun to realise that Lyya had an uncanny way of correctly guessing her thoughts. Surely she was not that transparent? But then, what else had she to think about, even days later?

"I don't know," she said eventually. "I don't know much about souls and spirits. But it can never be right to take the life that the world itself has given you. I have tried to make sense of it all, but I can't."

"We have perhaps another morning's walk until we reach the Round Tower," Fauli spoke up. She looked Jaana up and down, not without sympathy. "For a healer, you do not look after yourself very well. You should eat more, and take your own potions."

Jaana laughed at that despite herself. "I will try, Fauli."

"I meant to ask you both before," Lyya spoke up, glancing from Fauli to Tyrameer, "but how did you come to be travelling together? You don't seem like lovers..."

"Would it be wrong for a *du-luyan* woman to take a human man as her lover?" Fauli said dangerously. Then, inexplicably, she laughed out loud. "Lyya, you must know so little of the world, if you see a man and woman together and assume they must be lovers! Have you spent much time beyond the borders of Ai-Loun?!"

Lyya looked down at the ground, embarrassed. "It *is* uncommon, that's all I am saying."

"Uncommon, are we?! Well, amongst *your* people I daresay we would be..."

"Stop it, Fauli." Tyrameer gave her a shove. "You are right, Lyya. It's not the most commonplace sight. We met in the *crommar* sity of Culvanhem eight years ago. We both happened to be passing through- I had an errand for a *crommar* friend of mine- and we got on so well that we

131

decided not to go our separate ways. We both have the wanderlust, it seems, and neither of us sees much sense in settling amongst our people." A shadow seemed to pass over him. "I see even less sense now. There's nothing left for me where I came from."

"I can understand that," Jaana murmured.

They cooked their meal over the flames, and Jaana found to her surprise that she had regained a little of her appetite. Afterwards, as she lay down to rest and drift off to sleep curled up under a blanket, she stared up into the mist and wondered briefly whether the next few days would at last bring more answers than questions.

"You are a healer of some repute," Fauli suddenly said to her the following morning, as they were clearing their camp and preparing to leave their ramshackle shelter.

Startled, Jaana did not know what to say at first. "I don't think so," she ventured at last. "A healer, yes, but there are many like me."

But the *du-luyan* woman continued regardless, "I wondered where I had heard of you before. Your name is not a common one in the middle lands. Then I remembered that your name had been mentioned in a few of the places I passed through last year. And of course, when you said you were a healer... well! I like a puzzle, but that was almost no challenge at all."

"What does it matter now?" Lyya demanded warily, but Fauli chose to ignore her.

"I'm not sure what I am any more," Jaana said eventually, slinging her pack over her shoulder. She avoided looking at either of them as they walked out of their shelter and to the path where Tyrameer had already packed and awaited them. "Perhaps I did some good now and again, but more recently I found the illness I could do nothing about. We've already talked about it. A healer who cannot heal needs to think about doing something else with her life." She turned and stared at Fauli, suddenly angry. "I don't want to talk about this again."

"As you wish." Fauli shrugged as if she had suddenly lost interest in the matter, but Jaana knew better.

They made good progress that morning. The breeze lessened, and the fog eventually lifted to give them a good view of where they were headed. Towards noon the sun broke through what remained of the cloud cover, and Jaana thought she could see something glitter in the distance. As they drew slowly closer, she realised that it came from a window of a tower nestled at the foot of a hill, the summit of which was hidden in cloud. *This must be where the Crescents truly begin,* Jaana thought to herself, *and I suppose that building must be...*

"Fistelkarn's tower," Tyrameer proclaimed, pointing to it.

"I could never live in such a place- all stone and shadow," Lyya remarked.

"What's the matter, *luyan*? Afraid of the dark?" Fauli called across, and Lyya scowled at her.

"Our friend finds the stone and the shadows good company," Tyrameer said as they continued on across the moorland. "He once lived in the southern city of Emberton, but chose to leave that life behind decades ago."

"How did you come to know him?" Jaana asked.

"He gathered a group of people together once," Fauli said, "to find an artefact that had been lost for centuries. Friends of his who ran a historical Guild in Nisstar had sought it out for many years, and it was the subject of a hundred or more different rumours and myths."

"Did you find it?"

"No!" Fauli laughed. "Such things are very seldom found. But in time that hardly seemed to matter, as we spent so long in the attempt and went through so much together that some of us became good friends." Her smile faded. "I hear that now the Guild has been burned to the ground, as punishment for some perceived slight against the ruling church. The good people of Nisstar seem desperate in their desire to destroy knowledge and enlightenment. At least, those who rule over them do."

*I must remember never to go there,* Jaana thought with a shudder.

As the tower loomed nearer, she wondered if she might be able to ask Fistelkarn about the disease that had defeated her efforts. He might not have any answers, nor indeed might he want to speak to her or even listen to what she had to say, but she had best be prepared. If he had some idea about what might have caused it then that was a start. Then she might have some idea what had to be dealt with. Maybe they could find a cure, or even a way to stop it from spreading.

*And once I've done as much as I can, what then?* she wondered. *A quiet life somewhere, perhaps with a new name, given that even Fauli had heard of me. That would be best- peace and anonymity.*

"The yardgate is open," Tyrameer observed as they drew closer, and then, as they neared the courtyard, he stopped and exchanged glances with Fauli. Jaana could see plainly through the open gateway leading into the little courtyard that the door that lead into the tower was wide open and creaked gently in the breeze.

Tyrameer quietly unbuckled and drew his sword, and they advanced into the courtyard, as far as the open entrance. No sound issued from within. They waited and listened intently, but heard only the creaking back and forth of the door and the breeze that whistled around the tower wall.

Tyrameer advanced into the small, gloomy hallway beyond, and the others followed quietly behind. Jaana heard her own blood pulse in her ears. She took a deep breath and willed herself to be calm. Three doors opened from the hallway into various rooms, all of them untidy. Papers, books

134

and ornaments arranged haphazardly about the place and a faintly musty smell, like books and old food, hung heavy in the air. Lanterns had been lit in each room and gave out a faint glow to mingle with the late afternoon light that sifted through the windows.

"He has not been gone long," Fauli commented, as Tyrameer turned back to close the entrance behind them.

"Does he often venture out?" Lyya asked tentatively. Fauli glanced round at her. "Sometimes. But I've never known him leave his *door* open for people to wander in. There is too much of value here. No, someone has found- or *forced*- their way in."

They cautiously looked into each of the rooms. One was obviously a study, another a kitchen, though it looked as if it served as a main chamber as well, and possibly even a bedchamber. As she looked at the state of the place, Jaana could not help but wonder if the old man had simply wandered out and forgotten to shut the door behind him. Despite Fauli's words to the contrary, it seemed like something a man who lived amongst all this clutter might do.

"Upstairs, then," Tyrameer murmured once their search on the ground floor had been exhausted.

They carefully ascended the spiralling staircase that ran from the end of the hallway up into indeterminate gloom. Windows had been built into the outer wall of the stairwell and they opened out either sheer onto the tower wall, or onto tiny little balconies. Jaana peered out through one of them and noticed that it had started to snow again, a little more heavily this time.

The next floor held just another bedchamber and a store-room where piles of books lay piled on an old table as well as shelves placed against each of the walls. The shelves had begun to buckle under the weight of the books. Jaana saw a long-legged spider scuttle along one of them, hurrying from one shadowy hiding place to the next.

The staircase continued to wind on up through the tower. Suddenly they heard a faint sound, of something being dragged, as if across the floor, from somewhere above. Tyrameer glanced questioningly at Fauli, who gripped her twin longknives even more firmly and shook her head. "Someone else," she whispered. "I *knew* someone must have broken in."

The two of them walked up the stairwell once again. Their soft boots made almost no sound. Fauli turned briefly to Lyya and Jaana, cast almost completely in shadow. "Stay here if you wish," she whispered. "There is no need for you to come with us."

"We are coming with you," Lyya whispered back, as fiercely as she dared, and glanced at Jaana, who nodded reluctantly. She hoped that whoever was up there was merely a thief, or perhaps, contrary to Fauli's belief, even Fistelkarn himself, lost in his own dwelling and heedless to his open front door.

Fauli shrugged as if she could not care less, and they walked on up the spiral until they reached the small, dusty landing that marked out the top of the tower, where doors led into two chambers, one on each side. One of the doors stood slightly open, and they could hear sounds of furniture and other items being moved from within the chamber beyond. Tyrameer and Fauli nodded to each other, and kicked the door wide open, then walked in.

The *du-luyan* girl kneeling by a broken-open wooden chest in the middle of the room scrambled to her feet in shock and looked wildly around as Tyrameer and Fauli came to a standstill.

"*Ai chkaan luoddor!*" Fauli exclaimed, and pointed one of her blades at her. "*Luoddor fe naal!*"

The thief- for judging by the upturned state of the room, this was surely what she was- looked frantically around for a moment, and then ran straight between Fauli and Tyrameer with incredible speed, somehow able to get past them in her haste. Lyya tried to stop her but was thrown back as the girl pushed her aside and made for the door.

Cursing, Fauli chased after her as she reached the landing, but the other *du-luyan* ran straight through into the other chamber- and threw herself against the window.

As the window shattered, the wind swept in to send fragments of glass everywhere and blow papers and even books all over the room. Fauli stopped in disbelief and then ran over to the broken window, her boots crunching on broken glass, and peered out.

"I can't see her anywhere," Tyrameer muttered as he joined her, then leaned out further. "Gods!" he whispered. "How can she do that?"

As Jaana leaned forward to peer over the sheer window ledge, she could see, far below, the *du-luyan* girl swiftly descend the tower wall. Somehow she was able to find handholds and footholds where it seemed there were none.

"That's not as remarkable as it looks, Tyrameer," Fauli said dryly, "but nonetheless we should have stopped her! *Damn!*"

"We still can," Tyrameer grimly replied, and began to make his way down the stairwell, but Fauli shook her head. "She's already reached the base of the tower. Unless you can conjure a horse from somewhere, chances are that she is fleeter of foot in her clothes than you are in yours, so I would suggest we barricade this window before the wind blows everything out through it."

They set about putting a couple of boards securely in place. "I think she will have been scared off in any case," Fauli muttered, "but we'd best be on the safe side."

They made their way downstairs and into the larger study, and Fauli stoked up the dying embers of the fire. She stabbed at the remnants with a poker and then added a few more logs. "I still cannot fathom why the door was left open," she muttered. "If that girl broke in, why did she leave her entrance so obvious? Perhaps in her haste she forgot."

"No one has ever managed to break into the tower before," Tyrameer remarked. "Fistelkarn was always proud of the fact."

"We shouldn't have let her escape," Fauli sighed as she squatted by the flames and warmed her hands. "We could have been questioning her right now. But I didn't expect her to..." She shrugged. "I suppose I was outwitted. But if I ever see her again..."

"She was fast," Jaana spoke up, "and desperate also. I thought she looked terrified when she saw us."

"Ha! She *would* have been terrified if I'd captured her," Fauli exclaimed, then turned suddenly. "I hear sounds outside. Someone is coming."

Jaana could hear nothing at all except the crackle of logs in the fire, but a short while later, the main entrance door creaked open and they could hear a purposeful, steady walk in the hallway. Then the door to the study opened, and, judging by the relieved reactions of Fauli and Tyrameer, Fistelkarn stood before them.

He did not by any means form the image that Jaana had conjured up for herself of a well-known and respected scholar, not that she had met any before. His thinning, wispy white hair was snow-dampened, as was his untidy, almost yellow beard. He wore a heavy, faded fur cloak and boots and trousers that had both seen far better days. His eyes were a mild, almost milky blue, surrounded by smile wrinkles, but as he first looked at each of them in surprise he seemed like a man bearing the weight of the world.

"Well, well. Good company to come back to!" he remarked, closing the door behind him. His voice had warmth to it, and both Jaana and Lyya relaxed. Somehow Jaana knew there and then that he was not about to react badly to their intrusion, however surprising it clearly was.

Tyrameer glanced uncomfortably back at the old man. "I do apologise, Fistelkarn. We were waiting for you to return... we thought we had best look after the place for you. You see, there was..."

"An intruder. Yes, I know- as you would have done if you'd bothered to examine the lock carefully enough. I expect the thief had been waiting for a long while for me to go out, and then..."

"The intruder was *du-luyan*," Fauli spoke up. She seemed ashamed of the fact, as if none of her people had been known to turn to thievery.

"Yes. A trace of the power used to wield the key she had in her possession still remains," Fistelkarn agreed. "A female, if I am not mistaken. The patterns are different when a female uses a shifting key."

"Do you know who she was?" Fauli asked with added interest.

Fistelkarn nodded. "Yes, I believe so. But that's for me to think about and deal with." He drew up another chair and draped his damp cloak over the back of it to dry as he moved it nearer to the fire. As he sat down, suddenly he seemed older, more tired. He gazed at Jaana and Lyya in turn. "As my good friends have not seen fit to introduce you, I'll let you fulfil the task yourselves."

"My name is Jaana," Jaana spoke up hesitantly, and gestured to Lyya. "This is Lyya."

"Jaana is a witch, and a healer," Lyya added, and Jaana felt the heat rise to her cheeks as she glared at Lyya. "I'm neither. Well, I was a minor healer and an apprentice to Ellen of Knarlswood. I went to her to seek her help- people were falling ill, mad in a village where I was staying... but..." She glanced at Fistelkarn, and stopped in shock as she saw the compassion in his eyes. "She's dead. Yes, I know," he said softly.

"But...how..."

139

Fistelkarn leaned forward. "A week ago, a messenger arrived- a bird, to be precise. She would have sent it knowing full well of her coming demise. So I knew then that that would be the last time I would hear from her." He sighed. "Her time had come, as they say. Only it ought not to have been."

"She took her own life." Jaana could not keep the bitterness from her voice. "She even *planned* to do so!"

Fistelkarn regarded her in silence for a moment. "No," he said finally. "Oh, she knew what was coming. But I think she could do nothing about it."

Everyone stared at him. "Forgive me," Lyya said eventually, "but we saw her body the next morning. She had taken redweed."

Fistelkarn's expression became yet grimmer. "What you saw and what *happened* are two separate things. I knew Ellen for fifty years. I knew her well enough to know that she would not, *could* not, take her own life. But something was going to take it from her, and there was nothing she could do to stop it. Some powerful sorcery had been put in motion, and nothing could prevent it from working its weave, until the task for which it had been created was done."

Jaana put her head in her hands, reeling from the shock. Once again her world tumbled away from her. "I understand less and less of this. Others had tried occasionally to break into Ellen's land, to steal or even to kill- but they all perished, every one of them. How could *anything* reach into her domain, past her wards, and *kill* her? What could possibly be powerful enough to do such a thing?"

Fistelkarn did not answer, but walked over to kneel by the fire, watching sparks whirl up into the chimney. Outside the tower, the wind had picked up further, and howled like some lost, tormented creature.

"The taint of Aona's past," he said eventually. "Ellen and whatever destroyed her were different sides of the same coin. This is the essence of the Old Power, as some still call it- the weavings of the world. Neither light nor dark, in itself..." Abruptly he turned and stared directly at Jaana, a sudden intent look in his eyes. "Tell me something truthfully," he said quietly. "Were you *there* that night? Sleeping in her abode the night she died?"

Jaana felt her heart sink like a stone into darkness. Surely he did not think she had killed Ellen? She swallowed, unable to speak. Panic rose through her.

But he saw the truth, regardless of her inability to answer. He said to her, "Whatever it was, it spared your lives- or perhaps it *could not* kill you. It may be that she wove some protection about the two of you. Or something else..." He shook his head, and turned to Fauli and Tyrameer. "And what about the two of you- were you two there that night?"

"No- we hadn't met them at that point," Fauli ventured. Even she seemed a little nervous.

Fistelkarn turned back to Jaana and Lyya. "So, for some reason you were spared. Not just spared, but allowed your freedom." He shook his head. "You are part of some plan I know nothing of."

Jaana and Lyya stared blankly at each other. Fistelkarn retired to his chair and remained deep in thought for a long time. No one dared speak.

"Tell me, all of you," the sorcerer said eventually. "Have you ever heard the word *marandaal?*"

Everyone glanced nervously at one another. A gust of wind suddenly rattled one of the nearby windows. They all jumped, apart from Fistelkarn, who seemed far too wrapped up in his own words to pay any mind to the weather.

"I have heard the name," Lyya said quietly, glancing at Jaana. "Ellen spoke of it, that night."

Fistelkarn nodded. "And do you know what it means in the Old Hastian, Lyya?"

141

"Ellen said it was something about a light- a light out of darkness." Lyya grimaced. "I should have remembered, but I don't."

"She was right enough," Fistelkarn agreed. "The oldest known translation describes them as *they who come bathed in light, from out of the dark.*"

"What are they?" Tyrameer asked.

"A better question than you can possibly imagine, Tyrameer." Fistelkarn frowned. "The truth is that no one really knows what they were. They were simply the *marandaal.*"

"From the little I have read," he continued, "they were revered as Gods by some of the people of that time. As they came into the world, countless thousands fell into delirium, fever, madness... countless *other* thousands knelt in worship. And were then destroyed as the *marandaal* crushed the life from the world. Or nearly did."

"Do you think..." Jaana began. She had no need to say anything more, for Fistelkarn shrugged wearily and replied, "Who can say? There are signs wherever one chooses to look. The world wakes."

"The world wakes?" Fauli stared worriedly at him. "What does that mean?"

"Exactly that, Fauli. Aona's ancient powers now stir, for which there must be a reason. The Races thought for thousands of years that they had gone away for all eternity. But it did not happen like that. No, it was more like the tide going out. The Old Powers have two sides, and the darker of the two perhaps grows stronger now."

"Strong enough to..." Jaana blinked and stared back at him. "Could it be that something of the Old Powers grew strong enough to reach out and destroy Ellen?"

"It is possible." Rubbing his hands together thoughtfully, Fistelkarn continued, "Signs manifest themselves throughout the land. There are murmurs of strife wherever one looks. I too have heard of the madness, Jaana-it's more widespread than you might have thought. Some fall ill and cannot be wakened, others who were perfectly lucid and sane become gibbering idiots or lunatics, who wander aimlessly and shout their madness. But that's not all. Nisstar is a law unto itself now, a city run by madmen. In Rockmire, because of the laws passed in Nisstar, *luyan* and *crommari* and the Gods themselves know who else are gathering, determined to wage a war on the place. There are strange happenings far to the north too, beyond the Crescents. Talk of conflict, of war between tribes, of disappearances and sacrifices. The tales invariably become confused by the time they reach me. Still, whatever each case may be, they point to something. A *stirring* beneath the face of it all."

Fistelkarn stared into the flames, lost in thought for a while. When he spoke again it was of something else entirely.

"I believe I know what it was. Yes, the more I think about it, the more..." He glanced around and smiled. "The shaping, or the essence of it, left by whoever unlocked the door. It had that peculiar resonance, not used now for over a century..."

"She was just a *du-luyan* girl, a thief," Tyrameer put in, and Fistelkarn nodded. "I would have known if she had been anything else. And that makes it all the stranger..."

Abruptly he returned to the previous matter. "I intend to find out whatever lies at the heart of these... *changes*". He seemed deeply troubled. "It is gathering pace. I will go to the *crommar* city of Culvanhem, to the west."

"Why Culvanhem?" Tyrameer asked.

"The *crommari* hold captive a renegade dreamreader by the name of Ludas," Fistelkarn said. "A bitter enemy of mine, for reasons we have no need to discuss. But the *crommar* prisons are terrible places of cold stone, set deep into the mountains and far from any human territory, so he won't have escaped. If he still retains a hold on his sanity,

143

then I may be able to broker a deal for his release. In return for his help, of course."

"How would he be able to help us?" Jaana asked, but immediately she knew the answer. Fistelkarn nodded as he saw the look in her eyes. "As I said, he is a dreamreader of some power. If anyone can delve the truth from those who have fallen ill or mad, then he can."

"We will accompany you to Culvanhem," Fauli said, then glanced questioningly at Jaana and Lyya, who both nodded.

"Good," Fistelkarn said briskly. "Sleep soundly if you can. There's a spare room at the back. We will leave at dawn."

Throughout the night, Jaana's sleep was fitful. On several occasions during the dark hours she woke suddenly and stared up at the ceiling. She wondered what she might have seen, looming in the darkness of Ellen's hut, if she had been awake the night of her mentor's death.

# V - Amongst the Fallen

## I

Shambler, the doorkeeper at Tuin's Ale House, felt his heart sink at the sight of the *du-luyan* assassin, and knuckled his forehead in what he hoped would be taken as a gesture of humility as Iyoth strode into the tavern. Iyoth, for his part, barely acknowledged the fat doorkeeper, although he smiled inwardly at the greeting, for amongst his own people it signalled a challenge to a fight.

He gave the tap-room and its assortment of ragtag regulars a cursory glance and then headed straight for the bar. Tuin, perhaps cursing his decision to serve tonight, attempted to smile. "My friend, it's good to see you," he began. "Indeed, it has been..."

"I'm not your friend," Iyoth interrupted. "I am here for my gold. Then I will leave your sorry excuse for an alehouse alone."

"Of course." Tuin scratched at his moustache. "I..." He dropped his voice to an almost conspiratorial whisper. "I have it upstairs. Too much to keep down here. You understand of course..."

"Fetch it then." Iyoth's cold glare was constant; it was almost as if he never blinked.

Tuin smiled and nodded, and slipped quietly to the end of the bar and up the rotting wooden stairs to the upper floor. Iyoth leaned against the bar and stared contemptuously around. Anyone who accidentally looked his way quickly found more interesting subjects in other directions. He watched in disgust as Tuin's excuse for entertainment- tonight a slave-girl copulating with an eager mongrel dog- took place on the far side of the room. Men, most of them Tuin's shadowy friends, laughed and cheered in

145

between gulps of pissy ale and puffs of some foul brain-rotting mixture. Iyoth could not be entirely sure what it was, but it made even the dank and sulphurous air outside seem almost enticing. The cold breeze sighed around the walls, carrying Ethanalin Tur-morn's unrelenting stench to every corner of the town.

Of all the human settlements he had visited, Iyoth considered this to be the worst. An unsustainable huddle of hastily-made houses and stores, the town had been built by shiny-eyed prospectors eager for their reward. As the decrepit silver and crystal mines yielded less and less and cost more and more to run, so the people seemed to care less and less about their dismal situation.

Iyoth knew his history well enough, and recalled that decades ago this place had thrived, or had at least enjoyed a decent flow of money. The town had expanded month on month as more and more people flocked to the area, eager to get their grasping hands on what they thought would be easy wealth. But in recent times, those lucky enough to own sufficient funds, or with relatives in better places, had cut their losses and moved away, leaving behind the several thousand or so people who remained dependent on the dwindling returns from the sale of silver and crystal ornaments to the few merchants who still came this way.

Iyoth held in his heart a vague contempt for humans, and had initially found the ineptitude and petty violence of the Tur-mornian people amusing, but after a month spent here, it had started to grate. Although it was an irrational, typically *human* response, he now found it increasingly difficult to resist the temptation to slice the throat of anyone he caught looking at him oddly. Of course, furtive and worried looks were only to be expected- black skin and dark orange eyes were a rarity here, and he was *du-luyan* on top of that. How long had it been since the last of his people had come here? And more to the point, why would they have bothered? If they craved silver and crystal so much, they

146

would have mined it themselves rather than travel here to scrounge cast-offs from the humans. He had come only for the money, and as soon as he had that, he would be out of here as quickly as his horse and the weather permitted.

Two men had died at his hand at the bequest of Tuin, silently and possibly without even comprehending their fate. That was the way it should always be done- calmly, efficiently, without torture or prolonged suffering. After all he had borne no grudge against his victims, so why should he enjoy their demise?

Still, he would enjoy spending the reward.

Iyoth saw an old man shuffle past outside and then suddenly stop and turn to stare up into the sky and mutter something to himself. He licked at wind-chapped lips before he smiled suddenkly and nodded as if in obedience to some unseen master. As he turned, Iyoth saw the dark wetness of a fresh wound on the side of his head.

When the man outside finally turned his attention from the empty sky he happened to glance into the tavern, and his eyes met Iyoth's. They sparkled with amusement, and then suddenly they turned cold, even as the twitching smile returned.

*Now in his case,* Iyoth surmised as the maddened creature walked away, *the swiftness of steel against flesh would be a real mercy. But I don't do mercies.*

He heard the stairs creak as Tuin made his laborious way down them, and grabbed the cloth bag from the tavernkeeper as soon as it was presented. Tuin protested weakly as Iyoth tipped the coins noisily onto the bar and began to count. A few heads turned to look, but then turned swiftly away again. Iyoth's business was not theirs.

"I do apologise, Tuin," Iyoth said mildly without looking up as he deftly sorted gold crescents into little piles, "but I must be sure."

147

The coins numbered twenty and three, which was the correct amount. Satisfied, Iyoth tied a knot in the bag and put it in his belt pouch beneath his black tunic.

"There is something else," Tuin said suddenly. "I was told to make sure you knew of it by Father Dulorn, the archpriest."

Iyoth laughed. "I have done enough for you, Tuin, and spent too long in this grimy little town. And I hold no regard for your false Gods and the idiots who follow them."

Tuin paled at that casual blasphemy but continued, "There is gold in it for you. Far more than this reward."

Iyoth stared at him. "That must be all the gold in Ethanalin Tur-morn. But I forget- your Church surely *holds* almost all the gold in this town."

Tuin ignored the jibe. "He needs someone who can fight in darkness better than anyone else, someone who would be at home in the mines…"

"I am certainly *not* at home in your mines." Iyoth frowned. "They were built by imbeciles, and now they are looked after by idiots. What task is this?"

Tuin shrugged unhappily and wrung his hands. "I wish he had told me more, so that I might enlighten you, but he didn't. I expect you will have to go to him, if you're interested. All I know is that it is not an assa... not a *task* that you would normally undertake."

"Then the price must be negotiated," Iyoth told him as he turned and made his way to the door. "After all, I've looked forward to leaving this town ever since I got here."

He walked as far as the town stables where his horse was being kept, mindful of the snow underfoot which had started to turn into slippery slush. Iyoth had made a habit of checking daily that his horse was being fed and watered properly whilst he was here, and, for that matter, that no one had seen fit to sell it on or butcher it for meat. Everything imaginable had a price here, and that price rarely amounted to a fortune.

Luckily, his reputation had spread quickly. The horse remained in good health, unlike the downtrodden beasts that occupied the other stalls, so he gave the stable hand a cursory nod by way of approval. The relief in the man's eyes was so great that Iyoth thought he might burst into tears.

Tuin's words had made him restless. Iyoth went and stood outside the stables, sighed and tapped irritably on the pommel of one of his longknives. His cheeks already felt numb from the persistent northerly wind. *More snow coming soon,* he mused, without needing to look to the north and observe the cloud patterns. *I ought to leave. Powers know I can't buy anything of consequence here with my gold.*

And yet... and yet it made sense to see what this fool priest wanted, though in his heart he knew idle curiosity rather than good sense nagged at him. He did not want to ride south without knowing what it might have been, wondering what desperation had driven the church to offer up possibly almost all their money.

Iyoth cursed absently and made his way down the slippery track- dark with muddy, half-melted snow- to the squat little church that nestled in the lap of Tur-morn Hill.

Some kind of service or ritual that consisted of a low murmur and chant was taking place when he pushed open the door to the church. The warmth inside was welcome, but not the close odour that accompanied it. An associate of his- Iyoth did not have friends- had once remarked, *Humans do not just bleed like pigs, they smell like them too. I expect they even taste like them.* Iyoth reckoned that was unfair; he liked pigs.

He waited calmly at the back of the church as aged Father Dulorn, who had noticed him, quickly called an end to proceedings and ushered the five members of the congregation- all male, all middle-aged, all fat, Iyoth noticed with amusement- out of the church. They glanced briefly at Iyoth as they scuttled past, with expressions that varied

149

from loathing to fear to plain curiosity. Iyoth liked curiosity best; it was the easiest to turn into one of the others.

Father Dulorn waited until they had departed and gone their various ways into the warren of little tracks that wormed their way through the town. Then he shut and barred the door, presumably to avoid any disturbance.

"Well?" Iyoth said irritablyas he moved near to one of the wall brackets where a torch burned brightly. "I hear you're willing to dig deep into your church coffers, so desperately do you crave my services. What is this mysterious task that even your good friend Tuin knew so little about?"

"There is something inside the mines," Father Dulorn said bluntly. Iyoth had not expected such a straight reply, and attended a little more closely as the priest continued, "We don't know what it is, but it has slain a dozen miners and pathfinders already. We can't afford for the mines to shut. Many months have passed since we last found a new vein, and months also since the last crystal cluster, so matters are not proceeding well... but if our miners are too terrified to go down into the dark, then this town is as good as dead, regardless of the dividend from the rock. It could not have happened at a worse time. We *depend* on it, Iyoth. This town was built on the promise of such wealth. We have nothing else to sell."

"You people would sell your own mothers for a silver bit," Iyoth retorted. "Has anyone seen this creature and lived?"

"No. It has ripped apart a dozen men already, as I said. And the fear that this has caused will only spread. I'm at a loss. I need men who can fight underground, and you are..." He smiled anxiously. "You are a weaponsmaster. Everyone knows it."

"You have others," Iyoth pointed out. "They are cheaper."

"True, but none of them have your skill."

"And you expect me to go down there by myself?"

"Of course not! Two men of the town militia will come with you. They volunteered themselves for the task, and they know the layout. They will at least take you part of the way..."

"I wonder if they are being paid as handsomely as me," Iyoth mused, and a look of panic leapt up in the priest's eyes. "Don't speak of such things to them, I beg you! The church cannot afford to pay them such amounts. I am offering you five hundred in gold, Iyoth. That's all I can afford. That's all the *church* can afford."

Iyoth just about managed to conceal his surprise. Five hundred in gold was far more than he'd been paid for anything in his life. *I wouldn't even have to work for three years,* he thought. *Five hundred!*

"I suppose that will have to do," he said blandly. Father Dulorn's eyes widened. "Then you will do it? You will find this creature?"

"I will try. And I have certain conditions." The *du-luyan* stared meaningfully at Father Dulorn. "First, *I* oversee this task, and *I* will be in charge of the men that accompany me. Second, if either of them display the slightest hint of treachery, they will die by my hand, and I will not suffer any charge against my person for their deaths. Is this much understood, godsman?"

The priest swallowed, and wrung his hands. "I am in no position to dictate terms to you," he admitted finally.

"No," Iyoth agreed. "You are not. When are we to seek out this *creature* you speak of?"

"Come to the main entrance of the mines at sunset today."

Iyoth nodded, turned and left the church. As he made his way back up the hill, it occurred to him that he had made his decision almost without thought. *Greed,* he scolded himself. *It has done for these humans as they scrabble in the*

151

*earth for their metals, and it will do for you unless you clear your mind.*

He glanced back over the lower town, the ugly assortment of grime-blackened little buildings, mine shafts and workshop chimneys. *I could forget the entire episode, with my curiosity mostly sated,* he considered, *and I could ride out of Ethanalin Tur-morn.*

But he knew the kinds of creatures that crept through the darkness of mines and catacombs. They bore only a passing resemblance to the fairy-tales and legends that were passed down amongst the humans as they fortified their collective fear of the dark and the unknown. True, some of them looked horrifying enough, as did many things that scrabbled around in a world of darkness, and some of them were dangerous if cornered or frightened. They would fight if they had to. But that could be said of many beings. And twelve miners and pathfinders? The majority would have been unarmed, or at the most would have had nothing but unwieldy picks and axes to defend themselves with. The first ones at least would not have expected such an attack. They would have provided an easy meal.

Iyoth smiled to himself. He sat on a nearby boulder, looked out to the west where the lines of the distant hills rose and fell, and waited for sunset.

Iyoth had always prided himself on his punctuality, and he reached the mine entrance just as the last trace of the sun had slipped behind the jagged western skyline. Father Dulorn was nowhere to be seen, but two militiamen, kitted out with short swords and drab leather armour cobbled together from disparate pieces, waited at the entrance.

"I am Ghorith, sergeant-at-arms," the older and taller of the two spoke up. He looked nervous; Iyoth wondered how long it would take him to panic in the pressing warm darkness. It had happened to far better men. "And this here is Harran," Ghorith continued.

152

Harran, a muscular young man with an impressive array of scars upon his face, merely stared unflinchingly at Iyoth, who shrugged. "Names are names. Shall we get moving?"

"You speak our language well, *du-luyan*," Ghorith commented as they made their way down the entrance tunnel to the chain-lift.

"Why should I not?" Iyoth retorted, and the sergeant fell silent.

As they descended through the mine shaft in the creaking lift, Ghorith's face looked even more terrified by the sickly yellow light of his lantern. Iyoth glanced contemptuously at him. How much use would this man be? He began to think he might have been better off coming here alone. *Well, if they get in the way, so be it,* he thought. *I won't haul their bodies back up to the surface for a burial.*

An unpleasant idea occurred to him then. What if he was to slay both these men, sometime after they reached the bottom, wait a while, then return to the church to claim to have killed the creature that obstructed the business of Ethanalin Tur-morn? Dulorn would have to give him the money, surely- even if he brought no evidence up with him. The priest had not, after all, specifically asked for him to bring back the creature's severed head as might a storybook hero. *Perhaps he should have,* Iyoth thought, and smirked into the gloom, his face turned sufficiently from his restless companions.

That would hardly be a feat to be proud of, however. Perhaps these two would put up some resistance, perhaps not, but either way they would be no match for him. Still, it would be the quickest way to return to the surface for his money and leave this sorry, dirty town forever. And to think he had only stopped here out of curiosity on his way south.

Iyoth sighed, undecided. It was murder, and not even a *good* kind of murder.

They reached the bottom level of the mine, where a warm, earthy passage led off and sloped gradually downwards. The companions' lanterns flickered uncertainly in the close air as they set off. Ghorith chose the left fork when the passage split in two, and Iyoth made a mental note accordingly, then again when Ghorith chose the left fork at the next junction. He observed tools that had turned slowly to rust here and there, and markings in the rock that meant nothing to him. Perhaps they indicated areas that the miners thought might yield silver or crystal or whatever other materials they lusted after.

"Where were the most recent killings?" he asked impatiently. "This area looks utterly abandoned. I see no tracks."

"Further down here," Ghorith replied. He turned round to face Iyoth. There was something akin to panic in his eyes now. "We should make sure we're ready..." He drew his shortsword slowly, uncertainly, as if having heard something, pointed into the gloom in front of them- and then lunged at Iyoth.

The *du-luyan* had not expected his companions to dare attempt such treachery. The blade cut through his light armour and pierced his skin as he instinctively tumbled backwards. Mindful of Harran at his side as well as Ghorith in front of him, he whipped both longknives from his belt and slashed sideways and before him, as Ghorith and Harran tried to smash through his defences. The lanterns had crashed to the floor and faded fast.

"The light is going out!" he heard Harran shout desperately, as if that was the worst that would be happening to him. *You should really have thought of that when you planned this idiocy,* Iyoth silently told the man.

Within moments, Ghorith was on his knees. He clutched at his innards and uttered short, agonised gasps. Intestine gleamed faintly in what little remained of the lanternlight. Iyoth turned his cold fury on Harran, who had

154

begun to flee, though he turned back as he heard Iyoth's approach. Iyoth wasted no time finding out whether his foe intended to stand and fight, beg for mercy or forge some desperate attempt to make a deal with him. Both his blades cut through the scarred man's desperate defences in the same instant. One blow cut through the soldier's sword hand. He screamed and the sword went crashing into the wall.

As Harran staggered back, Iyoth pressed the dark blade of one of his longknives hard against the man's neck. "Who paid you?" he hissed, furious at having allowed himself to be fooled. "Who was it? The fat old priest?"

Harran, to his credit, spat at him and said nothing. Iyoth was impressed. "Brave boy," he whispered, and slashed the man's throat. Droplets of blood leapt through the air to wetly stain the passage wall.

As Harran joined his comrade on the floor, Iyoth glanced briefly at Ghorith, whose innards continued to slowly spill from him. A thin trickle of blood dripped from one side of the man's mouth. Ghorith's lips moved, but he uttered no sound except a faint wheeze.

"You misjudged me and you misjudged yourselves," Iyoth said, shaking his head in exasperation. "Why do you people never learn?"

Angrily he turned and strode back the way he had come. Dark thoughts flared in his mind. Had that idiot priest really thought two town militiamen could get rid of him? Coldly furious at himself as much as the priest, Iyoth strode on up the passageway. He would skin the fat godsman alive for this treachery, and put out his eyes. Then he would nail him to the wooden altar from which he spouted his nonsense.

He reached the point where the first passage had split in two, and it was here that he first became aware of some *presence*, a little way down the right fork. He stared in that direction, feeling the hairs rise on his skin. Something *loomed* there- not human, *luyan* or *du-luyan* or anything else he knew of.

*So,* he thought, *is there truly a predator here? Did Dulorn think that if his militiamen failed against me, this unseen creature would do their job for them?*

Whatever this being was, it made no sound, and he could not see it, but Iyoth knew it steadily approached. He continued to make his way back towards the lift but glanced back every half-dozen steps. The presence did not gain on him, but neither did it allow him to get further away. *Soundless,* Iyoth thought over and over, *and invisible too?*

But then, when he was still twenty paces or more from the lift shaft, it came into view, slipping out of the deeper shadow in one smooth, liquid movement.

*It's made of stone and earth,* was Iyoth's first bewildered thought.

It had a body, a head, arms and legs, but there its resemblance to anything Iyoth had ever seen ended. Its entire form shimmered as if unseen light reflected off its surface, yet that surface remained blacker than the shadows. The arms, too long, too thin, hung as low as the earthy floor. The legs, also painfully thin, surely could not have supported the mass to which they were entrusted, yet this apparition moved with silent, easy grace. Iyoth could see no eyes in its head, yet he *knew* that it watched him, and he knew for certain that it could smell his desperate, sudden fear and hear his shortened breaths. It measured and tasted his growing panic.

Iyoth could feel sweat trickling down his forehead and back. He took deep, measured breaths, each one sounding horribly laboured, and tried desperately not to take his eyes from this entity, although his every instinct screamed at him to flee. Somehow he knew that if he looked away even only for an instant, then the next moment it would be at his side. It would reach stone fingers into his

156

body like some dreadful golem and pull him into the earth to be as one with the darkness it inhabited.

Iyoth reached the lift, and heaved on the chain to start the mechanism, which shrieked slowly into life. As the lift basket rose from the floor with painful slowness, Iyoth stared down, and saw the creature's head upraised. It peered eyelessly up at him, or past his trembling form and on towards the opening far above. He feared for a moment that this nightmare would climb the lift shaft and tear him limb from limb, but it came no closer. Iyoth deliberately forced his gaze to the squealing cogs of the lift mechanism, beyond which a few fragments of night sky could be seen. Suddenly all he wanted was the opportunity to spend another night under the stars.

When he emerged from the mine and made his way back into the town, all traces of the sunset had long gone. The oil-lanterns that lined the sides of the streets creaked in the cold breeze, their sickly yellow flames fluttering as if about to go out at any moment.

Iyoth realised suddenly that he had started to mumble to himself. He stopped and took a deep breath. His hands trembled uncontrollably. Even more worryingly, all notions of retribution had fled his mind. He had no stomach for slaughter, only escape. Incomprehensibly he did not even want to visit the church for his payment. Did the townspeople *know* that this creature lurked in their mine? Had he been directed into these depths to be slain by it? Powers, did some of them even *worship* the thing?

He no longer cared.

Iyoth ran up the hill to the stables, paid the groom for his services by flinging far too much gold in his direction, and then rode as fast as he could up the dirt track. Soon he thundered south-west towards the broken hills under the brightness of Ildar's pale glow. His horse panted frantically as if infected with the assassin's panic.

157

The *du-luyan* man had no idea where he would end up, nor did he care, but he knew one thing for an absolute certainty. Never again would he set foot in Ethanalin Turmorn.

# VI - Earth Shadow

## I

"There was something I had to remember," Vornen whispered.

He spoke to himself, not to the woman who shared his bed, but she stirred at the faint sound. "Hmm," she said, neither listening nor caring in the softness of her slumber, and presently she turned over and away from him. Vornen heard none of this, for his thoughts were elsewhere.

The setting sun cast a light like fire through the large window of her bedchamber. It occurred suddenly to Vornen how odd it was to be in bed, having just woken up with the sun about to go down, but a moment later even that thought was gone. He found himself distracted by the temporary beauty of the sunlight and the long shadows cast by neighbouring buildings, so he wandered over to the window. Some way off from the track, a group of children were busy making their snowman as tall and wide as possible. Vornen smiled faintly at their concerted efforts, until one of the younger children added a vaguely sword-shaped stick to their creation.

In a metal tray by his side of the bed, a small mound of *kyush* ash gave off a faint but acrid odour. Slowly he turned to look at it. *Was it you?* he thought, idly at first, but then with a certain tired fury. *Have you started to take my mind apart again, brick by brick? What happens when you take the whole wall away? Will I even care? How was it that I found you again?*

A moment passed; a while passed. He returned to the bed. The sun went down, and soon afterwards the room began to darken with the dusk. Vornen stirred unwillingly and lit one of the lanterns, and by its soft light the woman woke and sat up.

Vornen sat on the edge of the bed, restless. Something turned his gaze to the southern sky, invisible but insistent. The woman watched him for a while and then she asked, "Do you think they'll find him? The man who killed all those people?"

"How should I know?" he said absently, but then the memory of what he had seen in the marketplace hurtled back. He sighed and closed his eyes, for all the good that might do.

"Rocan's men are after him," she mused, but then she changed the subject entirely. "You were upset. I've never seen a man so upset."

He remembered it then, the bloodshed and the silent shock of the aftermath. Still his recollection remained fractured and piecemeal, but he recalled that he had walked away from the market square once Rocan's men had arrived to help contemplate the horror that had cut through the morning.

He had walked for a long while, numb, cold and heedless, until eventually he had found himself at the *Last Oak* tavern, where he drank for the remainder of the day. He listened and watched a second grim scene unfold as the news spread throughout the town, and people came and went from the alehouse, each one the carrier of a different dark rumour. Only a few things were known to be true- that the murderer was an outsider, and that Rocan's men had gone after him, out of the town and south, for that was where his tracks led.

*Ah, but tracks or no tracks, you'll never find him,* Vornen thought. *I remember that much. I remember that man, perhaps no man at all but part of some sorcerous weaving. How could he have found his way into Ruan-Tor after days out in the winter storms? Rocan will need all his gods and idols, for that tainted boy will outpace him and all his horsemen and likely even drive them to their deaths.*

"I don't remember your name," he said bluntly as the young woman handed him a prepared *kyush* pipe from the table on her side of the bed.

"Lena," she told him as he stared down at the offering. "I know *your* name."

"Everyone knows me, or presumes to," Vornen said. "I had given the *kyush* a wide berth, but now..." He shrugged. "It makes you forget things. But I've already forgotten too much about some things. And not enough about others. Ah, if only we could pick the memories we wanted to keep..."

"You needed something to blunt it," Lena said, and that suddenly reminded him. "Did I say anything to you last night?" he asked, turning to face her. "Something about a secret, a task, a..." He shook his head. "Gods, I don't know. Some knowledge I must pass on..."

"You spoke of what you'd seen in the morning," Lena said, "and then we came up here after a while, and you talked- well, ranted, in truth- at length about a woman called Suli. I don't remember her, but my older sister does. She vanished many years ago and never came back."

Vornen shrugged, smiled to himself without knowing why, and took the *kyush* pipe. Lena dressed and left him up there whilst she worked downstairs in the tap room. When she returned in the small quiet hours, he was fast asleep.

*Trouble,* she thought as she recalled what Vornen had said the previous night. *He said to me- I am trouble and you'd do well to stay away from me.* But he hadn't seemed like trouble to her, despite being an obvious scatterbrain with a penchant for saying the oddest things. *Troubled,* certainly. She put her pouch of unused *kyush* back in her bedside drawer and wondered if she ought not to have given him any.

A few of the patrons downstairs in the tap room had voiced their fears that Vornen had brought ill luck to the town. Lena could not see how that was so. She knew of his reputation and past misdeeds- didn't everyone?- but she took the view that the shadow-man who had found his way into Ruan-Tor and dispatched entire families in moments was more likely to be something to do with the disturbing stories she had heard of events out in the Plains, some of which were not unlike this morning's killings. *How is it,* many had said, *that Vornen Starbrook makes an appearance after all this time, and a mere few days later, some darkness seeps in from the howling winter?*

*Coincidence, I expect,* the barwoman had thought to herself. But Lena had not voiced her appraisal of the situation. She knew that her job was to be seen and not heard, to serve ale and wine and not opinions. So she had remained silent on all such matters and wandered with a fixed smile through the blue-grey smoke of pipeweed and the sour odour of spilt ale.

## II

The following morning, Vornen wandered outside and set off up the road towards the east town, leaving Lena asleep.

As he strode along, his mind feeling a little sharper now, he wondered if Rocan had considered the same things that he, Vornen, had mulled over concerning the havoc Larien had wreaked. Vornen felt certain that the sword was something truly powerful, though how he had come by it was anyone's guess.

*And crafty too,* Vornen thought with a shudder. *To all intents and purposes, nothing but a wooden sword, a toy for children playing a game of knights and beggars. And surely it controls him- Larien seemed like a man whose mind itself had been robbed. Did he wilfully conduct that massacre in the market place, or did the sword, streaming with some destructive force? What might happen if Larien is captured and killed, and one of Rocan's men claims that weapon in his stead? What if the sword is brought back to Ruan-Tor? Surely*

162

*the best course of action is to find Larien, put him out of his misery and slavery if they can overcome him, and then bury that sword in a deep hole.*

The snow began to swirl thick and fast as he trudged along. Eventually Vornen turned and made his way back to the *Last Oak.* He wondered if he could make some swift earnings by helping with the morning cleaning and clearing. Any such task would keep his mind from other matters, and surely Lena and the other serving women would be happy enough to pass over some of their more tiresome chores if the innkeeper himself allowed it.

He humbly offered his services, and spent the remainder of the day clearing the back yard of ice and snow so that the privy could be safely used.

That evening, the skies cleared just before sunset, and Vornen sat and watched the event from his bedchamber window. He listened to the sounds of drunken merriment in the common room below- of people determined to be merry whatever their situation, laughing too hard at jokes they had all heard a hundred times before. He absently wished he could immerse himself in such frivolity. *It must be more than a year since I last bedded a woman,* he thought suddenly, thinking of Lena as he heard her voice upraised downstairs, perhaps admonishing some over-eager patron. *I can't even remember the last one before Lena.*

That thought turned, as he knew it would, to an aching for Suli, which itself turned, as he realised the hopelessness of such sentiment, to a more physical aching for any woman.

Vornen considered wandering downstairs, if nothing other than to keep half an eye on Lena's customers. But something troubled him, and it had nothing to do with anyone downstairs, or anyone at all for that matter.

It was a nagging sensation that something, some alignment of forces, was just *wrong.*

163

As he wandered over to the window and tried once again to work out what the feeling was and *why* it was, Vornen's gaze wandered southwards. It focussed on the horizon, and it was then that he managed to grasp an inkling of what it might be.

*Gates,* he thought suddenly. *I am drawn to those things. I always have been. I remember that much.*

It felt as if all the lines of force he knew about, those threads that linked Gates as well as the natural phenomena of all Aona, were being gently pulled, manipulated in some way, and their own focus and direction changed. The only book he had read that so much as mentioned Gates had a word for it: *realignment.* He stood trapped in the outer part of a vast cobweb, attached to a number of miniscule threads that trembled and pulled gradually towards one another from the centre.

*This is what I started to feel yesterday evening,* he reminded himself. *But it's stronger now.*

Vornen tried to tear his eyes from that distant, invisible place, some unknown point beyond the horizon, and when he could not, he closed his eyes until his awareness of the realignment ebbed enough for him to turn away from the window. For a moment he imagined that the air thickened, *changed* somehow. He sank to the floor and looked in the opposite direction, at the far wall, then concentrated on the random cracks and patterns.

*Not again, not as it once was,* he prayed, and eventually that *pull* from the distant south faded a little. Vornen allowed himself a small sigh of relief.

*Where is it?* he pondered. *Somewhere in the south, but where exactly? And what kind of change is it? What's happening?*

He realised dully that there was so little he knew about the force that had consumed his life and which had made a cruel leash for itself around his neck. His understanding of what happened to him and what it might

164

mean remained useless, more like the nonsensical parts of a dream than any coherent understanding. The sheer possibility of all that he might need to know but did not, itself made a frightening prospect.

*And does it mean anything at all anyway?* he asked himself. *Is it not just a mesh of forces and openings and worlds causing ripples in other worlds? I'm just a man, incapable of understanding such things. So why does this web reach out to me? What purpose can it possibly serve, except to slowly erode my being?*

He did not dare look southwards for the moment, but he allowed himself a hopeful thought: *Perhaps it will fade away entirely. They do that, sometimes. I remember I travelled towards one many months ago, only for it to vanish from the world before I reached it.*

*But might this one become stronger? Too strong?*

Vornen deliberately did not even contemplate that possibility any further. It was a concept too dark and wide to think about this late in the day, with the night sky opening up and the promise of warmth and *kyush* in Lena's company.

Still, other thoughts came unbidden as he crouched in the silence. *I could leave Ruan-Tor, against my promise to Lord Vothangrane. I could race on horseback across the snowbound plains- weather permitting- and allow myself to be drawn like a lodestone to wherever this realignment is happening. But to what end? To be drawn in, consumed, torn apart? I've gone to them before, but only when no other choice has existed and the pull has been too great.*

Vornen began to fear that the next time he witnessed the opening of a Gate or even found himself near one would be his last, the one that would finally snap his weary mind like a twig.

*You have been nearer than you remember,* a voice spoke up quietly inside him. *You barely recall, but you have been so near.*

165

*And seen inside?* He could not remember, but perhaps he had caught a glimpse of something- something he had then forgotten.

*Might others feel the same pull?* he wondered. *Might others make whatever discovery is there to be made?*

Although he faced towards the door, he did not even notice Lena until she was inside the bedchamber and speaking to him. "Are you praying?" she asked.

Vornen laughed out loud at that. "No," he said finally, looking up at her. "No, Lena. I'm not praying."

"Why does that amuse you so?" she frowned. "Why would anyone not pray in times like this?"

"I don't begrudge you your faith," he told her, "but I can't bring myself to share it. I never could."

Lena did not know what to say to this. She lit one of the lanterns, unbuttoned her shirt and trousers, and sat crosslegged on the bed. Carefully she filled and prepared her *kyush* pipe. "Let's share this instead, then," she remarked as Vornen watched and admired her deftness. *I'm all shivers and doubts, and she's a creature of smooth movements,* he observed. "Will you stay tonight?" Lena asked him.

"I would like to," he admitted.

"Good." She smiled briefly, sadly. "You're not the man that many make you out to be, I think."

"Am I not?" he rejoined, surprised. "What would *you* say I am, then? Unlucky perhaps? Cursed, in some low and pointless way?"

"Hmm. Like most men you have a penchant for self-pity," she noted, and passed him the *kyush* pipe. "But you may stay here for as long as you wish. I should like you to."

"Thank you," he said, touched and surprised at the gesture.

Yet even as he took the pipe with a faint smile of gratitude, Vornen knew on some base level that even if his mind tried to flee the vast presence beyond the horizon, one day soon his body would still face that unutterable darkness.

166

Lena's touch drew him gently from his dream, where he had been locked in a church with no one for company, listening to distant sounds of warfare as wind howled around the four walls and a too-bright Ildar cast cold light upon the granite floor but no shadows.

As he breakfasted, a messenger arrived from the council's fortress and requested his audience with Lord Vothangrane within the hour. After he had finished breakfast, Vornen left the *Last Oak* and made his way up the road, wrapped up in his cloak. Lena watched him go as she wiped down the tables, and wondered to herself why he had been summoned.

*Three days,* Vornen mused as he walked, *and no word from Rocan and his men, as far as I'm aware.* There should at least have been a messenger bird, everyone said. Had he forgotten to take them? No, two were missing from the aviary. Then why the silence? Had a bird been sent and then attacked by carrion, desperate and hungry for its flesh? That was unlikely. The messenger birds were tough, fearsome creatures, and the crows and rooks that wheeled through the bitter sky always gave them a wide berth.

From what Vornen had been able to tell during his work in the tavern, disquiet in the town had turned to a wider unease that fed upon itself, and rumours about what might have happened had begun to spread. They originated from the most morbidly inventive souls and moved swiftly, embellished with each telling. Few sought to dispel them. Meanwhile the snowstorms had become much less frequent, but the temperature had sunk further and turned the slushy roads to slopes of jagged ice that few dared to tread.

When Vornen was admitted to his chambers later that morning, Lord Vothangrane looked like a man who bore

167

the worry of every man, woman and child in Ruan-Tor. "They should have returned by now, with or without their quarry," he said by way of greeting. "I gave Rocan specific orders to return three days hence, regardless of what happened. He would not have failed me, had he the choice. They were in pursuit of a man on foot. *On foot.*"

"There's the matter of the sword," Vornen said quietly.

"You think one crazed man could have bested all of Ruan-Tor's finest knights?"

"I think... perhaps the *sword* could have, my Lord." Vornen bit his lip. He had not wanted to venture down this avenue of conversation, but now that he had been witless enough to mention the sword he felt forced to explain himself. "I saw the last of the... the killing, and felt sure it had something unnatural about it."

"Unnatural."

"It looked as if the sword led the man on a bloody dance through the people in the marketplace."

The Lord Protector stared at him. "I wish you had told me this before," he said finally.

"Would it have made sense then, when it makes no sense now?" Vornen shrugged unhappily. "I was in no state to recount what I had witnessed, my Lord. Rocan and some of his men arrived shortly after I did. There was nothing I could have done. Those in authority took charge of the situation. Rocan would not have thanked me for my meddling, as he might see it."

Lord Vothangrane rested his head in his hands. Vornen noticed how his fingernails looked dark grey and bruised and recent scars criss-crossed his hands. He could not recall them being there several days ago ago, and yet they looked more than a tennight old.

The overseer of Ruan-Tor pushed a goblet of wine across the table towards him. "Have a look at this," he whispered.

168

Vornen took the goblet and peered at its contents. "My Lord, I'm not sure I understand."

"What do you see in there?"

"Red wine..." Vornen sniffed it a little more carefully. "Watered, no herbs. What should I be seeing, my Lord?"

"It's black," Lord Vothangrane said tightly as he stared directly back at him. "Black as eternity."

The silence in the room became almost suffocating. Vornen struggled for an age to think of anything to say. Finally he ventured, "Begging your pardon, my Lord, but it's a medium red as far as I..."

The Lord Protector held his right hand up as if telling him to stop speaking. His gaze wandered from place to place around the room, as if he watched the random motions of some pet bird that had escaped and flitted from one area to another. *Gods, he is far from well*, Vornen thought. *Has he been seen by a physician? Perhaps I should arrange it, if I can find one who'll listen to me. Surely one of the Council members will help me, if he or she sees the state the man is in.*

"I cannot afford to send more men out," Lord Vothangrane said eventually, almost making him jump. "All we can do is reinforce our defences, Vornen. We know that even some of the larger villages have been attacked- have been *destroyed*. We can reasonably assume that our time will soon come. So we need to ensure that as many people as possible are armed and have the ability to defend themselves. Those who cannot must come under the protection of those who can. Attacks have been made on settlements in almost every direction from here in the last few months. And we know so little, because... because..."

"There are never any survivors," Vornen said quietly.

There was no response at first. Finally Lord Vothangrane said, "You must play your part, and assist in the fortification as far as possible. I will send officers out to ensure that everyone is as well-prepared as they can be. I

169

would appreciate it if you could lend all your expertise and help them however you can."

"Some would call it an opportunity to repay my debt to Ruan-Tor." Vornen smiled mirthlessly.

"That was the purpose of your exile." Lord Vothangrane waved a hand in dismissal of the notion. "That debt was paid. I'll hear no more about it."

They fell silent. Eventually Vornen spoke up once again. "I will do whatever I can, my Lord."

The Lord Protector nodded. "That's all anyone can ask." But he had become distracted once again, as if he listened not to Vornen but to an invisible third person.

## IV

Rocan drew his horse to a standstill and wearily raised his left hand in a motion for the men following behind to halt. Even that felt like an arduous task, the movement leaden.

Grimly he surveyed the village in the valley below. After a moment, he took the spyglass from his pocket- a costly but useful device which he had procured some years ago from a southland merchant- and used it to evaluate the place in greater detail. Their map showed that this remote place was Klan-tur, a settlement about as far from any major town as was possible, remote even by the standards of the Plains.

Smoke trailed lazily upwards into the cold, still air from hut chimneys. Here and there people wandered along the one main track that meandered through the settlement. In several of the fields around the village, workers attempted to dig and hammer into the ice-hardened ground, sending hard chips of frozen earth up into the air.

Rocan pocketed his spyglass and chewed his lip thoughtfully. What were they trying to do? He could think of no reason why anyone would want to dig holes in a field in the heart of winter. Of course there would be a fair number of deaths, as there always were during this harsh season, but they were digging in the fields, not in the graveyard to the west of the settlement. Had the graveyard already been filled? Possibly, but why not dig new graves adjacent to the existing site? And, although he personally found the idea uncomfortable, why not cremate bodies if they could not be buried?

His lieutenant, Kovin, coughed politely at his side. "Sir, I know I have said this before, but..."

"We are not going back without some answers, Kovin," he interrupted. "I'm aware of our orders. I'm also aware that if we return to Ruan-Tor with neither this murderous youth nor any knowledge about the killings out here, we may as well never have left at all. In all likelihood, the man we're hunting is a part of the wider unrest." He glanced briefly at his lieutenant. "You can thank our good friend Vornen Starbrook for us being out here in a winter like the five hells. I suspect Vornen knows more than he has chosen to tell anyone about this Larien."

"You think he's in league with him, sir?" Kovin said in surprise. "But we saw him in the aftermath- he didn't look or behave like an accomplice. He was clearly as shocked as we all were."

Rocan smiled bitterly. "Never trust the words of a madman, Kovin, especially one who has already brought shame upon Ruan-Tor and its people. You cannot tell what the man will do from one moment to the next."

He noticed more movement in the valley below and placed the spyglass to his eye once again. With its aid he saw six men move from one of the larger houses to a nearby field, where a large pile of firewood had been assembled. It struck Rocan as particularly foolish to waste that much wood on a single fire- and outside at that!- but then his heart sank as he realised that another, more sinister reason existed for the woodpile.

171

One of the six men, he now realised on closer scrutiny, was a young woman, and the other five bore her roughly towards the waiting woodpile. One of the other men who waited near the pyre had lit an oil-doused rag tied to a stick, and was waiting for their approach.

"The rule of law extends less far than it used to," he murmured, half to himself. Kovin gave him a puzzled look, and Rocan silently handed him the spyglass. After a moment, Kovin turned his pale face to his captain once again. "What should we do, sir?"

"We do what the village warden and his men- wherever they might be- should be doing," Rocan muttered. "Those people will need some very good reasons..." He glanced round at the other men gathered behind him. "We'll head down to the village. Be on your guard."

They rode down at a cautious pace along a muddy trail that led onto the village's track. By the time they had reached the field, a good crowd had gathered at the woodpile. Faces turned towards the knights, and the crowd parted reluctantly to allow the horses through as Rocan led his men directly to the group that held the woman captive. He observed grimly that she had been beaten almost unconscious and stripped naked from the waist up. Three open whiplash wounds adorned her left side and gleamed wetly in the fading light.

"I am Rocan of Ruan-Tor," he said coldly by way of introduction. "Where is your warden? Why are there no militiamen here?"

They glanced at each other and all around, as if they half-expected those men to materialise. No one said anything in response, but a murmur of disquiet rippled through the crowd.

Raising his voice, Rocan continued, "Perhaps someone other than these animals can tell me why you see fit to *burn* people? Execution by fire has been outlawed

172

throughout the North for more than three centuries. What has this woman done to deserve such punishment?"

"If you don't wish to burn also, *sir knight*," one man from the crowd spoke up, "you'd best be headed back up the hill and return whence you came."

Rocan stared levelly at the speaker- a grubby, lean man approaching his middle years- and then allowed his gaze to take in the rest of the crowd. The afternoon sun had dipped below the western skyline and cast much of Klan-tur in curiously deep shadow alleviated only by the expanse of snow covering the fields. In that diminished light and the perfectly still air, the villagers looked quietly malevolent, hateful stares directed at him. Thin and poorly-dressed, they stood like skeletons covered in sallow skin. Here and there he saw the glimmer of longknives and pitchforks, and after a moment a harsh scratch of metal against metal cut through the chilly quiet. A mutter of anger began to rise.

Rocan took a deep breath, and walked his horse up to the group of men who still held tightly to their prize, then drew his greatsword and levelled it at the nearest of their number. "Release her if you want to live," he said quietly, and only just hid his relief when they reluctantly did so. They pushed her towards his own men so that she fell stumbling to the ground.

"Kovin, pick her up. Put her in the saddle with you and make sure she can't fall off," he said, without taking his eyes off the men. "As for *you,* I would have answers. If I am not satisfied, you'll come back with us to answer for your actions at a court in Ruan-Tor."

"No one goes anywhere with you," one of them spat back at him. "What can you do? You have no rights here. This is not your territory. You do not know this land. Take the bitch and leave."

"She'll die soon anyway," another of the men added with a brown-toothed grin. "She's been marked."

173

Rocan quickly estimated the number of people gathered in the field. There were perhaps upwards of two hundred, and a few stragglers who still emerged from their huts elsewhere in the village. Even though his men numbered just twenty, they would surely emerge victorious from any fight. But that sort of slaughter was exactly what he sought to end. Aside from that, he could ill afford any losses or severe injuries on his side. They were far from home.

*And if word were to spread that a band of Torian Knights had arrived in a village and slaughtered its entire people...*

"She is faithless," called a voice from the crowd, several rows back and cast too deep in shadow for Rocan to make her out. "All the faithless will be struck down. They will drown in their own fear." A murmur of assent rose into the chill air.

"We put her to the test," one woman spoke up, "and we saw that she was poisoned by the lightdreams. Take her, and you invite that madness into your arms."

"We should go, Rocan." Kovin rarely used his captain's first name, and only when desperate to impress something upon him. Rocan understood, and silently agreed, though he did not glance at Kovin. He wanted nothing more than to be away from this dark valley of murderous peasants, far away and riding back north to the sanity and sanctity of Ruan-Tor.

"When we return, answers will be sought. That I promise you," he said to the assembled crowd, and then signalled for his men to turn and slowly leave.

*When?* he reasoned silently as they departed. *In the spring? How many others will be chosen for sacrifice by then? No, we're powerless to do anything. But don't let them know that. Leave them fearful that they may still see you at the crest of the hill sometime after winter's passing.*

174

Something else about Klan-tur bothered him as they made their way back up the slushy track to the ridge where they had first noticed the settlement, but it was only when Kovin spoke that he realised what it was.

"Did you notice, sir?" Kovin had the young woman wrapped in a blanket and balanced before him in the saddle, one strong arm wrapped about her as she slumped witlessly forward. Rocan hoped his lieutenant would ride with due care- it was doubtful that in her state she would survive any fall to the ground. "Did I notice what?"

Kovin glanced back, and then made a warding gesture in the air. His hands trembled in the failing light. "There were *no children* in the village."

V

Vornen stared helplessly out of his window into the starlit south and wished he could sleep instead.

The longest and most prominent line of force in the North had always been that which followed the Great Old Road- except in truth it was the road itself that had been built to follow the line. The architects of that ancient paved highway- now in deep disrepair, cracked and split apart with weeds when spring came- had not exactly known what they were doing in that regard, but Vornen believed that they had been driven to create it along that path. The force-lines affected everyone's minds, he was certain of that, although often in very subtle ways.

Vornen now felt himself driven towards wherever this new Gate manifested itself. It could only be a Gate, he had decided, and that was a terrifying prospect, because he still could not remember anything of use from when he had last encountered such a thing.

*I remember now that I peered into its depths. Once I thought I'd walked through such a Gate and been spat out half-dead through another one. But it was the one and the*

175

*same. Where was that? Somewhere in the west, somewhere near the Chor Valley. I was healed afterwards. I remember being healed. I almost died out there in the cold as the night came.*

Vornen rested his head on the windowsill. For just a moment, with his gaze averted from the night he could think a little more clearly. He wondered briefly where the exact location of this new Gate might be. South of course, but perhaps a little towards the east as well. How far? Thirty, forty leagues, perhaps fifty? It was almost impossible to say. What lay in that direction? Mostly empty land, dotted with villages here and there. Further on, the town of Ethanalin Tur-morn and its mines. Then the hills, which to the south became the Crescents and to the east the borderlands between Aphenhast and the abandoned realm of Alhar. Rumour had it that no one lived in Alhar, that it had become impossible to eke out any kind of living in a land that had become desert.

Sighing, he put the matter of Alhar to one side. It was a distant land, too distant to hold this beacon of horror that burned somewhere in the south, whatever other secrets it might hold. The Gate was nearer. Much nearer.

Vornen jumped as a loud knock sounded upon the door. He opened it to reveal a timid-looking servant.

The girl did not meet his eyes. "You are to go to Lord Vothangrane, sir," she said quietly and took a couple of steps back as if he might strike her for some perceived slight. "His Lordship demands audience with you as soon as possible."

"Again?" Vornen frowned. "So soon?"

"If you please sir," she mumbled, then hung her head and stared at the floor.

"Thank you. I will be there as soon as I can." Vornen closed the door and listened to the girl swiftly descend the stairs. Should he tell Lord Vothangrane of the Gate and what it meant? What good would that do?

*No*, he decided. *It means nothing, and I can't talk of such things, even to him. Most townsfolk already think me half-mad.*

In any case, the Lord Protector had enough to worry about.

He made his way outside to find that the snow had started to swirl down again. Vornen pulled his cloak tightly about him and set off up the hill towards the Council fortress. Absently he brushed snowflakes from his face and tried to mind his way as he negotiated the icy track. The pull of the Gate- and now of something else, much more distant but also to the south, that he couldn't fathom- was of course stronger outside. It would have been stronger still had the night been clear.

Eventually he reached the fortress gates, and was admitted into the cobbled courtyard. The guards made him wait a fair while here as they engaged in their pretence of formalities. Vornen knew enough of protocol to realise that they simply chose to waste his time and make him wait so they could tell their friends they had done so. He gritted his teeth, said nothing and waited as patiently as he could.

The guardsmen wasted no time speaking to him, however. So tightly wrapped in their scarves were they that he might not have heard what they said anyway. The entrance hall was almost as cold as the courtyard, and Vornen shivered as he made his way up the several flights of stairs to the Lord Protector's chambers, tramping snow from his boots onto the carpet.

No guards had been posted outside Lord Vothangrane's chambers. Perhaps they had been moved to join the increased number of sentries at the outer gates of the fortress and Ruan-Tor itself. Everyone seemed to believe firmly that an attack was imminent. It was, they agreed, simply a matter of how soon.

Lord Vothangrane sat facing the large arched window on the other side of his study. He did not turn when

177

Vornen quietly announced himself. Vornen waited patiently for a while, then made his way over to where the Lord Protector sat. Perhaps he had dozed off.

When he walked around the chair to face him, Vornen realised numbly that if he had indeed fallen asleep, he would never wake.

Lord Vothangrane lay slumped with his throat slit almost from ear to ear. Blood soaked him from his throat down to his stomach and had started to drip from the chair to form a sodden patch in the carpet. His eyes stared through the window, out into the darkness, wide as if with bewilderment.

Vornen could not be sure how long he spent by the body of Ruan-Tor's leader, but eventually he heard a faint sound from near the doorway and saw a servant there. The man walked forward a few steps, tentatively, and then his expression changed, perhaps because of the look on Vornen's face. Vornen knew exactly what that expression meant. The servant had seen the blood, had seen Vornen's panicked expression, and was doubtless convinced that he had killed Lord Vothangrane.

Vornen had a split second in which to think. If the alarm was raised, that would be the end of him. Far swifter than the servant could turn, never mind flee the hall, Vornen flung his shortsword straight at him and skewered the man onto the wooden post behind.

Astonishment flared in the servant's eyes, swiftly followed by a lifeless glaze. His head drooped and his body twitched momentarily. A trickle of blood fell in a gentle patter to the floor.

Vornen took one last look at Lord Vothangrane, who still stared straight ahead as if in puzzlement that anyone could have slain him. "At peace," he whispered. "At peace, my Lord." Gently he placed a hand over his eyelids- that terrible stare was too much to bear- and then he strode out of the hall. He willed himself not to look at the impaled body of the servant. *Survive now and regret later,* he reminded himself. *I was seen going in, and if anyone sees what has happened here, I will be named as guilty. Everyone may be busy preparing for attack, but they'll find time to hang me.*

Vornen had reached the top of the staircase when he heard bells begin to chime some distance away, both within the fortress itself and out in Ruan-Tor. As those sounds rang out, a faint memory stirred within him, a vague, nagging recollection of his having heard those same bells in the same place, before. *Years ago,* he thought. *They're not used often, hardly ever at all...*

Vornen took a deep breath and leaned against the wall for a moment. He had to think clearly. If he did not, then he might as well give up now.

*What would be worse?* he thought blackly. *To die at the hands of a screaming mob, or frozen out in the wilderness, alone?*

*The latter,* he decided almost instantly.

Vornen hastened down several flights of stairs, and strode down the long corridor that led to the main reception hall, and forced himself not to break into a run. A horrible calm had come over him.

He made his way out into the grounds, and from there back out onto the road that led down to the middle of the town. *I should buy a horse,* he thought briefly. *If I leave on foot, they will catch me within hours.*

Vornen hastened to the stables that stood next to the *Traveller's Rest.* A boy was busy feeding the horses their rations of hay. He turned, startled, as his unexpected visitor walked in. "I have to travel to meet with Rocan and his men," Vornen said, and offered a brief smile in an attempt to put the boy at ease. "I'll need one of these horses. A good strong one."

The boy scratched his head nervously. "I... I don't think I should..."

179

"This is important business," Vornen said firmly. "I have been instructed by Lord Vothangrane to head out to find out what has happened to Rocan. I'm sure I don't need to tell you how important that is."

The boy bit his bottom lip and looked nervously about the stable as if in vain hope that someone else here could advise him. Vornen thanked all the Gods that the boy was alone.

Eventually the stable boy patted the horse next to them, a black stallion with a proud look about him. "You can take Stepthorn, sir. He's fleet of foot, and strong besides."

"Good. That's what I need." Vornen dug into his pockets for money. The boy's eyes widened as five silver crescents were pressed into his hands. "Tha... thank you, sir," he stammered, and hastily stepped back as Vornen grabbed a nearby saddle and began to fit it. He had not ridden in a while, and an even longer time had passed since he'd needed to fit a saddle himself, but thankfully he remembered enough to make a half-decent job of it.

The boy stood by and looked increasingly troubled as Vornen jumped up into the stirrups. "I should speak to my master," he said suddenly. "Please, sir, wait a moment. I'll be in trouble for accepting this much money, and for letting you..."

"No time for that," Vornen said, and spurred Stepthorn into action. He galloped up the slushy track and headed for Ruan-Tor's southern gates. In the distance the mournful tolling of bells could still be heard. To Vornen they sounded like funeral bells, but of course it was far too soon for that.

Vornen had no idea what he might say to the guardsmen at the gates any more than he had known what to say to the stable boy. As the gatehouse loomed up before him figures emerged and raised their arms, shouting at him to stop. Reluctantly he drew his mount to a halt.

"Lord Vothangrane has instructed me to find Rocan and his men," Vornen spoke up clearly. "Open the gates if you please. I have no time to lose."

He hardly dared believe his luck when two of the sentinels began to push open the old town gates. A thought flashed briefly. *Here I am again. Only this time there can be no return. I'll never again set foot in Ruan-Tor. But I'll live on in their thoughts and in their stories- tales of a coward and a murderer. How they'll rue the day they ever let me come back. Lena- what will she make of me? She'll be relieved I didn't slit her throat wide open too, I expect.*

Vornen sat astride Stepthorn and waited for them to open the gates sufficiently and step out of the way; all the time that cloak of utter calm lay upon him like a shroud, cold and still. Somewhere further back in his mind, faint but worrisome questions formed. Had someone deliberately slain Lord Vothangrane and then sent him the message, intending for him to walk into Vothangrane's chambers and be caught looming over the body? If that was the case, then why had only the one servant appeared? Why was he being allowed out of Ruan-Tor? Surely the guardsmen would have been informed of what he had supposedly done, and told to apprehend him?

So immersed did Vornen become in these frantic thoughts that one of the sentinels had to remind him the gate was open. "M'lord?"

"Thank you," he murmured, and rode through. He listened to them close the gates behind him. *M'lord?* he thought, confused. *Since when has anyone in Ruan-Tor ever called me that?*

He rode on only for a short distance before something- some higher sense- made him slow his mount and turn around to face the southern gates of Ruan-Tor.

He could make out a figure behind the gates, someone who was not one of the sentinels. The light at the

181

gatehouse was poor, and it took Vornen a moment or two before he realised who it was.

The chief guardsman, Ulan. A member of the Council.

Ulan stared at him for a moment, and then turned away to walk back through the mud and the snow. The sentinels had already gone back into the gatehouse. It was as if they had all but forgotten about him.

Vornen knew by now that something far beyond his understanding had happened here. *But the gates to Ruan-Tor are shut forever now,* he thought. *I have slain one of Lord Vothangrane's guardsmen. I concocted a story to flee the town. I am as wanted as Larien. No, more so.*

Deep foreboding settled within him. Something terrible had stirred within Ruan-Tor, and Vornen felt suddenly certain that Ulan had something to do with it. *Why did he allow me to leave?* he asked himself. *Why not have me captured, tried and executed? Surely he could have done that. The alarm must have been raised by now. Lord Vothangrane and the dead servant will have been found.*

Vornen turned his horse and stared into the southern darkness. He had nothing all now. *How does it feel,* he asked himself harshly, *to be a murderer? How old was the sentinel you murdered? Old enough to have a young family of his own. No doubt about that. Well, if his family hunt me down I'll turn and kneel before them, let them finish me off. That's the very least I could do.*

Caught up in sudden despair and overwhelming guilt, Vornen turned to look back towards the town. *Let them kill you,* came his mind's voice.

But a while passed, and the call of the Gate came to him again, a silent cry that implored him for attention. Vornen smiled bitterly as he leaned forward in his saddle. *What else is there in the world?* he asked himself again, and the answer came quickly. *For you, Vornen, there is nothing. You were always meant to die facing the void, mind and body*

182

*torn asunder. One way or another, this was your fate. Diversions and distractions are at an end now. Next time you behold a Gate, you may even step helplessly into it and make an end of your unfortunate story.*

He rode south along a branch of the Great Southern Road. At times during that night, it seemed that the Gate reached out to him like a long-lost friend, joyous at his imminent arrival.

*How I have missed you!* cried a voice in his head, over and over, and eventually Vornen had no idea whether it was even his own.

## VI

Rocan had not seen such fear in anyone's eyes before.

His map told him that this settlement was Fanlur, formerly a trading post for other nearby villages, a communal market and meet. But it lay abandoned now. He had decided that this would be their last stop before they gave up their futile chase and made haste back to Ruan-Tor.

Rocan was a proud man, and did not relish the idea of reporting his failure to catch Larien. Yet he was not entirely driven by his emotions, and knew that the bitter winter they'd seen so far was merely a precursor to what would soon sweep in out of the forever frozen lands beyond the Pinnacles. It was time, therefore, to return as fast as possible to Ruan-Tor, admit his failure and help prepare his town for whatever the winter might bring.

Fanlur had been stripped almost entirely bare, as if the furnishings of each dwelling had vanished along with all the people. The table at which he sat, opposite the girl they had rescued from Klan-tur, was one of the few left in the place, along with two chairs. His best trackers, Jorath and Glan, had set about an attempt to discover what had happened to Fanlur's people, but they had found nothing

183

that cast light on events here, however long ago they might have been.

"Alsa," he said gently, "it must be difficult to recall what happened to you in Klan-tur. But we must know what occurred there. Why did they call you *faithless*? Many of our people follow the old Gods- I'm one such man- but nowhere in the scriptures is execution without trial permitted, and certainly not by a group of..."

He stopped himself, and looked uncomfortably away. The look in her eyes continued to unsettle him. It was as if she looked not at him but inside herself.

"They are my people," she murmured, and nothing more. The chilly wind sighed around the building as if in sympathy.

*Your people,* he thought. *You call them your people, after they attempt to burn you alive? They're no one's people. They serve some evil I can't fathom.*

He wondered for perhaps the hundredth time what had happened to the children, and shuddered involuntarily as he recalled the holes being dug in the surrounding fields.

"How many of their own have they butchered?" Rocan said grimly. He leaned forward, and she shrank back in her seat at that, so he sat back again with a sigh of resignation. "I don't mean to frighten you, Alsa. I only mean to find the truth. What happened to all the children in Klan-tur? What was done to them?"

Alsa gave him a sudden sharp look and leaned forward as if about to reveal some terrible secret. *Let's hope we have the truth from you,* Rocan silently prayed.

"A sacrifice is demanded from all the faithful," she whispered, "but I am not faithful. I don't see the shadows. So I become a sacrifice myself."

"The shadows." Rocan frowned. "What shadows?"

"They see them from the corners of their eyes, only for a moment," Alsa said. "The old ways have never gone away. It's just that they went back into the world, but now

**Your mind has a peaceful, calm default setting.**

And the less you fiddle with it and try to fix, the easier it returns to this.

Always.

**Midlife.**

**Old enough to reflect back over the years to uncover our patterns, and cast light on our blind spots.**

Mature enough to recognise what to accept and live with and what's worth changing.

Young enough to create a new, inspiring way of being.

**I wandered lonely as a cloud and then thought what the heck!**

You can stuff that for a lark!

I'm off to party, to see the night through with dear friends, a bottle of wine (and a selection of great nibbles wouldn't go amiss either).

Laughter, shared silliness and dancing.

**Where your thoughts are when
you are stressed/ anxious**

**and when you're calm**

**Even in the midst of suffering, we also know that the pain will pass and eventually the feelings will move on.**

Once we let go of the preference for this or that experience - preferring joy over boredom, excitement over frustration, each emotion simply becomes another part of the rich experience of life.

Taken from Ditch Your Midlife Stress From the Inside Out: Dawn Robinson.

Self care isn't about spa days, massages and bubbly baths (although these can be lovely).

It's about looking after yourself and doing what you need to do to treat yourself well in every moment.

the times have changed. That's what folk say." She shook her head, puzzled. "But if all that is true, why can I not see them?"

"So I must be mad, and tainted," she whispered before he could even think of a response. Her eyes wide as they fixed on the knight-commander, she continued, "The tainted shall be punished. I've seen things, in my dreams, and sometimes in the day, and thought myself gone mad. But not the *same* things. Not the same."

"Did they murder all their children?" Rocan knew with a dread certainty that they had, but he could still not quite bring himself to believe it fully. Could there be any more awful crime than that? What could drive an entire community to such atrocities?

Alsa sat back and pulled her robe more tightly over her thin frame. She said nothing. After a short while, she began to rock gently back and forth and quietly whispered an old nursery rhyme that Rocan barely remembered.

He cursed quietly to himself and strode out into the little courtyard where powdery snow swept around in the breeze. His lieutenant was talking quietly with some of the men as they poured out hot water into cups near the fire they had made. "Kovin! See if you can get any sense out of her."

Kovin raised an eyebrow. "Do you not think she would be best tended to by a healer first, sir?"

"Perhaps, but if she can tell us something of importance, then we may not go home empty-handed after all. We may have failed in one duty, but if we can glean something of events in the outlands then that's something, perhaps. Alsa's people may even have had some involvement in it. If you get nothing from her, then so be it- tell the healer to do what he can to make her lucid. Then we'll try again. I must have answers."

Kovin nodded reluctantly, and ducked inside the old alehouse to talk with Alsa, who now wept pitifully at the

185

table. *If she says anything at all now,* Rocan thought briefly and bitterly to himself, and he gathered his cloak about him as he glared morosely around the silent village.

To confirm his gloomy prediction, Kovin came out of the alehouse a while later, thoroughly subdued.

"Well?" Rocan demanded.

His lieutenant shook his head. "She'll say nothing of what happened. And when I asked her about what had happened to the children... she just cried even more. Our questions make her worse, sir. She needs to be healed. Worse than that, I fear it's not just her body but her mind."

Rocan nodded grimly. "Yes. We'll do that. Then perhaps we can set about finding the truth."

"If she even knows the truth anymore," Kovin said. "Ask someone with a damaged mind for the truth and you're liable to be drawn further from it."

"Maybe." Rocan was in no mood to argue.

They had headed east, and now north again, back towards Ruan-Tor, for days now, and stopped at three other settlements along the way. All had been abandoned. No sign of any massacre could be found but neither could any clue as to where the people had gone. Rocan's trackers had searched extensively around these villages and had found no evidence that anyone had come or gone from the place. Rocan found that deeply disturbing. How could an entire community simply disappear without trace?

Jorath made his way across the village square to where Rocan stood brooding. His face bore a look of frustration. Rocan knew that look. "Nothing here then, either?"

Jorath shook his head glumly and scratched at his nose. "I cannot make sense of it, sir. Unless they all learned how to fly."

A vision came to Rocan of winged plainspeople rising into the grey sky, black shapes that circled amidst a coming storm. Abruptly he forced the picture from his mind,

186

disturbed by the clarity with which it had come to him. It was nonsense of course, but at the same time it did not feel like *entire* nonsense.

*I wish I could forget the look in all their eyes,* he thought. *That silent, deep hate.*

Rocan cursed to himself. His mind had begun to wander on its own fanciful journeys over the last few days. Perhaps the sheer cold and emptiness of the land had caused it. Or perhaps he had merely pushed himself too hard. It had happened before. Either way, supplies had run low, they were possibly a great many leagues from their intended quarry by now, and he had had enough of this madness.

"Back home," he said abruptly, two words that raised a faint but heartfelt cheer from the weary men gathered in the courtyard.


Four days later, Ulan watched from his window high in the Council fortress as Rocan's men wearily made their way down Ruan-Tor's main north-south street, greeted by a small but vociferous crowd who no doubt cheered simply out of relief that they had returned at all.

Ulan had known they would fail as soon as he had learned of their mission, but the way they rode back into Ruan-Tor would have convinced him that they had failed anyway. His masters had drawn the sword here by force of will, borne by its human host, and they had spirited both artefact and host away again. Mortal men might as well chase the ends of rainbows as find and trap the darkness that had erupted so violently in Ruan-Tor.

His lip curled contemptuously. *They should have known they could never find their quarry. But Rocan never did know when to give up. I wonder how many times he prayed whilst they were out there in the Plains? I wonder if he feared that his Gods might not be listening to him? If such deities ever existed, they turned their backs on the likes of him centuries of centuries ago.*

Ulan smiled at the sight of Rocan slumped tiredly in his saddle, misery and defeat etched upon his countenance. *The greater the pride, the worse failure hurts,* Ulan thought, *and was there ever a more prideful man than Rocan?*

The figure at the other side of the room moved slightly, a faint rustle and whisper. Ulan flinched in fear and turned to face it once again. He remained uneasy about keeping such company anywhere, but especially here.

*Vornen Starbrook heads south to his death,* it said quietly. Ulan found it difficult to look at the being's features, as they underwent subtle changes the whole while. Throughout their discussion, those features had changed completely, many times. Ulan marvelled at whatever sorcery it was that could do such a thing, but still he feared it as would any sane man.

Still, if he was to succeed, if he was to *survive,* he would have to get used to such things, and that included negotiations with entities that belonged only in scare-tales.

"He will have gone south, Lord," Ulan agreed respectfully, "and he will meet his death in Ethanalin Turmorn, as you said. I expect he will embrace it willingly."

*Perhaps you should have had him executed. Yet I suspect you are fearful of him.*

"It was easier and quicker to let him go, to give him an excuse to run. The entire town is certain that he killed Vothangrane. It took little more than the whisper of a rumour for the story to spread." Ulan took a deep breath and found a little courage from somewhere, although he turned his attention back to the events down in the streets, not wishing to meet his companion's ever-shifting eyes. "Let me manage the affairs of Ruan-Tor."

*As you managed the holder of the key?*

Ulan blinked in puzzlement. For a moment it seemed that his companion became darker, larger, less a shadow and more a black wave about to crash over him. Ulan swallowed. "I don't know what you mean, Lord. Forgive me, but..."

188

*The boy with what appears as a sword, fool. But that has worked well, for he also is on his way to the place you call Ethanalin Tur-morn. His role in this matter is important. And so I shall allow you to continue managing the affairs of this place, for as long as this town remains yours. Others will arrive soon, and you will then do as bidden.*

"Others?"

*Of your kind, but enlightened. This world has reached out to touch them. If you are strong enough, perhaps you will join them. I trust you understand.*

Ulan bowed. "I understand, Lord." He did not, but that was hardly the answer to give. In any case, his heart and his belly told him that he would find out soon enough. He had become a part of this now, heart and soul. He had agreed the blood-price for the assistance that would now be given. Ulan wondered briefly what was being done with Lord Vothangrane's body.

When he turned again, the *choragh* had vanished, leaving nothing but a gathering of gloom in the corner where it had stood.

# VII - Blood and Power

## I

The small hours were racing towards first light when the rider came to the northern gates of Darkenhelm, distracting the night watch from their game of fourdice and pots of Kyransan beer. The thump of hooves and then the harsh ring of a blade upon the bars of the outer gate had them scrambling quickly for their positions.

As they peered through the thick iron bars of the outer gate, the rider- unarmoured, and clad in thin robes for the cold, wet night he had ridden through, took from his pocket a plain scroll, protected all around with wax, and passed it through a bar of the gate without so much as a word. One of the sentries tentatively took it, and the other men gathered around him by the wan light of their lanterns as he carefully made a slit down the length of the wax cover with his knife.

The fact that the scroll bore the personal seal and signature of Kown Malakray and instructed the gatekeepers to admit its bearer with neither question nor comment, was more than enough to gain entry, and the cloud of late-night torpor evaporated swiftly from their senses as they sought to open the outer and inner gates for their silent visitor, valiantly attempting to hide their inebriation.

The rider waited patiently, almost statuesque in the saddle, and then urged his horse through the gates. He vanished as quickly as he had appeared, a shadow that fled down the street, and the sight and sound of his passing sank into the haze of cold mist.

Malakray had not slept that night, although that was far from unusual. He considered sleep to be largely a waste of time and rarely succumbed to it for more than an hour or two. Curiously, he had found that the less he slept, the less he needed to sleep, and he looked forward to the night when he would need it no longer.

In full regimental uniform- for he considered himself a military man before all else, whatever fate and ambition had made of him- he made his way to the meeting room where he waited for his visitor, and ordered the servant to leave as soon as the fire had been stoked up and the room was warm enough to bear. Gods, but it was cold tonight, without a doubt the coldest night of the season. It felt as if the sleet out in the city had somehow seeped into the Palace, despite the fires and torches that had been lit wherever possible.

The sleet had begun to fall again, and pattered faintly on the windows. *When was the last time Darkenhelm had weather like this?* he wondered absently.

The guardsmen outside the room knocked and called to advise that his visitor had arrived, and Malakray went to sit at his desk, hands folded and a calmly neutral expression upon his face as the door opened and the cloaked, rain-dampened figure was admitted.

Malakray waited patiently until the heavy oak doors had been fully shut once again, then spoke up quietly as the visitor showed him a small ring on the middle finger of the right hand, a simple twisting design with a delicate mark that only he would recognise. "You bring news?"

His visitor pulled back the hood of the robe. Malakray was mildly surprised to see a young woman with mousy brown hair and cautious blue eyes stare calmly back at him. He tried to put a name to the face, but could not, which was always a good thing. Xeth Korriston was, of course, too clever to send anyone remotely recognisable into Darkenhelm. It was quite possible that she had never even been here before, and had had to use maps to find her way.

"I bring instructions," she responded. Malakray was surprised to hear a distinct Harnian accent to her voice. Where was she from? Luudhoq, most probably. *Well, well,* he thought. *He finds them here, there and everywhere.*

"Xeth Korriston has decreed that this occupation will draw to an end," the messenger continued. "The Council has issued its command to Emberton's army, and the march to Darkenhelm will commence."

Malakray nodded, his expression unchanged. None of this came as any surprise to him whatsoever. The entire operation had been planned many months ago, and the plan had been honed further in the time since. As the overseer of all military regiments in Darkenhelm, it had of course been one of his duties to talk at length with Xeth Korriston during his many visits to the Queen and her family. Quite how Korriston had sought him out- a man who by his own, if secret, admission would kill his own mother for a large enough fee- was one of the many remarkable things about Korriston, a man who had about him a *feel* for the way people thought and acted, an innate knowledge of the reasons that lay behind actions.

Malakray supposed that that was just another reason why Xeth Korriston was leader of the Council of Priests and effectively the overseer of Aphenhast whereas he, Malakray, played the role of temporary ruler in a city-state soon to be returned to the control of that same Council.

Of course, a favour would now be due him for instigating this coup. Some of his men- a few of his best warriors, in the renowned Death's Head Regiment- had died during the storming of the Palace, and although he cared about as much for their lives as he did for the dirt under his boots, their demise had stung his pride. And relinquishing the position he now held would not be an easy task. Xeth Korriston had known this, and even brought it up during one of their late-night conversations deep within his barracks headquarters months ago.

"You will be handsomely rewarded," Korriston had told him. "I need good leaders of men around me, men with sound military experience and a quick mind. Men who are unafraid to take whatever action is necessary in any situation. A role awaits you in my circle of advisors, once the matter of the Queen and her family is dealt with."

And he had dealt with them in no uncertain manner. The arrangement of heads- Elysa's included- on the spikes of the main Palace gates had shocked the populace into submission more than all the other acts of brutality that followed the coup. For weeks those heads had remained there until at last they became empty and flyblown.

"I understand," he said to the woman. "We will join in battle at the northern walls."

"That battle is to last less than a full day," she reminded him. "At sundown, when you realise how heavily outnumbered your forces are, you will signal the full and complete surrender of Darkenhelm. You will throw open the gates, cast down your weapons, and let the men of the Council Fortress pass unhindered into the city."

He nodded. That was almost exactly what Xeth Korriston had said months ago, word for word. He might as well have been speaking to the man right now. In a way, he wished that he was. There were questions he had wanted to ask the Council of Priests' leader for a long time, not that he expected straight answers to any of them.

She might have been reading his mind as clearly as the lines that furrowed his brow. "Do you wish to ask me anything, Kown Malakray?"

He frowned further at that. Nobody in Darkenhelm dared address him by his first name- it meant *follower* in the all but forgotten Old Hastian, and he detested that fact- but he had to remember that this woman knew full well that she would ride out of here tonight unscathed and untouched, and within a few days find herself safely back in Emberton, to report back to Korriston. He itched to instil a little fear into

193

this arrogant messenger, but couldn't. That, he reminded himself, was not part of the plan.

"I have nothing to ask," Malakray said. Idly he wondered what protection this messenger had to call upon, if she should fall into difficulties during her journeys here and back. Korriston would have considered that, of course. He had a ruthless, thorough intelligence that Malakray admired, much as he also envied and hated the man for what he had achieved. One way or another, any attempt to assassinate her during her lonely journey back to Emberton would be traced back to him.

She smiled at that, and the expression accentuated a faint scar on her right cheek. She took from the inside pocket of her robe another scroll and rolled it across to him over the desk. "What's this?" Malakray demanded.

"It contains certain technical details concerning the assembly of your forces and the resistance they will put up, when our forces arrive. You may expect them about two weeks from now."

"Can you be any more specific?" he asked.

"No," she said coldly. "You should know the logistics of forces on the move as well as anyone else. You will ensure that your own men are in place in plenty of time to defend the citadel. Now, have you anything else to ask me?"

"Nothing," he said. Without a further word, she rose from her chair, turned and rapped upon the door to be let out. Malakray remained seated. A quiet rage burned inside him even after the messenger had departed. *Was* Xeth Korriston truly a man of his word? Would he reward him for all his effort in the overthrow of the ruling family in Darkenhelm, effectively making him the supreme leader of the entire land? Korriston *owed* him!

His gaze fell on the sealed scroll. So these were his orders. Although he felt oddly tired and the hour was late- he reckoned he might even stray into a fourth hour of sleep tonight, whether he liked it or not- his hand strayed to the scroll.

Sighing, he broke the seal and carefully unravelled his instructions from Xeth Korriston.

Malakray stared at the opened scroll for what seemed an age, but no more than a moment could have passed by. For some reason he could not understand any of the words inked on the parchment. In fact, he failed to recognise any of the letters. The sigils swam before his eyes, senseless, pointless. Blinking, he put the scroll down on his desk. A sudden nausea overcame him. Something was wrong.

All over his body, tiny pinprick-sized droplets of blood appeared. They grew swiftly and soaked his clothes. In a sudden, terrified panic, he staggered to his feet and ripped off his shirt to behold the horror that had suddenly risen inside him, and tried to scream for help. He could feel his own blood writhe inside him and surge like a thousand tiny streams, through and over his skin.

Malakray's scream became nothing more than a faint choke. His mouth flooded with hot blood which, a moment later, he drowned in.

On the other side of the door to Malakray's chambers, Nia listened to the faint sounds of his death throes, then carefully stepped over the bodies of the two guardsmen- who had collapsed to the floor either side of the door almost as soon as she had left Malakray's meeting room.

She made her way downstairs. The task was not even a quarter done. She had other names on her list. They would all meet their end tonight, in silence. Already the insidious sorcery that she had brought with her would have started to work on her victims, lulling them to a sleep from which they would never wake. She toyed with the idea of waking one or two of them before she made the quick cut across the throat- that unique look in the eyes of the damned

195

had always fascinated her. Maybe she would, or maybe she would not.

It was time to make a choice.

Nia flipped a silver coin as she reached the bottom of the stairs, and smiled as it fell in her hand with the Queen's head facing upwards.

## II

Yui woke suddenly, startled by a sound. Quickly she peered through the gloom of the cell to see if she could catch a glimpse of whatever had made it. *Maybe it was a small animal, a rat or something,* she decided as no movement caught her eye.

Misery settled into her once again as she remembered where she was. In her dream she had wandered through a forest, and then up a mountain. Yui had never been outside Darkenhelm, nor had she ever had a book with pictures of woodlands in it, but somehow she knew exactly what a forest looked like, just as she knew exactly what the view from the top of a high mountain looked like.

Knowing the words to whisper, to bring those visions sharply into being, had always been enough. The rest was as simple as willing herself to sleep and allowing the dreams to take over. Of course, sometimes they were bad dreams, nightmares about black things that opened up under her feet or in front of her, as if the world around her was just a painting and someone or something from outside of it had ripped through the canvas from that other side. But the good dreams made up for them, sometimes.

It made it all the harder to come back from such a dream, to this cold cell.

She had felt her father's terror as the guards beat him, and now, as she sat up and glanced across at him, she felt something of his pain.

196

Phyqor, who sat propped up against the wall, stirred at that moment. His face was still horribly swollen. Yui thought maybe one of his eyes might be damaged. *I hate them for what they did,* she swore to herself, and moved tentatively over to sit with him.

"Yui," he murmured, and she began to cry. She couldn't help it. They were stuck here in this horrible prison, her father had been beaten so badly she could barely recognise him, and now they were probably going to have their heads chopped off like the Queen and her family. She remembered that she saw the heads briefly one time, a few weeks ago, before they had both been arrested.

"Don't cry," Phyqor murmured. The words struggled thickly from his mouth, barely intelligible.

"I'm scared!" she sobbed. "I don't want to die!"

"Be brave." He gazed at her with his one good eye. "We don't know what will happen. We just have to wait and see."

"For how long?" Yui wiped angrily at her tears.

"I... don't know." He sat back again, his remaining strength having fled. He paused for a long while, then added, "I'm sorry. I should have... should have..." Yui waited for him to finish, but it became evident that he wasn't going to. He had lost consciousness again.

*I know what he was trying to say,* she thought. He had said it before, perhaps a day ago, perhaps longer. *I should have taken us from the castle at the first sign of unrest. I should have taken the back route, out through the kitchens and the cellars and under the palace, under the city and through the sunken streets of the Old Town.*

She held his hand and wept quietly to herself. They were locked up here for the rest of their lives, she decided. If they somehow escaped the executioner's blade, they would probably end up dying and rotting away in this prison, remembered and mourned by no one.

197

Yui heard soft footfall in the corridor outside their cell. Each pace was measured, slow, as if whoever approached took the time to look at each of the cells in turn. Inspecting them, but not in the same way a guard might. She felt a sense of dread as the footsteps grew closer out in the narrow passageway between the blocks of cells. Even Phyqor stirred in his slumber and muttered something incomprehensible before his head lolled to one side again.

Presently a face appeared at the grille in the cell door, of a woman with light brown hair and blue eyes. Yui stared at her, and a moment later to her astonishment she saw a *man* instead, with similar features. He could have been the woman's brother.

Yui gazed open-mouthed, certain that she had started to imagine things. *Am I going mad?* she wondered.

The man stared back at her, an expression of sudden shock upon his face. *He knows,* Yui thought, not knowing quite how she could tell. *He or she has a secret. It's to do with the way she can change between being a woman and a man, just like that. But she didn't expect me to see her change just now. No one else has ever seen it happen, I'm sure about that. Now she isn't sure what to do.*

A key turned in the lock and the door swung open. Yui felt sudden fear rise like a flood within her. "Please..." she whispered, or tried to whisper; the word died soundlessly in her throat. The young man crouched down in the doorway and stared intently at her. "Powers around us- you can *see* me," he said softly. "How is that possible?"

Then, as if a ripple of shadow passed over his face and body, he transformed again and Yui saw the woman staring intently at her instead.

"How do you do that?" Yui whispered. *I must be dreaming,* she thought at the same time. *I've fallen asleep in the dirt, I'm dreaming the mad dreams that people have when they die.*

The woman walked a little further into the cell, and regarded her in silence. "You're seeing it, and yet I'm *not* changing," she said quietly. "I only *thought* about it. Remarkable.".

"I won't tell anyone," Yui said quickly. "You don't want anyone to know, so I won't tell anyone."

A hint of amusement in the woman's eyes mingled with a different expression. Yui could not tell what it was. "There's no one to tell," she said. "Now, I think you should not be here at all- someone of your gifts!- so it's only right that you should be the first out."

The apparition left the door open and wandered on down the passageway. A short while later she had disappeared to some other part of the palace dungeons. Yui stared at the open doorway. *It's a trick,* she decided at first, but knew that it was no such thing. *It's a dream,* she thought after that, which seemed altogether more likely.

With considerable effort she roused her father, and they began a slow and painful journey through the prison tunnels. They had to stop frequently, and all the while, Yui feared that they would be discovered by one of the guards as they dragged their way through the narrow tunnels, but soon she came to the firm conclusion that she *had to be* dreaming.

Every guard they came across was already dead and still, and their way out into the city remained unhindered.

III

Alexia stared down through the grimy little window of her bedchamber at the street below. The rain pattered incessantly upon the glass. No traders had braved the marketplace at the end of the road. These days only a few ventured out even when the weather was good, and when the heavens poured like this they were nowhere to be seen. Trade was one of the last things on people's minds at the moment. Three ships from the southern island of Kyransa

199

had been anchored in Darkenhelm Bay for weeks now, their crew waiting patiently to do business with the new masters of the citadel. They knew full well the dangers of remaining where they were but were attracted to the lucrative possibilities that trade with Darkenhelm had always offered. Imported goods had become high-priced rarities now, and as trade with the outlying towns and villages of southern Aphenhast had also dried up- nobody wanted to enter Darkenhelm for fear of being unable to leave again- even necessities were about to become rarer.

Still, Alexia reminded herself, none of this was her problem. Not once she found a way out of Darkenhelm, anyway.

For perhaps the twentieth time or more, she considered wandering the streets of the citadel to gather all the information she needed. After all, there were few people who knew her face- she supposed she ought to be thankful for her habit of staying away from the public eye as much as possible- and she looked even less of a princess now with her hair hastily chopped to a crude, almost boyish length, and her clothing much the worse for wear.

*That said, who would so much as bid good-day to a down-and-out?* she reminded herself. *These days, no one in the city speaks a word to anyone unless they need to.* Besides, there was every chance that Malakray's militia employed men and women throughout the city to comb the streets and look for both her and her sister Maria. It was common knowledge that the two of them had been absent from the palace during the bloody coup.

*Quite an irony really,* Alexia thought. *I choose to spend most of my days immersed in my studies deep within the palace libraries, and then one day when I need to visit a Guild library instead...*

And yet, oddly, she felt little grief when she thought about that day. She had heard about the arrests and executions, and then the next day, before she fled into hiding, she saw for herself the heads upon the gate barbs, hair fluttering in the breeze, sightless eyes overfilled with dried blood. She had felt horror, yes, and then sudden panic that she might be caught, but not grief as such- just a guilty feeling that she *ought* to be grieving.

Alexia had never been especially close to anyone in her cold, disinterested family. When it became clear as Alexia grew up that she would never fit in with their endless social gatherings, parades and ceremonies, they developed a certain cruelty towards her- the subtle but effective cruelty of words and belittlement. For her part, she had simply backed away further from their world of pointless artifice and buried herself in her studies.

But whatever they had said and done, none of them had deserved the brutal fate meted out to them.

Alexia walked over to the mirror and stared appraisingly at herself. Her hair hung lank and forlorn, unwashed for more than a tennight. She looked tired, plain and somewhat pale, as if she had been deprived not only of sleep but also food. *And perhaps I will, if famine hits the city before I can leave,* she thought. She wore a plain cotton shirt and trousers, both of which were grimy and had about them a worryingly beggar-like odour. Her boots had worn almost through in the heels and toes.

*I look like a mercenary without a sword,* she thought with a sardonic smile, and as an afterthought, slotted her knife into her belt and looked herself over again. *No, I look like a common footpad. And perhaps that's what I'll be, in time. I'll do whatever it takes to survive.*

And survival would be an achievement no one else in her family could claim, except perhaps her older sister.

*I was lucky to come here without being seen, weeks ago,* Alexia thought as she recalled her exit from the Guild and panic-stricken journey through the gathering dusk and the shadowy back-streets of Darkenhelm, to Phain's cure-all shop. *But at least I was not alone in my panic that day.* The news of what had happened in the Palace, having already reached the libraries of the Guild, had spread like wildfire through the rest of the city.

She had made her way to Phain's shop for a few very good reasons. Not only had he long been a steadfast friend- he had also helped with some of her studies- but she also felt certain that no one else within the Palace knew of their friendship. It was not a relationship any of them would have approved of, had they known.

Suddenly restless, Alexia made her way down the narrow, wooden stairs to the cluttered kitchen area where Phain was busy concocting stew for breakfast. She had learned in the time she had been here that Phain's diet left much to be desired. It consisted mostly of stew or soup or something in between, regardless of the time of day. She would have thought an apothecary or potionmaster, or whatever it was he called himself these days, would have had the skill to prepare something with a little more imagination, but apparently he did not.

Nevertheless, she remained more than grateful for his hospitality, and she had no one else in the entire city who could be trusted. Phain was an absent-minded, vague old man but he loyal to the bone, and nowhere near as daft as he sometimes appeared.

He turned and bobbed his head in greeting as she walked into the kitchen. "Good morning, ah... er, Alexia." Even now, weeks after she had first told him not to use it, he still occasionally addressed her by her title. Her *former* title, Alexia reminded herself as she sat at the table. A title she had never really used and certainly never would in the future.

"Good morning, Phain," she said tiredly. "That smells nice," she added with a smile, although it did not.

Phain grinned at the compliment. "This is a slightly different recipe to my usual one. A little less spice, but I added a few new herbs into the mixture."

202

"Has there been any news?" Alexia asked. Phain had left the shop early in the morning to gather information from his various eyes-and-ears around the city. Usually he came back with as much information as he had left with, but occasionally he managed to pick up snippets of interesting rumours and stories. Alexia knew well enough that similar-sounding rumours and accounts could be pieced together to make a half-decent picture of events, so she listened and made a mental note of everything he told her, even when it seemed irrelevant. And she knew he would hold nothing back, unless of course he forgot that detail before his return.

Phain shrugged. "Nothing as such. The mood in the city is one of deep unease, but that's hardly news. People seem to think that the Council of Priests will send their armies to Darkenhelm, that there will be fighting in the streets. I think there might be fighting in the streets long before then if the food shortage worsens."

"All the more reason for me to leave," Alexia sighed.

Phain looked at her with sudden alarm. "*Leave?* But how? Nothing comes in or out of Darkenhelm now, so it's not as if you can even hide in a grain cart or a barrel! I can't see a way. No, you'd best lay low and wait for an end to this situation."

"I'll not wait for an end to it. Who knows when that might happen? There must be a way, Phain. Even if I have to jump into the bay and swim to one of those Kyransan vessels still anchored out there."

Phain shook his head. "Even if that were possible, the port is well guarded. Our lords and masters look out for anyone foolish enough to make a bid for freedom- or, as is more likely, a bid for the food stocks on those ships."

He stirred the pot of stew with a big ladle and lapsed into thought. "You know," he said thoughtfully after a long silence, "if the Council of Priests do send their army, then the city will fall. Those men are well paid, and motivated by a sense of duty rather than fear. A force will be sent here, in

203

a matter of tennights or even days. It's what happens before then that worries me. Something will give. The frustration that simmers in the streets will boil over into something far worse."

Alexia thought for a moment. "Is there any mention of me on the streets? Anything at all? I don't expect there is, but the less people talk of my family the better. Whatever happens now, our time has passed."

"I've heard nothing."

"And Maria? That would be more likely? She always enjoyed public attention."

Phain looked agitated. "Nothing of Princess Maria either. But once the Council's army gains control here, matters will be put right, or at least as right as can be. To be more precise, Maria will be crowned. Unless she has been captured."

"Two things, Phain," Alexia said grimly. She was beginning to tire of his persistent hope that her family would somehow rule in Aphenhast once again. "Maria was in Emberton at the time, and as far as I know she still is. She will be in hiding if she is sensible, because the Council priests cannot be trusted. Korriston is a snake like his father before him, only three times as devious. Secondly, I have no desire to return to Palace life even if it ever becomes possible."

"But you can't remain in hiding for the rest of your life," Phain persisted.

"I have no intention of being a fugitive exactly," she told him, "but if I *do* find the opportunity to leave Darkenhelm, then I will do so, and perhaps change my appearance a little more."

"But what will you do, Prin... ah, er, Alexia?" As ever, Phain forgot about what she had told him concerning her former title when he became flustered.

Alexia shrugged wearily. "Do? I suppose I will travel, and maybe settle down somewhere, then make myself useful if I can. A town big enough for me to settle in without causing much notice, but small enough not to remind me of Darkenhelm. I never want to be reminded of this place, and I never want to be reminded of the life I once led. In fact, I would quite like to become an archivist or a researcher- if I can do so as far from here as possible. There are Guilds and places of learning in other cities. You know that as well as I do."

Phain stared at her and blinked. "Well, I..." Seemingly having forgotten what he was about to say, he returned his attention to the stew and frowned into its murky depths as if about to add another ingredient. "You must do what you think best," he said eventually, clearly unhappy with her decision.

"Do you honestly think life in Darkenhelm will ever be the same again, after all that's happened?" Alexia asked the old physician. "After my mother, grandmother, two brothers and three cousins have had their heads stuck on the barbs of the palace gates and their headless bodies dragged through the streets by the very militia that was thought to be loyal above all others?"

"I suppose not," Phain mumbled. He winced at her brutal words, and no doubt wished he had kept his thoughts to himself. He poured some stew into two cracked porcelain bowls and brought them over to the table, where he sat with a sigh.

"No. And *I* suppose not either," Alexia said, not without bitterness. "That time has passed, Phain. I am afraid you will never again take pride of place with your wares in the Inner Market," she added with a smile, and he stared seriously at her. "That was the last thing on my mind! I would dearly love the throne to be reclaimed, by yourself, or Maria as may be the case, but I hadn't given any thought to my own situation..."

Alexia laughed out loud despite herself. "I know, Phain. I know. Well, if my sister wants the throne and the

205

Council army liberates Darkenhelm then it's hers. But if Maria can keep a cool head for once, she'd be well advised to lie low and trust as few around her as she can. I intend to leave it all behind when I leave this city."

"You would make a more just Queen." His tone was mild, but held a hopeful edge. Phain rarely gave up hope once he had a notion about something. *But he'll be disappointed on this occasion,* Alexia told herself.

"I would make a terrible Queen, and if you thought about it properly for a moment, I think you would be forced to agree," she told him sternly, and took her first mouthful of stew. It was not bad at all and much better than its smell had promised. Having a guest in his house had certainly improved Phain's cooking as time went on. "I don't know the first thing about affairs of the state. I went out of my way not to learn, and in the end they gave up on me and left me alone to my own studies."

"Then you have some skill in getting your own way," Phain remarked, and stirred his stew thoughtfully, giving the impression all the while that he still intended to find a way to make her reconsider. *Think all you want,* Alexia told him silently, scowling into her stew, *because I will not be moved.*

The steady rain which had persisted all morning eased off shortly after they finished lunch, and Phain went out to gather information as usual. Alexia sat upstairs in the back bedchamber and began to read one of the old man's books on civil history, but she grew increasingly restless. She *had* to leave the city; already she had hidden herself away too long, and the fact of her being here put Phain's life at risk. The Council troops might arrive next week or the week after, or instead there might be negotiations that went on for days or even weeks and led nowhere. But she would be out of Darkenhelm long before then. One way or another.

She must have allowed her thoughts to wander for a long while, because she still pondered what her life might be like far from Darkenhelm when eventually Phain returned and called her downstairs almost as soon as he had shut and bolted the door.

"Matters have begun to move quickly," he said as soon as she reached the bottom stair. A sparkle of merriment gleamed in his eyes. Alexia smiled despite herself. "What is it? What's happened?"

"From what I can gather," Phain told her, "the Death's Head Regiment and all their guards have been slain! A small contingent of the Council's army- apparently from an encampment just east of the city- have marched in and started to assume control." He shook his head. "It all happened so quickly! And no one seems to have heard any fighting. Still, this is what we have waited for! A bloodless end to the situation!"

Alexia felt suddenly cold inside. An inexplicable feeling that some strange plan had been put in motion came to her, like vast ancient wheels that had started to turn or boulders that began to rumble down a hill.

"I must remain in hiding," she said, raising a hand immediately as Phain opened his mouth to argue. "Don't even *think* to protest otherwise. Whether Maria still lives or not, the Council will want me for whatever machinations come next. They must not know I am here."

Phain nodded, openly frustrated but unwilling to argue the point. It was an argument he would lose.

"I need to think about what I do next," Alexia said shortly, and turned and made her way upstairs, as all manner of notions raced through her head.

*Should I leave Darkenhelm amidst the confusion which is probably now rife throughout the city?* she wondered. *Or do I remain here and wait for that same confusion to blow over? Should I find somewhere else to stay? I've burdened Phain for long enough even though he'd keep me cooped up here for months if I asked him to. My very being here endangers him, I'm sure of it. But where else can I go? I can't think of anyone else I can trust, someone who would risk the so-called justice of the Council of Priests for harbouring me and not delivering me into their safe keeping.*

Alexia sighed. Every choice seemed a poor one. She lay down on her mattress and stared up at the ceiling, unable to decide what the best option would be. She normally prided herself on her ability to think her way through a problem- *No puzzle is without an answer,* she had always told herself- but eventually, frustrated and tired, she fell asleep.

A dull pounding upon the front door of the shop woke her suddenly. It stopped, and then sounded again. Five knocks came, and each sounded more impatient than the last. *And made with the pommel of a sword or other weapon,* she noted as she sat up. Her heart raced. Who would come to the shop at this late hour and knock upon the door with a weapon?

Alexia glanced at her window and noted that night had fallen. She got up and walked out of the room and as far as the top of the stairs, and a feeling of deep unease clawed its way up inside her. Then she heard Phain bustle through from the back room. "Could be Marc or Garron, from the Guild," he muttered to himself up as he reached the foot of the staircase. "I spoke with them earlier. They said they might come by. One thing's for sure, it won't be the Death's Head regiment on the hunt! Ha!"

*Don't answer the door,* she thought in sudden panic, as she listened to Phain as he drew back the bolts, whistling tunelessly to himself. *Whoever it might be, don't answer it!*

But Phain opened the door, and she heard someone- perhaps two people- push their way in.

"You are Phain D'hyyrn?" a man spoke up. His voice sounded imperious, impatient; this was someone in a hurry for formalities to be done with.

"I am, officer." Phain seemed perfectly calm, if a little more bewildered than normal- a half-trick that almost never

208

failed, although this time it was surely no trick. *Officer,* Alexia thought numbly. *But they're all supposed to be dead, everyone believed so. I should have known the rumour was too good to be true. Some would have survived, and somehow they have found me at last.*

Alexia got up and moved silently back to the bedchamber, and over to the window which overlooked the back yard. Slowly she opened the window, wincing in fear of it making a noise, though all she could hear was her own blood as it pounded madly. An old ale-keg stood just below the window- Phain was fond of his ale- and another had been set against the far wall. If she managed to get down into the yard, and then stood on that second keg then she might be able to scale the wall. As far as she knew there was just an alleyway beyond it. It was too late to check now though.

As she stared down into the yard she heard the man's voice drift up the stairs again, more faintly. "I am Captain Harrin Liss of the Council of Priests. I am here to ensure the safety of Her Highness, Princess Alexia."

*Oh, Gods,* Alexia thought, her knees almost giving way. *They've found me! How?!*

"But why would you look for her here, officer?" Phain began in puzzlement. "I have never so much as seen Her Highness. I know her name of course, but..."

Alexia heard him gasp suddenly. A dull thud sounded, followed by something even worse; the sounds of the soldiers kicking him around the shop floor. A few jars and bottles fell off shelves and shattered. "Careful, you idiots!" she heard Captain Liss shout. He had almost reached the bottom of the stairs.

Whatever else happened, she could not be found and then ensnared in whatever schemes the Council of Priests, or even Maria if she was still around, had in store for her. Alexia jumped down into the yard and hobbled across to stand on the ale-keg by the far wall. She managed to heave herself onto the top of the wall and then jump down into the alleyway beyond, her whole body trembling.

Alexia gasped in pain as she fell to her knees; red-hot pain scythed through her, and for a moment she struggled to even breathe. Then, as she heard a sudden bellow of "Find her!" from the window of the bedroom, she staggered to her feet and half-ran, half-hobbled through the evening mist.

She had no idea where she would go only that she had to get away, that she could not, *would* not be captured by anyone ever again.

# VIII - A Coin, Light and Dark

## I

The weather had improved since their departure from the Round Tower, and a welcome warmth tinged the breeze, but Jaana's weather sense was as good as anyone's and she knew it to be a brief respite. The companions had made good progress as they headed west across the Crescent foothills, helped by their procurement of horses from a small village along the way, and they reached the grey slate town of Morlan after just three days' travel, which was when it became decidedly colder once again.

"We're about halfway to Culvanhem," Fistelkarn had told them, and Jaana thought, not for the first time, that he seemed distracted. Perhaps he was far from certain that this old enemy of his could be coerced into helping them, even in return for his freedom. *Or perhaps he simply cannot bring himself to trust the man if he does free him*, she considered. *No doubt there's much to the situation that I know nothing about.*

Jaana wondered how and why they had come to be such bitter foes, but decided it would be better not to ask. The matter was none of her business.

Morlan was a grim-looking but sturdy place of squat stone buildings built low and wide, its people polite enough but wary of the outsiders in their midst. Fistelkarn received a few cordial bows and calls of welcome- which he seemed to find embarrassing, although he acknowledged each one with a weary smile and a nod- as they rode slowly down the main street on the lookout for a stable and inn for the night. Jaana, rode anonymously towards the rear, thankful that no one recognised her so far from the Hastian midlands. She had never ventured this far north before, and there was no reason why word of any healer short of a miracle-worker should have travelled this far.

*Yet I'm still looking for cures,* she reminded herself, *even though I've tried to leave that life behind. I suppose this is too hard to walk away from. Especially as I have nothing else to walk towards.*

The rain that had started to fall felt as cold as sleet with the stiff breeze that blew across them. Jaana's stomach rumbled as she pulled forward the hood of her robe. It would be good to sit down with a roof over her head, she mused, and to have some food and drink inside her. Her appetite had returned a little over the last few days, although Ellen's fate preyed on her mind continually. Everything seemed more confused than ever after Fistelkarn had spoken about her, and she couldn't even begin to think what to believe. *Time to put it behind you then,* she scolded herself. *Isn't that what Ellen would have wanted?*

But she then recalled the words of her mentor, that evening before her death. *You will have to be strong.*

Jaana shivered, as if the cold had sunk into her a little further.

They retired to the *Stone's Throw,* a large, comfortable inn set a little way back from the main street, as light began to fail and a heavier onslaught of rain pattered down onto the slate roofs and flagstoned roads. Over distant hills in the west, Jaana saw lightning play amongst the leaden clouds as she hurried inside.

Dinner turned out to be a rare treat- a hog roast and vegetables of the late season, served at a large table near the hearth where they were drying their cloaks. It was one of the finest meals Jaana had ever eaten, and afterwards, especially after several cups of delicious wine, she almost felt content. She must have smiled to herself without realising, because Lyya leaned over and commented on the fact.

"I feel a little better perhaps," she admitted, as her smile faded. "I can't do anything about what's happened. But

212

I've been thinking more and more about that night in Ellen's hut."

Lyya looked pensive. Finally she said quietly, "I think the truth will find us sooner or later, Jaana. I would say sooner."

The following morning, a short while after they had left Morlan, the weather took a turn for the worse, and snow quickly began to cover the ground. The road petered out to a rough track, which would have been impassable by cart given the number of ruts and holes that marked the way ahead. It sloped gradually upwards so that they were well within the hills by dusk, yet the companions struggled to keep up the pace they had managed for the previous three days, mindful of the need to progress without risking injury to the horses.

"We draw near to *crommar* territory now," Fistelkarn said as they prepared a fire, sheltered partly by the edge of a barren-looking copse. The snowfall had eased, but dark grey clouds massed in the north and the east, heavy with the promise of more. To the north the ground sloped gradually down into a shallow valley between broad hills, occupied by a large, slate-shored lake. It looked every bit as barren as the hills around it.

"What kind of place is Culvanhem?" Jaana asked him, before she realised the ambiguity of her question. "I mean, does it look similar to one of our own cities?"

"It's a *stronger* place," Fistelkarn said after a moment's consideration. "Architecturally sounder- fashioned from stone and a little harshwood pretty much throughout. There are nowhere near enough trees that high up, and besides, the *crommari* prefer to fashion from stone."

"It was built five thousand years ago," Fauli remarked, "and much of the original city has stood since that time. Attempts have been made down the centuries to conquer Culvanhem, but all of them failed. The only way to overwhelm such a place would be from within, I think. It's

213

far too well-defended to succumb to any other attack. And the *crommari* are a tightly-knit race to say the least. Unrest of the sort needed for Culvanhem to fall from within..." She shook her head. "Unthinkable."

Jaana dozed off as she listened to her companions' conversation. She was dimly aware of Lyya placing a thick blanket over her at some point, and a little after that the murmur of voices faded and she fell into a deep, dreamless slumber.

She woke suddenly into the small hours of the night. The snow clouds had moved on, but oddly the air didn't feel cold at all. A slight breeze blew from the south and gently rustled the withered bushes nearby. Both Ildar and Archaon had risen, the red moon Archaon clinging ponderously to the low southern sky as the brighter face of Ildar arced through the high heavens.

Jaana glanced around at each of her companions, and realised suddenly that they were all asleep: no one kept watch. *I suppose I shall if I can't sleep,* she thought. She no longer felt tired, nor did she feel the need to huddle under her blanket with the night breeze being so warm.

She sat and let her thoughts wander as she gazed at the moons and the stars. *I should like to visit the South Ocean Islands one day,* she thought. *I remember Mother telling me that the stars in their sky are different. Does that mean they have different moons as well?*

As she contemplated the possibilities of the cosmos, something like a whisper came to her, as if a snatch of far-off conversation had been carried by the breeze, although it came from behind her, down by the lake.

She heard it again. It sounded more like a rhythm than a whisper of words, a chanted repetition driven by a distant voice. Jaana got up and stared in the direction of the lake. The waters shimmered faintly in the moons-light, but she could see nothing move, nor could she hear anything.

214

*There's nothing there,* she reasoned, but at the same time some faint memory stirred within her, and she remembered words that belonged to her mother, spoken long ago, that had never made sense: *You will know when you see them.*

Quietly she took a dozen paces or so away from the camp. She glanced back and saw that her companions slumbered on peacefully.

*When I see what?* she silently echoed, bewildered that she should have remembered those words after all these years. *There's nothing there.*

But she found herself walking slowly on, drawn by some curiosity, and with each step she took, Jaana found that she walked a little faster, a little more sure-footedly.

As she drew closer to the lake, Jaana suddenly noticed two figures that stood by the shoreline, where tiny waves lapped quietly against the slate and gravel. Both figures were draped in ragged, clinging robes. The taller of the two had a hand upon the shoulder of the smaller one. Both appeared perilously thin, their arms like the branches of winter trees.

She stopped, terrified. *I must go back,* she decided, but she could not. Another part of her, quiet but filled with rage, rejoined, *I have seen these things before, in another life. I have killed them before. I will tear them apart.*

Jaana willed the babbling in her head to cease, but when it did, an altogether different sound drifted across the night air, a rough, low chant that filled her with dread.

Yet still she drew closer, down the gentle slope towards the lake shore. Her feet squelched in the muddy ground under the thin layer of snow. The wind chased itself across the lake and rippled the surface.

Jaana had walked to within fifty yards of the almost skeletal figures- and still these creatures seemed to know nothing of her presence, for they had not turned or even moved- when she felt a sudden mad pulse and movement, as

215

if her blood had been agitated and now began to swirl in strange directions. Jaana felt her heart thump painfully. *What are they?* she thought desperately.

The taller of the two figures looked down at its companion- though in truth Jaana could see no eyes, only the hood under which they must be hidden- and pointed across the water to the distant far shore. Then it spoke, and the voice, carried across the wind, was one of bestial cunning, the crunch of rotting bones.

"From the beginning, to the end, from the first blood to the last, *hear us,* our masters." The words were uttered almost as a vile song, in symphony with the lap of wavelets against the shore. *And I hear you too,* Jaana thought, almost delirious with the sudden heat behind her eyes and in her limbs. She felt certain that she would melt through the snow, even through the muddy earth beneath. *I hear you, and I feel every beat of your rotten hearts.*

The smaller figure turned as if to peer up at its companion. Although Jaana could see little detail, she knew that something *misshapen* existed under the cloak of the smaller figure, something that had changed the very form of the body and rended bone and tissue slowly apart. As she closed her eyes, she could even *hear* it.

The tall figure laughed again, and with terrifying ease, reached under the hood of its companion's robe and tugged a handful of hair from the head of its companion, then scattered it in the breeze with a laconic gesture. "Time below and time above..."

Then the other being spoke up. "I sleep. I wake. I sleep..." It was not any kind of voice Jaana could recognise. Entrenched with filth, mud or slime, it was a hoarse, choking gurgle, spoken through a broken throat, an evil sound that hid inside a broken body. Worse still, it changed in pitch the whole while, as if that noise was nothing more than a reflection of something chaotic happening to this wretched form.

216

*I will send you back under the earth,* came that mad, hot voice from within her again. They both turned in the same instant, as if they had heard those unspoken words. Jaana could *feel* the taller figure smile as if in welcome, although it had no face, let alone a mouth.

She raised a hand as if to defend herself, and the wave of rage inside overwhelmed her completely.

In utter agony, she clapped her hands over her ears and fell to the ground, but even through what blood-rimmed sight remained she saw the smaller figure burst into flames. The other one howled as if in anguish. The creature's cloak billowed as it turned to face the waters of the lake again. It raised both thin, bony arms to the sky as if to exalt some unseen god.

The cloak simply fell to the floor in a heap. Of its wearer no sign remained, though ripples of darkness like a scattering of deep shadows over the lake mingled with the water. A moment later all that remained was the motionless body on the lake shore. Flames licked at the still form, but within only a few of Jaana's short, frightened breaths it became ash. As she sat up in the mud and snow, the breeze carried those remains across the waters of the lake in an angry swirl.

Jaana sat as her body eventually calmed itself and the cold worked its way into her. *I felt something dark and unspeakable that moved between the two of them,* she thought.

But events here would be something to mention much later, if at all. She could hardly bear to think about everything that had just happened.

Jaana dragged herself back up the slope towards the camp. She did not dare to look back, yet she felt a brooding malevolence behind her, as if the surviving abomination still watched with hateful eyes through the icy waters of the lake.

217

## II

Jaana woke under her blanket. She barely remembered having returned to the camp at all. She glanced fearfully towards the lake, but in the early morning light it looked entirely unthreatening. *I had a powerful dream, nothing more,* she decided, but knew those words for a lie.

"You don't look well, Jaana," Fauli pointed out with characteristic bluntness as she filled a kettle with snow and placed it over the fire.

"I slept poorly," she said, which was the truth.

"We'll be in Torrom this evening," Fauli said, which Jaana supposed was a form of encouragement. Lyya gave her a sidelong glance which could have meant anything.

*I should tell them,* she thought. *I should tell them everything. Who knows how important it may be? Fistelkarn may know what those creatures were. What if I see them again? What if others of their kind attack us as we sleep?*

But she could not tell her story, not unless she told half of it only. *What might they make of the* thing *that burst into flames,* she thought, *at the same time as I thought I would be enveloped by fire? What would they say if I spoke of the mad words that danced around in my head, which those creatures seemed to hear?*

So she said nothing, and they rode on after breakfast. Gradually the way ahead took them towards one of the distant hills and a well-marked stony trail.

Daylight had begun to fade when they reached the village of Torrom, which Tyrameer pointed out was the last settlement before they entered *crommar* territory. A small crowd of villagers gathered and murmured amongst themselves as the companions made their way into a nearby tavern, although no one asked to know their business.

They sat at the rear of the tap-room. Tyrameer bought drinks and meals for them and also paid for rooms for the night. The companions' mood remained pensive and

218

nobody seemed to have as much appetite as he or she ought. Jaana could eat nothing at all.

They decided to retire shortly afterwards, and were shown to their rooms by one of the night servants. Only three chambers were available, so Lyya and Jaana agreed to share the third.

As Lyya lit the lamp by the bedside, Jaana looked around the low-ceilinged little room. It was a little cramped, but seemed comfortable enough and clean. Tiredly she sat and removed her boots, trousers and shirt, and lay back on the bed with a groan. She felt tired enough to sleep for a week. Riding did not suit her- though of course it would have been impossible to walk this- and she did not even want to think about rising so soon in the morning.

*But neither do I look forward to sleeping,* she thought, *because I think I know what I'll dream of.*

Lyya took her boots off and tossed them to one side. "Are you really all right, Jaana?" she asked as she turned to face her friend.

"Why do you ask? What do you think is wrong?" Jaana bit her lip, wishing she had the sense not to leap to her own defence whenever questioned. That old trait of hers would take a while to lose.

"You said this morning that you slept poorly," Lyya said, "but in truth you were sleepwalking."

Jaana's heart almost skipped a beat. "Sleepwalking?" she said faintly.

"You must have wandered off," Lyya continued. "I woke up just as you came back."

"I probably had to pass water."

"Hmm. I spoke to you on your return, but you didn't hear me."

Jaana forced a smile. "I would sometimes sleepwalk as a child. I do it less often now, but I suppose it still happens sometimes." *Lie upon lie,* she thought, *but perhaps if she only saw me come back from the lake...*

Lyya said nothing as she took off her shirt and trousers and lay down next to her. She took deep breath and wrinkled her nose. "I think we both need a bath, Jaana."

Jaana laughed out loud at that despite herself. "Perhaps we can, tomorrow."

She fell asleep after only a moment or two. One hand clutched at the nearest bedpost as if to anchor her safely to the world of dreams.

Jaana was startled awake by a loud rap upon the door, followed by Fauli's strident tones. "Jaana! Lyya! Get up!"

Shielding her eyes from the bright sunlight that poured in through the bedroom window, Jaana blearily made her way over to the door and threw back the bolts. As soon as she opened the door a little way, Fauli pushed past her, a grim look on her face. "Get up! There's little time," she said abruptly.

Lyya scowled at her as she began putting her outer garments on. After a moment Jaana did the same, and dressed in haste for fear of Tyrameer or Fistelkarn also being nearby. "Do any of you *du-luyan* possess manners?" Lyya snapped.

Fauli ignored the question. "Tyrameer has saddled the horses ready for our departure. We'll breakfast quickly and take some provisions, then go."

"And since when did you become our leader, Fauli?" Lyya demanded. The other woman gave her a level stare. "Since Fistelkarn left," she said.

"What?!" Jaana exclaimed, as Lyya stared open-mouthed. "Why would he leave? And where has he gone?"

"He has a good reason, usually." Fauli showed her a scrap of paper that she took from her pocket. "When he chooses to give one at all, that is. This was pushed under our door at some point in the night. Normally I would have heard- I barely sleep at all some nights if I'm indoors- but if Fistelkarn wants to come and go undetected then he will. I

220

don't know where he has gone; that is his business. He'll tell us when we need to know."

Jaana took the paper and sat down on the bed. The message had been written in an untidy, hasty scrawl and ink blotches marked the paper here and there.

*I will meet you again as soon as I am able to. In the meantime, I need you to continue to Culvanhem with all haste.*

Jaana showed Lyya the paper. Lyya read the message and then silently handed it back to Fauli. "If you want to part company with us, so be it," the *du-luyan* woman told them. "But I would prefer it if you remained. Both of you. Four people can look out for each other better than two in foreign territory," she added, and glanced at Lyya, who nodded stiffly. "If Jaana is willing to, then so am I."

"Of course," Jaana put in. "We've already come this far. I have nowhere else to go anyway. Do we wait for him in Culvanhem?"

Fauli smiled wryly. "If I know Fistelkarn- and I think I know him better than most- then he will arrange for another instruction to be left for us there, or he'll be in the city already." She paused, a troubled look in her eyes. "I only hope he knows what he's doing."

III

Davvin Glain waited patiently at the head of the valley as snow began to drift down. The steep slopes on either side of him were marred and pitted with broken paths, jagged rocks and deep crevices. Even tough hillgrass found it hard to grow here, and most other plants had long given up. It was not a part of the Territories that he or anyone else walked out of choice. Many unfortunate myths and tales were entangled with this area, and although rarely mentioned they remained common knowledge amongst his people. Even to

221

speak of them in passing was frowned upon, yet neither could anyone deny their existence.

*Poison metal,* he thought gloomily as he stared up at the slopes and noted the reddish-brown hue to the rocks. *But there's always been more than that. All the stories say that the dead were buried in unmarked graves here, twenty hands down, and were never brought back to Culvanhem. Left to seep into the earth and never interred within their Family Halls, because the poison that had cursed them would last forever.*

He bowed politely as his visitor rode up and stopped ten paces from where he waited. The correct protocols always had to be observed, whatever one might think of one's visitor. This had always been *crommar* territory, but a guest was a guest and this one had sent word ahead to his masters, who had requested his help. Davvin was not sure what he thought of sorcerers in general and human ones in particular, but he had managed to put such worries to the back of his mind. After all, he had been given a job to do, and that was something he took very seriously. It would not have been his personal choice to seek the help of any human, but a majority of the *crommar* lords thought differently and that was what mattered.

*I'll do my job,* he thought, not for the first time that morning, *and I'll be back in the city by nightfall.*

He pointed to the tethering post nearby, a lingering remnant of the settlement that had once existed here before the sickness and the poisonings. "We must go the rest of the way on foot. Are you well enough?" He looked doubtfully at the old man and wondered how many decades he had seen.

Fistelkarn's smile held more than a little anger. "I am perfectly well enough." Still, he looked uncomfortable as he dismounted, and after he had tethered his horse Davvin decided to set a less than furious pace as they set off along one of the zigzag paths that led up the western slope of the valley.

"Do you know why you are here?" Fistelkarn asked him between laboured breaths as they made their way up over the broken ground. Every now and then they dislodged a few stones that tumbled and crashed to the bottom of the valley.

"I was told to escort you to the place of the sighting," Davvin said simply. "Nothing more. I follow my orders, and I leave questions and speculation to others."

"Wise fellow," Fistelkarn muttered.

They reached an area close to the ridge within a couple of hours. The path they now followed wound between tall, precarious cliffs of slate and shale, an ancient way-path carved into being thousands of years ago in the days when the *crommari* had followed nature-gods. Paths such as these still existed on many of the mountain ridges and summits, though they were seldom walked now, perhaps because of what they had once signified, which the *crommari* sought to disown and deny.

They came out onto an exposed area of the ridge. Fistelkarn cursed quietly as the harsh wind cut through him like a knife. Davvin, oblivious like all his kind to whatever the elements might throw his way, led him calmly over the flat plateau to a curious mound of rocks, some of them thirty or forty hands high, which had been twisted and somehow *melted* into odd shapes. In the centre of this mass of deformed stone there loomed a crack in the ground, utterly dark, about five yards across in both directions at its widest. Davvin came no nearer than a dozen yards away, and hung back with sudden nervousness. He fiddled with his tribal necklace and cast sudden glances up into the sky, his weather-beaten countenance set in a scowl.

Fistelkarn bent down and stared into the fissure for a long time. Finally, he picked up a small stone from nearby, held it over the chasm at its widest point, and dropped it in. He had counted slowly to fifty-seven by the time he heard

223

the faintest of sounds from within the chasm, of the stone at last coming to rest.

"Black shapes came forth from here," he said, quoting the message he had received whilst in Torrom, "and cast a burning frost upon the ground."

He touched the ground next to the gaping fissure, and closed his eyes. Almost immediately he could *feel* those same shapes, writhing their way into the sky, like slivers of darkness cutting through the winter air. He knew better than to keep his eyes closed for more than a moment, however. *Yes,* he thought grimly. *That is what happened. Some powerful weave cut through from the underearth and set free...*

He feared even the name, but there was no avoiding it. *The Old Dark.*

Davvin said nothing, but he looked even more eager to head back. "What does it mean?" he said eventually. He asked the question with a seeming reluctance. After all, he had claimed to be a follower, not a questioner.

Fistelkarn did not look up. "The old powers of the world begin to stir," he said. "Those who once ruled, in the dark times before our Races ascended. It's as I feared. And if they..." He shook his head. The wind was so cold it felt as if it would numb his brain. He felt so tired that thinking anything through had become a struggle. "But why? What could have awakened them?"

Davvin had no response to give, but Fistelkarn nodded, having answered his own question. "*Marandaal,*" he said. "As I thought. They *know* about them. They always have." He looked up and across at his worried guide. "The old ways work their way into the world again, *crommar.* Do you know about them?"

"We don't speak of such things." Davvin found that he could not help but stare at the great fissure, and with an effort he forced himself to look away.

"A coin, both light and dark. But when the *marandaal* last found this world, the coin fell dark-side up. The *choragh* smiled heavenwards as the world released them into its wider self, and a war the like of which no world has ever seen ensued. *That* is the legend. Or a version of it."

Davvin shifted uncomfortably. The words were unfamiliar but moved him nonetheless. The hand that clasped his necklace shook with fear. He needed to be away from this place. Some strangeness in the air made the hairs on the back of his neck stand up and coaxed beads of sweat from the skin of his back despite the icy wind. "Have you seen enough?" he demanded, taking a step back to show that *he* had, whatever fascination this man might have for the phenomenon before them.

For a moment Fistelkarn seemed not to have heard the question, and Davvin began to despair. Finally he nodded. "This is all there is to see- the remnants. Whatever *was* here, is now somewhere else."

After they descended the slope once again, Davvin bade him a curt farewell and made his way through the valley, following the path of the frozen river with what looked like undue haste.

Fistelkarn watched the sturdy *crommar* for a short while, then turned his attention to the jumble of thoughts that clamoured for attention in his mind.

There was something else, an important puzzle which he had overlooked, or neglected to solve. He frowned, thought hard for a moment, and then it suddenly came to him.

The shaping spell that had been used to gain access to his tower- or what remained of it when he returned- had had about it a certain taint, a unique pattern, as if it had been created by someone but then, perhaps unknowingly, changed by someone or some*thing* else before it had been used.

*Was the thief sent by a* choragh? Fistelkarn wondered. He quickly dismissed the idea. But the taint had somehow reminded him of such a fell creature. He thought instead of *where* the spell could have been created. Many sorcerers could have brought such a weave into being, but surely none could have co-operated with a *choragh* or other such creature. Unless they had not precisely *known* about it. *First came the spell, perhaps,* he mused, *and then came the taint, and the two together were carried all the way to my home.*

*Where?* Fistelkarn thought. *Where would be the most likely place in the world for the old order to manifest themselves? Which place has been hidden away from the younger, newer parts of the land for longest? Which place, if overcome, would represent the sweetest victory for the Old Dark?*

He considered the matter a little more, and then suddenly realised. The more he thought about the possibility, the more it became a certainty.

*Mirkwall.*

Abandoned, laid forgotten, a cursed and ancient castle where the bitterest of struggles had taken place dozens of centuries ago. Mirkwall. And someone who lurked there had brought into being a spell to gain access to the Round Tower.

It had to be Shimlock, and that was a shock in itself, for everyone- Fistelkarn included- had thought him long gone from this world.

But that still did not explain *why.* Why would Shimlock be so desperate to gain access to the Tower?

*What does Shimlock know about me?* Fistelkarn wondered as he sat wearily on a boulder and nibbled on some rations, though he had no appetite at all. *Was he perhaps searching for knowledge about the* choragh, *in desperation? Or perhaps he has nothing to do with this. Perhaps the old man is dead, and the* choragh *and their minions now rule in*

226

*Mirkwall. Could they have sent one such creature out into the wider world? And if so, why to my tower?*

Yet another matter that needed his attention. Bent forward against the wind, a deep ache in every bone, Fistelkarn began to feel even older than his many years.

IV

As they reached the summit of a windswept, near-barren hill of rock and heather, Jaana gained her first glimpse of the *crommar* city of Culvanhem, and for a moment, she utterly forgot everything else as she stared at the vastness of the place, which was still perhaps a league away from them.

"Plenty of time to look around when we get there," Fauli called to her impatiently, having somehow sensed her dawdling without needing to look back.

*She has been here before,* Jaana recalled as she gently urged her horse to catch up with the others, *so even this grand sight means less to her.*

She continued to drink in the scene as they made their way along a gently sloping path towards where Culvanhem nestled. The vast city had been built into and in places *made of* the vast mountain. Greys and whites intermingled across the battlements, parapets, towers, spires and fortresses that stood tall and wide everywhere she looked. The hard beauty of the place bewildered her. What was it Fauli had said the other evening? Culvanhem had never fallen to any invaders. Given its location, it would have been difficult to invade in any case, but the sheer height of the outer inner walls in the south, from which any attack would almost surely have to come, was breathtaking, and would require siege engines the like of which had never been built.

*How long did it take to fashion this place?* she wondered. *Many decades, I'm sure. Centuries even?*

227

Lyya appeared to be similarly overcome by the sight of the place. "Few of my people have ever seen Culvanhem," she commented at one point. "Not because of any enmity, but because we have always held to our own lands, and rarely need to visit *crommar* territories." She smiled to herself. "So I'll have a story worth telling when I return."

"I don't think many of my people have seen it either," Jaana said. "From the little I know they're not welcome in these territories."

"Few are welcome in Culvanhem, unless they have good reason to be here," Fauli spoke up. She shrugged. "But at least they deal with visitors of all races on their own particular merits."

They were less than a half-thousand paces away when a vast gateway in the base of the outer wall opened up with a low grating and deep rumble. Presently a small contingent of *crommari* guards made their way slowly towards them on foot. "I will talk with them," Fauli said sharply as they drew nearer. *As if anyone else had been about to,* Jaana thought, and saw Lyya glare at the *duluyan*'s back as she led them at a slower pace down the path.

When no more than a couple of hundred paces separated them, the group of four *crommari*- tough-looking, muscular men with shaved heads, as was normal- drew to a standstill, and remained still and silent as the companions drew up to them and stopped. Each one of them wore hide armour almost the colour of grey granite, and each carried a shortsword and mace at their side. Their dark eyes looked almost like black gemstones set into unyielding, leathery faces.

Fauli said something to them in their own language. Jaana understood one word- *Fistelkarn*- and the name itself seemed to unsettle the guardsmen. One of them, a scarred, grim-looking man who stood a little taller than most *crommari* but had the same lean, muscular look, took a few steps forward and bowed formally to each of them in turn.

228

"You are welcome to Culvanhem," he told them, although the harsh tone of voice he used indicated otherwise.

The *crommari* remained silent as they led their guests to the vast gateway in the outer wall, though Jaana noticed a few glances being exchanged between them. Two of them exchanged furtive, complex hand signals that might have meant anything. She knew next to nothing of these people.

The companions reached the door, which stood well over one hundred hands high and almost as wide, dotted with iron squares each as large as someone's head. One of their guides stepped forward and hammered upon the one of the squares with his mace, then stepped back. After a short while the door opened down the middle to reveal a group of six more *crommari* who strained as they pulled in opposite directions to open a wide enough space for the newcomers to pass through.

Jaana looked up at the battlements, where dozens of archers had appeared. A forest of arrows waited to be released, black barbs held against the grey sky. She could not see any faces- just glimpses of watchful eyes behind visored helmets- but she felt certain that many of them would quite enjoy letting fly.

Jaana looked away, suddenly troubled. They had no friends here, and would make none.

Their guides led the four of them through into a courtyard surrounded by high walls of white, grey and black stone in every direction. A hundred paces ahead of them stood the inner wall into Culvanhem, even taller and thicker than the outer wall. The *crommari* allowed them no time to gape, however; they were instructed to dismount and give up their horses, and without further ado they were then ushered through one of the gates in the inner wall, which led them down a wide passageway and through into the citadel itself.

Narrow and cobbled streets wound away up steep gradients, some of them so steep that they looked almost impossible to climb, although many *crommari* folk made their way up and down them seemingly without breaking sweat- though that would have been difficult enough anyway in this chill air. To the north, the city appeared to go on forever, built on tier after tier of land, with roads that curled and meandered their way up between the bewildering array of houses, fortresses and towers, almost as high as the clouds.

As they followed their guides up one of the streets, *crommari* going about their daily business stopped and stared, most of them openly suspicious. Some exchanged words with one another, pointed and nodded, as if they had reached swift agreement that the outsiders were unwelcome in their city and that the sooner they were sent away the better.

Jaana had little time to drink in the sights, sounds and smells of that small part of Culvanhem through which they walked, but she noticed that almost every window here had been fashioned from coloured glass, something that was a rarity everywhere else she had been, and every door that led into a house or a shop bore a bronze plaque with writing upon it, in some cases nothing more than a single, complex symbol. Jaana guessed that this was simply a way to provide information about the people who lived in that particular house or the people who traded at that particular shop. *I'll not ask the question though,* she thought, mindful of the glares thrown in their direction, not least by their impatient chaperones.

They were led up one of the many steep, winding roads, and struggled at times to keep up with their guides. Jaana noticed something else odd. Although she had seen a couple of stables so far, the *crommari* did not seem to have any horses themselves, nor did they use any beasts of burden as far as she could see. Carts, many of which looked

230

dreadfully heavy, were pulled by teams of muscular *crommar* men up and down the hills. Jaana wondered briefly if they were slaves, or if pulling carts was just another job to do in this place where everyone seemed to have an occupation.

The fortress to which they were led stood over a south-west facing part of the city, rounded with turrets and parapets each of which held at least three black-clad guards armed with crossbows. It was at the entrance to this place- an archway that loomed more than fifty spans above- that their guides abruptly passed them on to a dozen heavily-armed sentries. Immediately and without a word of explanation, they were ushered onwards and into the shadowy fortress.

Jaana had guessed that they were being taken to someone who had authority in the city, but when they were shown to the marbled hall where he awaited them, she was taken aback. The man waiting for them was surprisingly young, or appeared to be, although how young he might be in *crommar* terms was a different matter. One of his arms, crippled and wizened, was about half the size of the other. It took her only a moment to realise that the limb was entirely useless. It lay curled against his body, darker-skinned than its counterpart, and mottled with scars and blemishes. The fingers at its end were abortive and misshapen, one of them more like a claw than a finger. Jaana took all this in swiftly and then made a conscious effort not stare at it again. To do so in any company would be rude- to do so here might be thought of as some sort of crime.

The young *crommar* man did not rise from his high-backed chair at the table, nor did he smile in greeting. It seemed that smiles were not something the *crommari* offered readily. He merely gestured to the empty seats around the square marble table, and waited for them to be seated before he spoke.

"I am Garon Ferrhun," he said simply by way of greeting. "I represent the People's Council and speak on their behalf."

Fauli introduced each of them in turn. Garon remained impassive, glancing briefly at each of them as they were named, sitting back in his chair cast half in shadow. Finally he nodded and said, "I understand you came here because of Ludas. Fistelkarn has told us that much. We find it interesting that he wishes to have dealings with that man."

"Ludas may be able to assist us," Tyrameer put in. "You see, he..."

"Whatever you need from him is none of my business, if you take him outside our territories," Garon cut across abruptly. "Assuming a deal is struck for his freedom." He fell silent then and pondered something, before he roused himself again. "You have travelled far. I expect you are hungry."

They were led, with the guardsmen following at a discreet distance, down several more passageways and into a large open hall, brightly-lit and colourfully decorated. Around the edges of this hall, various stalls held foodstuffs of all kinds, the aromas of which were mouth-watering. The central area, the floor of which was slightly lower, held a number of long granite tables for eating from, each of which were supplied with large flagons of wine and ale.

"You may eat and drink." Garon gestured to the offerings. "I shall return later, and you will be taken to see Ludas."

"We're to see him before Fistelkarn arrives?" Fauli frowned.

"That is what he told the Council," Garon said. He turned abruptly and left, although several of the guardsmen remained some distance away, one in each archway leading from the eating-hall. "I think we'll see them wherever we go here," Lyya said.

232

"We're outsiders, and none of you have been here before." Fauli's tone was dismissive. "This is exactly how they respond when any newcomers arrive in Culvanhem–which is not often, so if they seem over-zealous then that's why. Do nothing to rouse their suspicions further, and in return they will do nothing to harm you, *luyan.*"

Lyya for once could not muster up a retort. The companions selected food and drink from one of the stalls, and then sat at a table to eat in weary silence.

A while later, Garon returned, and led them as far as a lower hall where he summoned a guardsman and instructed him to lead the four of them to Ludas' cell.

"It seems a strange gamble by Fistelkarn, to seek the help of such a man," he remarked. "Ludas is known well for his deceit." This was the first time Garon had shown any kind of interest whatsoever in their affairs and to Jaana it seemed like a casual attempt to gather information from them.

"We cannot speak for Fistelkarn," Fauli responded smoothly. "But we thank you for allowing us to see Ludas."

Garon pursed his lips at that, and then gave a little nod, then turned abruptly and walked back the way they had come. His steps echoed harshly on the marble floor. Their new guide, meanwhile, had already set off down the passage, and by the time they had caught up with him he had reached the top of a stairwell that led down in a wide spiral.

The stairwell was lit by oil-lanterns that hung on ropes from iron brackets in the ceiling. They cast a faint, reddish-tinged light that did little to make the shadows shrink back. At its base, passageways ran off in three different directions. Each one looked much the same in the gloom. The one that their silent guide chose had rows of iron doors on both sides. A dank, close odour hung in the air. Jaana thought at first that it might be mould, but it smelled stronger and even more unpleasant.

233

They were led for perhaps a hundred paces down the passage before the guardsman stopped and unlocked one such door, with a large black key. Then he pushed at it, and as it swung open Jaana could not help but recoil at the stench that suddenly hit them. Yet her next reaction was one of pity mingled with disgust.

The man who sat shackled to the back wall of the cell, naked and squatting in his own faeces, was painfully thin, with a long yellow beard and dark, sunken eyes. He looked up briefly and then cowered, looking nervously into each corner of his prison as if he expected shadows to fly at him from out of the walls.

"This is Ludas?" Fauli inquired.

"This is the great man himself," the guardsman responded with a hint of a smile upon his lips.

Jaana could keep silent no longer. "Why do you keep him in these conditions? I realise he's a prisoner, but he's hardly a threat to..."

"Do we criticise the way you run your own prisons?" their guide coldly interrupted. "No, we do not. You would be wise to respect the customs of your hosts. Furthermore, I suspect you know nothing of the circumstances that surround his crimes."

Jaana gritted her teeth at that but kept silent. She threw a warning glance to Lyya, who looked equally ready to challenge their *crommar* guide.

Fauli cautiously walked into the cell a little way. "We need your help," she said quietly.

Ludas laughed softly at that, a faint wheezing sound. "I am in no condition to help anyone, *du-luyan*."

"I hope you are wrong, *dreamreader*," Fauli responded, and his head snapped up at that, a sudden keen wariness in his eyes. He threw a fearful glance at the *crommar* guide, who remained impassive.

"You forget that I'm a prisoner here," Ludas said eventually. His chains rustled faintly as he moved his arm.

"What will you do, melt these shackles from my limbs and let me escape through the walls?" He coughed harshly and droplets of blood flecked his beard. "Many's the time I have dreamt of doing just that. Perhaps I will when I'm dust at last and I seep through the ramparts."

"We are here to negotiate your freedom."

"Why would you want to do that? Why this sudden pity from strangers?"

"We are friends of Fistelkarn," Fauli told him, and Ludas shrank back as if the guardsman had suddenly decided to beat him to a pulp.

"Fistelkarn will not harm you," Fauli said patiently. "The truth is, we need your help, and we cannot have that without your freedom."

"Or my consent." Jaana saw a sudden gleam in his eyes. Did Ludas presume to bargain with them, if they successfully freed him? "But of course I will help, if you can heal me, feed me, let me breathe the open air again. I am *yours,* if Fistelkarn swears to leave me unharmed."

"I am certain that he will."

Ludas said nothing for a while, and sat and stared into space. "You will have to drive a hard bargain. The *crommari* are as hard and cold as the stone they make their home," he stated finally.

"Everyone has their price." Fauli stood up. "We will discuss that price with them."

Ludas nodded, then began to shake. It took Jaana a moment to realise that he was in fact laughing, but almost silently. "Your chances... I don't..." His words drifted into silence, and he bowed his head as if in exhaustion.

The guardsman ushered them out, and the door was locked and bolted again. They began their walk back to the stairway.

They had covered about half the distance to the stairs when Jaana felt as if something *rippled* through her, an invisible nauseous wave that caught her so unawares that she staggered to her knees. Instantly she recognised the sensation. *It's the lake all over again,* she thought, horrified, *but far worse this time. Something more powerful has come for us. Something we have no hope of withstanding. Why didn't I tell the others, warn them? Why...*

"Jaana!" Lyya cried out. "Are you all right?"

She could not speak. Everything around her seemed distant. Lyya's voice sounded as if it came from the top of a well, as she sank through darkness to the bottom.

As Lyya tried in vain to pull her to her feet, Jaana saw shadows move at the end of the corridor, emanating from the gloom of the stairwell. They created a deeper darkness that detached itself from its surroundings, given sudden life.

As the gathering of shadows became one, the entity that moved before them took one form and then another, and pulled into itself what little light remained. Jaana glanced around from where she helplessly lay, and saw that their *crommar* guide had vanished.

She knew what they faced now. As the *choragh* moved towards them, savage pain cut through her. The corridor, her companions and even the enemy itself faded from her sight as her face pressed against cool flagstone. Everything around her became silent and black, nothing more.

Her world flickered back into view as Fauli screamed in pain, and dropped the shortbow she had tried to load. It burst into flames as it hit the ground.

Jaana became dimly aware that she sat against the side wall of the passageway. She could now see almost nothing at all. The periphery of her vision blurred and flickered darkly as the *choragh* manifested itself before them.

Lyya cut at the being with her longknife, a glitter of light in the gloom. Jaana saw the motion and the light, dimly recognised Lyya's swiftly moving form, but even that had

236

begun to fade. It was if the *luyan* woman sliced at the shadows. Wherever she stabbed or cut, there was nothing but the lightless air. The ephemeral darkness that clung to anything of substance moved, and gathered itself elsewhere. Then the *choragh* shimmered, reached out, and Lyya howled in agony as it flung her back down the passageway.

*This is it,* a small voice spoke up in Jaana's mind. Her sight of Lyya's motionless form faded entirely.

Then, as the *choragh* turned its attention to her, her vision became suddenly, painfully clear, as if the entire world was composed of searing light and black shadow and nothing existed between those extremes. It loomed towards her, a myriad faces twisting and turning. Jaana stared back at it. She no longer felt anything at all, and waited to be torn apart.

*I have waited for you my entire life,* she thought, as all hope emptied out of her. *Now I know what my mother was afraid of, what she hoped to protect me from. It was you, and all others like you. She was an enemy of yours, and her ancestors, my ancestors, were enemies of yours.*

*The other side of the coin.*

And then the *choragh* spoke.

The voice was like a distant whisper spoken through layers of ancient earth, and yet she heard every word clearly. No mouth moved; it was almost as if the sound of the voice came from within her.

*I see the ancient gifts still run true.*

Jaana could not speak. She tried to open her mouth and her teeth chattered violently.

*You exist only to steal. What you think is yours, is ours. In time, you will come to us.*

The *choragh* turned suddenly, and as if it had been the only thing that held back the dark, Jaana's vision faded and she slumped back onto the cold stone. This time she did not wake.

# V

Jaana woke suddenly with a clamour of voices in her head. She opened her eyes and managed to raise her head a little from where she lay, unable to work out if those urgent sounds had been from her dream or not.

The door into the sparse, white-walled little chamber lay wide open. Beyond it, a long passageway led away, narrow and high-ceilinged. Lanterns all along its length gave out a greenish-hued light. About halfway down the corridor, two *crommari* were deep in quiet but intense conversation, perhaps an argument about something.

Abruptly, they both looked in her direction at the same time, as if they had heard her stir. Jaana felt her skin crawl as their cold, disparaging gaze swept over her. *Where am I? Why am I here?* she thought desperately. *Why...*

Her vision faded, and she sank back into unconsciousness.

Sometime later, perhaps many hours, she opened her eyes to the sight of more unfriendly faces.

The three *crommari* stood and talked together across the room, but they glanced furtively towards her on occasion as if they suspected her of eavesdropping. When they realised she was awake, they ceased their discussion entirely, and one of them took a few steps towards where she lay in the bed.

Jaana could still not remember how she had ended up here. *The prison,* she thought. *We were taken to see Ludas in his cell. And then... I remember nothing after that... did we return to the hall? Did I fall and faint? Why can't I remember?*

"Have I been ill?" she asked weakly.

The *crommar-* female, stout and with a firm, squarish face- looked dispassionately down at her. "Ill? Not precisely. I shall inform your friends that you are awake. You seem strong enough to talk, at any rate."

238

"What happened to me?" Jaana spoke up. She tried to raise her head, but that caused a sudden, savage pain in her neck so she lay back again, trembling with the exertion.

None of them answered. The *crommar* who had spoken gave her a long, unreadable look, and then the three of them filed out of the little chamber and closed the door behind them.

Jaana sighed and took in more detail of her surroundings. The room was sparse and austere, the walls fashioned from rough-hewn rock painted white. One tiny window about six feet high in the wall to her left let the grey daylight in. The room looked disconcertingly like a prison cell, if a clean one.

Perhaps many hours passed before the door opened and Fistelkarn entered and quietly closed the door behind him. He listened intently at it for a moment before he then walked over and dragged a stool from the corner over to Jaana's bed.

"I didn't know you had arrived," Jaana murmured. "Why am I here, Fistelkarn? I asked them if I'd been taken ill, but all they..."

Fistelkarn shook his head. "Never mind what the *crommari* say or fail to say. That's their way, and it always will be."

Jaana noticed the drawn, haunted look in his eyes-the eyes of a man fashioned from wrinkles and shadows. "What happened to me?" Jaana asked him. Suddenly, and without any reason she could think of, the memory of her encounter at the lake came sharply back to her, and her heart began to race. *Was it something to do with that?*

Fistelkarn sat with his head bowed, lost in thought, and remained silent for a long while. Jaana began to wonder if he had even heard her question. She was about to cautiously ask him again when he looked up and stared at her.

"How do you feel?"

239

"Tired," she murmured. "Well, exhausted. I don't know why. I just wish I could..."

"Remember?" He smiled faintly. "Of course. But for now, it's probably best that you do *not* remember."

"Why?" Alarm spread through her. "Why can't I recall anything that happened?"

"The four of you were attacked. And it is likely," he continued quietly, "that there are many here in Culvanhem who wish us harm. Therefore, we are working quickly to secure Ludas' release. If we can do so, we'll make haste away from this place."

Jaana silently recalled their visit to Ludas' grim cell. She tried to recall more, and this time she remembered that Fauli had spoken to him. *And before then, I argued for his better treatment,* she thought. *I should have kept my mouth shut. Might those words have brought harm to us?*

"We're beset on all sides by enemies, Jaana," Fistelkarn spoke up, as if he could see her thoughts race to piece together her recollection, "and Ludas is probably the least of them."

He raised a hand before she could say anything further. "Something has happened here, and worked its way through Culvanhem into the very fabric of the *crommari* people. Still, we can do nothing but remain on our guard until we leave. I would have had one of us watch over you, but they would not permit it."

Jaana lay back, puzzled and confused by what he had told her, and even more by what he had not. "I'll let you rest now," he said, and then he left.

She didn't remember falling asleep, but sometime later she was shaken gently but insistently awake. Her eyes flickered open to behold Fauli staring down at her. "Are you strong enough to walk, I wonder?" the *du-luyan* woman said. "They've asked me to take you to the others, if you can at least take a few steps."

"I'll try," she ventured. Fauli nodded, and helped her out of the bed. As Jaana got unsteadily to her feet the *duluyan* woman looked her up and down. "You're as unsure as a newborn calf, Jaana. Still weak at the knees," she commented. "Lean on my shoulder. Put your arm over my other shoulder," she added as they began their slow walk down the corridor.

"Are you going to tell me what happened?" Jaana asked. "Fistelkarn wouldn't." Fauli's description of her condition was not short of the mark, she thought ruefully. Her legs felt as if they had forgotten how to work properly.

"In a while. When you're stronger." Fauli gave her an odd look- Jaana felt there might be fear mingled with sympathy in her expression, though she had no idea why- but said nothing more, and Jaana felt too tired and confused to press the issue.

They walked along corridors and down several flights of wide wooden stairs, which Jaana found difficult to negotiate. Now and again they rested, and to her credit, Fauli remained resolute and patient with their slow progress. A few *crommar* servants and guardsmen passed by every now and then, though they paid the two of them scant attention and offered no help. Word of their visit had probably spread to every stone corner of Culvanhem by now, Jaana thought.

She tired rapidly and felt ready to drop by the time they arrived in a great hall where Fistelkarn, Tyrameer and Lyya waited, seated at a long table. They were not alone; five *crommari*, two men and three women, also sat at the table and leafed through documents and parchments. *Are these the Councillors of Culvanhem?* she wondered. *Why is the other one not here, the one with the withered arm?*

Tyrameer rose and helped guide her to a seat at the table. It was a relief to sit down, although the feeling was short-lived as she saw the icy gazes of the five *crommari* upon her. Suddenly she felt angry- angry that no one had

241

told her anything, coupled with a deep frustration at her own inability to remember what had happened after their meeting with Ludas. To the coldly dismissive *crommari,* she might as well have been an insect to be crushed against the marble floor.

"You will learn everything soon, Jaana." Fistelkarn seemed to have already read her thoughts, or perhaps her expression gave her away. "I have explained to our good hosts that the sooner we agree a price for Ludas, the sooner we will be away from Culvanhem. It has not escaped my attention that our presence here is perhaps... inconvenient." He made a respectful little nod of the head, but if anything, the demeanour of the five *crommari* became frostier than ever.

"A shame that Garon could not attend," Fistelkarn remarked, and one of the male *crommari,* old and pale for one of his kind, spoke up. "Garon is otherwise engaged this day. You deal with the Council of the People regardless of which representatives choose to hear your plea."

"You have some odd bargaining chips, Fistelkarn," one of the women spoke up. "And we find it strange to say the least that you should choose to not only free your bitter enemy, but *pay* for his freedom. I ask you again- what is it you want with him?"

"I believe he will be of use to me, and it's plain enough that he's of no use to you," Fistelkarn said as he leaned back in his chair. "That's all you need to know, and I'm willing to say no more as to *why.* After all, I have my own agenda."

"When did any sorcerer *not?*" she countered.

Fistelkarn smiled thinly. "What advantage does it give you to incarcerate this man in your dungeons in silence and squalor? You have neither need nor reason to interrogate him. If you had a need to prise information from him, I am sure you would have done so by now- your methods in that area are legendary. And I am equally sure

242

that he would be of considerably less use to me, after such... laborious interrogation. What is he to you? A thief, a peddlar of forbidden goods, nothing more.

"I, however, *do* have a need for Ludas. That is why I offer you a not inconsiderable sum of money- as gemstones, naturally- in return for passing him over to my care."

As the *crommar* officials glanced wordlessly at each other, Fistelkarn continued in an almost matter-of-fact way, "I hear that bad times are upon the land. Rumours speak of unrest, a gathering of the races in the middle lands, and even war. I know of no better way to coax the far-flung races of the land to your side than by the use of precious items. Wealth moves many people, does it not?"

They bristled visibly at that, and one of the women looked as if she might get up and either stalk out of the hall or draw a blade. Fistelkarn remained impassive. He may as well have commented on the weather.

"As you say," the old *crommar* man spoke up eventually, "wealth moves many people. We, however, are more concerned with our own protection. You are correct. A war may indeed be imminent, and we prepare accordingly as you might expect. But as you point out, we have no need for Ludas. You are willing to pay for his release. Are we willing to accept your payment? It is a simple choice."

He turned to the other four, none of whom looked in the slightest bit happy with the way the conversation was going. Nevertheless, they nodded and murmured assent, albeit reluctantly. "The fee will be of some use- limited use, I might add- when the thaw eventually comes and the trade routes open in the south," one of the female *crommari* ventured unenthusiastically, and another turned to glance at their guests. "I suspect they intend to exact their own form of justice on Ludas. Whatever the case may be, he will no longer be our responsibility."

The old *crommar* said no more, but pushed one of the many documents across the table towards Fistelkarn, who read it in silence for a while. "This passes him over to my care, and relinquishes all claims you have to him," he commented finally.

"It does," the *crommar* responded.

"You appear to have added a condition." Fistelkarn tapped a finger on the paper. "It states here that whether or not Ludas is given to us, under no condition may any of us return to Culvanhem or any *crommar* territories. If we do, we are to be summarily executed."

"That is part of the price. We do not seek the company of humans, nor indeed *luyan* and *du-luyan*. The fewer outsiders who come to Culvanhem the better. Invariably you bring trouble, or trouble finds you here. In short, Fistelkarn, you and your assortment of strange companions are to leave Culvanhem with Ludas and never return, or you leave without him and never return. The choice is a simple one."

"How times have changed." Fistelkarn sat back in his chair and gave a grim little smile.

"Times *must* change," the *crommar* responded. "As you so quickly pointed out, war is coming. Your prized citadel of Nisstar is soon to fall."

"Prized? Not by the likes of me."

"A gathering of the Races masses to the west of it. This is no time to for us to be entertaining such as you."

They stared at each other for what seemed an age. Finally Fistelkarn nodded, and without further ado he took the proffered quill and pot of ink and signed the paper. The *crommar* man made a gesture to the sentinels at one of the many doors leading into the hall, and the door was opened. Two more guards from the other side pushed a bound and gagged Ludas into the hall, and he was marched to the table where he stood unsteadily, head bowed and eyes averted. Jaana barely recognised him at first. The prisoner had evidently been prepared for departure; he had even been washed, shaved and clothed.

244

The *crommar* shrugged when Fistalkarn looked at him. "As I said, the choice was a simple one."

The companions were marched under heavy guard as far as the outer perimeter wall and reunited with their horses. Throughout the journey, citizens of Culvanhem stopped and stared, whispered to one another, and some even spat at Ludas, who said nothing at all and stared straight ahead as if oblivious to the entire scene. He appeared to be either lost in his own world or still stupefied to find himself under open skies.

They headed directly south into the lowlands with the wind at their backs. Only when they had ridden two leagues away from the stone city did Ludas hoarsely demand that they stop. Tyrameer, with whom he rode, drew his mount to a halt, and as the others did likewise and warily regarded their new companion, Ludas motioned for water to be provided. Hesitantly Tyrameer offered him his canteen, and Ludas drank thirstily. "They will seek you out, and one way or another you will take a side," he said after gulping the water down.

"Enough of your riddles, Ludas." Fistelkarn's mood had been black since their departure from Culvanhem.

To her shock, Ludas pointed directly at Jaana. "This girl- she's strong in the old ways. I heard everything that happened from my cell, Fistelkarn, as I cowered and wept in my corner, fearful that the *choragh* those *crommari* bastards had invited into their city would melt through the wall and rip my insides out. It left her untouched, sorcerer. *Untouched!* It would have taken more than one of their kind to finish her off. I saw it all without needing to look. I saw it start to fade. The blood must run particularly strong in her!" Ludas stared wildly at Jaana, who feared suddenly that she had drifted into another horrifying dream, and that she still slumbered in her rest-chamber in Culvanhem.

245

Abruptly he turned his attention to the others. "Ha! So none of you saw fit to tell her, or perhaps you simply do not remember the detail. Well, the *choragh* gain in power day by day as they fight their way back to this world. Doubtless they will find a use for her. What they cannot destroy, they subvert…"

As Jaana felt her consciousness ebb away, the last thing she heard was Lyya urging her horse next to hers.

"They will have to kill me first," Lyya said softly as she caught her, and those were the last words Jaana heard as she drifted away, like flotsam on an ocean of madness.

# IX – Departures and Circles

Tears of rage and frustration rolled down Kian's cheeks as she leapt up onto the window ledge and remained straddled there, one leg either side. She peered into the gloom of the castle chamber, and then out into the greyish half-light of the Mirk. She dared not go any further at this point, not until she had gathered her thoughts and perhaps found herself an excuse.

Shimlock awaited her return. Kian shuddered as she thought of him. He would sit in his decayed inner chambers, and chose neither to eat nor even move for days on end, wearing the rictus-like smile of a man who had lived too long in shadow.

She was his eyes and ears to the world, but he seldom seemed to listen to any of the tales she brought back to the Mirk of events elsewhere. And in turn, the world had long since ceased to remember Shimlock, let alone any of those he had once known. To the people out in the surrounding lands, the Mirk was simply that- a vast swampland clad in the perpetual grey of a mist that never lifted. Perhaps it held the remnants of an old city, perhaps not. Maybe, like whatever lay below the waterline- and even Shimlock could not remember that with any clarity- everything that still reached out into the mist would in time be reclaimed by the swamp.

Kian shivered and hugged herself as tendrils of fog snaked into the bare chamber. Shimlock might well be furious at her failure to bring back anything of note from Fistelkarn's tower, if he was sufficiently lucid. He showed patience when it came to awaiting her return. He knew that the journey there and back would have been be a long and arduous one. But that patience would swiftly evaporate when he found out that all she had managed to bring back were the useless trinkets she had absently stuffed into her pockets before conducting her search properly.

Kian had always known that she would never feel entirely comfortable here in Mirkwall. She was twenty-two years old, barely full-grown for a *du-luyan*, and had been brought here, according to Shimlock, by a man and woman- her parents- who had for some reason given up their child to the decrepit sorcerer and then either left or become lost forever in the Mirk. During her dark moods she occasionally wondered why they had abandoned her. Had she been hideous in some way? She cautiously thought of herself as pretty enough whenever she looked into the mirrors here, but perhaps she had been less becoming as an infant. From what she knew, it happened quite often that ugly children grew up to be pretty whereas those blessed with looks in their first years might easily become plain as they matured. And she knew *du-luyan* to be a proud, vain people. She might not have grown up amongst her kin but she had met half a dozen of them.

Kian sighed. This was far from the first time she had pondered the matter and it would not be the last, but the answer remained as remote as ever.

She thought briefly of the people who had disturbed her and ruined her chances of leaving Fistelkarn's tower with anything useful. She had never seen *du-luyan* and humans together before, and certainly not *du-luyan,* humans and *luyan* all together. That was especially odd. Someone- a human woman- had once told her that the *luyan* were the enemies of her race. Human folk all seemed to think themselves experts in everything- certainly they held opinions on everything- but Kian reckoned they were no better than average in almost every area.

She had often contemplated never returning to the Mirk. One day, she told herself, she would travel and learn more about the world. Only the thought of what Shimlock had done for her- he was terrifying, otherworldly even, but he *had* raised and protected her- kept her from doing just that.

Kian had no idea how old he was- he claimed to have lived for centuries- but he grew increasingly frail in the twilight of his long life. Whenever she looked at those haggard features, Kian wondered if he had bought more years, more decades even than his body could reasonably bear, making use of whatever strange forces he called upon to prolong his dismal life. In her gloomier moments she would wonder why he persisted at all in the grey silence of a mostly-abandoned fortress. She had no idea whether he would last another month or another year. Perhaps, to a point, it was up to him.

His temper- weaker though it had been of late- worried her, but nowhere near as much as the *creatures* that she had noticed at the periphery of her vision, around the castle. Creatures that were there one minute and gone the next, shadows that flitted away before she could figure out what they were. Shimlock denied that they existed, and would say no more about them.

On very rare occasions she had caught a proper glimpse of one or two of them, and wished immediately that she hadn't. They took the form of odd, constantly shifting shapes that looked like long, voracious worms that glistened deep red and moved with a deadly grace and horrifying speed.

Kian took a deep breath and willed herself into the castle chamber and then down the long, lonely corridors in search of her stepfather. Once, Shimlock had told her, these passageways had been grand and opulent, and men and women other than himself had wandered their lengths. Kian had asked what became of them, but Shimlock could not remember, or perhaps chose not to. *The Mirk takes us all in the end,* he had said with bitterness. *Whatever we do and for however long we persist.*

*I'll challenge it to claim* me, Kian had sworn to herself on numerous occasions, in part to lend herself courage during those times when despair closed in along with the mist. She knew the obscure pathways in and out of the Mirk, routes that Shimlock had made her memorise over and over, as soon as she had been old enough to comprehend their importance. She could leave, and never return. Only the mad, shambling being that had raised her made her return again and again, perhaps out of conscience or duty, or guilt, or even morbid curiosity.

Despite the half-hidden creatures.

She found her stepfather in one of the lower bedchambers, a thin mass of bony flesh almost buried in a profusion of damp-smelling blankets. His eyes were open, but he seemed not to recognise her at first. "Kian," he said eventually. The word was spoken in a paper-dry whisper. She drew nearer, reluctantly. The odour of damp decay clung to him like a shroud. His eyes, deeply sunken into their sockets as if about to be reclaimed from within, turned languidly to focus on her as she stood at the foot of the bed.

"You brought the book... for me? And... the crystals?" It was almost as painful listening to him as it must have been for him to utter those words.

Kian swallowed down her rising panic. Even bedridden and unable to reach out to her, still he somehow had the capacity to terrify. "I couldn't," she said eventually. "I gained access to the tower easily enough, but some people arrived, so I had to escape." She paused and then, hoping that it might encourage some leniency on his part, she added, "If I'd let them capture me, I might never have returned."

Shimlock remained silent for so long that Kian began to wonder if he had fallen into a deep, blank reverie as he often did. His breathing, harsh, forced and irregular, slowed. Finally the dry lips parted, and he said quietly, "I was wrong to send you there."

Silence filled the dank bedchamber again, until Kian tentatively asked, "What... what shall I do now?"

"Do as you wish, child. It is over." Shimlock's words had about them an almost dreamlike quality. Kian wondered if he was, in a way, asleep and awake at the same time, and shivered. He often seemed that way- in both of two possible states, be they awake and dreaming... or alive and dead. She already wanted to be away from here, heading back through the Mirk's twisting paths and out into the sunlight.

Kian remembered being terrified almost out of her wits by the sunlight, the first time she had reached the outskirts of the Mirk as a child. Yet as time went on she grew to tolerate it, and now she even yearned for the sight of it occasionally, or at least for the pleasurable warmth it sometimes gave. There had been little of that warmth over the last few months, however.

The scant colour and life in Shimlock's countenance seemed to have drained from him. Guilt and panic in equal measure stirred within Kian. "I'm sorry," she said quietly, then added, though it had always seemed wrong to address him thus, "I'm sorry, Father."

He barely stirred. Eventually one arm raised itself and his hand waved her away in a weak and faint dismissal. Kian felt the heat of shame rise to her face. She turned away and left for her own chamber, as her stepfather stared fixedly upwards into the gloom.

Anger came to the fore as she reached her own sparse quarters. *I was wrong to send you there,* he had said. Might that have been some sort of tired apology? She couldn't remember him ever having apologised for anything before. More likely he had realised to himself that she would fail in her duty. He had been wrong to send her there because he should have known that she would fail to carry the task through properly. Never mind the fact that those people had turned up suddenly. *What were the chances of that happening?* Kian thought bitterly. *There was nothing*

251

*around there for leagues! Just hills and moorland that went on forever.*

Despite herself, Kian smiled as she thought about the changes in the weather on the way there. She had lain on her back looking up at the blue sky, the faintest warmth from the sun coming down. She had tasted the bitterness of the cold north wind. She had stared up at thousands of stars mapping out the night sky. And at some point soon, she would be back there again. Somewhere.

She took a book from the shelf to read. She had built up a small collection of books over the last few years, having found them in various studies or libraries around the castle and, through diligent care, rescued some of them from a mouldering demise. At first she had asked Shimlock for permission to read them and keep the more interesting books in her chambers, but when it became evident that he had no interest whatsoever in such things- in fact her stepfather had loathed books recently, despite having instructed her to steal one from the tower- she had simply taken one at will if its title and contents had piqued her curiosity.

Kian tried hard to immerse herself in her reading, but as the hours went on she found it increasingly hard to maintain her concentration. She was used to the deep silence of Mirkwall, comfortable with not hearing the sounds that filled the rest of the world with their bewildering clamour. Now though it felt different, and again and again she felt her thoughts drawn back to Shimlock's drawn, haggard visage, the frail form lying in bed as if...

*As if he was waiting for something,* she decided. *But not me.*

Over the last few years Shimlock had *done* less and less and become withdrawn, a man who had learned to accept whatever fate awaited him with barely a whisper in response. But tonight, he had appeared *more* than accepting. All his remaining strength had deserted him. It was as if his

252

life itself seeped slowly out into the dank room where he lay in the darkness.

Kian put her book down on a nearby chair with a sigh. She couldn't settle. Suddenly the need to go to him and make peace, and perhaps ask all the questions that had gathered in her mind down the years, rushed through her.

She went out into the corridor outside, welcomed by the silence and archway after mournful archway that stretched into the distance. She began to walk, and with each step it seemed to Kian that the quiet, fluttering panic inside her grew and grew. She walked faster and eventually broke into a run. A part of her screamed that whatever she was raced to prevent she was already too late, and the wheels of some hideous plan had been put in motion.

The stone slatted floor of the corridors was damp and Kian almost slipped a number of times as she hurtled on, barely slowing down at corners, heedless even to the areas that lay in deep shadow, their torches having flickered out.

The door to Shimlock's bedchamber stood open a little way. She could not remember whether if she had shut it on her way out. Kian's heart hammered as she pushed the door open further and peered into the room. The greasy oil-lantern burned low and cast languid yellow light and shadow upon the walls. It was on the verge of burning out entirely.

Kian willed herself a few yards into the room, and then realised that Shimlock had passed away.

She had no need to step further into the room to know this. She simply *knew*. Numbly she stared at him for what could have been an eternity and tried desperately to work out how she should feel. And worse even than that was her inability to decide what she ought to do.

Something moved on the mildew-spotted eiderdown. Kian swallowed and took a few trembling steps back, then stopped. This was not one of the creatures she feared and loathed.

It was *dust*.

Kian's eyes widened as she took in the sight of motes of dust that gathered and moved across the pillows, the blankets, to form something at the foot of the bed. "No," she whispered. She had seen bizarre miracles performed before on occasion, but those had been by Shimlock's hand. This could not be Shimlock's work, surely. Nothing remained of the man except the body.

The dust formed a scrap of parchment and upon that parchment Kian saw letters appear, in the simple common script. She tried to steady her nerves and approached a little nearer, although she didn't dare to peer too closely, just near enough to read the script.

*There is nothing here for you now. Leave and never return.*

As the fear subsided, a cold fury took its place. Kian clenched her fists and stared at Shimlock's lifeless form as tears blurred her eyes. *Why?* she almost shouted. *After all this time, is that all you can say to me? No answers? You simply send me out into the Mirk and beyond, and now you send me again one last time with nothing to tell me?*

Tentatively, her hands shaking, Kian reached out to pick up the piece of parchment, but it fragmented before she could even touch it. The pieces became smaller and smaller until nothing remained of the message except the dust from which it had been formed.

A sound from somewhere near the roof of the chamber caught her attention, and she peered up at the ceiling. As ever, it lay in gloom but she caught a glimpse of something- a slithering, red form that writhed along the surface of the cold rock. Kian could see the roof of this chamber more clearly as her eyes adjusted further to the gloom, and as she watched another red, almost serpentine form emerged from a hole in the ceiling, near the corner. She saw that a whole cluster of holes had been made in that part of the ceiling, and *something* moved behind each one.

She stepped fearfully back. Her legs trembled violently. *What's happening? Have they come for him? Have they been waiting all this time? Waiting for his power to wane? Is this what happened to all the others who lived here, so many decades ago?*

Two of the dark, reddish forms slipped from the cavities near the corner, and then a couple more. They clustered together, and at that moment the oil lamp at Shimlock's bedside table flared up, as if in one last act of defiance against the inevitability of darkness. The shadows melted back, and Kian stared in open-mouthed horror as she saw there were even more holes in the walls than she had thought. In places barely enough stone remained to hold the remaining structure together. The red monstrosities writhed as if in anticipation.

*Soon the flame will die out, and then they will feed.*

Kian turned and ran as fast as she could. She didn't stop until she had reached her chambers. Once there she crammed rations and books into one of her packs, then heaved it over her shoulder.

Even though her lungs screamed for more air, she ran as fast as she could towards the distant eastern edge of Mirkwall, where she had entered earlier as the day's gloom turned to darkness.

Complete darkness still reigned as she reached the easternmost tower, though she knew the skies would lighten soon. Kian took one last look back into Mirkwall, with nothing but fear and resentment in her heart.

*Tomorrow I will sleep under the stars*, she swore, and made her way down the stone steps into what had been lush gardens in past centuries. She stepped out over the watery grounds. She headed along the eastern path that would take her through and out of the Mirk, and into whatever lonesome future waited.

## II

The sun had set the following day and clouds gathered ominously in the south when Kian first became sure that something was following her.

Whenever she stopped and looked around, she saw nothing out of the ordinary, only the windswept low hills along which she had walked, covered here and there with patches of snow, clumps of heather and stunted bushes that bowed before the wind. *More snow or sleet will come soon,* she thought, and shivered as she wrapped her cloak about herself more tightly. The garment was woefully inadequate, but she had failed to consider such things in her haste to be gone from Mirkwall.

Kian wondered how easy it would be to find shelter tonight. A vast forest lay to the east- Knarlswood was its name, she remembered- but that was a place where she might easily become lost. Despite having read a little about it on occasion she still knew almost nothing about that woodland. Certainly she did not trust her outdoor skills enough to find safe shelter and hunt for game.

She walked wearily on for a little longer, until she heard, from perhaps a few hundred yards behind her, a faint screeching noise, and turned again, pulling her longknife free in a panic.

This time she saw the creature.

It looked like some kind of wildcat, although Kian had never seen one quite as big as this. The head seemed too large, the legs too long and thin, the stomach grossly distended. She wondered if it was starving, and the thought caused her to panic even more. It was lean and perhaps once muscular although now, even from this distance, it looked like skin stretched over bone, and the face leered almost painfully at her.

Kian continued onwards, and made sure to stop and look back frequently. Every time she looked, the wildcat had gained on her a little, although it did not appear to be moving any more quickly. *Is it just cautious?* she wondered. *Or can it not run?*

She disregarded the second possibility. It simply followed patiently and waited for her to tire. It would not dare attack her yet, but it would continue to follow her until she grew too tired or fell asleep.

Kian glanced around and considered her options. On every side except the south, rough moorland spread out, interspersed here and there with hills. She could run, but she could hardly move quickly through the thick grass and heather. There was little doubt that even a starving wildcat could catch her easily, and when it did she would be in no condition to put up a fight against a creature so desperate for a meal.

As she moved on, Kian decided that it sensed her desperation and had decided to act. One furtive glance back told her all that she needed to know; the creature had increased its pace and padded relentlessly towards her, a glint of hunger in its eyes.

When Kian turned to face it again a moment later, the creature was only a dozen yards or so away and about to spring at her. She yanked her longknife free. *If it springs at me, maybe I can cut the underbelly,* she thought swiftly. *Maybe it hasn't thought about the knife. Maybe it's careless with hunger. If it goes for me now...*

Kian had no time to scream or even think about struggling as she was pushed to one side and saw from the corner of her eye a loaded crossbow pointed directly at the beast's head.

She raised her head from the ground and turned just in time to see the bolt smash into the wild-cat's skull. Ragged pieces of gore fell on some of the rocks nearby. The creature bellowed in pain, then turned, staggered and fell to the ground as its legs gave way. It did not rise again, nor

257

even move. Kian stared at it for a while, barely daring to believe it had been stopped in its tracks.

The *du-luyan* man walked over to the corpse and plucked the bolt from its head, then calmly wiped it with a cloth and placed it back in his quiver. Then and only then did he turn his attention to Kian. He looked handsome in a cold, grim way, and moved with a lithe, unconscious grace.

"*Ko hyyr uyal dam or,*" he said with a faint smile, and then, when Kian merely gaped at him, he frowned and added, "*Ai yuul do mor! No kashen in du-luyan?*"

Kian shrugged warily. She could still not be entirely sure if she was out of danger. "I don't speak your language," she tried to explain, and then as she realised the oddness of her words, she qualified them with, "I don't speak the language of my own people." The heat of shame rose to her cheeks and she looked down at the ground. This was not the first time she had had to explain to a member of her own Race that she could not speak their language, but it never felt anything less than humiliating.

"How strange," he said in the common language, as he squatted down and peered at her. "You *do not* speak your own language? Why not?"

Kian shifted uncomfortably and rubbed at her shoulder where it had hit the ground. He had shoved her with unnecessary force, she thought. "I was not brought up by my own people."

He stared at her. "Again, why not?" He frowned suddenly, an angry look in his eyes. "Were you enslaved? By humans perhaps?"

She hesitated, and he seemed to take that as affirmation, for his expression grew grim. "They have so much blood to answer for."

Kian shook her head. "No. I have never been a slave. I lived in Mirkwall. Have you heard of it?"

He stared at her, entirely bewildered by the question, and then spoke. "The castle hidden by mists? Where Shimlock lives?"

"Yes," Kian said, but then a cold feeling swept through her. "I mean, no. He has passed away now. So..." She shrugged. "I couldn't stay there any longer."

"Of course." Finally he extended a hand in greeting. "I am Iyoth."

"My name is Kian," she said as they shook hands.

A while later, as the sky began to darken, snow drifted down again. Without a word, Iyoth got up, slung his pack over his shoulder, then strode down the slope towards the nearby forest. Kian swiftly scrambled to her feet, snatched up her pack and ran to catch up with him. Iyoth turned calmly to face her as she caught up. "You will need to learn to fight a little better if you're to survive."

Kian brushed hair away from her face. The wind had become stronger as well as colder. Where would she sleep tonight? Did Iyoth know of somewhere to shelter? "Thank you. I will try to bear that in mind." She willed herself to remain even-tempered. Brusque and rude he might be, but this man had probably saved her life.

Iyoth said nothing. He continued to walk down the slope towards the edge of the woodland, and after a moment Kian followed. As they followed an overgrown path into the depths of the forest, he set such a furious pace that even Kian had to occasionally run to keep up with him. "Where are we going?" she gasped at one point.

"*I* am going to a place I know of, to shelter from the storm and keep warm," he retorted. "*You* can do as you will." He did not even turn around, nor did he cease his relentless pace.

Little snowfall reached down here under the thick canopy of evergreen, but a few flakes still drifted down from far above. Kian could hear the wind howl as it shook the tops of the trees and even snapped some of the lesser branches.

259

She shuddered, colder than ever. This was not the season to be out in the wilderness. In previous winters she had often spent months on end cooped up in Mirkwall, reading or exploring. There had always been new books to read and new areas with which to familiarise herself.

Yet she had been given no choice but to flee. Mirkwall and whatever dwelt there now had forced her hand. Kian wondered briefly how long that *presence* in Mirkwall had been present, moving inexorably inward while Shimlock declined, as if his powers had been the only thing that held it back.

Much to her relief, Iyoth eventually slowed his pace, but he kept a longknife in his hands and occasionally used it to cut through errant bramble or thorn, the motion nothing more than a silvery flash in the gloom. He said nothing.

The two *du-luyan* pressed on through the swiftly darkening afternoon. The shallow brooks they crossed had frozen solid almost all the way through, and ice crunched like glass under their boots as they carefully negotiated each one in turn. Some especially overgrown areas- particularly the deeper ravines through which frozen rivers cut a path- seemed darker than they ought, or so Kian believed.

On an impulse she tried to decide whether or not Iyoth could be trusted. She had no idea what to make of him. She had tagged along simply because she had no idea what else to do, and in the hope that he would allow her to share his shelter, wherever that turned out to be. That fact alone made her feel wretched and helpless.

*But I'm alive,* she reminded herself. *I'm still alive.*

Dusk had almost melted into absolute darkness when they arrived at a cliff of crumbling granite, dotted here and there with weatherworn trees and shrubs that clung grimly to its jagged surface. A damp-looking cave loomed at the base of the cliff, and Iyoth made his way inside.

"Well?" he said, and turned around as Kian stopped doubtfully at the entrance and wrinkled her nose at the dank smell. With a sigh she made her way in and managed to find a relatively dry spot on the stone floor. Immediately she was struck by how warm the place was, and said as much. Iyoth smirked at that. "Of course it is! The last remnants of the witchery that once threaded through this place are still good for something."

"Witchery?" Kian exclaimed, and almost scrambled to her feet in alarm. "Is it safe to be here?"

"It's as safe as anywhere else. I have slept here several times before, when I happened to travel through Knarlswood, and each morning I woke with my mind and body intact. What more can one ask for?"

"A little comfort," Kian said ruefully, and Iyoth scoffed at that. "Comfort? Life in Mirkwall has softened you."

Kian shivered despite the warmth of the cave. "I never thought life was soft in Mirkwall. Often it frightened me."

"Why?" Iyoth's voice was sharp. "Because of Shimlock?"

"No, although he scared me enough sometimes. No, it was..." Kian sighed. "It was Mirkwall itself. I always thought it had a meaning of its own that was nothing to do with me. The history of the place, the things that had happened there many centuries ago. And there were... there were *other* beings there. Shimlock was all that stood between them and Mirkwall itself."

She told him of her last visit to Shimlock's bedside, and what she had witnessed in that chamber. Iyoth maintained his stony silence throughout and sharpened his knife on a whetstone as if he expected to have to use it at any moment. Finally, after Kian had spoken of her fleeing Mirkwall, he said quietly, "There are older and stronger forces than those of the younger Races. No matter how resilient Mirkwall may once have been or how great the people who built and occupied it so many centuries ago, the

261

tide will always come back in eventually, to coin a seafarer's phrase."

Kian knew of each Race only what she had learned from reading books in Mirkwall's mouldering libraries, and none of those tomes had told her anything about older and stronger forces. Perhaps she had simply not read enough from the right books.

Iyoth put his knife away- much to Kian's relief- and collected some wood for the fire. When Kian pointed out afterwards that the wood he had collected was damp, he gave her a derisory look and scattered some black powder from a pouch onto the twigs he had gathered together in the small hearth in the side wall of the cave. The first spark he created from his tinderbox lit the entire bunch of twigs in a moment and flung back the shadows in the cave. Instantly the place felt a lot warmer.

Kian noticed that the fire was almost completely smokeless. "How did you do that?" she asked suspiciously.

"You've lived in the shadow of a great sorceror," Iyoth said dismissively. "You shouldn't need to ask such questions."

Kian said nothing. A long while passed before Iyoth spoke again, his voice now more thoughtful, almost detached. "Throughout the centuries, the races that seek to shape things have grown further and further apart. But in the beginning, this is how they were. They hid in caves and used fire to defend themselves against the dark and hidden forces of the world. Aona is a place of terrible secrets, Kian, and as the Ages come and go the balance between the order created by the sorcerers, witches and warlocks and so on, and the chaos of the true Old Powers, rampant and unbridled, ebbs and flows as if it was itself a live creature. In a sense, I suppose it is."

"Is that what happened in Mirkwall?" Kian asked.

"Not just there. Something far greater has happened." He shuddered, suddenly uncomfortable. "I have seen it myself. I wasn't sure at the time, but..."

Iyoth suddenly whipped both longknives from his belt and stood. He stared out beyond the fire and into the misty, impenetrable darkness. "Show yourself," he said calmly.

Kian had neither seen nor heard anything, but a figure stepped slowly into view, hands raised. Kian was surprised to see a human woman of middle age with lank, grey hair. At her side a wolf stood silently, eyes like dark pools that reflected the firelight. Kian recalled her encounter earlier and shrank back towards the fire, her heart pounding. She just about resisted the temptation to snatch up a branch-end from outside the flames' reach.

"I have no quarrel with you, *du-luyan*," the woman said calmly. Iyoth looked her up and down, gave the wolf a cursory glance and said, "What about your friend?"

"He'll not harm you. Why would he?" The woman stared at him for a while and then continued, "I would not spend any longer here than you have to."

"Why should we not?" Iyoth demanded, but both woman and wolf turned and melted back into the damp darkness. Iyoth stood where he was for a moment and frowned as if unable to decide whether or not to follow and challenge them. Then he made his way back into the cave and sat down, silent and thoughtful.

Not knowing what else to say, Kian asked him if he knew who the woman was, but he ignored the question and stared out into the night as if it was a live thing that could reach in and tear them limb from limb. Eventually Kian succumbed to her exhaustion and fell into a fitful slumber.

Iyoth stared for a long time into the darkness, before finally he retreated to the fire and placed his longknives crosswise against each other in the ancient sign of warding and luck.

263

He stared for a long while at Kian as she lay curled up near the fire, as the light from the flames danced and rippled across her body.

*So he looked after her and she became his eyes and ears to the world,* he thought. *And now she must face the world with nowhere to go back to- no safe haven. A world where the powers and enlightenment of the Races- for all their quarrels and wars with one another- has held sway for many centuries, but which now ebbs away in a return to the lightless ancient ways.*

*What a time to find your way in life.*

*I should leave,* he tried to tell himself. *I can do no good here, and it's hardly my place to do good anywhere.*

Yet he remained exactly where he sat for the rest of the night, by the glowing embers of the fire, watching over his daughter's sleeping form.

# X – The Gate

## I

With the wind sending snow again from the north, Vornen drew Stepthorn gently to a halt. The stallion whickered softly, ears pricked, and his eyes darted warily about the place, as his rider dismounted. Vornen patted him gently, knowing something of what he must have sensed.

"Well," he said softly, as he wiped wet snow from his hair and looked towards the town, "It's *worse*."

Ethanalin Tur-morn was as bleak and as forbidding as the snow-swept hills and rolling plains that lay beyond it. The huts, taverns and storehouses that made up this sorry muddle of a town showed plainly how the place had been created in the first place, as a hastily-constructed settlement whose existence owed everything to the once-rich silver mines. Almost every building was coloured a drab grey or black, and the tracks that ran between them were packed with mud and slush. A few of Ethanalin Tur-morn's citizens walked slowly through the muck, wrapped up in several layers of cloaks and shawls so that little of them could actually be seen.

"Welcome!" someone called across to him, and Vornen already had his hand on the pommel of his sword before he turned to look at the newcomer, a man perhaps a little older than him, dressed in a thick robe over tough travelling clothes. *Not a Tur-mornian, for certain,* he thought as he glanced at the man's pack and well-worn boots, and relaxed a little. The newcomer smiled as he walked slowly over through the slush. "Heading into town?" he inquired.

"I am," Vornen said, and shivered. The persistent stench of waste from the barely-functioning gutters wafted up in the chill breeze. He looked across to the other side of the town, towards the east where the clouds massed almost black with the promise of thunder. Ailach Tor, known more commonly as Tur-morn Hill, loomed over the settlement. Vornen could see a small number of townspeople dotted about on the slope, and in an instant he knew why. Soon, more would go there, drawn inexorably by the Gate. He had known that that would happen as soon as he became aware of how powerful this one would become. Here, its influence would touch everyone.

*What thoughts go through their minds as they wait?* he wondered suddenly. *Are they any more able to escape than I am? But from what I've already seen and heard, on the way here, they probably have no thoughts of escape. Instead their minds will be filled with some sort of crazed salvation.*

He jumped suddenly when he realised that his new companion had moved to stand uncomfortably close to him. "The dream has brought so many here," the man said conversationally. "The taverns are full to bursting, so many of the storehouse owners have found space for the pilgrims in their buildings. I doubt I shall find somewhere comfortable to sleep." He looked almost happy at the prospect.

"I wouldn't worry about sleep," Vornen said, and the traveller reached out to touch his arm. "*Nobody* need worry," he agreed, smiling.

The smile remained fixed even as Vornen firmly removed himself from the man's grasp. "I met some other pilgrims on the way here," he continued, falling in alongside as Vornen began to make his way down towards the town's main arterial road. "My name is Artur," he added, and offered his hand in greeting. Vornen reluctantly shook hands with him and listened with growing disquiet to Artur's heedless rambling. "Good men they were, good men and women. Well blessed also- do you know why?"

"I don't," Vornen admitted, "but I expect you'll tell me."

"Three of them dreamed of the Great Light without sleeping! Can you imagine that?"

266

*Dreams without sleeping,* Vornen thought, and shivered as he recalled some of the men, women and children he had seen in other, smaller settlements on the way here. A few of them had spoken of the Great Light, or the New Light, or the Age of the Light. *They were the same as those who had grown sick and senseless to the world,* he thought suddenly. *The same cause, surely, but the symptoms vary so much. But what is that cause? Could the imminence of the Gate have done all that?*

He shook his head, bewildered.

"I cannot either," Artur confessed, mistaking his response. "But if I can sleep tonight and be strong for tomorrow..." He grinned. "We live in astonishing times. How appropriate that this deprived and neglected settlement should bear first witness to a new dawn!"

The little road they followed grew steep as it twisted downwards towards the heart of the town. It deteriorated to little more than a rough path in places, where the surface of the road had been worn away and slabs of rock sank into the surrounding muck. Lopsided gravestones and bone markers dotted the hill in places, the newer pits and mounds crammed in at the edges. It did not surprise Vornen at all that Ethanalin Tur-morn's dead had outgrown their town.

*Soon now,* he thought suddenly, and his gaze moved helplessly to the flat summit of the hill. He felt a lurching pain and a strange pull, as if some force tried to pull his skin from his body. He looked away with an effort, and the sensation lessened, though it did not cease completely. It never would, now.

*It will pull me in this time,* he thought. *When it appears, it will pull me in and that will be the end of that. It's about time.*

Halfway down the hill, he spotted a stable that still appeared to be working and occupied. "I must feed my horse," he explained with a polite smile.

Artur nodded and gave a cheery wave as he continued towards the middle of the town.

Vornen was reluctant to part company with Stepthorn. The stable was a filth-ridden place and the stable hand a sullen, suspicious-looking man who looked as if he had as much empathy with horses as he probably did with people. "Look after him well and I shall pay you extra," Vornen encouraged him.

"When?" came the immediate response, both wary and interested.

"When I leave," Vornen said, and smiled to himself a moment later as he remembered that he would not be leaving this place. *If a small Gate can almost kill me, in the face of a much larger one I will crumble to ash,* he thought, *as will all these others who are drawn to its potential. Gods, who could imagine such a thing, which doesn't yet exist and still can bend the wills of men and women, infiltrate their dreams?*

A tavern whose sign had disappeared or been stolen stood nearby, in a state of considerable disrepair. What little paint remained had peeled swiftly away, no glass remained in the windows and the door had been struck with what may well have been a large hammer, judging by the large, gaping hole that adorned the centre of it. The door itself leaned slightly open, and the smell of stale, spilt ale, mingled with far worse odours, drifted from the dank interior.

As Vornen stood and stared absently at the place, the door creaked open further, and a small, skinny little man, naked from the waist down despite the intense cold, emerged, a *kyush*-pipe held in one badly shaking hand. His skin was scarred in more places than Vornen had thought possible, with two large gashes forming an X upon his chest.

"You look for somewhere to stay?" the man asked, and puffed greedily on the pipe. Pungent *kyush* fumes drifted through the air.

"Possibly," Vornen said. "But not here." With a vague smile he politely bade the half-naked man good-day and hastened away from the place. He headed down the slope at a good pace and only stopped when he found a rest-house that looked a little safer and whose owners had clothed themselves appropriately.

The place was almost empty. Presumably many of those who might otherwise be here had already departed for the hill. Vornen bought a tankard of watered wine and sat wearily to one side of the tap-room. Silently he watched as the snow started to fall again and his view of Tur-morn Hill disappeared in a white and grey haze.

He had enough coins left to pay for a room, and after a second tankard of wine to warm him a little more, he trudged upstairs. Days of riding had made him sore and desperately tired. His stomach was empty and tight as a clenched fist, but he had no desire to eat. Somehow he had gone beyond hunger. In any case, eating felt pointless now.

It took him a while to open the door, his hand clumsy as it struggled with the key. Finally he found his way in and searched carefully around for a lantern. There would be one on the small table near to the door, so the bartender had said.

Something pounced on him, hands pressed against his neck and a moment later a boot kicked him viciously in the groin. One blow sent him flying back into the wall, and the next kick to his groin almost made him pass out with the pain.

He crashed to the floor and his senses grew swiftly fainter. Then, suddenly, the grip on his throat eased and his attacker moved away, almost soundlessly.

Gasping for breath, Vornen raised his head briefly, but he saw nothing more than a vague shape that moved towards the table on the other side of the room.

Instinctively his hand reached for his sword, until he remembered that he had removed it, and like a fool had left

269

it by the door. The figure lit the lantern on the table, and as light flared up suddenly around the room and long shadows across the walls, he saw his assailant for the first time.

Instantly he forgot all about his sword and everything else in the world, even the Gate.

Suli smiled as he stared open-mouthed at her.

She looked much the same as when he had last seen her, Vornen thought at first. Her hair was perhaps a little shorter, and maybe she was somewhat thinner, her cheekbones more pronounced, and there were wrinkles around her eyes and mouth. But otherwise...

*No,* Vornen realised suddenly. *She is not the same at all.*

The smile on Suli's face was nothing less than venomous. Her eyes shone with an unhealthy light. Her skin was pale, more so than he remembered, and yet a frantic, mad heat infected it- so much so that he could detect it even from where he lay.

Vornen's heart sank. She had changed, and he recognised the change.

"The fever," he murmured. "The *light.*"

Suli gazed at him for an age, that dark hunger in her eyes the whole while.

Vornen swallowed hard. He could taste blood in his throat. Her nails had made shallow gouges on his neck. "I never expected to see you again," he managed to say eventually.

"No. And yet here we are. Such a strange world this is." Suli leaned against the wall, a lithe shadow amongst shadows. "Perhaps I should have killed you after all, Vornen."

He moved to sit at the edge of the bed. For a long while he found himself without any idea what to say to her. How long had it been? It felt like a lifetime, even someone else's lifetime. *We were both different then,* he reflected. *When we were young, before the world ruined us.*

270

"You've changed, Suli," he said eventually, and then as an afterthought he continued, "Why didn't you kill me?"

"What would be the point?" A trace of a smile played upon her lips. "You've come here to die in any case."

Vornen said nothing, but eventually he nodded. "I suppose I have."

"Have hope, Vornen. Perhaps the *marandaal* will spare us."

*That word,* he thought suddenly, all else forgotten in that instant.

A moment later he understood how he knew it, and instantly after *that,* Vornen recalled what he had seen and heard an age ago, before he lay broken and freezing on a hillside. He stared straight ahead at the wall, everything but that memory forgotten.

*I heard them. I stared into the Gate, into the heart of a storm of stars, and heard them coming. Their voices crawled through my head. I knew they would come to Aona. I knew they had spent eons searching for a way back. I even felt their thoughts, if they think. The words...*

"A special place," he whispered. "The heart of the Existence. The heart of the Existence." He repeated it again three more times, until he became aware of Suli once again. He stared at her. "How do *you* know? How can you know about them?"

Suli only grinned at that, a savage expression that told Vornen all he needed to know. Dull realisation settled like lead into him. *Strange how I should find her after all this time, only to find that she's now little more than any of the rabid townspeople who gather on the hill. Except that she must have caught a glimpse as I did, and learned the name from within the Void. But now she dreams...*

He glimpsed again the crazed sparkle in her eyes. *She dreams without sleeping. But she knows their true name. Everyone else calls them the Great Light, or something akin to those words.*

271

"Ah well," he murmured. "The sooner the better."

She wandered over and sat next to him, then traced a long-nailed finger down his cheek. Vornen flinched, expecting her to draw blood, but she did not. Yet her touch was like fire.

Suli looked him up and down with cold amusement. "I am not sure what to do with you now, Vornen."

"I could say the very same thing." He asked her, "What did you do after you left Ruan-Tor, all those years ago?"

"I travelled some of the time, or I stayed in some place or other and found employment if I could. I put Ruan-Tor behind me. I thought about you a few times, but then I forgot you utterly, even as I was pulled along the lines and made to witness those little flashes of broken sky. Each time, they took a part of me." She grimaced. "Not much left now. Even less, soon."

"You forgot me utterly? I doubt you, Suli."

"Don't flatter yourself!" Icy rage filled her voice. "True enough, then- I thought about you many times over the years. But there was no going back. I couldn't bear it any longer."

"Perhaps now you know how I felt," Vornen retorted, and she slapped him hard on the cheek. "Do not judge me! I am here now because this is where I'm *meant* to be- and yes, also because I can't resist the fever for much longer. The dream is *killing* me, Vornen, piece by piece. I can't even *remember* three of the five days I have supposedly been here."

"Are you afraid?" he asked her softly.

"I'm not afraid of death, especially as there's so little time left to be afraid of it. No, it's *life* I'm afraid of. Of losing my mind before I die."

"Did you truly think about killing me just now?"

Suli frowned in puzzlement, and Vornen realised with shock that she had no recollection of what she had done

272

mere moments ago. Slowly he raised his neck a little and pointed out the gouge marks on his neck. Suli studied them briefly, her expression growing more and more bewildered. Suddenly she stood, and strode to the door.

"Wait!" Vornen cried, but she opened the door and ran down the stairs, almost tripping in her haste.

He sat and stared at nothing for a long while. *Poor Suli. How long has she been like this? It would have been bad enough with Gates alone, but now...*

A wild idea occurred to Vornen. What if he attempted to leave Ethanalin Tur-morn and took Suli with him- if he could track her down, for she had probably fled the resthouse by now- to some other place where perhaps a healer could tend to her. But he knew it was too late for that, and there were no healers who could do anything about this madness in any case.

They had become locked into this place like lodestones, held in position like flies in amber. No way out of Ethanalin Tur-morn existed for them. Not until the Void opened to herald an age of destruction.

II

Three grey-robed men- all of them priests of some kind judging by the odd medallions around their necks- stood and talked in the otherwise deserted town square, oblivious to the bitterly cold wind that lashed at them from the east. Occasionally the wind would catch the bottom of one of their robes and lift it up enough for Amethyst to see, even from her distant vantage point at the window of the tavern, that they were wore nothing underneath. Quite how they had stood and talked for as long they had in such conditions was beyond her, as was their reason for stumbling through deepest winter in such a state.

That said, it was not the maddest thing she had seen here, in this town that could have been fashioned from a

273

nightmare. *I wonder if everyone in the world has lost their mind,* she thought moodily to herself, and somehow that notion was the only one that didn't seem insane.

Since her arrival in Ethanalin Tur-morn she had realised that almost everyone here was what Craddan and his bloodthirsty plainsfolk would have called a *lightdreamer.* Likely, this would have been the place where Fenmor would have taken his people had they survived. They would have come here to await the Great Light of the East, or whatever he called it.

Amethyst idly traced a fingernail through a gouge in the table where she sat and tried to figure out how it could be that the tribes of the Plains dreamed of the Earth Lords, yet the people in places as diverse as this filthy, rotting town and the castle where she had taken such a wrong turn, spoke and dreamed of nothing but the Light, the enemy of the Earth Lords and their followers.

She had eventually concluded bleakly that no reason could be found in either their behaviour or in her interpretation of it. *This is madness,* she had thought to herself, over and again. *It's madness without an end, or they will butcher one another until they make an end of themselves.*

That had led to an even more terrible thought- that whatever insanity had swept the north and set folk against one another, would or already had spread into the middle lands, and even further south all the way to Darkenhelm.

*I wanted to see my family again,* she thought, as tears of frustration and sudden panic brimmed in her eyes. *I wanted to go back before it's too late. What can I do, if I somehow return there to find Mother and Father, and Lona, all entrapped by this same madness?*

Amethyst recalled Elluron's words before they had parted company. *He seemed sane enough,* she recalled, *but then he also thought these opposing powers were real.* She had decided, in the days that followed, that perhaps they had

274

been real once- maybe they still were- but she had never believed that Gods touched and manipulated the lives of mortals in such a way, and she could not bring herself to believe such a thing now.

Outside in the square, one of the priests had produced a heavy-looking symbol on a gold chain- Amethyst could not make out the precise shape of it- and now, with a gesture of great ceremony, he placed it around the neck of one of his companions. *What is he doing?* she wondered. *Making him a priest? A priest of what, exactly? Did his dreams instruct him to ordain his fellow-man?*

The three of them walked off down the street towards the town's eastern end, holding hands. *How sweet,* Amethyst thought dryly, although even that sentiment failed to cheer her one iota. The childlike gesture held a sinister quality. *May your Great Light shine upon you,* she thought, and hoped that they might slip on the slushy ice underfoot.

Snow began to drift down from the uniformly grey sky, nothing but a light flurry that swirled haphazardly in the wind. Amethyst wondered how the townsfolk would survive the winter. *It wouldn't surprise me,* she decided, *if the people of this town set fire to all their food stocks and danced a merry jig around the flames. It would almost be expected behaviour from people who babble nonsense about the coming of the Saviours, and dream of unseen Gods.*

But despite all that, she could not shake off the nagging certainty that *something* might be about to happen. Amethyst considered that she would almost rather be somewhere out in the wilderness than Ethanalin Tur-morn, but to travel anywhere now would be suicidal.

*And I can go no further east anyway,* she reminded herself. After arriving here, she had taken a cursory look around the place and decided to continue...

*Then it changed,* she recalled. *Suddenly it no longer compelled me to go eastwards. The further I went in that direction, the more the pain flared up again.*

She had walked south, north and west also, a short distance out of the town each time, only for the same thing to happen. Finally, she had walked back into Ethanalin Turmorn, her mind racing as she tried to work out what this sudden change might mean.

*Either the girl that witch-woman seeks is right here in this town,* she had decided, *or I'm simply trapped here by something else. Or more likely, both.*

But finding her would surely be impossible in this sprawling chaos of a settlement, whose streets and tracks bore no visible names, whose people gradually migrated to the great hill in the east.

The light began to fail. Every now and then townsfolk would wander across the square or down the nearby streets. Some were silent, others suddenly ranted at someone or something she could not see. Some were clothed and others, incredibly, stumbled naked through the gathering darkness. Occasionally they would stop, stare up into the low sky and smile.

Amethyst watched these scenes with morbid fascination for a while, until eventually she could bear it no longer and turned away, thankful for her sanity. Perhaps it was all she had left.

"It will be tomorrow," someone nearby spoke up, causing her to jump almost out of her skin. "Everyone says tomorrow is to be the day."

She turned to see a thin, middle-aged man sitting at the table next to hers. He smirked at her as she glanced in his direction, then continued stuffing a dirty bone pipe with *kyush* weed.

"Tomorrow. Yes, I expect it will be," she agreed cautiously, and politely excused herself. He merely smiled at her, yellowish eyes hungry and as dirty as his shaking hands.

Amethyst glanced back as she reached the foot of the stairs, to see him still staring at her.

**Pause, relax awhile.**

Just take a moment to take in the
beauty of this world, the gifts already
in your life.

# How overthinking causes stress and miserableness

## Unhelpful thinking

How am I going to cope?
What will I do if that happens?
Who's going to look after me?
What's everyone going to think of me?
How will I manage if..........?
That's really going to stress me out!
I'll never manage that!

## Helpful thinking

What do I need to do now?
What's the next step I need to take?

**Stress doesn't mean anything about you.**

There's nothing wrong with you.

You don't need fixing, you're not damaged and you're not broken.

All you're suffering from is a trick of the mind and once you see what's really going on, you'll relax into living differently.

Taken from Ditch Your Midlife Stress From the Inside Out: Dawn Robinson.

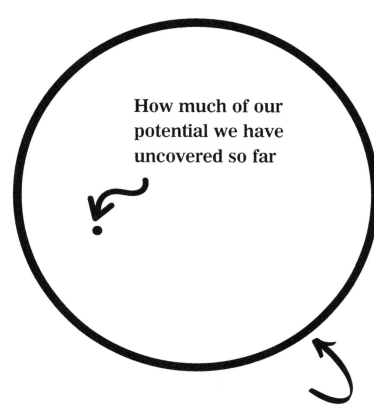

How much of our potential we have uncovered so far

How much more there is for us to discover about our talents and abilities

This might sound strange but the idea of being locked up Rapunzel-like in a tall tower with a load of books frequently looks incredibly attractive to me.

## Acknowledgements.

A huge thank-you to all my peers and colleagues who have guided and supported me over the last few years (whether you've known it or not).

James Abbott, Lexie Bebbington, Charlie Crossman, Vicki Montague, Tracey McBeath and Tracey Swainson.

**And as the final credits roll and we come to the end of Hot Flourishes, its time for the final advert.**

 Are you a midlife, menopausal woman who seems to have misplaced her joy in living in the frantic busyness of life?

**Struggling to calm down and enjoy the moment? Looking for a way of helping your body and your mind gently slow down and regain that feeling of inner serenity?**

What you need is **The Hot Flourishes Relaxation** - a gently calming audio journey to soothe your body and mind.

The Hot Flourishes Relaxation the marvelously delectable, **FREE** guided meditation can be yours now.

Just scan the square thingy below or visit www.theflourishingmidlife.com/hotflourishes

## A final request.

If you've found this book

- moderately supportive, inspirational or comforting
- loved it
- best book ever,

I'd be really grateful if you could leave me a review on Amazon to prevent it from being squashed, unloved and forgotten amongst all the other titles there.

Huge thanks
Dawn x

## About the author

 Dawn Robinson is an author, a coach and she runs online courses for midlife women.

She spent over one and a half decades working in organisations in HR and as a management trainer and then a number of years as an Alexander Technique teacher helping people use their bodies with more ease and less strain.

She lives in the UK with her husband and daughter and when she's not working she is often roaming the countryside armed with a map and a slab of cake.

For more details of current programmes and books, please visit

**www.theflourishingmidlife.com**

## III

As the sun struggled over the distant eastern mountains the following morning, an opaque smear against the light, high cloud that now covered the sky, Vornen came to a church.

By now the town had become all but deserted. Those who had not yet set up camps on Ailach Tor had made their way to the great hill with the first hint of daylight. Vornen wondered briefly if Suli might be amongst the many hundreds, perhaps thousands camped out on the slope, waiting. *I would like to see her again, one last time,* he thought suddenly. *Perhaps the haze of madness will lift, just for an instant. I just want to hold her, see recognition in her eyes, one last smile, a kiss, anything.*

But he knew it to be an idle, wistful thought, and with a heavy heart Vornen put it to one side. He looked at the symbol etched into the wide iron-studded doors that led into the church and tried to think where he had seen it before. It did not belong to any faith he knew, but Aphenhast was infested with a great many belief systems, some of which only scholars of religion would ever have known about. *Perhaps it's from the lightdream,* he thought, and looked swiftly away.

Just as he moved to pass by the church, a cry of abject pain and misery came from within. Vornen stopped and frowned. It struck him as odd that anyone should have been overlooked during this exodus from the town. Even the bedridden and those rendered incapable by illness had been borne along with the fervent crowds, as if to be cleansed and cured.

After a moment he made his way up the path to the door, and quietly pushed his way into the church.

The place had been lit by candles and lanterns, and there were some on the floor also, hacked to pieces and shattered. The pews had also been attacked, possibly with a sword or other sharp-bladed weapon judging by the deep gouges made. Some had been hacked into splinters.

At the altar, lying sprawled across the marble dais was Larien.

Vornen took a deep breath and approached, his footsteps echoing softly.

Larien's body twitched and writhed as if buffeted by some unfelt wind. His mouth opened and a trickle of blood dripped from it on both sides. His stomach gaped open and its contents glistened faintly in the dim light.

The black sword lay at his side. Vornen flinched as he saw it and kicked it away, though he was certain now that Larien would never be able to wield it again. Silently he knelt by the young man.

"...*not the strength*," Larien whispered. His voice sounded thick with blood.

Vornen surveyed the clumsy disembowelment that had taken place. Larien's innards did not smell of freshly presented flesh. They exuded a grim, pungent odour that had no place in a man who still lived, if only barely. "I think perhaps you were doomed, my friend," he said softly, "even if your blade had not turned on you."

Larien said nothing. *This is the end to all things now,* Vornen thought, and felt oddly calm. *The day grows dim. May rest come to me soon. It will come sooner to Larien.* Aloud he continued, "Where did you find that sword? How did you come by it?"

Larien merely smiled faintly, and Vornen looked again to the sword that lay upon the cold marble floor. "When you found or were given this thing, what were you told to do with it? Were you to roam the land, killing and mutilating?"

"No." Larien's voice grew ever fainter. "To... kill... the *marandaal*..."

Vornen shook his head. He could make no sense of this. Someone had given Larien this sword and sent him

278

here to defeat the *marandaal* as they emerged from the Gate? What kind of desperation was that?

He thought about bringing a healer, if one could be found who had not already hurried to his or her oblivion on the slopes of Ailach Tor, but another quick survey of Larien's ruined body convinced him that his time was up. "Do you remember when we met before?" he asked. "Out near the Great Old Road to the north? I was headed for Ruan-Tor. We walked together, for a while."

"No," Larien whispered. "I... don't know... who you..."

"As I thought," Vornen murmured. When he glanced at Larien a moment later, the young man's eyes were unseeing and glassy. His body became still.

Vornen sighed, and got to his feet. He wondered who Larien had been before he became the unfortunate bearer of that sword. Perhaps he had friends and family somewhere. Vornen remembered him saying he was from Ethanalin Turmorn, but perhaps in his confusion the boy had simply told him where he was headed.

Vornen did not remember picking the sword up and replacing his own with it, nor did he even realise that he had the weapon in his possession until he left the old church and made his way back to the now-abandoned tavern. When he looked down and found it at his side, he was alarmed for a moment at this subtle thread of sorcery being woven around him, but not as much he would normally have been.

After all, like everyone else in this town of death and depravity, he was doomed, and there would be little time for the sword to work its insidious power upon him before the Gate opened and tore everything asunder.

The clouds had blackened still further. The air felt curiously warm, and prickly sweat dotted his forehead and gathered under his eyes. In the distance, beyond the mountain peaks in the east, lightning played. No thunder could be heard. But the centre of the storm swiftly approached, to circle around Ailach Tor.

Vornen had seen on other occasions the phenomena played out across the skies whenever a Gate manifested itself. It ripped through the mesh of natural forces that held the elements together. *Like a stone when it plunges into a lake,* Suli had once said. Except that the ripples created in the natural forces were never exact and smooth, and their effects often unpredictable.

*This time they might very well tear the sky apart,* Vornen thought briefly. *Is the earth itself furious at the opening of this door? Or is it simply the forces around the Gate that cause the storm? I suppose it's too late to study such things now.*

He shivered and absently rubbed at his arms and shoulders, which had started to itch. He felt as if there were grubs that burrowed under his skin. He was being twisted and turned, and made to face the monolithic horror that stood on the summit of Ailach Tor.

"I tried to leave," Suli said from behind him.

He turned swiftly, bewildered to find that the sword was out of its scabbard and in his hands before he had even drawn breath. With an effort, he slid it back and removed his shaking hand from the hilt. It felt blistered, but nowhere could any marks be seen to indicate any damage.

Suli's eyes seemed lost, unable to focus. Her gaze took in everything and nothing and wandered without purpose until eventually she looked at him. "I feel like my insides have burned up, Vornen. As if there's nothing but blackness and char inside me. *I tried to leave.*"

She walked up to him and reached out her hand. It felt hot and fevered. "You would have tried too if you had any desire to live," she whispered. "I suddenly wanted to survive. I thought I might have had a chance if I was strong enough. But it tore at me. It pulled me here."

Vornen smiled faintly. "It's good to see you again, Suli. I had hoped to be with you today."

She smiled bitterly. "A little too late for everything now. I've hated you for as many years as I loved you. Perhaps more. The past feels like a bridge forever being eaten away behind me. I no longer know how I feel about anything, Vornen, which is just as well, because neither of us has very much time left."

Vornen could think of nothing to say. A storm to end all storms gathered its fury around the summit and forced him to watch. It pulled at every fibre of his being. He shrugged wearily. "I am going to the bottom of the hill," he said finally. "Will you come with me?"

Suli nodded. As they made their way along the track that wound out of the town and down to the snowdrifts at the base of Ailach Tor, she spoke up. "Where did you get that sword with which you nearly slew me, Vornen?"

"Oh, this?" He tried to force a casual tone into his voice. "From a dying man. I think the blade is cursed, somehow. But as you said, it's a little late now for all things-curses included."

"Cursed is right. Your hand is becoming the same colour as the blade."

Vornen raised his right hand. It looked as if it had been beaten for hours until every bit of flesh lay ruined over his bones, battered and bruised beyond repair. For a moment he thought of Larien, dying a lonely and painful death on the cold tiles of the church, his body and mind having given up at last. The sorcery woven around the sword had feasted well on his misery.

"Not long either way," he murmured, and for a moment felt a flash of anger, at nothing more tangible than fate, and ill luck, and the sheer humiliation of being nothing more in life than a lodestone and a spectator, at the last. *Is this it?* he wondered, knowing that it was. *All these years of nightmares, addiction, banishment and betrayal, hatred and*

281

*worthlessness, all to be brought here, to witness the coming of the* marandaal?

They reached Ailach Tor, where dozens of townspeople still made the arduous climb. Many of them slipped and floundered in the snow and the mud. Lightning tore through the sky and struck the great stone at the summit. Light and dark swirled and crackled around each other and then the grey gloom returned, darker than ever now.

Wherever they looked, Vornen and Suli saw only lunacy. The low and mindless chants, the occasional cries of exultation, and the shouts of joy, were suffused with an underlying malignance, a light that shone in the eyes of everyone. Men, women, children, the young and the old, all had about them a feverish excitement, as if the storm had whipped them up into frenzy.

*The lightdream,* Vornen reminded himself. *If ever something could signify the end of the world itself, surely that must be it- a mind-burning madness that transcends possibility itself, that reaches out and touches the minds and bodies of all these people, even from somewhere across the Existence. It's impossible, but I see it and I know it to be true.*

Vornen felt the ground suddenly sway beneath his feet, and his legs gave way. His head felt as if it had caught fire inside. Suli tried to pull him to his feet. He looked up and saw that her eyes were red with blood. *Not light,* he thought. *Not light but blood.*

"We will be cremated here on this hill," he said hoarsely. Now his entire body felt as if it was burning up.

Suli knelt by him and stared at his side. "The sword, Vornen," she whispered. She pointed at it, and veins bulged obscenely in her shaking hand.

Vornen touched the hilt, and cried out as the heat cut savagely into his hand. He tried to remove his hand from the sword, but could not. The odour of burned flesh drifted into the air. As if that stench was itself a lodestone, those people

282

nearest to them grew quiet and turned to watch. Vornen barely noticed. He pulled the sword free and struggled to his feet. All around, a hostile murmur started up. Whispers darted amongst the crowd. Fingers were pointed. Even amidst the white-hot pain, Vornen could hear every word, but he understood nothing they said.

Not one of them dared venture closer than they were, although even those further up the hill or to the sides ceased their exultations and turned their bright, mad eyes to the sword.

*Soon they will attack,* Vornen thought. *I only wish it could be now. Gods, let this end.*

The skies had darkened further overhead and a sudden crack of thunder rolled and echoed around the hill. Then a different sound, of splitting stone, louder even than the thunder, emanated from the summit of Tur-morn Hill. The townspeople suddenly lost all interest in Vornen and the sword, and their eyes turned to the crest of the hill where the great slab of black rock stood.

Then, as one they surged forward up the hill. They slipped in the snow and slush and turned the slope to half-frozen muck in their desperation to reach the summit.

Vornen and Suli continued, until they were less than two hundred strides from the Gate, drawn helplessly towards it. Suddenly Vornen screamed in pain and dropped the sword to the ground. It melted the snow for a dozen yards around and scorched the mud and grass beneath.

The rumble from the top of the hill grew louder, a sound so low that it could be barely be heard, yet it resonated through every person gathered there.

Suli held onto Vornen as he staggered. "The Gate is opening!" she shouted. "I can see stars, Vornen..."

"There are always stars," he muttered. Nevertheless, he was forced to raise his head to look. As the faithful rushed onward towards the Gate, arms outstretched, Vornen saw the vastness of the void. Familiar and terrible, an emptiness yawned from out of the stone, dotted with distant points of light.

Vornen forced himself to look away, but something just as terrible took place in front of him. Something that could only be described as blackness had begun to spread from the sword. It cut through the snow and the earth beneath and reached *into* the earth, then emerged again. Vornen stumbled back, and as an afterthought tried to pull Suli with him. She turned briefly to look at him, her eyes no more than crimson pools.

"The song of the earth," she whispered as she collapsed to the ground.

From the blade, slivers of blackness rose into the air and then dove into the trembling ground. Dozens, then hundreds, appeared, like a swarm of carrion. They rose far into the sky and then swooped down, sometimes to cut through one of the maddened, howling people who still desperately made their way up the slope. Then, as one, they rushed to the top of the hill and gathered as a single mass of writhing darkness, above the monolith where the Gate had opened.

*What is it?* Vornen wondered, stupefied at the sight. *What kind of magic came from the sword? What kind of beings are those? Why are they here?*

A moment later, and in that moment only, he understood.

A shimmering form fashioned from pure light appeared in the Gate, and drowned out the light of the distant stars. As it gathered in intensity, the crowd that had gathered at the summit screamed in adulation and agony, and the *marandaal* took its first stride into Aona.

Then the twisting cloud of black shapes flung themselves at the *marandaal* and into the Gate. They swirled and turned and drowned out the light wherever it appeared. There were more than hundreds now. Many thousands appeared and poured in and out of the Void. *To do*

284

*battle with the* marandaal, Vornen thought numbly as he collapsed to his knees.

The *marandaal* that had emerged from the void writhed briefly, and then disappeared completely, as if cut to fragments and enshrouded by the darting shadows. Still more of these shapes flooded into the Gate, and from within, light and darkness danced and intertwined. In the void beyond, others waited. A battle both here and somewhere else ripped both skies apart.

Those people who had gathered on Ailach Tor to witness the arrival of their Gods fell to the ground, their screams now of nothing but sheer terror. Some were attacked and rent apart by the slivers of blackness, their bodies cut through as easily as paper. Others were dragged into the earth itself, screaming until the ground made itself anew over their flailing forms. Still others were flung into the air to be sliced in a dozen horrific ways, and their bodies fell as a rain of meat to the ground. They died touched by either light or darkness, or both.

The ground shook. Thunder rolled. Lightning played endlessly around the summit of Ailach Tor. Black shapes circled in the sky, and slowly the light from the Gate grew dim.

Then the Gate exploded. Molten rock hurtled into the air, and Vornen tumbled down the hill as the savage pain of endless, searing light cut through his mind.

## IV

A world of mud and snow greeted his opening eyes.

He could see no more than several yards ahead, beyond which everything melted into a violent white haze. Vornen struggled to his feet only for them to give way under him. His outstretched hands sank more than six inches into snow. With an effort he stood up again and walked several

285

painful yards before he came across a body half-buried in snow.

*Suli. Is she at peace now?*

He lifted her wrist and felt for a pulse. Eventually he found one, weak but steady. Vornen lifted her, and with Suli's body leaning against him he struggled on.

He came across other bodies in the snow, one or two of which were not yet still. Others had not moved for some time, and a light powdering of snow had already begun to settle on them. Vornen stepped over and around the corpses and those people who would soon become corpses, shutting out the faint cries and pleas as he made his way past.

The snow grew deeper. Immense pain welled up in his legs. Cold and fatigue threatened to pull him down. Vornen knew that if he did fall he would lack the strength to get back up again, and he and Suli would be buried together. *Isn't that what I wanted?* he asked himself, but he continued regardless.

Eventually he reached the track that led back towards Ethanalin Tur-morn. Only the guidestones, tall chiselled standing rocks arranged sporadically at the sides of the track, gave any indication that it was there, under the snow. At this rate of snowfall, perhaps they too would vanish as the elements conspired to cover this nightmare.

Vornen struggled slowly back into the town, and only stopped when he reached an inn, abandoned with its door half-open. He dragged his way inside and pulled Suli with him, then kicked shut what remained of the door. Glass that had been clinging on dislodged and fell to the floor. Vornen pushed aside some of the chairs and tables and laid Suli down. He almost collapsed with exhaustion.

*Need to keep warm,* he thought. *Blankets. Robes. Fire.* After a moment he made his way slowly upstairs to see if he could find some extra clothing for them.

When he returned downstairs to the tap-room, Suli had somehow roused herself and moved near to the hearth, although that was as cold as every other corner of the room. The ragged remains of curtains billowed at the windows and broken glass glittered in the faint light. Suli sat and hugged herself. She shivered and stared into the hearth as if by imagining flames she might warm herself.

Vornen draped a couple of robes over her. She did not respond at first, then pulled them tighter. "Suli," he murmured. She shivered, and said nothing.

They needed food and warmth. For all he knew they might need a whole winter's-worth of food and warmth. Vornen found some dried fruit and cured meat in a storeroom at the back of the building, and a water pump whose contents were not yet entirely frozen.

He then began the laborious task of smashing chairs to create firewood, moving tables against the windows to block out the worst of the icy wind, and building up a fire in the hearth. It took an age to light, even with the firepowder he found in a drawer. Finally the few scraps of dried parchment he had found caught alight, and he sank down next to Suli and drew a ragged sigh of relief that almost turned into a sob. Never in his life had he been so relieved simply to have lit a fire.

Vornen quickly went through the options in his mind. This was a place of utter isolation now, with neither a way in nor a way out. There might be other survivors on Ailach Tor, although he had seen none that looked likely to live any great length of time. There might or might not be enough food and firewood to last through the winter, although that also depended on how many people were left to scavenge the supplies. Vornen's heart sank as he wondered how many weeks- or indeed how many months- travel might remain impossible for.

Next to him, Suli began to shake, head bowed. Vornen glanced worriedly at her for a moment, then realised that she was simply weeping.

"Suli," he said gently, and placed his arm around her.

A long while passed, until eventually she raised her head. Tears made a track through the grime on her face, and more glimmered in her eyes. "You make a good fire, Vornen," she said brokenly, and gave a little laugh.

"We are going to be here for a while, I think," Vornen murmured. "We will need to find some more food stores. And firewood. We have a whole winter ahead of us, if we live."

"We should have died," Suli whispered.

"But we lived," Vornen rejoined.

She laughed at that. "You know, I was looking forward to the end of it all. I had no idea what was happening to me. I'm not sure I do now either."

"Do you recall anything at all?" he asked. "All I remember was the sword... the Gate... nothing more than that."

Suli glanced around at his other side. "Good. I see you no longer have the sword."

Vornen shuddered, and looked quickly around as if he expected it to come hurtling through one of the windows. "No," he said, then gave a short laugh. Somehow, they had been incredibly lucky, and that sword had had much to do with it. *Evil lends a helping hand*, he thought bleakly.

"Others may have survived," he said after a while. "They may set upon each other, and perhaps upon us. This is the worst of winters, and if there are other survivors, they may be tempted to eat whatever and whoever they can. We need to be prepared."

Suli laughed softly. "I don't think I can even stand up, Vornen, let alone defend myself. If someone wishes to gnaw the poisoned flesh from my bones, they are welcome to it."

Amethyst had managed to walk perhaps fifty yards through the blizzard before she realised that she was not the only survivor. She passed by small groups of people, some of whom bore such terrible injuries that there was no doubt

288

they would die soon. A few cried out to her as they saw a faint shadow or movement pass somewhere near them. Others shrank away and gibbered with fear or hid their faces. Still others did nothing at all, other than sit in the snow and the freezing mud as their insides gradually turned to ice.

The wind numbed her face and howled in her ears. Amethyst reached up to brush snow from her hair, and was not entirely surprised to feel a sticky wetness on one side of her head. She felt only a little pain, but when she took her hand away and stared down at it, it was almost completely red with her blood. *I'm still walking,* she reminded herself. *But for how much longer?*

She could remember very little about what had happened over the last day, since she had wandered to the slopes of Ailach Tor, walking with everyone else as if she too had finally experienced the *lightdream.* The lightning, the vast stone at the top of the hill- although even she knew it was much more than that- the earthquake...

She had no idea if the day had just begun, or if dusk was about to fall. Nor could she tell which direction the town lay in, so she was more than relieved to see the first buildings looming up in front of her, so much so that she began to cry softly to herself.

The track that led up to the centre of the town was covered in thick snow, under which a layer of ice lurked, causing her to slip and fall several times.

Eventually she reached the abandoned central square, by which time the blizzard had abated somewhat. Silence greeted her as she stared around at the houses, shops and inns. Doors stood wide open and snow piled up on thresholds. Here and there lay bodies or other, less determinate bundles, disappearing fast in the snow. It looked as if anyone still able to walk had made their way to the slaughtering ground that Ailach Tor had later become, and those who lacked the strength and had no one to carry them, had simply fallen to the ground and frozen.

Amethyst was about to call out, to see if there was, after all, someone left here who was still alive and able to help her, but she stopped herself.

What else, then, was she meant to do?

As the hopelessness of the situation sank into her, Amethyst's legs gave way and she sank kneeling in the snow, as if in desperate prayer. *What a stupid, pointless end,* she thought.

Across the square, the door to one of the many abandoned buildings opened. She saw a man staring across at her, as the wind whipped up the snow again, and another flurry descended, as if the elements were rushing to bury Ethanalin Tur-morn and its horrors once and for all.

Vornen sat and watched the women as they slept, and warmed his aching hands near the fire. The melted snow in the kettle hung over the fire gradually heated up.

The young woman he had seen in the snow was exhausted, and her head wound had looked serious at first, but once he had cleaned it up it had revealed itself to be shallow, her skull not even fractured. *A glancing blow from something,* he thought. *A lucky blow, if one can call it that.* He wondered briefly where she was from. The far south perhaps, judging by her dark hair and tan-coloured skin. Perhaps he would ask her when she woke.

For a while he lapsed into thought, until a faint scraping sound came from somewhere behind him.

Somehow, he knew what had made the sound without needing to turn to face it. The hairs on the back of his neck stood up, and suddenly he felt far colder than he could ever have done outside, as if all the warmth and the will to live had drained from his body.

Vornen knew he had to turn to look eventually.

290

Like a sliver of jagged darkness, the sword waited for him in the gloom, resting upon the bar.

Vornen put his head in his hands and gave vent to his despair, until eventually his cries turned to uncontrolled laughter that echoed round the dank walls of the ruined alehouse, almost as if alive.

When Amethyst woke some hours later, she knew immediately that something had changed, but it took her a moment to work out what it was. When the realisation came to her, she was numb with shock.

"Gods," she murmured, failing to notice the man across the room as he stared at her. "It's *gone*. The pain has *gone away*."

She wept in relief. The crippling agony had been a part of her life for so long that she could do nothing else now that it had gone entirely.

For a long while she remained thus, hugging herself with pure relief, until she heard footfall upon the stairs that led down into the room. Even before she lifted her head to look, she knew who it was and laughed to herself, her thoughts at last free of pain, her body free of enslavement.

"Vengeance," Amethyst whispered, and finally she looked up, unable to help the unpleasant smile upon her lips.

# XI – The Hands of Gods

## I

*Truth or madness?*

Morthanien could not decide. His hand strayed to the stonework of the window ledge and from there to the smooth surface of the wall, where he fancied that some faint pulse resonated through the rock.

*There it is.*

A complex rhythm coursed within the cold stone against which he kept his hand pressed. He listened and tried to interpret its nature.

*I have been here so long,* he thought, *that I thought this place had only one pulse. But now there is something else that calls to me, calls to the castle itself.*

He knew that by now something calamitous had happened in the east. He had learned of the light-dreams and the blood-dreams, a twin rising that he of all people should have foreseen. *Vornen spoke the truth,* he mused. *What bitter irony that I sent that wretch away and disbelieved his ill-remembered mumblings. But regardless, he will have been pulled east to the event if he's the hapless lodestone he claims to be. He'll be more than likely dead now, consumed by whatever has happened there.*

Morthanien moved to the north-facing window and stared towards the vastness of the Pinnacles, a great wave of rock and ice that rose to scrape the heavens. Thoughts of the *marandaal* and the *choragh* vanished from his mind as he glimpsed for a fleeting moment a flash of light and colour, more vibrant even than the stark brilliance of the snow and jagged black outline of rock. It was gone as quickly as it had appeared and left nothing in its wake.

*Nothing,* Morthanien reminded himself, *except this residual response from my home. The elements themselves dance to more than one tune.*

He thought swiftly as his weary heart started to race. *Could it be that the* illeagh *have finally returned, despite their ancient promise to turn their backs on the so-called enlightened world?*

He scarcely dared hope for such a thing. That the *choragh* were rising was a fearful notion, even in response to the arrival of the *marandaal*. It meant a return to the previous Age, or worse. But if the *illeagh* had returned, what might that mean? Would they rise up against their once-brethren, the *choragh?*

*I must go to them.*

Morthanien almost jumped at the suddenness of that thought, as if someone had whispered it to him. He retreated from the window, troubled in a way he could not describe, and sat at his table to stare at the motes of dust in the air as they danced in the late afternoon sunlight. The castle remained as silent as always, but if he closed his eyes he could *feel* a whisper move back and forth through the foundations and course along the walls, stopping at the windows as if its owner desired to peer in at the tired old man who sat alone alone to watch the afternoon fade.

*They have returned,* he decided, *and I must go to them.*

This time the thought was more forceful, and persuasive.

Morthanien found his sturdy walking boots, and put them on with hands that shook. *Be cautious,* he told himself. *If you find nothing, if there are no more signs in the mountains, then turn back.*

*But there will be,* he thought as, a short while later, he made his way along the narrow path that led north and into the heart of the Pinnacles.

293

He walked on. Once he saw a flash of light, but it could have been the last of the afternoon sunlight reflecting off the surface of a frozen lake. Another time he fancied that the same whisper he had heard within his fortress was now being carried by the wind. It sounded louder, clearer, more urgent. Morthanien listened attentively to it, more certain now than ever.

The sun disappeared, and as clouds gathered in the sky the afternoon grew swiftly darker. Morthanien hastened onwards, stopping only for breath and to tell himself that yes, these were indeed potent signs, and that yes, he must go to the *illeagh*.

After some time, he drew to a halt. Archaon had risen in the east, visible faintly through thin and high cloud, giving almost no light. Morthanien sat on a boulder and took deep, measured breaths, then winced as a savage pain cut into his side. *Stupid old man,* he scolded himself. *You walk out into the mountains for the first time in many years- you should expect pain and fatigue.*

He looked northwards where a wide valley ascended. A half-dozen streams and small rivers carved silver streaks through the landscape, all of them frozen. The wind numbed his face and drove an errant tear across his cheek. Morthanien waited for the pain to subside.

*You believed in us,* came the whisper on the wind.

This time it was so clear, so *strong,* that Morthanien almost leapt to his feet despite his aching legs and overburdened heart. "Yes," he murmured, although the wind snatched the word away. For a moment he *saw* them, little instances of colour and light here and there, waiting out in the night. Relief almost overwhelmed him.

He slid from the boulder, knelt upon the hard ground and wept.

A while later footfall sounded nearby, the harsh crunch of boots upon the frosted path. Morthanien could not move, but a hand stole under his chin so that he looked up.

The man's touch was like hot, smouldering iron. The sclera of his eyes held a red hue, redder even than the great moon Archaon looming above. Morthanien knew an awful truth in that moment.

*Choragh and their dark kin,* he thought numbly, and tried to open his mouth. A single word was all he needed to wither this bloodfeeder where he stood. But he could not open his mouth, for the man's hand had moved upwards to cover his lips, and Morthanien could feel his unwilling flesh being pulled, *changed,* so that in a moment he would have no mouth at all.

"Two hundred and twelve years," the man said, as he removed his hand from the smooth skin where Morthanien's mouth had been. "Who has the right to live that long?" He looked to his left, and as Morthanien tried to follow his glance, something hard and sharp struck him on the side of the head. He heard bone shatter. A moment later, as the remains of his vision swam bloody and fading, he saw others, some of them humanlike, some impossible to describe in words.

Morthanien had been born to the sound of cyclic chanting, a low sonorous repetition whose purpose was to ensure an infant's calm and peaceful entrance into the waking world. He now died to a similar sound, the purpose of which could not have been more different.

They stripped the skin from his flesh. They hung his glistening remains above a smoking pyre. The night grew ever darker as Archaon set and clouds hid the stars. Celebrating their triumph in a raucous cacophony, the *kin* sat around their death-fire and ate sorcerer meat for the first time in a thousand years.

## II

In Knarlswood, the rain poured without end. Grass and earth turned to mud, and the air became thick with the misery of grey mist and spray from the downpour.

Serina sat, nearly oblivious to this mingling of the elements, and read the epitaph of a man called Ilumor, who once, in a past life, had been touched by the darker side of the Old Powers, and condemned to an existence of confusion and life after life, each one befuddled by memories of the last.

The stone before which she sat was not exactly what it appeared to be. It bore his epitaph, it spoke truly enough of him, but it did not mark his grave. As far as she knew, Ilumor had no grave. He lingered in the Silver Road, to be called back by one power or another, whether that might be for good or ill. Once, for a short while, Serina had broken his will and put him to use, gathering information for her Circle of witches. She did not know for certain what would happen when he was brought back, or even if he could be compelled by such as her, given what had happened before.

But times grew desperate.

*There is no one else now, no one I can reach or talk to about this,* she reasoned, *so I alone must take the risk.* The other women of the Circle, who might each have had the power to do such a thing and make it bind, were as good as ashes in the wind now, the few survivors of their number scattered through many lands.

*I suspect I am now the last of them all,* she thought, *now that Imiera has gone.*

Only ten years had passed since the demise of the Circle, but already it felt as if a century had opened up since the breaking of that ancient gathering.

Serina sighed and absently wiped a few strands of wet hair away from her eyes.

*What would my old companions think of me now, if they were still alive?* she wondered. *Would they laugh at my dream of a new Circle? Would they shake their heads in disapproval at the methods I employed, in my search for those whose talents I've dreamed of, who themselves have called to me without knowing? Would they even try to stop me, fearful that the breaking might happen again?*

She recalled the moment last night, when she had been suddenly pulled from her sleep by a clamour of *something* inside her head, a sudden snapping of the tenuous link between her and the southern girl she had entrapped. The link had been severed forever, which meant one of two things- either she had died, or she had found the girl that Serina had directed her to find.

*If she has found her, what now? Will she seek me out, bent on vengeance?*

Serina hoped so. She thought it likely that after all her suffering the southlander would want retribution, and would come for her. But Serina also hoped that the girl would keep her new find close at her side, fearful that if she let her go or if anything happened to her, the crippling pains would return.

*Powers, let that be her reasoning,* Serina thought fervently. *Let her believe that I may still reach her.*

She stared at the standing stone for a long while as the rain came down harder than ever, almost painfully cold. Gaan, her lupine companion, sat patiently nearby, fur soaking wet and head bowed. He liked this place even less than she did.

She knew the terrible risks of invoking such a restless and unpredictable being, but she had no idea what else to do. Without the strength to bring to her side all those who might help forge the new Circle, she needed every ally she could find.

*It must be now,* she told herself, *or I will lack the courage ever after.*

Serina reached forth and touched the stone, closed her eyes and felt herself descend into a kind of darkness that few people could reach, as if the earth itself opened up to envelop her. "May all the Powers preserve me," she whispered, an old saying once used as a ward against the unknown. Then she slumped forward and whispered the recital that might reach into the world within the world, the in-between place that existed as a parallel of the one that most people knew. The Silver Road.

Gaan howled softly and paced back and forth in agitation, but he knew better than to try and nudge her from the deep, unknowing state to which she had descended.

Sometime later, Serina raised her head from the sodden ground. Sinew and bone creaked with effort. The earth had almost taken her. She tore her hands and head away from wet, muddy roots.

All light had long since fled from the sky and a cold mist suffused the air to make the night even closer. Serina breathed it in and listened to the hammering of her heart, the pulsing of blood in her head.

No more than a hundred paces away, something made a sound amongst the trees. It was not the sigh of the wind, nor the call of a creature of any normal kind. It drifted across the still air, and instinctively she recognised the sound.

*It is him,* she thought, though she hardly dared to believe that she still had the power to call him from the twilit other-place of the Silver Road he had inhabited for years. Gaan snarled nearby, hackles raised.

"Ilumor," she breathed, as a figure made its way slowly from out of the cover and into the mist-laden clearing where she crouched. *What have I done?* she thought as sudden panic seized hold of her. *What will he do? All my strength has fled. Will I beg his forgiveness for past misdeeds? I've enslaved so many others, in different ways, but*

*I sorely regret ever bending him to my will. Yet that's what I've just done, again.*

Ilumor, still little more than a sound and a shadow in the dark, drew nearer. *How much will he remember?* Serina wondered fearfully.

When finally he loomed near- still as dreadful and as handsome as in the Age that had given him birth- Serina found hersel dumbfounded, unable to speak. His perfectly black, obsidian eyes took in the sight of her as she crouched in the mud before him. The thin, grey lips parted like a reopened scar and he knelt down, smiling at her.

"Do you forgive me?" she blurted out. "Will you help me?"

Ilumor reached out a hand and gently stroked her cheek. The touch burned like ice, and she flinched back. "I knew you would come to free me," he murmured. "A great kindness, Serina. All is forgiven. The past is the past."

"And... you will..."

"Help you? I think perhaps I should like *you* to help *me*. We could call it the return of a favour, or a kind of penance."

"The... the Circle," Serina stammered desperately. "The Circle must be made anew, but I cannot do such a thing alone..."

"Ah, the *Circle*." He sounded almost wistful. "We have no need of it, Serina. The world moves on. The Age draws to a close."

Ilumor reached out again, this time to gently lift her chin and force her to look at him. A different touch altogether, it felt as if flames ate at her skin, but she could not scream, much less struggle. Her view of him blurred as tears of agony brimmed in her eyes. Then suddenly everything came back into focus.

And when Serina saw the other figures, those who had gathered behind him, she sobbed and bowed her head to the mud, and wished she had fled this place and never even

299

dared to contemplate this deed, the most terrible of her many wrongdoings.

## III

Far to the west, in the ancient and secretive realm of Harn stood the city of Luudhoq, a bastion of order and civilisation, ruled with an iron grip by the Seven.

At the centre of this great city stood the Fortress of the Seven, known also as the Sanctum. This place was the symbol of law and order, progress and enlightenment, of which the Watchers had for a thousand years been the guardians.

Seated within a chamber on the fourteenth floor of this great fortress, a Watcher looked up from his paperwork, suddenly perturbed, although no sound or movement had occurred to disturb him.

Instantly he looked around at every one of his instruments and keys, scales and clocks. He silently observed and waited for an action or reaction that would confirm a disturbance of some sort. But his devices remained as before, still and silent. No one and nothing could come near to his inner chambers without the appropriate device making its characteristic chime, a specific resonance and volume for each particular event.

He calculated and reasoned, but could arrive at no useful conclusion. Nothing, as far as sense and observation dictated, had happened. So why the absolute certainty that something had?

*The instruments*, he thought suddenly. Were all the instruments working as they should? He walked around the chamber three times amd placed a hand near to each of them in turn to feel the resonance peculiar to each device. *No disturbance*, he reasoned. *Therefore, nothing of consequence has happened.*

*Unless it happened beyond the range of all these keys-*
*but they were made to sense that which we cannot, so why*
*would I have perceived some change and yet the patterns*
*formed by each of these instruments remain unchanged? That*
*should not be possible.*

Yet something foreign to him, a sense that some
might have called *fear*, lurked at the very edges of his
senses. For some reason that he could not even hope to
understand, he felt the urgent need to speak with his
master, Omir of the Seven.

Instinct was not familiar to Watchers. It held no role
in their world of sharp logic and routine. It was contradictory
to their nature. And yet instinct- or whatever Watchers
owned in place of such a characteristic- guided him now.

On an impulse, he abandoned his preparations for
the Sunset Ceremony, which he had worked on all morning,
and raced up the tower staircase to Omir's quarters.

The door opened for him as soon as he stood before it.
A moment later, he stood in the middle of the darkly-painted
room with Omir's cold white-rimmed eyes surmising him
from where he stood by the fireplace.

"Forgive me, master..." he began, but he had no way
to describe the impulse that had driven him here. For any
Watcher to act thus, on *impulse*, was unheard of. Surely
some punishment would be meted out to him for this
transgression.

But something *had* brought him here and superseded
all logic. That thought, that *certainty,* would not leave him.

Omir raised a hand to demand silence from his
underling. "I know. I sensed it also."

The Watcher gaped at him.

"Something has shifted. The earth pours forth
demons, and the paths that once brought us here have
conspired to bring destruction. We knew that sooner or later
this day would come."

Omir walked to the window and gazed out over the city. "Those of us who travelled here, long before such as you were pulled from the Void, knew this world to be different. We knew it had its own peculiar dangers. Sooner or later, much as we tried to deny the eventuality, we knew *they* would come. To destroy us, to destroy Aona itself."

The Watcher remained lost for words.

Omir smiled to himself and looked down on the vast city and the throngs of people going about their daily business. "We make ideal defenders for this world, against the *marandaal*," he said softly, and turned to his minion. "Would you care to know why?"

"Because there is no power greater than the Seven," the Watcher said automatically, although he had no understanding of the word *marandaal*.

But he had given the wrong answer, and Omir laughed. "No," his master said, eyes drawn once again to the vastness of Luudhoq, dominion of the Seven for over a thousand years. "Because *we created them.*"

If you enjoyed *Oblivion's Forge*, the next book in the Aona series, *Secret Roads*, is available on Amazon and from paperback publisher Completely Novel – www.completelynovel.com.

Please also take the time to review this book on Amazon and Goodreads and any other book review websites.

If you'd like to keep up to date with news from the author, subscribe to the newsletter at www.simonwilliamsauthor.com